Nicholas Sparks and J.K. Rowling are the only contemporary authors to have a novel spend more than a year on both the *New York Times* hardcover and paperback bestseller lists. *The Notebook*, *Nights in Rodanthe*, *The Rescue*, *A Bend in the Road*, *True Believer*, *At First Sight* and *Dear John* have all reached the number-one spot. All Nicholas Sparks's novels have been international bestsellers and have been translated into more than thirty languages. *Message in a Bottle*, *A Walk to Remember* and *The Notebook* have been adapted into major films.

Nicholas Sparks lives in North Carolina with his wife and family.

For more information, visit www.nicholassparks.com

Praise for Nicholas Sparks

'Will have you weeping for the joy and tragedy of it all'
Daily Mail

'A page-turner . . . Sparks's fans won't be disappointed'
Glamour

'Deeply moving, beautifully written'
Booklist

'Extremely powerful'
Borders.com

'Sparks addresses the difficulties and struggles of people adjusting to sharing their intimate lives'
Irish News

'Very moving'
Closer

'Sparks's writing is superb'
Woman

Also by Nicholas Sparks

The Notebook
Message in a Bottle
A Walk to Remember
A Bend in the Road
Nights in Rodanthe
The Guardian
The Wedding
True Believer
At First Sight
Three Weeks with My Brother
(with Micah Sparks)
Dear John
The Choice

THE RESCUE

Nicholas Sparks

SPHERE

First published in the United States of America in 2000 by
Warner Books
First published in Great Britain in 2001 by Bantam Books
This paperback edition published in 2006 by
Time Warner Books
Reprinted in 2007 by Sphere
Reprinted 2008

A CIP catalogue record for this book
is available from the British Library.

ISBN 978-0-7515-3890-8

Typeset by Palimpsest Book Production Limited, Polmont, Stirlingshire
Printed and bound in Great Britain by Clays Ltd, St Ives plc

Papers used by Sphere are natural, renewable and recyclable products made from wood grown in sustainable forests and certified in accordance with the rules of the Forest Stewardship Council.

Sphere
An imprint of
Little, Brown Book Group
100 Victoria Embankment
London EC4Y 0DY

An Hachette Livre UK Company
www.hachettelivre.co.uk

www.littlebrown.co.uk

This book is dedicated with love to
Pat and Billy Mills. My life is better because
of you both. Thank you for everything.

Acknowledgments

Again, I'd like to thank my wife, Cathy, who had to be more patient with me than usual while writing this novel. What a wild eleven years we've shared, huh?

My three sons (Miles, Ryan, and Landon) also deserve my thanks, simply because they help me keep everything in perspective. It's fun watching you guys grow up.

My agent, Theresa Park, of Sanford Greenburger Associates, has been with me every step of the way, and it's been my good fortune to have worked with her. I can never say it enough: Thank you so much for everything—you're the best!

My editor, Jamie Raab, of Warner Books, has also been great to work with—again! What can I say? I'm lucky to have your guidance—don't ever believe that I take it for granted. I hope we work together for a long, long time.

Many thanks to Larry Kirshbaum, the number one guy at Warner Books, who also happens to be a really nice guy, and Maureen Egen, who is not only a gem, but a brilliant gem. You both changed my life for the better and I'll never forget it.

And finally, a wineglass raised in toast to the rest of those people who help me every step of the way: Jennifer Romanello, Emi Battaglia, Edna Farley, and the rest of the publicity department at Warner; Flag, who designed all my fabulous book covers; Scott Schwimer, my entertainment attorney; Howie Sanders and Richard Green at United Talent Agency, two of the best at what they do; Denise DiNovi, the fabulous producer of *Message in a Bottle* (the main character in this novel is named for her, by the way); Courtenay Valenti and Lorenzo Di Bonaventura at Warner Bros.; Lynn Harris at New Line Cinema; Mark Johnson, producer . . .

Prologue

It would later be called one of the most violent storms in North Carolina history. Because it occurred in 1999, some of the most superstitious citizens considered it an omen, the first step toward the end of time. Others simply shook their heads and said that they knew something like that would happen sooner or later. In all, nine documented tornadoes would touch down that evening in the eastern part of the state, destroying nearly thirty homes in the process. Telephone lines lay strewn across roads, transformers blazed without anyone to stop them. Thousands of trees were felled, flash floods swept over banks of three major rivers, and lives changed forever with one fell swoop of Mother Nature.

It had begun in an instant. One minute it was cloudy and dark, but not unusually so; in the next, lightning, gale-force winds, and blinding rain exploded from the early summer sky. The system had blown in from the northwest and was crossing the state at nearly forty miles an hour. All at once, radio stations crackled with emergency warnings, documenting the storm's ferocity. People who could took cover inside, but people on the highway, like Denise Holton, had no place to go. Now that she was firmly in its midst, there was little she could do. Rain fell so hard in places that traffic slowed to five miles an hour and Denise held the wheel with white knuckles, her face a mask of concentration. At times it was impossible to see the road through the windshield, but stopping meant certain disaster because of the people on the highway behind her. They wouldn't be able to see her car with time enough to stop. Pulling the shoulder strap of the seat belt over her head, she leaned over the steering wheel, looking for the dotted lines in the road, catching a glimpse here and there. There were long stretches during which she felt as if she were driving on instinct alone, because nothing was visible at all. Like an ocean wave, rain poured across her windshield, obscuring nearly everything. Her headlights seemed absolutely useless, and she wanted to stop, but where? Where would it be safe? On the side of the highway? People were swerving all over the road, as blind as she was. She made an instant decision—somehow, moving seemed safer. Her eyes darted from the road, to the taillights in front of her, to the rearview mirror; she hoped and prayed that everyone else on the road was doing the same thing. Looking for anything that would keep them safe. Anything at all.

Then, just as suddenly as it had started, the storm weakened and it was possible to see again. She suspected she'd reached the front edge of the system; everyone on the road apparently guessed the same thing. Despite the slick conditions, cars began to speed up, racing to stay ahead of the front. Denise sped up as well, staying with them. Ten minutes later, the rains still evident but slowing even more, she glanced at the gas gauge and felt a knot form in her stomach. She knew she had to stop soon. She didn't have enough gas to make it home.

Minutes went by.

The flow of traffic kept her vigilant. Thanks to a new moon, there was little light in the sky. She glanced at the dashboard again. The needle on the gas gauge was deep into the red shaded area. Despite her fears about staying ahead of the storm, she slowed the car, hoping to conserve what was left, hoping it would be enough. Hoping to stay ahead of the storm.

People began to race by, the spray against her windshield wreaking havoc with her wipers. She pressed onward.

Another ten minutes passed before she heaved a sigh of relief. Gas, less than a mile away, according to the sign. She put on her blinker, merged, rode in the right-hand lane, exited. She stopped at the first open pump.

She'd made it but knew the storm was still on its

way. It would reach this area within the next fifteen minutes, if not sooner. She had time, but not a lot.

As quickly as she could, Denise filled the tank and then helped Kyle out of his car seat. Kyle held her hand as they went inside to pay; she'd insisted on it because of the number of cars at the station. Kyle was shorter than the door handle, and as she walked in she noticed how crowded it was. It seemed that everyone driving on the highway had had the same idea—*get gas while you can*. Denise grabbed a can of Diet Coke, her third of the day, then searched the refrigerators along the back wall. Near the corner she found strawberry-flavored milk for Kyle. It was getting late, and Kyle loved milk before bedtime. Hopefully, if she could stay ahead of the storm, he'd sleep most of the way back.

By the time she went to pay she was fifth in line. The people in front of her looked impatient and tired, as if they couldn't understand how it could be so crowded at this hour. Somehow it seemed as if they'd forgotten about the storm. But from the looks in their eyes, she knew they hadn't. Everyone in the store was on edge. *Hurry up*, their expressions said, *we need to get out of here*.

Denise sighed. She could feel the tension in her neck, and she rolled her shoulders. It didn't help much. She closed her eyes, rubbed them, opened them again. In the aisles behind her, she heard a mother arguing with her young son. Denise glanced over her shoulder. The boy appeared to be about the same age as Kyle, four and a half or so. His mother seemed as stressed as Denise felt. She was holding on tightly to her son's arm. The child stomped his foot.

"But I want the cupcakes!" he whined.

His mother stood her ground. "I said no. You've had enough junk today."

"But *you're* getting something."

After a moment Denise turned away. The line hadn't moved at all. What was taking so long? She peeked around those in front of her, trying to figure it out. The lady at the cash register looked confused by the rush, and everyone in front of her, it seemed, wanted to pay with a credit card. Another minute crawled by, shrinking the line by one. By this time the mother and child got into line directly behind Denise, their argument continuing.

Denise put her hand on Kyle's shoulder. He was sipping his milk through a straw, standing quietly. She couldn't help but overhear the two people behind her.

"Aw, c'mon, Mom!"

"If you keep it up, you'll get a swat. We don't have time for this."

"But I'm hungry."

"Then you should have eaten your hot dog."

"I didn't want a hot dog."

And so it went. Three customers later Denise finally reached the register, opened her pocketbook, and paid with cash. She kept one credit card for emergencies but seldom, if ever, used it. For the clerk, making change seemed more difficult than swiping credit cards. She kept glancing up at the digital numbers on the register, trying to get it right. The argument between mother and son continued unabated. In time Denise finally received her change and put her pocketbook away, then turned toward the door. Knowing how hard it was for everyone tonight, she smiled at the mother behind her, as if to say, *Kids are tough sometimes, aren't they?*

In response, the woman rolled her eyes. "You're lucky," she said.

Denise looked at her curiously. "Excuse me?"

"I said you're lucky." She nodded toward her son. "This one here never shuts up."

Denise glanced at the floor, nodded with tight lips, then turned and left the store. Despite the stress of the storm, despite the long day driving and her time at the evaluation center, all she could think about was Kyle. Walking toward the car, Denise suddenly felt the urge to cry.

"No," she whispered to herself, "you're the lucky one."

Chapter 1

Why had this happened? Why, of all the children, was Kyle the one?

Back in the car after stopping for gas, Denise hit the highway again, staying ahead of the storm. For the next twenty minutes rain fell steadily but not ominously, and she watched the wipers push the water back and forth while she made her way back to Edenton, North Carolina. Her Diet Coke sat between the emergency brake and the driver's seat, and though she knew it wasn't good for her, she finished the last of it and immediately wished she'd bought another. The extra caffeine, she hoped, would keep her alert and focused on the drive, instead of on Kyle. But Kyle was always there.

Kyle. What could she say? He'd once been part of her, she'd heard his heart beating at twelve weeks, she'd felt his movements within her the last five months of her pregnancy. After his birth, while still in the delivery room, she took one look at him and couldn't believe there was anything more beautiful in the world. That feeling hadn't changed, although she wasn't in any way a perfect mother. These days she simply did the best job she could, accepting the good with the bad, looking for joys in the little things. With Kyle, they were sometimes hard to find.

She'd done her best to be patient with him over the last four years, but it hadn't always been easy. Once, while he was still a toddler, she'd momentarily placed her hand over his mouth to quiet him, but he'd been screaming for over five hours after staying awake all night, and tired parents everywhere might find this a forgivable offense. After that, though, she'd done her best to keep her emotions in check. When she felt her frustration rising, she slowly counted to ten before doing anything; when that didn't work, she left the room to collect herself. Usually it helped, but this was both a blessing and a curse. It was a blessing because she knew that patience was necessary to help him; it was a curse because it made her question her own abilities as a parent.

Kyle had been born four years to the day after her mother had died of a brain aneurysm, and though not usually given to believing in signs, Denise could hardly regard that as a coincidence. Kyle, she felt sure, was a gift from God. Kyle, she knew, had been sent to replace her family. Other than him, she was alone in the world. Her father had died when she was four, she had no siblings, her grandparents on both sides had passed away. Kyle immediately became the sole recipient of the love she had to offer. But fate is strange, fate is unpredictable. Though she showered Kyle with attention, it somehow hadn't been enough. Now she led a life she hadn't anticipated, a life where Kyle's daily progression was carefully logged in a notebook. Now she led a life completely dedicated to her son. Kyle, of course, didn't complain about the things they did every day. Kyle, unlike other children, never complained about anything. She glanced in the rearview mirror.

"What are you thinking about, sweetie?"

Kyle was watching the rain as it blew against the windows, his head turned sideways. His blanket was in his lap. He hadn't said anything since he'd been in the car, and he turned at the sound of her voice.

She waited for his response. But there was nothing.

Denise Holton lived in a house that had once been owned by her grandparents. After their deaths it had become her mother's, then eventually it had passed on to her. It wasn't much—a small ramshackle building set on three acres, built in the 1920s. The two bedrooms and the living room weren't too bad, but the kitchen was in dire need of modern appliances and the bathroom didn't have a shower. At both the front and back of the house the porches were sagging, and without the portable fan she sometimes felt as if she would bake to death, but because she could live there rent-free, it was exactly what she needed. It had been her home for the past three months.

Staying in Atlanta, the place she'd grown up, would have been impossible. Once Kyle was born, she'd used the money her mother had left her to stay at home with him. At the time, she considered it a temporary leave of absence. Once he was a little older, she had planned to go back to teaching. The money, she knew, would run out eventually, and she had to earn a living. Besides, teaching was something she'd loved. She'd missed her students and fellow teachers after her first week away. Now, years later, she was still at home with Kyle and the world of teaching in a school was nothing but a vague and distant memory, something more akin to a dream than a reality. She couldn't remember a single lesson plan or the names of the students she had taught. If she didn't know better, she would have sworn that she'd never done it at all.

Youth offers the promise of happiness, but life offers the realities of grief. Her father, her mother, her grandparents—all gone before she turned twenty-one. At that point in her life she'd been to five different funeral homes yet legally couldn't enter a bar to wash the sorrow away. She'd suffered more than her fair share of challenges, but God, it seemed, couldn't stop at just that. Like Job's struggles, hers continued to go on. "Middle-class lifestyle?" *Not anymore*. "Friends you've grown up with?" *You must leave them behind.* "A job to enjoy?" *It is too much to ask.* And Kyle, the sweet, wonderful boy for whom all this was done—in many ways he was still a mystery to her.

Instead of teaching she worked the evening shift at a diner called Eights, a busy hangout on the outskirts of Edenton. The owner there, Ray Toler, was a sixty-something black man who'd run the place for thirty years. He and his wife had raised six kids, all of whom went to college. Copies of their diplomas hung along the back wall, and everyone who ate there knew about them. Ray made sure of that. He also liked to talk about Denise. She was the only one, he liked to say, who'd ever handed him a résumé when interviewing for the job.

Ray was a man who understood poverty, a man who understood kindness, a man who understood how hard it was for single mothers. "In the back of the building, there's a small room," he'd said when he hired her. "You can bring your son with you, as long as he doesn't get in the way." Tears formed in her eyes when he showed it to her. There were two cots, a night-light, a place where Kyle would be safe. The next evening Kyle went to bed in that small room as soon as she started on her shift; hours later she loaded him in the car and took him back home. Since then that routine hadn't changed.

She worked four nights a week, five hours a shift, earning barely enough to get by. She'd sold her Honda for an old but reliable Datsun two years ago, pocketing the difference. That money, along with everything else from her mother, had long since been spent. She'd become a master of budgeting, a master of cutting corners. She hadn't bought new clothes for herself since the Christmas before last; though her furniture was decent, they were remnants from another life. She didn't subscribe to magazines, she didn't have cable television, her stereo was an old boom box from college. The last movie she'd seen on the silver screen was *Schindler's List*. She seldom made long-distance phone calls to her friends. She had $238 in the bank. Her car was nineteen years old, with enough miles on the engine to have circled the world five times.

None of those things mattered, though. Only Kyle was important.

But never once had he told her that he loved her.

On those evenings she didn't work at the diner, Denise usually sat in the rocking chair on the porch out back, a book across her lap. She enjoyed reading outside, where the rise and fall of chirping crickets was somehow soothing in its monotony. Her home was surrounded by oak and cypress and mockernut hickory trees, all draped heavily in Spanish moss. Sometimes, when the moonlight slanted through them just right, shadows that looked like exotic animals splashed across the gravel walkway.

In Atlanta she used to read for pleasure. Her tastes ran the gamut from Steinbeck and Hemingway to Grisham and King. Though those types of books were available at the local library, she never checked them out anymore. Instead she used the computers near the reading room, which had free access to the Internet. She searched through clinical studies sponsored by major universities, printing the documents whenever she found something relevant. The files she kept had grown to nearly three inches wide.

On the floor beside her chair she had an assortment of psychological textbooks as well. Expensive, they'd made serious dents in her budget. Yet the hope was always there, and after ordering them, she waited anxiously for them to arrive. This time, she liked to think, she would find something that helped.

Once they came, she would sit for hours, studying the information. With the lamp a steady blaze behind her, she perused the information, things she'd usually read before. Still, she didn't rush. Occasionally she took notes, other times she simply folded the page and highlighted the information. An hour would pass, maybe two, before she'd finally close the book, finished for the night. She'd stand, shaking the stiffness from her joints. After bringing the books to her small desk in the living room, she would check on Kyle, then head back outside.

The gravel walkway led to a path through the trees, eventually to a broken fence that lined her property. She and Kyle would wander that way during the day, she walked it alone at night. Strange noises would filter from everywhere: from above came the screech of an owl; over there, a rustle through the underbrush; off to the side, a skitter along a branch. Coastal breezes moved the leaves, a sound similar to that of the ocean; moonlight drifted in and out. But the path was straight, she knew it well. Past the fence, the forest pressed in around her. More sounds, less light, but still she moved forward. Eventually the darkness became almost stifling. By then she could hear the water; the Chowan River was close. Another grove of trees, a quick turn to the right, and all of a sudden it was as if the world had unfolded itself before her. The river, wide and slow moving, was finally visible. Powerful, eternal, as black as time. She would cross her arms and gaze at it, taking it in, letting the calm it inspired wash over her. She would stay a few minutes, seldom longer, since Kyle was still in the house.

Then she'd sigh and turn from the river, knowing it was time to go.

Chapter 2

In the car, still ahead of the storm, Denise remembered sitting with the doctor in his office earlier that day while he read the results from the report on Kyle.

> The child is male, four years eight months old at the time of testing . . . Kyle is a handsome child with no obvious physical deficiencies in the head or facial area . . . No recorded head trauma . . . pregnancy was described by mother as normal . . .

The doctor continued for the next few minutes, outlining the specific results from various tests, until finally reaching the conclusion.

> Though IQ falls within the normal range, child is severely delayed in both *receptive* and *expressive* language . . . probably *central auditory processing disorder (CAPD)*, though cause can't

be determined . . . overall language ability estimated to be that of a *twenty-four-month-old* . . . Eventual language and learning capabilities unknown at this time . . .

Barely that of a toddler, she couldn't help but think. When the doctor was finished, he set the report aside and looked at Denise sympathetically. "In other words," he said, talking slowly as if she hadn't understood what he'd just read, "Kyle has problems with language. For some reason—we're not sure why—Kyle isn't able to speak at a level appropriate for his age, even though his IQ is normal. Nor is he able to understand language equal to the level of other four-year-olds."

"I know."

The assurance of her response caught him off guard. To Denise it seemed as if he'd expected either an argument, an excuse, or a predictable series of questions. When he realized she wasn't going to say anything else, he cleared his throat.

"There's a note here that says you've had him evaluated elsewhere."

Denise nodded. "I have."

He shuffled through the papers. "The reports aren't in his file."

"I didn't give them to you."

His eyebrows rose slightly. "Why?"

She reached for her purse and set it in her lap, thinking. Finally: "May I be frank?"

He studied her for a moment before leaning back in his chair. "Please."

She glanced at Kyle before facing the doctor again. "Kyle has been misdiagnosed again and again over the past two years—everything from deafness to autism to pervasive development disorder to ADD. In time, none of those things turned out to be accurate. Do you know how hard it is for a parent to hear those things about her child, to believe them for months, to learn everything about them and finally accept them, before being told they were in error?"

The doctor didn't answer. Denise met his eyes and held them before going on.

"I know Kyle has problems with language, and believe me, I've read all about auditory processing problems. In all honesty, I've probably read as much about it as you have. Despite that, I wanted his language skills tested by an independent source so that I could know specifically where he needed help. In the real world, he has to talk to more people than just me."

"So . . . none of this is news to you."

Denise shook her head. "No, it's not."

"Do you have him in a program now?"

"I work with him at home."

He paused. "Does he see a speech or behavioral specialist, anyone who's worked with children like him before?"

"No. He went to therapy three times a week for over a year, but it didn't seem to help. He continued to fall further behind, so I pulled him out last October. Now it's just me."

"I see." It was obvious by the way he said it that he didn't agree with her decision.

Her eyes narrowed. "You have to understand—even though this evaluation shows Kyle at the level of a two-year-old, that's an improvement from where he once was. Before he worked with me, he'd never shown any improvement at all."

Driving along the highway three hours later, Denise thought about Brett Cosgrove, Kyle's father. He was the type of man who attracted attention, the kind who'd always caught her eye: tall and thin with dark eyes and ebony hair. She'd seen him at a party, surrounded by people, obviously used to being the center of attention. She was twenty-three at the time, single, in her second year of teaching. She asked her friend Susan who he was: she was told that Brett was in town for a few weeks, working for an investment banking firm whose name Denise had since forgotten. It didn't matter that he was from out of town. She glanced his way, he glanced back, and their eyes kept meeting for the next forty minutes before he finally came over and said hello.

Who can explain what happened next? Hormones? Loneliness? The mood of the hour? Either way, they left the party a little after eleven, had drinks in the hotel bar while entertaining each other with snappy anecdotes, flirted with an eye toward what might happen next, and ended up in bed. It was the first and last time she ever saw him. He went back to New York, back to his own life. Back, she suspected even then, to a girlfriend he'd neglected to mention. And she went back to her life.

At the time, it didn't seem to mean much; a month later, while sitting on the bathroom floor one Tuesday morning, her arm around the commode, it meant a whole lot more. She went to the doctor, who confirmed what she already knew.

She was pregnant.

She called Brett on the phone, reached his answering machine, and left a message to call; three days later he finally did. He listened, then sighed with what sounded like exasperation. He offered to pay for the abortion. As a Catholic, she said it wasn't going to happen. Angered, he questioned why this had happened. I think you already know the answer to that, she answered. He asked if she was sure the baby was his. She closed her eyes, calming herself, not rising to the bait. Yes, it was his. Again he offered to pay for an abortion. Again she said no. What did she want him to do? he asked her. She said she didn't want anything, she just thought he should know. He would fight if she demanded child support payments, he said. She said she didn't expect that from him, but she needed to know if he wanted to be involved in the child's life. She listened to the sound of his breaths on the other end. No, he finally said. He was engaged to someone else.

She'd never spoken to him again.

In truth, it was easier to defend Kyle to a doctor than it was to herself. In truth, she was more worried than she let on. Even though he'd improved, the language ability of a two-year-old wasn't much to cheer about. Kyle would be five in October.

Still, she refused to give up on him. She would never give up, even though working with him was the hardest thing she'd ever done. Not only did she do the regular things—make his meals, take him to parks, play with him in the living room, show him new places—but she also drilled him on the mechanics of speech for four hours a day, six days a week. His progression, though undeniable since she'd begun with him, was hardly linear. Some days he said everything she asked him to, some days he didn't. Some days he could comprehend new things easily, other days he seemed further behind than ever. Most of the time he could answer "what" and "where" type questions; "how" and "why" questions were still incomprehensible. As for conversation, the flow of reason between two individuals, it was still nothing but a scientific hypothesis, far beyond his ability.

Yesterday they'd spent the afternoon on the banks of the Chowan River. He enjoyed watching the boats as they cut through the water on the way to Batchelor Bay, and it provided a change from his normal routine. Usually, when they worked, he was strapped in a chair in the living room. The chair helped him focus.

She'd picked a beautiful spot. Mockernut hickory trees lined the banks, Christmas ferns were more common than mosquitoes. They were sitting in a clover patch, just the two of them. Kyle was staring at the water. Denise carefully logged his progress in a notebook and finished jotting down the latest information. Without looking up, she asked: "Do you see any boats, sweetie?"

Kyle didn't answer. Instead he lifted a tiny jet in the air, pretending to make it fly. One eye was closed, the other was focused on the toy in his hand.

"Kyle, honey, do you see any boats?"

He made a tiny, rushing sound with his throat, the sounds of a make-believe engine surging in throttle. He wasn't paying attention to her.

She looked out over the water. No boats in sight.

She reached over and touched his hand, making sure she had his attention.

"Kyle? Say, 'I don't see any boats.'"

"Airplane." *(Owpwane)*

"I know it's an airplane. Say, 'I don't see any boats.'"

He raised the toy a little higher, one eye still focused on it. After a moment he spoke again.

"Jet airplane." *(Jet owpwane)*

"Yes, you're holding an airplane."

"*Jet* airplane." *(Jet owpwane)*

She sighed. "Yes, a *jet* airplane."

"Owpwane."

She looked at his face, so perfect, so beautiful, so *normal* looking. She used her finger to turn his face toward hers.

"Even though we're outside, we still have to work, okay? . . . You have to say what I tell you to, or we go back to the living room, to your chair. You don't want to do that, do you?"

Kyle didn't like his chair. Once strapped in, he couldn't get away, and no child—Kyle included—enjoyed something like that. Still, Kyle moved the toy airplane back and forth with measured concentration, keeping it aligned with an imaginary horizon.

Denise tried again.

"Say, 'I don't see any boats.'"

Nothing.

She pulled a tiny piece of candy from her coat pocket.

Kyle saw it and reached for it. She kept it out of his grasp.

"Kyle? Say, 'I don't see any boats.'"

It was like pulling teeth, but the words finally came out.

He whispered, "I don't see any boats." *(Duh see a-ee boat)*

Denise leaned in and kissed him, then gave him the candy. "That's right, honey, that's right. Good talking! You're such a good talker!"

Kyle took in her praise while he ate the candy, then focused on the toy again.

Denise jotted his words in her notebook and went on with the lesson. She glanced upward, thinking of something he hadn't said that day.

"Kyle, say, 'The sky is blue.'"

After a beat:

"Owpwane."

In the car again, now twenty minutes from home. In the back she heard Kyle fidget in his seat, and she glanced in the rearview mirror. The sounds in the car soon quieted, and she was careful not to make any noise until she was sure he was sleeping again.

Kyle.

Yesterday was typical of her life with him. A step

forward, a step backward, two steps to the side, always a struggle. He was better than he once had been, yet he was still too far behind. Would he ever catch up?

Outside, dark clouds spanned the sky above, rain fell steadily. In the backseat Kyle was dreaming, his eyelids twitching. She wondered what his dreams were like. Were they devoid of sound, a silent film running through his head, nothing more than pictures of rocket ships and jets blazing across the sky? Or did he dream using the few words he knew? She didn't know. Sometimes, when she sat with him as he lay sleeping in his bed, she liked to imagine that in his dreams he lived in a world where everyone understood him, where the language was real—maybe not English, but something that made sense to him. She hoped he dreamed of playing with other children, children who responded to him, children who didn't shy away because he didn't speak. In his dreams, she hoped he was happy. God could at least do that much, couldn't he?

Now, driving along a quiet highway, she was alone. With Kyle in the back, she was still alone. She hadn't chosen this life; it was the only life offered to her. It could have been worse, of course, and she did her best to keep this perspective. But most of the time, it wasn't easy.

Would Kyle have had these problems if his father were around? In her heart she wasn't exactly sure, but she didn't want to think so. She'd once asked one of Kyle's doctors about it, and he'd said he didn't know. An honest answer—one that she'd expected—but she'd had trouble sleeping for a week afterward. Because the doctor hadn't simply dismissed the notion, it took root in her mind. Had she somehow been responsible for all of Kyle's problems? Thinking this way had led to other questions as well. If not the lack of a father, had it been something she'd done while pregnant? Had she eaten the wrong food, had she rested enough? Should she have taken more vitamins? Or fewer? Had she read to him enough as an infant? Had she ignored him when he'd needed her most? The possible answers to those questions were painful to consider, and through sheer force of will she pushed them from her mind. But sometimes late at night the questions would come creeping back. Like kudzu spreading through the forests, they were impossible to keep at bay forever.

Was all of this somehow her fault?

At moments like those, she would slip down the hall toward Kyle's bedroom and watch him while he slept. He slept with a white blanket curled around his head, small toys in his hand. She would stare at him and feel sorrow in her heart, yet she would also feel joy. Once, while still living in Atlanta, someone had asked her if she would have had Kyle if she had known what lay in store for both of them.

"Of course," she'd answered quickly, just as she was supposed to. And deep down she knew she meant it. Despite his problems, she viewed Kyle as a blessing. If she conceived it in terms of pros and cons, the list of pros was not only longer, but much more meaningful.

But because of his problems, she not only loved him, but felt the need to protect him. There were times each and every day when she wanted to come to his defense, to make excuses for him, to make others understand that though he looked normal, something was wired wrong in his brain. Most of the time, however, she didn't. She decided to let others make their own judgments about him. If they didn't understand, if they didn't give him a chance, then it was their loss. For despite all his difficulties, Kyle was a wonderful child. He didn't hurt other children; he never bit them or screamed at them or pinched them, he never took their toys, he shared his own even when he didn't want to. He was a sweet child, the sweetest she'd ever known, and when he smiled . . . God, he was just so beautiful. She would smile back and he'd keep smiling, and for a split second she'd think that everything was okay. She'd tell him she loved him, and the smile would grow wider, but because he couldn't talk well, she sometimes felt as if she were the only one who noticed how wonderful he actually was. Instead Kyle would sit alone in the sandbox and play with his trucks while other children ignored him.

She worried about him all the time, and though all mothers worried about their children, she knew it wasn't the same. Sometimes she wished she knew someone else who had a child like Kyle. At least then someone would understand. At least then she'd have someone to talk to, to compare notes with, to offer a shoulder when she needed to cry. Did other mothers wake up every day and wonder whether their child would ever have a friend? Any friend? *Ever?* Did other mothers wonder whether their children would go to a regular school or play sports or go to the prom? Did other mothers watch as their children were ostracized, not only by other children, but by other parents as well? Did their worries go on every minute of every day, seemingly without an end in sight?

Her thoughts followed this familiar track as she guided the old Datsun onto now recognizable roads. She was ten minutes away. Round the next curve, cross the bridge toward Edenton, then left on Charity Road. Another mile after that and she'd be home. The rain continued to fall, and the asphalt was black and shiny. The headlights shone into the distance, reflecting the rain, diamonds falling from the evening sky. She was driving through a nameless swamp, one of dozens in the low country fed by the waters of the

Albemarle Sound. Few people lived here, and those who did were seldom seen. There were no other cars on the highway. Rounding the curve at nearly sixty miles an hour, she saw it standing in the road, less than forty yards away.

A doe, fully grown, facing the oncoming headlights, frozen by uncertainty.

They were going too fast to stop, but instinct prevailed and Denise slammed on the brakes. She heard the screeching of tires, felt the tires lose their grip on the rain-slicked surface, felt the momentum forcing the car forward. Still, the doe did not move. Denise could see its eyes, two yellow marbles, gleaming in the darkness. She was going to hit it. Denise heard herself scream as she turned the wheel hard, the front tires sliding, then somehow responding. The car began to move diagonally across the road, missing the deer by a foot. Too late to matter, the deer finally broke from its trance and darted away safely, without looking back.

But the turn had been too much for the car. She felt the wheels leave the surface of the asphalt, felt the *whump* as the car slammed to the earth again. The old shocks groaned violently with the bounce, a broken trampoline. The cypress trees were less than thirty feet off the highway. Frantically Denise turned the wheel again, but the car rocketed forward as if she'd done nothing. Her eyes went wide and she drew a harsh breath. It seemed as if everything were moving in slow motion, then at full speed, then slow motion again. The outcome, she suddenly realized, was foregone, though the realization lasted only a split second. At that moment she blasted into the tree; heard the twisting of metal and shattering of glass as the front of the car exploded toward her. Because the seat belt was across her lap and not over her shoulder, her head shot forward, slamming into the steering wheel. A sharp, searing pain in her forehead . . .

Then there was nothing.

Chapter 3

"Hey, lady, are you all right?"

With the sound of the stranger's voice, the world came back slowly, vaguely, as if she were swimming toward the surface in a cloudy pool of water. Denise couldn't feel any pain, but on her tongue was the salty-bitter taste of blood. She still didn't realize what had happened, and her hand traveled absently to her forehead as she struggled to force her eyes open.

"Don't move . . . I'm gonna call an ambulance . . ."

The words barely registered; they meant nothing to her. Everything was blurry, moving in and out of focus, including sound. Slowly, instinctively, she turned her head toward the shaded figure in the corner of her eyes.

A man . . . dark hair . . . yellow raincoat . . . turning away . . .

The side window had shattered, and she felt the rain blowing in the car. A strange hissing sound was coming from the darkness as steam escaped from the radiator. Her vision was returning slowly, starting with the images closest to her. Shards of glass were in her lap, on her pants . . . blood on the steering wheel in front of her . . .

So much blood . . .

Nothing made sense. Her mind was weaving through unfamiliar images, one right after another . . .

She closed her eyes and felt pain for the first time . . . opened them. Forced herself to concentrate. Steering wheel . . . the car . . . she was in the car . . . dark outside . . .

"Oh God!"

With a rush, it all came back. The curve . . . the deer . . . swerving out of control. She turned in her seat. Squinting through the blood in her eyes, she focused on the backseat—Kyle wasn't in the car. His safety seat was open, as was the back door on his side of the car.

Kyle?

Through the window she shouted for the figure who'd awakened her . . . if there had been a figure. She wasn't quite sure whether he had been just a hallucination.

But he was there, and he turned. Denise blinked . . . he was making his way toward her. A moan escaped her lips.

Later she'd remember that she wasn't frightened right away, not the way she should have been. She knew Kyle was okay; it didn't even register that he might not be. He'd been strapped in—she was sure of it—and there wasn't any damage in the back. The back door was already open . . . even in her bewildered state, she felt certain that the person—whoever he was—had helped Kyle out of the car. By now the figure was at the window.

"Listen, don't try to talk. You're pretty banged up. My name is Taylor McAden, and I'm with the fire department. I've got a radio in my car. I'm gonna get you help."

She rolled her head, focusing on him with blurry eyes. She did her best to concentrate, to make her words as clear as possible.

"You have my son, don't you?"

She knew what the answer would be, what it should be, but strangely, it didn't come. Instead he seemed to need extra time to translate the words in the same way that Kyle did. His mouth contorted just a little, almost sluggishly, then he shook his head.

"No . . . I just got here . . . Your son?"

It was then—while looking in his eyes and imagining the worst—that the first jolt of fear shot through her. Like a wave, it started crashing and she felt herself sinking inward, as she had when she'd learned of her mother's death.

Lightning flashed again, and thunder followed almost immediately. The rain poured from the sky, and the man wiped his forehead with the back of his hand.

"My son was in the back! Have you seen him?" The words came out clearly, forcefully enough to startle the man at the window, to awaken the last of her deadened senses.

"I don't know—" In the sudden downpour, he hadn't understood what she was trying to tell him.

Denise struggled to get out of the car, but the seat belt across her lap held her fast. She unbuckled it quickly, ignoring the pain in her wrist and elbow. The man took an involuntary step backward as Denise forced the door open, using her shoulder because the door had crumpled slightly from the impact. Her knees were swollen from smashing into the console, and she almost lost her balance as she stood.

"I don't think you should be moving—"

Holding on to the car for support, she ignored the man as she moved around the car, toward the opposite side, where Kyle's door stood open.

No, no, no, no . . .

"Kyle!"

In disbelief, she bent inside to look for him. Her eyes scanned the floor, then back to the seat again, as if he might magically reappear. Blood rushed to her head, bringing with it a piercing pain that she ignored.

Where are you? Kyle . . .

"Lady . . ." The man from the fire department followed her around the car, seemingly uncertain of what to do or what was going on or why this lady who was covered in blood was suddenly so agitated.

She cut him off by grabbing his arm, her eyes boring directly into his.

"You haven't seen him? A little boy . . . brown hair?" The words were tinged with genuine panic. "He was in the car with me!"

"No, I—"

"You've got to help me find him! He's only four!"

She whirled around, the rapid movement almost making her lose her balance. She grabbed hold of the car again. The corners of her vision faded to black as she struggled to keep the dizziness at bay. The scream came out despite the spinning in her mind.

"Kyle!"

Pure terror now.

Concentrating . . . closing one eye to help her focus . . . getting clearer again. The storm was in full fury now. Trees not twenty feet away were difficult to see through the rain. It was absolute darkness in that direction . . . only the path to the highway was clear.

Oh God.

The highway . . .

She could feel her feet slipping in the mud-soaked grass, she could hear herself drawing short, rapid gasps as she staggered toward the road. She fell once, got up again, and kept going. Finally understanding, the man ran after her, catching her before she reached the road. His eyes scanned the area around him.

"I don't see him . . ."

"*Kyle!*" She screamed it as loud as she could, praying inside as she did it. Despite being nearly drowned out by the storm, the sound prompted Taylor into further action.

They took off in opposite directions, both shouting Kyle's name independently, both stopping occasionally to listen for sound. The rain, however, was deafening. After a couple of minutes Taylor ran back to his car and made a call to the fire station.

The two voices—Denise's and Taylor's—were the only human sounds in the swamp. The rain made it impossible for them to hear each other, let alone a child, but they continued anyway. Denise's voice cut sharply, a mother's scream of despair. Taylor took off at a lope, shouting Kyle's name over and over, running a hundred yards up and down the road, firmly caught up in Denise's fear. Eventually two other firemen arrived, flashlights in hand. At the sight of Denise, her hair matted with clots of blood, her shirt stained red, the older one recoiled for a moment before trying and failing to calm her down.

"You've got to help me find my baby!" Denise sobbed.

More help was requested, more people arrived within minutes. Six people searching now.

Still the storm raged furiously. Lightning, thunder . . . winds gusting strongly, enough to bend the searchers over double.

It was Taylor who found Kyle's blanket, in the swamp about fifty yards from the spot where Denise had crashed, snagged on the underbrush that covered the area.

"Is this his?" he asked.

Denise started to cry as soon as it was handed to her.

But after thirty minutes of searching, Kyle was still nowhere to be seen.

Chapter 4

It made no sense to her. One minute he was sleeping soundly in the backseat of her car, and in the next minute he was gone. Just like that. No warning at all, just a split-second decision to jerk the wheel and nothing would ever be the same again. Was that what life came down to?

Sitting in the back of the ambulance with the doors open while the flashing blue lights from the trooper's car illuminated the highway in regular, circular sweeps, Denise waited, her mind racing with such thoughts. Half a dozen other vehicles were parked haphazardly as a group of men in yellow raincoats discussed what to do. Though it was obvious they'd worked together before, she couldn't tell who was in charge. Nor did she know what they were saying; their words were lost in the muffled roar of the storm. The rain came down in heavy sheets, mimicking the sound of a freight train.

She was cold and still dizzy, unable to focus for more than a few seconds at a time. Her balance was off—she'd fallen three times while searching for Kyle—and her clothes were soaked and muddy, clinging to her skin. Once the ambulance had arrived, they'd forced her to stop. A blanket had been wrapped around her and a cup of coffee placed by her side. She couldn't drink it—she couldn't do much of anything. She was shivering badly, and her vision was blurred. Her frozen limbs seemed to belong to someone else. The ambulance attendant—though no doctor—suspected a concussion and wanted to bring her in immediately. She steadfastly refused. She wouldn't leave until Kyle was found. He could wait another ten minutes, he said, then he had no choice. The gash in her head was deep and still bleeding, despite the bandage. She would lose consciousness, he warned, if they waited any longer than that. I'm not leaving, she repeated.

More people had arrived. An ambulance, a state trooper who'd been monitoring the radio, another three volunteers from the fire department, a trucker who saw the trouble and stopped as well—all within a few minutes of each other. They were standing in a sort of circle, in the middle of the cars and trucks, headlights on. The man who'd found her—Taylor?—had his back to her. She suspected he was filling them in on what he knew, which wasn't much, other than the location of the blanket. A minute later he turned around and glanced at her, his face grim. The state trooper, a heavyset man losing his hair, nodded in her direction. After gesturing to the others to stay where they were, Taylor and the trooper both started toward the ambulance. The uniform—which in the past had always seemed to inspire confidence—now did nothing for her. They were men, only men, nothing more. She stifled the urge to vomit.

She held Kyle's mud-stained blanket in her lap and was running her hands through it, nervously rolling it into a ball and then undoing it. Though the ambulance sheltered her from the rain, the wind was blowing hard and she continued to shiver. She hadn't stopped shivering since they'd put the blanket over her shoulders. It was so cold out here . . .

And Kyle was out there without even a jacket.

Oh, Kyle.

She lifted Kyle's blanket to her cheek and closed her eyes.

Where are you, honey? Why did you leave the car? Why didn't you stay with Mom?

Taylor and the trooper stepped up into the ambulance and exchanged glances before Taylor gently put his hand on Denise's shoulder.

"I know this is hard, but we have to ask you a few questions before we get started. It won't take long."

She bit her lip before nodding slightly, then took a deep breath. She opened her eyes.

The trooper looked younger up close than he had from a distance, but his eyes were kind. He squatted before her.

"I'm Sergeant Carl Huddle with the state troopers office," he said, his voice rolling with the lullaby of the South. "I know you're worried, and we are, too. Most of us out here are parents, with little ones of our own. We all want to find him as badly as you do, but we need to know some general information—enough to know who we're looking for."

For Denise, the words barely registered.

"Will you be able to find him in this storm . . . I mean, before . . . ?"

Denise's eyes traveled from one man to the other, having trouble focusing on either. When Sergeant Huddle didn't answer right away, Taylor McAden nodded, his determination clear.

"We'll find him—I promise."

Huddle glanced uncertainly at Taylor, before finally nodding as well. He shifted onto one knee, obviously uncomfortable.

Exhaling sharply, Denise sat up a little, trying her best to stay composed. Her face, wiped clean by the attendant in the ambulance, was the color of table linen. The bandage wrapped around her head had a large red spot just over her right eye. Her cheek was swollen and bruised.

When she was ready, they went over the basics for the report: names, address, phone number, and employment, her previous residence, when she'd moved to Edenton, the reason she was driving, how she stopped for gas but stayed ahead of the storm, the deer in the road, how she lost control of the car, the accident itself. Sergeant Huddle noted it all on a flip pad. When it was all on paper, he looked up at her almost expectantly.

"Are you kin to J. B. Anderson?"

John Brian Anderson had been her maternal grandfather, and she nodded.

Sergeant Huddle cleared his throat—like everyone in Edenton, he'd known the Andersons. He glanced at the flip pad again.

"Taylor said that Kyle is four years old?"

Denise nodded. "He'll be five in October."

"Could you give me a general description—something I could put out on the radio?"

"The radio?"

Sergeant Huddle answered patiently. "Yeah, we'll put it on the police emergency network so that other departments can have the information. In case someone finds him, picks him up, and calls the police. Or if, by some chance, he wanders up to someone's house and they call the police. Things like that."

He didn't tell her that area hospitals were also routinely informed—there was no need for that just yet.

Denise turned away, trying to order her thoughts.

"Um . . ." It took a few seconds for her to speak. Who can describe their kids exactly, in terms of numbers and figures? "I don't know . . . three and a half feet tall, forty pounds or so. Brown hair, green eyes . . . just a normal little boy of his age. Not too big or too small."

"Any distinguishing features? A birthmark, things like that?"

She repeated his question to herself, but everything seemed so disjointed, so unreal, so completely unfathomable. Why did they need this? A little boy lost in the swamp . . . how many could there be on a night like this?

They should be searching now, instead of talking to me.

The question . . . what was it? Oh, yes, distinguishing features . . . She focused as best she could, hoping to get this over with as quickly as possible.

"He's got two moles on his left cheek, one larger than the other," she finally offered. "No other birthmarks."

Sergeant Huddle noted this information without looking up from his pad. "And he could get out of his car seat and open the door?"

"Yes. He's been doing that for a few months now."

The state trooper nodded. His five-year-old daughter, Campbell, could do the same thing.

"Do you remember what he was wearing?"

She closed her eyes, thinking.

"A red shirt with a big Mickey Mouse on the front. Mickey's winking and one hand has a thumbs-up sign. And jeans—stretch waist, no belt."

The two men exchanged glances. *Dark colors.*

"Long sleeves?"

"No."

"Shoes?"

"I think so. I didn't take them off, so I assume they're still on. White shoes, I don't know the brand. Something from Wal-Mart."

"How about a jacket?"

"No. I didn't bring one. It was warm today, at least when we started to drive."

As the questioning went on, lightning, three flashes close together, exploded in the night sky. The rain, if possible, seemed to fall even harder.

Sergeant Huddle raised his voice over the sound of the pounding rain.

"Do you still have family in the area? Parents? Siblings?"

"No. No siblings. My parents are deceased."

"How about your husband?"

Denise shook her head. "I've never been married."

"Has Kyle ever wandered off before?"

Denise rubbed her temple, trying to keep the dizziness at bay.

"A couple of times. At the mall once and near my house once. But he's afraid of lightning. I think that might be the reason he left the car. Whenever there's lightning, he crawls into bed with me."

"How about the swamp? Would he be afraid to go

there in the dark? Or do you think he'd stay close to the car?"

A pit yawned in her stomach. Fear made her mind clear just a little.

"Kyle isn't afraid of being outside, even at night. He loves to wander in the woods by our house. I don't know that he knows enough to be afraid."

"So he might have . . ."

"I don't know . . . maybe," she said desperately.

Sergeant Huddle paused for a moment, trying not to push her too hard. Finally: "Do you know what time it was that you saw the deer?"

Denise shrugged, feeling helpless and weak. "Again, I don't know . . . maybe nine-fifteen. I didn't check the time."

Instinctively both men glanced at their watches. Taylor had found the car at 9:31 P.M. He'd called it in less than five minutes later. It was now 10:22 P.M. More than an hour—at the least—had already passed since the accident. Both Sergeant Huddle and Taylor knew they had to get a coordinated start right away. Despite the relative warmth of the air, a few hours in this rain without proper clothing could lead to hypothermia.

What neither of them mentioned to Denise was the danger of the swamp itself. It wasn't a place for anyone in a storm like this, let alone a child. A person could literally vanish forever.

Sergeant Huddle closed his flip pad with a snap. Every minute now was precious.

"We're going to continue this later, if that's okay, Miss Holton. We'll need more for the report, but getting started with the search is the most important thing right now."

Denise nodded.

"Anything else we should know? A nickname, maybe? Something he'll answer to?"

"No, just Kyle. But . . ."

It was then that it hit her—the obvious. The worst possible type of news, something the trooper had never thought to ask.

Oh God . . .

Her throat constricted without warning.

Oh, no . . . oh, no . . .

Why hadn't she mentioned it earlier? Why hadn't she told him right away, when she first got out of the car? When Kyle might have been close . . . when they maybe could have found him before he got too far away? He might have been right there—

"Miss Holton?"

Everything seemed to wash over her at once: shock, fright, anger, denial . . .

He can't answer them!

She lowered her face into her hands.

He can't answer!

"Miss Holton?" she heard again.

Oh God, why?

After what seemed like an impossibly long time, she wiped her tears away, unable to meet their eyes. *I should have told them earlier.*

"Kyle won't answer if you simply call his name. You'll have to find him, you'll have to actually *see* him."

They stared at her quizzically, not understanding.

"But if we tell him that we've been looking for him, that his mom is worried?"

She shook her head, a wave of nausea sweeping through her. "He won't answer."

How many times had she said these words before? How many times had it simply been an explanation? How many times had it really meant nothing when compared with something like this?

Neither man said anything. Drawing a ragged breath, Denise went on. "Kyle doesn't talk very well, just a few words here and there. He . . . he can't understand language for some reason . . . that's why we were at Duke today."

She turned from one man to the other, making sure they understood. "You'll have to find him. Simply shouting for him won't do any good. He won't understand what you're saying. He won't answer . . . he can't. You'll have to find him . . ."

Why him? Of all the children, why did this have to happen to Kyle?

Unable to say anything else, Denise started to sob.

With that, Taylor put his hand on her shoulder as he'd done earlier.

"We'll find him, Miss Holton," he said with quiet forcefulness. "We'll find him."

Five minutes later, as Taylor and the others were mapping out the search pattern, four more men arrived to help. It was all that Edenton could spare. Lightning had sparked three major fires, there had been four auto accidents in the last twenty minutes—two with serious injuries—and downed power lines were still a hazard. Calls were flooding in to police and fire departments at a furious pace—every one was logged by priority, and unless a life was in immediate jeopardy, they were informed that nothing could be done right away.

A lost child took priority over nearly everything.

The first step was to park the cars and trucks as close to the edge of the swamp as possible. They were left idling, headlights set on high beams, about fifteen yards apart. Not only would they provide extra light necessary for the immediate search, but they would also serve as a beacon in case one of the searchers got disoriented.

Flashlights and walkie-talkies were handed out along with extra batteries. Eleven men (including the trucker, who wanted to help) would be involved, and the search would start from where Taylor found the blanket. From there they would fan out in three directions—south, east, and west. East and west paralleled the highway; south was the last direction Kyle had appeared to be headed. It was decided that one man would stay behind, near the highway and the trucks, on the off chance that Kyle would see the headlights and return on his own. He would send a flare up every hour on the hour, so that the men would know exactly where they were.

After Sergeant Huddle had given them a brief description of Kyle and what he was wearing, Taylor spoke. He, along with a couple of the other men, had hunted in the swamp before and laid out what they were up against.

Here, on the outer fringes of the swamp near the highway, the searchers were told that the ground was always damp but not usually underwater. It wasn't until half a mile farther into the swamp that water formed shallow lakes above the ground. Mud was a real danger, though; it closed in around the foot and leg, sometimes holding it like a vise, making it difficult for an adult to escape, let alone a child. Tonight the water was already half an inch deep near the highway and would only get worse as the storm wore on. Mud pockets combined with rising water would make for a deadly combination. The men grimly agreed. They would proceed with caution.

On the plus side, if there was one, none of them

imagined that Kyle could have gotten far. Trees and vines made the going rough, hopefully limiting the distance he might have traveled. A mile, maybe, definitely less than two miles. He was still close, and the sooner they got started, the better chance they would have.

"But," Taylor went on, "according to the mother, it turns out that the boy probably won't answer if we call him. Look for any physical sign of him—you don't want to walk right by him. She made it very clear that we shouldn't depend on him answering us."

"He won't respond?" asked one of the men, clearly baffled.

"That's what his mother said."

"Why can't he talk?"

"She didn't really explain it."

"Is he retarded?" another asked.

Taylor felt his back stiffen at the question.

"What the hell does that matter? He's a little boy lost in the swamp who can't talk. That's all we know right now."

Taylor stared at the man until he finally turned away. There was only the sound of the rain coming down around them before Sergeant Huddle finally let out a deep sigh.

"Then we ought to get going."

Taylor turned on his flashlight. "Let's do it."

Chapter 5

Denise could see herself in the swamp with the others, pushing branches away from her face, her feet sinking into the spongy earth as she searched frantically for Kyle. In actuality, however, she was lying on a gurney in the back of the ambulance on the way to the hospital in Elizabeth City—a town thirty miles to the northeast—that had the nearest emergency room.

Denise stared at the ceiling of the ambulance, still shivering and dazed. She'd wanted to stay, she'd begged to stay, but was told that it was better for Kyle if she went with the ambulance. She would only hinder things here, they said. She'd said she didn't care and had stubbornly stepped out of the ambulance, back into the storm, knowing that Kyle needed her. As if in complete control, she'd asked for a raincoat and flashlight. After a couple of steps, the world had begun to spin. She'd pitched forward, her legs uncontrollable, and fallen to the ground. Two minutes later the ambulance siren had roared to life and she was on her way.

Aside from shivering, she hadn't moved since she'd

been on the gurney. Her hands and arms were completely, eerily still. Her breathing was rapid but shallow, like that of a small animal. Her skin was pale, sickly, and her latest fall had opened her head wound again.

"Have faith, Miss Holton," the attendant soothed. He'd just taken her blood pressure and believed she was suffering from shock. "I mean, I know these guys. Kids have been lost around here before, and they always find 'em."

Denise didn't respond.

"And you'll be okay, too," the attendant went on. "In a couple of days, you'll be on your feet again."

It was quiet for a minute. Denise continued to stare upward. The attendant began to take her pulse.

"Is there anyone you want me to call when you get to the hospital?"

"No," she whispered. "There's no one."

Taylor and the others reached the spot where the blanket was found and began to fan out. Taylor, along with two other men, headed south, deeper into the swamp, while the rest of the search team headed east and west. The storm hadn't let up at all, and visibility in the swamp—even with the flashlight—was only a few yards at most. Within minutes Taylor couldn't see or hear anyone, and he felt a sinking sensation in his gut. Somehow lost in the adrenaline surge prior to the search—where anything seemed possible—was the reality of the situation.

Taylor had searched for lost people before, and he suddenly knew there weren't enough men out here. The swamp at night, the storm, a child who wouldn't answer when called . . . fifty people wouldn't be enough. Maybe even a hundred. The most effective way to search for someone lost in the woods was to stay within sight of the person to the right and left, everyone moving in unison, almost like a marching band. By staying close, searchers could canvas an area thoroughly and quickly like a grid, without wondering whether something had been missed. With ten men that was simply impossible. Minutes after they'd split up, everyone involved with the search was on his own, completely separated from the others. They were reduced to simply wandering in the direction of their choosing, pointing the flashlights here and there—anywhere—the proverbial search for a needle in a haystack. Finding Kyle had suddenly become a matter of luck, not skill.

Reminding himself not to lose faith, Taylor pressed forward, around trees, over the ever softening earth. Though he didn't have any children himself, he was godfather to the children of his best friend, Mitch Johnson, and Taylor searched as though looking for one of them. Mitch was also a volunteer fireman, and Taylor wished fervently that he was out here searching as well. His main hunting partner for the past twenty years, Mitch knew the swamp almost as well as he did, and they could use his experience. But Mitch was out of town for a few days. Taylor hoped it wasn't an omen.

As the distance from the highway lengthened, the swamp was becoming denser, darker, more remote and foreign with every few steps. Standing trees grew closer together, rotted trees lay strewn across the ground. Vines and branches tore at him as he moved, and he had to use his free hand to keep them away from his face. He pointed his flashlight at every clump of trees, at every stump, behind every bush, moving continually, looking for any sign of Kyle. Several minutes passed, then ten.

Then twenty.

Then thirty.

Now, deeper in the swamp, the water had risen past his ankles, making movement even more difficult. Taylor checked his watch: 10:56. Kyle had been gone for an hour and a half, maybe more. Time, initially on their side, was rapidly becoming an enemy. *How long would it take before he got too cold? Or . . .*

He shook his head, not wanting to think beyond that.

Lightning and thunder were regular occurrences now, the rain hard and stinging. It seemed to be coming from all directions. Taylor wiped his face every few seconds to clear his vision. Despite his mother's insistence that Kyle wouldn't answer him, Taylor nonetheless kept calling his name. For some reason it made him feel as if he were doing more than he actually was.

Damn.

They hadn't had a storm like this in, what, six years? Seven? Why tonight? Why now, when a boy was lost? They couldn't even use Jimmie Hicks's dogs on a night like tonight, and they were the best in the county. The storm made it impossible to track anything at all. And simply wandering out here blindly wasn't going to be enough.

Where would a kid go? A kid afraid of storms but not afraid of the woods? A kid who'd seen his mother after the accident, seen her injured and unconscious.

Think.

Taylor knew the swamp as well as, if not better than, anyone he knew. It was here that he'd shot his first deer at the age of twelve; every autumn he ventured forth to hunt ducks as well. He had an instinctive ability to track nearly anything, seldom returning from a hunt without something. The people of Edenton often joked that he had a nose like a wolf. He did have an unusual talent; even he admitted that. Sure, he knew what all hunters knew—footprints, droppings, broken branches indicating a trail a deer might have followed—but those things didn't fully explain his success. When asked to explain his secret skill, he simply replied that he tried to think like a deer. People laughed at that, but Taylor always said it with a straight face, and they quickly realized he wasn't trying to be funny. *Think like a deer? What the hell did that mean?*

They shook their heads. Perhaps only Taylor knew.

And now he was trying to do the same thing, only this time with much higher stakes.

He closed his eyes. Where would a four-year-old go? Which way would he head?

His eyes snapped open at the burst of the signal flare in the evening sky, indicating the turn of the hour. Eleven o'clock.

Think.

The emergency room in Elizabeth City was crowded. Not only those with serious injuries had come, but people who simply weren't feeling that well. No doubt they could have waited until the following day but like a full moon, storms seemed to bring out an irrational streak in people. The larger the storm, the more irrational people became. On a night like this, heartburn was suddenly a heart attack in the making; a fever that had come on early in the day was suddenly too serious to ignore; a cramp in the leg might be a blood clot. The doctors and nurses knew it; nights like these were as predictable as the sunrise. The wait was at least two hours long.

Due to her head wound, Denise Holton, however,

was taken in immediately. She was still conscious, though only partially. Her eyes were closed, but she was speaking in gibberish, repeating the same word over and over. Immediately she was taken in for an X-ray. From there the doctor would determine whether a CAT scan was necessary.

The word she kept repeating was "Kyle."

Another thirty minutes passed, and Taylor McAden had moved into the deeper recesses of the swamp. It was incredibly dark now, like spelunking in a cave. Even with a flashlight, he felt the beginnings of claustrophobia. Trees and vines grew even closer together, and moving in a straight line was impossible. It was easy to wander in circles, and he couldn't imagine what it was like for Kyle.

Neither the wind nor rain had let up at all. Lightning, however, was slowly lessening in its frequency. The water was now halfway up his shin, and he hadn't seen anything. He'd checked in on his walkie-talkie a few minutes earlier—everyone else said the same thing.

Nothing. Not a sign of him anywhere.

Kyle had been gone now for two and a half hours.

Think.

Would he have made it this far? Would someone his size be able to wade through water this deep?

No, he decided. Kyle wouldn't have gone t
not in a T-shirt and jeans.

And if he did, they probably wouldn't find him alive.

Taylor McAden pulled the compass from his pocket and pointed the flashlight at it, figuring his bearings. He decided to go back to where they'd first found the blanket, back to square one. Kyle had been there . . . that's all they knew.

But which way had he gone?

The wind gusted and trees swayed above him. Rain stung his cheek as lightning flashed in the eastern sky. The worst of the storm was finally passing them by.

Kyle was small and afraid of lightning . . . stinging rain . . .

Taylor stared up at the sky, concentrating, and felt the shape of something there . . . something in the recesses of his mind slowly beginning to emerge. An idea? No, not quite that strong . . . but a possibility?

Gusting wind . . . stinging rain . . . afraid of lightning . . .

Those things would have mattered to Kyle—wouldn't they?

Taylor grabbed his walkie-talkie and spoke, directing everyone back to the highway as quickly as possible. He would meet them there.

"It has to be," he said to no one in particular.

* * *

Like many of the volunteer firemen's wives who called into the station that evening, concerned about their husbands on this dangerous night, Judy McAden couldn't resist calling. Though Taylor was called to the station two or three times a month, as Taylor's mother she nonetheless found herself worrying about him every time he went out. She hadn't wanted him to be a fireman and told him so, though she finally stopped pleading with him about it once she realized he'd never change his mind. He was, as his father had been, stubborn.

Still, all evening long she'd felt instinctively that something bad had happened. It wasn't anything dramatic, and at first she'd tried to dismiss it, but the nagging suspicion persisted, growing stronger as the hours passed. Finally, reluctantly, she'd made the call, almost expecting the worst; instead she'd learned about the little boy—"J. B. Anderson's great-grandkid"—who was lost in the swamp. Taylor, she was told, was involved in the search. The mother, though, was on the way to the hospital in Elizabeth City.

After hanging up the phone, Judy sat back in her chair, relieved that Taylor was okay but suddenly worried about the child. Like everyone else in Edenton, she'd known the Andersons. But more than that, Judy had also known Denise's mother when they were both young girls, before Denise's mother had moved away and married Charles Holton. That had been a long time ago—forty years, at least—and she hadn't thought about her in years. But now the memories of their youth came rushing back in a collage of images: walking to school together; lazy days by the river, where they talked about boys; cutting the latest fashion pictures out of magazines . . . She also remembered how sad she'd been when she'd learned of her death. She had no idea that her friend's daughter had moved back to Edenton.

And now her son was lost.

What a homecoming.

Judy didn't debate long—procrastination simply wasn't in her nature. She had always been the take-charge type, and at sixty-three she hadn't slowed down at all. Years earlier, after her husband had died, Judy had taken a job at the library and had raised Taylor by herself, vowing to make it on her own. Not only did she meet the financial obligations of her family, but she did what it usually took two parents to do. She volunteered at his school and acted as room mother every year, but she'd also taken Taylor to ball games and had gone camping with the Scouts. She'd taught him how to cook and clean, she'd taught him how to shoot baskets and hit baseballs. Though those days were behind her, she was busier than ever. For the past dozen years her attention had shifted from raising Taylor to helping the town of Edenton itself, and she participated in every aspect of the community's life. She wrote her congressman and state legislators regularly and would walk from door to door collecting signatures for various petitions when she didn't think her voice was being heard. She was a member of the Edenton Historical Society, which raised funds to preserve the old homes in town; she went to every meeting of the town council with an opinion on what should be done. She taught Sunday school at the Episcopal church, cooked for every bake sale, and still worked at the library thirty hours a week. Her schedule didn't allow her to waste a lot of time, and once she made a decision, she followed it without turning back. Especially if she felt certain she was right.

Though she didn't know Denise, she was a mother herself and understood fear when children were concerned. Taylor had been in precarious situations his entire life—indeed, he seemed to attract them, even at a young age. Judy knew the little boy must be absolutely terrified—and the mother . . . well, she was probably a basket case. *Lord knows I was.* She pulled on her raincoat, knowing with absolute certainty that the mother needed all the support she could get.

The prospect of driving in the storm didn't frighten her; the thought didn't even enter her mind. A mother and son were in trouble.

Even if Denise Holton didn't want to see her—or couldn't because of the injuries—Judy knew she wouldn't be able to sleep if she didn't let her know that people in the town cared about what was going on.

Chapter 6

At midnight the flare once again ignited in the evening sky, like the chiming of a clock.

Kyle had been gone for nearly three hours.

Taylor, meanwhile, was nearing the highway and was struck by how bright it seemed compared with the murky recesses he'd just emerged from. He also heard voices for the first time since he'd split up with the others . . . lots of voices, people calling to one another.

Quickening his step, Taylor cleared the last of the trees and saw that more than a dozen extra vehicles had arrived—their headlights blazing with the originals. And there were more people as well. Not only had the other searchers returned, but they were now surrounded by those who'd heard about the search through the town grapevine and had come out to help. Even at a distance Taylor recognized most of them. Craig Sanborn, Rhett Little, Skip Hudson, Mike Cook, Bart Arthur, Mark Shelton . . . six or seven others as well. People who'd defied the storm, people who had to work the following day. People whom Denise had probably never met.

Good people, he couldn't help but think.

The mood, however, was gloomy. Those who'd been searching were soaking wet, covered with mud and scrapes, exhausted, and dejected. Like Taylor, they'd seen how dark and impenetrable it was out there. As Taylor approached them, they quieted. So did the new arrivals.

Sergeant Huddle turned, his face illuminated by the flashlights. His cheek had a deep, fresh scratch, partially hidden by splattered mud. "So what's the news? Did you find something?"

Taylor shook his head. "No, but I think I have an idea of which way he headed."

"How do you know?"

"I don't know for sure. It's just a guess, but I think he was moving to the southeast."

Like everyone else, Sergeant Huddle knew of Taylor's reputation for tracking—they'd known each other since they were kids.

"Why?"

"Well, that's where we found the blanket, for one thing, and if he kept heading that way, the wind would be at his back. I don't think a little boy would try to fight the wind—I just think he'd go with it. The rain would hurt too much. And I think he'd want to keep the lightning at his back, too. His mother said he was afraid of lightning."

Sergeant Huddle looked at him skeptically. "That's not much."

"No," Taylor admitted, "it isn't. But I think it's our best hope."

"You don't think we should continue searching like before? Covering every direction?"

Taylor shook his head. "We'd still be spread too thin—it wouldn't do any good. You've seen what it's like out there." He wiped his cheek with the back of his hand, collecting his thoughts. He wished Mitch were with him to help make his case—Mitch was good at things like this.

"Look," he finally went on, "I know it's just a guess, but I'm willing to bet I'm right. We've got, what? More than twenty people now? We could fan out wide and cover everything in that direction."

Huddle squinted at him doubtfully. "But what if he didn't go that way? What if you're wrong? It's dark out there . . . he could be moving in circles for all we know. He might have holed up somewhere to take shelter. Just because he's afraid of lightning doesn't mean he'd know enough to move away from it. He's only four years old. Besides, we've got enough people now to head in different directions."

Taylor didn't respond as he considered it. Huddle

made sense, perfect sense. But Taylor had learned to trust his instincts. His expression was resolute.

Sergeant Huddle frowned, his hands jammed deep in the pockets of his rain-soaked jacket.

Finally Taylor spoke: "Trust me, Carl."

"It's not that easy. A little boy's life is at stake."

"I know."

With that, Sergeant Huddle sighed and turned away. Ultimately it was his call. He was the one officially coordinating the search. It was his report, it was his duty . . . and in the end he would be the one who had to answer for it.

"All right," he finally said. "We'll do it your way. I just hope to God you're right."

Twelve-thirty now.

Arriving at the hospital, Judy McAden immediately approached the front desk. No stranger to hospital protocol, she asked to see Denise Holton, her niece. The clerk at the front desk didn't question her—the waiting room was still filled with people—and hurriedly checked the records. Denise Holton, she explained, had been moved to a room upstairs, but visiting hours were over. If she could come back tomorrow morning—

"Can you at least tell me how she's doing?" Judy interrupted.

The lady shrugged wearily. "It says she was taken

in for an X-ray, but that's all I know. I'm sure more information will be available once things begin to settle down."

"What time do visiting hours start?"

"Eight o'clock." The lady was already reaching for another file.

"I see," Judy said, sounding defeated. Over the clerk's shoulder, Judy noticed that things seemed even more chaotic than they were in the waiting room. Nurses were moving from room to room, looking harried and overwhelmed.

"Do I have to stop here before I go up to see her? Tomorrow, I mean?"

"No. You can go in the main entrance, around the corner. Just head up to room 217 tomorrow morning and inform the nurses at the station when you get there. They'll direct you to her room."

"Thank you."

Judy stepped away from the desk, and the next person in line moved forward. He was a middle-aged man who smelled strongly of alcohol. His arm was in a makeshift sling.

"What's taking so long? My arm is killing me."

The clerk sighed impatiently. "I'm sorry, but as you can see, we're really busy tonight. The doctor will see you as soon . . ."

Judy made sure that the lady's attention was still focused on the man at the desk. Then she exited the waiting area through a set of double swinging doors that led directly to the main area of the hospital. From previous visits to the hospital she knew that the elevators were at the end of the corridor.

In a matter of minutes she was sailing past a vacated nurses' station, heading for room 217.

At the same time Judy was making her way to Denise's room, the men resumed their search. Twenty-four men in total, with only enough distance between them to allow them to see the neighboring flashlights, they stretched nearly a quarter of a mile wide. Slowly they began moving to the southeast, shining lights everywhere, oblivious of the storm. Within a few minutes the lights from the cars on the highway were swallowed up once more. For the people who'd just arrived, the sudden darkness was a shock, and they wondered how long a young boy could survive out here.

Some of the others, however, were beginning to wonder if they'd even be able to find the body.

Denise was still awake because sleep was simply an impossibility. There was a clock on the wall alongside her bed, and she was staring at it, watching the minutes pass with frightening regularity.

Kyle had been missing for nearly four hours now. *Four hours!*

She wanted to do something—anything but lie there so helplessly, useless to Kyle and the searchers. She wanted to be out looking for him, and the fact that she wasn't was more painful than her injuries. She had to know what was going on. She wanted to take charge. But here, she couldn't do anything.

Her body had betrayed her. In the past hour the dizziness had abated only slightly. She still couldn't keep her balance long enough to walk down the hall, let alone participate in the search. Bright lights hurt her eyes, and when the doctor had asked her a few simple questions, she'd seen three images of his face. Now, alone in the room, she hated herself for her weakness. What kind of mother was she?

She couldn't even look for her own child!

She'd broken down completely at midnight—Kyle had been gone for three hours—when she realized she wouldn't be able to leave the hospital. She'd begun to scream Kyle's name over and over, as soon as the X-ray had been completed. It was a strange relief to just let go, to scream his name at the top of her lungs. In her mind, Kyle could hear her, and she was willing him to listen to her voice. *Come back, Kyle. Come back to where Mommy was. You can hear me, can't you?* It didn't matter that two nurses were telling her to be quiet, to calm down, while she struggled violently against their grip. Just relax, they said, everything's going to be okay.

But she couldn't stop. She just kept screaming his name and fighting them until they'd finally brought her here. By then she'd screamed herself out and the screaming had turned into sobs. A nurse had stayed with her for a few minutes to make sure she'd be okay, then had to respond to an emergency call in another room. Since then Denise had been alone.

She stared at the second hand of the bedside clock.

Tick.

No one knew what was going on. Before she'd been called away, Denise had asked the nurse to call the police to find out what was happening. She'd begged her, but the nurse had gently refused. Instead she'd said that as soon as they heard anything, they would let her know. Until then the best thing she could do was to calm down, to relax.

Relax.

Were they crazy?

He was still out there, and Denise knew he was still alive. He had to be. If Kyle was dead, she would know it. She would feel it deep down, and the feeling would be tangible, like getting hit in the stomach. Maybe they had a special connection, maybe all mothers shared it with their children. Maybe it was because Kyle couldn't talk and she had to rely on instinct when dealing with him. She wasn't exactly sure. But in her heart she believed she would know, and so far her heart had been silent.

Kyle was still alive.

He had to be . . .

Oh please, God, let him be.

Tick.

Judy McAden didn't knock. Instead she opened the door slightly, noticing the overhead light was off. A small lamp glowed dimly in the corner of the room as Judy quietly made her way inside. She couldn't tell whether Denise was asleep or not but didn't want to wake her if she was. As Judy was closing the door, Denise turned her head groggily and peered at her.

Even in the semidarkness, when Judy turned and saw Denise lying in the bed, she froze. It was one of the few times in her life that she didn't know what to say.

She knew Denise Holton.

Immediately—despite the bandage around her head, despite the bruises on her cheek, despite everything—Judy recognized Denise as the young woman who used the computers at the library. The one with the cute little boy who liked the books about airplanes . . .

Oh, no . . . the cute little boy . . .

Denise, however, didn't make the connection as she squinted at the lady standing before her. Her thoughts were still hazy. Nurse? No—not dressed right. The police? No, too old. But her face seemed familiar somehow . . .

"Do I know you?" she finally croaked out.

Judy, finally gathering her senses, started toward the bed. She spoke softly.

"Sort of. I've seen you in the library before. I work there."

Denise's eyes were half-open. *The library?* The room began to spin again.

"What are you doing here?" Her words came out slurred, the sounds running together.

What, indeed? Judy couldn't help but think.

She adjusted her purse strap nervously. "I heard about your son getting lost. My son is one of the ones out there looking for him right now."

As she answered, Denise's eyes flickered with a mixture of hope and fear, and her expression seemed to clear. She broke in with a question, but this time the words came out more lucidly than before.

"Have you heard anything?"

The question was sudden, but Judy realized that she should have expected it. Why else would she have come to see her?

Judy shook her head. "No, nothing. I'm sorry."

Denise pressed her lips together, staying silent. She seemed to be evaluating the answer before finally turning away.

"I'd like to be alone," Denise said.

Still uncertain of what to do—*Why on earth did I come? She doesn't even know me*—Judy said the only thing she herself would have wanted to hear, the only thing she could think to say.

"They'll find him, Denise."

At first Judy didn't think that Denise had heard her, but then she saw Denise's jaw quiver, followed by a welling of tears in her eyes. Denise made no sound at all. She seemed to be holding back her emotions as if she didn't want anyone to see her this way, and that somehow made it worse. Though she didn't know what Denise would do, Judy acted on motherly impulse and moved closer, pausing briefly beside the bed before finally sitting. Denise didn't seem to notice. Judy watched her in silence.

What was I thinking? That I could help? What on earth can I do? Maybe I shouldn't have come . . . She doesn't need me here. If she asks me to go again, I'll go . . .

Her thoughts were interrupted by a voice so low that Judy could barely hear it.

"But what if they don't?"

Judy reached for her hand and gave it a squeeze. "They will."

Denise drew a long, uneven breath, as if trying to draw strength from some hidden reserve. She slowly turned her head and faced Judy with red, swollen eyes. "I don't even know if they're still looking for him . . ."

Up close, Judy flashed upon the resemblance

between Denise and her mother—or rather, how her mother used to look. They could have been sisters, and she wondered why she hadn't made the connection at the library. But that thought was quickly replaced as Denise's words sank in. Unsure if she had heard correctly, Judy furrowed her brow.

"What do you mean? Do you mean to say that no one's kept you informed of what's happening out there?"

Even though Denise was looking at her, she seemed very far away, lost in a kind of listless daze.

"I haven't heard a thing since I was put in the ambulance."

"Nothing?" she finally cried, shocked that they had neglected to keep her informed.

Denise shook her head.

At once Judy glanced around for the phone and stood up, her confidence rising with the knowledge that there was something she *could* do. This must have been the reason she'd felt the urge to come. *Not telling the mother? Completely unacceptable. Not only that, but . . . cruel. Inadvertent, to be sure, but cruel nonetheless.*

Judy sat in the chair beside the small table in the corner of the room and picked up the handset. After dialing quickly, she reached the police department in Edenton. Denise's eyes widened when she realized what Judy was doing.

"This is Judy McAden, and I'm with Denise Holton at the hospital. I was calling to find out what's going on out there . . . No . . . no . . . I'm sure it's very busy, but I need to talk to Mike Harris . . . Well, tell him to pick up. Tell him Judy's on the line. It's important."

She put her hand over the receiver and spoke to Denise.

"I've known Mike for years—he's the captain. Maybe he'll know something."

There was a click, and she heard the other end pick up again.

"Hey, Mike . . . No, I'm fine, but that's not why I called. I'm here with Denise Holton, the one whose boy's in the swamp. I'm at the hospital, and it seems that no one's told her what's happening out there . . . I know it's a zoo, but she needs to know what's going on . . . I see . . . uh-huh . . . oh, okay, thanks."

After hanging up, she shook her head and spoke to Denise while dialing a new number. "He hasn't heard anything, but then his men aren't conducting the search because it's outside the county lines. Let me try the fire station."

Again she went through the preliminaries before reaching someone in charge. Then, after a minute or so, her tone becoming that of a lecturing mother: "I see . . . well, can you radio someone at the scene? I've got a mother here who has a right to know what's happening, and I can't believe you haven't kept her informed. How would you like it if it was Linda here and Tommy was the one who was lost? . . . I don't care how busy it is. There's no excuse for it. I simply can't believe you overlooked something like that . . . No, I'd rather not call back. Why don't I hold while you radio in . . . Joe, she needs to know now. She hasn't heard a thing for hours now . . . All right, then . . ."

Looking at Denise: "I'm holding now. He's calling over there with the radio. We'll know in just a couple of minutes. How're you holding up?"

Denise smiled for the first time in hours. "Thank you," she said weakly.

A minute passed, then another, before Judy spoke again. "Yes, I'm still here . . ." Judy was silent as she listened to the report, and despite everything, Denise found herself growing hopeful. *Maybe . . . please . . .* She watched Judy for any outward signs of emotion. As the silence continued, Judy's mouth formed a straight line. She finally spoke into the handset. "Oh, I see . . . Thanks, Joe. Call here if you find out anything, anything at all . . . Yes, the hospital in Elizabeth City. And we'll check back in a little while."

As she watched, Denise felt a lump rise in her throat as her nausea returned.

Kyle was still out there.

Judy hung up the phone and went to the bed again. "They haven't found him yet, but they're still out there. A bunch of people from the town showed up, so there are more people than there were before. The weather's cleared up some, and they think Kyle was moving to the southeast. They went that way about an hour ago."

Denise barely heard her.

It was coming up on 1:30 A.M.

The temperature—originally in the sixties—was nearing forty degrees now, and they'd been moving as a group for over an hour. A cold northern wind was pushing the temperature down quickly, and the searchers began to realize that if they hoped to find the little boy alive, they needed to find him in the next couple of hours.

They'd now reached an area of the swamp that was a little less dense, where the trees grew farther apart and the vines and bushes didn't scrape against them continually. Here they were able to search more quickly, and Taylor could see three men—or rather their flashlights—in each direction. Nothing was being overlooked.

Taylor had hunted in this part of the swamp before. Because the ground was elevated slightly, it was usually dry, and deer flocked to the area. A half mile or so ahead, the elevation dropped again to below the water tables, and they would come to an area of the swamp known to hunters as Duck Shot. During the season men could be found in the dozens of duck blinds that lined the area. The water there was a few feet deep year-round, and the hunting was always good.

It was also the farthest point that Kyle could have traveled.

If, of course, they were going in the right direction.

Chapter 7

It was now 2:26 A.M. Kyle had been missing for almost five and a half hours.

Judy wet a washcloth and brought it to the bedside and gently wiped Denise's face. Denise hadn't spoken much, and Judy didn't press her to do so. Denise looked shell-shocked: pale and exhausted, her eyes red and glassy. Judy had called again at the top of the hour and had been told that there still wasn't any news. This time Denise had seemed to expect it and had barely reacted.

"Can I get you a cup of water?" Judy asked.

When Denise didn't answer, Judy rose from the bed again and got a cup anyway. When she returned, Denise tried to sit up in the bed to take a sip, but the accident had begun to take its toll on the rest of her body. A shooting pain coursed from her wrist through her shoulder, like a surge of electricity. Her stomach and chest ached as if something heavy had been placed on top of her for a long time and now that it had finally been removed, her body was slowly coming back to shape, like a balloon being painfully reinflated. Her neck was stiffening, and it seemed as if a steel rod had been placed in her upper spine that kept her head from moving back and forth.

"Here, let me help," Judy offered.

Judy set the cup on the table and helped Denise sit up. Denise winced and held her breath, pursing her lips tightly as the pain came in waves, then relaxed as they finally began to subside. Judy handed her the water.

As Denise took a sip, she shot a glance at the clock again. As before, it moved forward relentlessly.

When would they find him?

Studying Denise's expression, Judy asked: "Would you like me to get a nurse?"

Denise didn't answer.

Judy covered Denise's hand with her own. "Would you like me to leave so that you can rest?"

Denise turned from the clock to Judy again and still saw a stranger . . . but a nice stranger, someone who cared. Someone with kind eyes, reminding her of her elderly neighbor in Atlanta.

I just want Kyle . . .

"I don't think I'll be able to sleep," she said finally.

Denise finished her cup and Judy took it from her. "What was your name again?" Denise asked. The slurring had lessened a little, but exhaustion made the words come out weakly. "I heard it when you made the calls, but I can't remember."

Judy set the cup on the table, then helped Denise get comfortable again. "I'm Judy McAden. I guess I forgot to mention that when I first came in."

"And you work in the library?"

She nodded. "I've seen you and your son there on more than a few occasions."

"Is that why . . . ?" Denise asked, trailing off.

"No, actually, I came because I knew your mother when she was young. She and I were friends a long time ago. When I heard you were in trouble . . . well, I didn't want you to think that you were in this all alone."

Denise squinted, trying to focus on Judy as if for the first time. "My mother?"

Judy nodded. "She lived down the road from me. We grew up together."

Denise tried to remember if her mother had mentioned her, but concentrating on the past was like trying to decipher an image on a fuzzy television screen. She couldn't remember one way or the other, but as she was trying to do so, the telephone rang.

It startled them both, and they turned toward it, the sound shrill and suddenly ominous.

A few minutes earlier Taylor and the others had reached Duck Shot. Here, the marshy water began to deepen, a mile and a half from the spot where the accident had occurred. Kyle could have gone no farther, but still they'd found nothing.

One by one, after reaching Duck Shot, the group began to converge, and when the walkie-talkies clicked to life, there were more than a few disappointed voices.

Taylor, however, didn't call in. Still searching, he again tried to put himself in Kyle's shoes by asking the same questions he had before. Had Kyle come this way? Time and time again he came to the same conclusion. The wind alone would have steered him in this general direction. He wouldn't have wanted to fight the wind, and heading this way would have kept the lightning behind him.

Damn. He had to have moved in this direction. He simply had to.

But where was he?

They couldn't have missed him, could they? Before they'd started, Taylor had reminded everyone to check every possible hiding place along the way—trees, bushes, stumps, fallen logs—anywhere a child might hide from the storm . . . and he was sure they had. Everyone out here cared as much as he did.

Then where was he?

He suddenly wished for nightvision goggles, something that would have rendered the darkness less crippling, allowing them to pick up the image of the boy from his body heat. Even though such equipment was available commercially, he didn't know anyone in town who had that type of gear. It went without saying that the fire department didn't have any—they couldn't even afford a regular crew, let alone something so high-tech. Limited budgets, after all, were a regular staple of life in a small town.

But the National Guard . . .

Taylor was sure that they would have the necessary equipment, but that wasn't an option now. It would simply take too long to get a unit out here. And borrowing a set from his counterparts at the National Guard wasn't realistic—the supply clerk would need authorization from his or her superior, who'd need it from someone else, who'd request that forms were filled out, blah, blah, blah. And even if by some miracle the request were granted, the nearest depot was almost two hours away. Hell, it would almost be daylight by then.

Think.

Lightning flashed again, startling him. The last bout of lightning had occurred a while back, and aside from the rain, he thought the worst was behind him.

But as the night sky was illuminated, he saw it in the distance . . . rectangular and wooden, overgrown with foliage. One of the dozens of duck blinds.

His mind began to click quickly . . . duck blinds . . . they looked almost like a kid's playhouse, with enough shelter to keep much of the rain away. Had Kyle seen one?

No, too easy . . . it couldn't be . . . but . . .

Despite himself, Taylor felt the adrenaline begin to race through his system. He did his best to remain calm.

Maybe—that's all it was. Just a great big "maybe."

But right now "maybe" was all he had, and he rushed to the first duck blind he'd seen. His boots were sinking in the mud, making a sucking sound as he fought through the ground's spongy thickness. A few seconds later he reached the blind—it hadn't been used since last fall and was overgrown with climbing vines and brush. He pushed his way through the vines and poked his head inside. Sweeping his flashlight around the interior of the blind, he almost expected to see a young boy hiding from the storm.

But all he saw was aging plywood.

As he stepped back, another bolt of lightning lit the sky and Taylor caught a glimpse of another duck blind, not fifty yards away. One that wasn't as shrouded as the one he'd just searched. Taylor took off again, running, believing . . .

If I were a kid and I'd gone this far and saw what looked like a little house . . .

He reached the second blind, searched quickly, and found nothing. He cursed again, filled with an even greater sense of urgency. He took off again, heading for the next blind without knowing exactly where it was. He knew from experience that it wouldn't be more than a hundred yards away, near the waterline.

And he was right.

Breathing hard, he fought the rain, the wind, and most of all the mud, knowing in his heart of hearts that his hunch about the duck blinds had to be right. If Kyle wasn't here, he was going to call the others on the walkie-talkie and have them search every duck blind in the area.

This time when he reached the blind, he pressed through the overgrowth. Moving around to the side, he steeled himself to expect nothing. Shining his light inside, he almost stopped breathing.

A little boy, sitting in the corner, muddy and scratched, filthy . . . but otherwise, seemingly okay.

Taylor blinked, thinking it was a mirage, but when he opened his eyes again, the little boy was still there, Mickey Mouse shirt and all.

Taylor was too surprised to speak. Despite the hours out there, the conclusion had seemed to come so quickly.

In the silence—a few seconds at most—Kyle looked up at him, toward the big man in a long yellow coat, with an expression of surprise on his face, as though he'd been caught doing something that would get him in trouble.

"Hewwo," Kyle said exuberantly, and Taylor laughed aloud. Grins immediately spread across both their faces. Taylor dropped to one knee, and the little boy scrambled to his feet and then into his arms. He was cold and wet, shivering, and when Taylor felt those small arms wrap around his neck, tears welled in his eyes.

"Well, hello, little man. I take it you must be Kyle."

Chapter 8

"He's okay, everyone . . . I repeat, he's okay. I've got Kyle with me right now."

With those words spoken into the walkie-talkie, a whoop of excitement arose from the searchers and the word was passed along to the station, where Joe called in to the hospital.

It was 2:31 A.M.

Judy retrieved the phone from the table, then sat it on the bed so that Denise could answer it. She was barely breathing as she picked up the receiver. Then all at once she brought her hand to her mouth to stifle the scream. Her smile, so heartfelt and emotional, was contagious, and Judy had to fight the urge to jump up and down.

The questions Denise asked were typical: "He's really okay? . . . Where did you find him? . . . Are you sure he's not hurt? . . . When will I see him? . . . Why so long? . . . Oh yes, I see. But you're sure? . . . Thank you, thank you all so much . . . I can't believe it!"

When she hung up the phone, Denise sat up—

this time without help—and spontaneously hugged Judy while filling her in.

"They're bringing him to the hospital . . . he's cold and wet, and they want to bring him in as a precaution, just to make sure everything's okay. He should be here in an hour or so . . . I just can't believe it."

The excitement brought the dizziness back, but this time Denise couldn't have cared less.

Kyle was safe. That was the only thing that mattered now.

Back in the swamp, Taylor had removed his raincoat and wrapped it around Kyle to keep him warm. Then, carrying him from the blind, he met up with the others and they waited in Duck Shot just long enough to ensure that all the men were accounted for. Once they were assembled, they started back as a group, this time in tightly knit formation.

The five hours of searching had taken their toll on Taylor, and carrying Kyle was a struggle. The boy weighed at least forty pounds, and the extra weight not only made his arms ache, it also made him sink even deeper in the mud. By the time he reached the road, he was spent. How women were able to carry their kids for hours while shopping in the mall was beyond him.

An ambulance was waiting for them. At first Kyle didn't want to let Taylor go, but Taylor, speaking softly, was finally able to coax him down to let the attendant examine him. Sitting in the ambulance, Taylor wanted nothing more than a long hot shower, but because Kyle seemed on the verge of panicking every time Taylor moved away, he decided to ride with him to the hospital. Sergeant Huddle led the way in his trooper's car, while the other searchers began to head home.

The long night was finally over.

They reached the hospital a little after 3:30 A.M. By that time the emergency room had calmed down and nearly every patient had been seen. The doctors had been informed of Kyle's imminent arrival and were waiting for him. So were Denise and Judy.

Judy had surprised the nurse on duty by walking up to the station in the middle of the night to request a wheelchair for Denise Holton. "What are you doing here? Don't you know what time it is? Visiting hours are over . . ." But Judy simply ignored the questions and repeated her request. A little cajoling was necessary—though not much. "They found her son and they're bringing him here. She wants to meet him when he arrives."

The nurse went ahead and granted the request.

The ambulance rolled up a few minutes earlier than predicted, and the back door swung open. Kyle was wheeled in as Denise struggled to her feet. Once inside the doors, both the doctor and the nurses stepped back so that Kyle could see his mother.

In the ambulance he'd been stripped down, then wrapped in warm blankets to get his body temperature back up. Though his temperature had dropped a couple of degrees over the last few hours, he hadn't been at real risk of hypothermia, and the blankets had done their job. Kyle's face was pink and he was moving easily—in every respect he looked far better than his mother did.

Denise reached the gurney, bending closer so that Kyle could see her, and Kyle sat up immediately. He climbed into her embrace and they held each other tightly.

"Hello, Mommy," he finally said. *(Hewwo, Money)*

Denise laughed, as did the doctor and nurses.

"Hi, sweetie," she said, whispering into his ear, her eyes tightly closed. "Are you okay?"

Kyle didn't answer, though this time Denise couldn't have cared less.

Denise accompanied Kyle, holding his hand as the gurney was rolled to the exam room. Judy hung back throughout all this, watching them go, not wanting to interrupt. As they disappeared from view, she sighed, suddenly realizing how tired she was. She hadn't been up this late in years. It had been worth it, though—there was nothing quite like riding an emotional roller coaster to really get the old ticker pumping. A few more nights like this and she'd be in shape for a marathon.

She walked out of the emergency room just as the ambulance pulled away and began to search through her pocketbook for her keys. Looking up, she spied Taylor talking to Carl Huddle near his patrol car and breathed a sigh of relief. Taylor saw her at the same time, sure at first that his eyes were playing tricks. He eyed her curiously as he started toward her.

"Mom, what are you doing here?" he asked incredulously.

"I just spent the evening with Denise Holton—you know, the child's mother? I thought she might need some support."

"And you just decided to come down? Without even knowing her?"

They hugged each other. "Of course."

Taylor felt a surge of pride in that. His mother was a hell of a lady. Judy finally pulled back, giving him the once-over.

"You look terrible, son."

Taylor laughed. "Thanks for the vote of confidence. I actually feel pretty good, though."

"I'll bet you do. And you should. You did something wonderful tonight."

He smiled briefly before turning serious again. "So

how was she?" he asked. "Before we found him, I mean."

Judy shrugged. "Upset, lost, terrified . . . pick your adjective. She's been through pretty much everything tonight."

He looked at her slyly. "I heard you gave Joe a piece of your mind."

"And I'd do it again. What were you guys thinking?"

Taylor raised his hands in defense. "Hey, don't blame me. I'm not the boss, and besides, he was as worried as we were. Trust me."

She reached up, brushing the hair from Taylor's eyes. "I'll bet you're pretty worn out."

"A little. Nothing that a few hours' sleep can't fix. Can I walk you to your car?"

Judy looped her arm through Taylor's and they started toward the parking lot. After a few steps she glanced at him.

"You're such a nice young man. How come you're not married yet?"

"I'm worried about the in-laws."

"Huh?"

"Not my in-laws, Mom. My wife's."

Judy playfully pulled her arm away. "I take back everything I just said."

Taylor chuckled to himself as he reached for her again. "Just kidding. You know I love you."

"You better."

When they reached the car, Taylor took the keys and opened her door. Once Judy was behind the wheel, he bent down to peer at her through the open window. "Are you sure you're not too tired to drive?" he asked.

"No, I'll be fine. It's not that far. By the way, where's your car?"

"Still at the scene. I rode with Kyle in the ambulance. Carl's gonna bring me back."

Judy nodded as she turned the key, the engine cranking over immediately.

"I'm proud of you, Taylor."

"Thanks, Mom. I'm proud of you, too."

Chapter 9

The following day dawned cloudy with sporadic rain, though most of the storm had already passed out to sea. The newspapers were filled with coverage of what had happened the night before, the headlines focusing largely on a tornado near Maysville that had destroyed part of a mobile home park, leaving four people dead and another seven injured. No coverage at all was granted to the successful search for Kyle Holton—the fact that he'd been lost at all wasn't learned by any reporters until the following day, hours after he'd already been found. The success had made it, in their vernacular, a non-event, especially when compared with the continual reports feeding in from the eastern part of the state.

Denise and Kyle were still in the hospital and had been allowed to sleep in the same room. Overnights were mandatory for both of them (or, rather, what was left of the night), and though Kyle could have been discharged the following afternoon, the doctors wanted to keep Denise in for an extra day of observation.

The noise in the hospital made it impossible to sleep late, and after another examination of both of them by the doctor on call, Denise and Kyle spent the morning watching cartoons. Both were on her bed, pillows behind them, wearing ill-fitting hospital gowns. Kyle was watching *Scooby-Doo*, his favorite. It had been Denise's favorite as a child, too. All they needed was some popcorn, but the very thought made Denise's stomach turn. Even though the dizziness had subsided for the most part, bright lights still hurt her eyes and she had trouble keeping food down.

"He's running," Kyle said, pointing at the screen, watching Scooby's legs turning in circles. *(Eez runny)*

"Yes, he's running from the ghost. Can you say that?"

"Running from the ghost," he said. *(Runny fraw ah goz)*

Her arm was around him, and she patted him on the shoulder. "Did you run last night?"

Kyle nodded, his eyes still on the screen. "Yes, eez runny."

She looked at him tenderly. "Were you scared last night?"

"Yes, he's scared." *(Yes, eez scairt)*

Though his tone changed slightly, Denise didn't

know whether he was talking about himself now or still talking about Scooby-Doo. Kyle didn't understand the differences among pronouns (I, you, me, he, she, and so on), nor did he use verbal tenses properly. Running, ran, run . . . it all meant the same thing, at least as far as she could tell. The concept of time (yesterday, tomorrow, last night) was also beyond him.

It wasn't the first time she'd tried to talk to him about the experience. Earlier she'd tried to talk to him about it but hadn't gotten very far. Why did you run? What were you thinking? What did you see? Where did they find you? Kyle hadn't answered any of her questions, nor had she expected him to, but she wanted to ask them anyway. One day maybe he'd be able to tell her. One day, once he could talk, he might be able to think back and explain it to her. "Yeah, Mom, I remember . . ." Until then, though, it would remain a mystery.

Until then.

It seemed as far away as ever.

With a slow push, the door squeaked open.

"Knock, knock."

Denise turned toward the door as Judy McAden peeked inside. "I hope I'm not coming at a bad time. I called the hospital, and they said you both were up."

Denise sat up, trying to straighten her wrinkled

hospital gown. "No, of course not. We're just watching TV. C'mon in."

"Are you sure?"

"Please. I can only take so many hours of cartoons without a break." Using the remote, she turned down the volume slightly.

Judy walked to the bed. "Well, I just wanted to come by to meet your son. He's quite the topic of conversation around town now. I got about twenty calls this morning."

Denise angled her head, glancing proudly at her son. "Well, here he is, the little terror. Kyle, say hello to Miss Judy."

"Hello, Miss Judy," he whispered. *(Hewwo, Miss Jeewey)* His eyes were still glued to the screen.

Judy pulled up the chair and sat beside the bed. She patted him on the leg.

"Hello, Kyle. How are you? I heard you had a big adventure last night. You had your mother really worried."

After a moment of silence Denise prodded her son. "Kyle—say, 'Yes, I did.'"

"Yes, I did." *(Yes, I di)*

Judy glanced at Denise. "He looks just like you."

"That's why I bought him," she said quickly, and Judy laughed. Judy turned her attention to Kyle again.

"Your mom's funny, huh?"

Kyle didn't respond.

"Kyle doesn't talk too well yet," Denise offered quietly. "He's delayed in speech."

Judy nodded, then leaned in a little farther as if telling Kyle a secret.

"Oh, that's okay, isn't it, Kyle? I'm not as much fun as watching cartoons, anyway. What're you watching?"

Again he didn't answer, and Denise tapped him on the shoulder. "Kyle, what's on TV?"

Without looking at her he whispered, "Scooby-Doo." *(Scoody-Doo)*

Judy brightened. "Oh, Taylor used to watch that when he was little." Then, speaking a little slower: "Is it funny?"

Kyle nodded exuberantly. "Yes, it's funny." *(Yes, eez fuh-ee)*

Denise's eyes widened just a little when he answered, then softened again. *Thank God for small favors . . .*

Judy turned her attention to Denise. "I can't believe it's still on the air."

"Scooby? He's on twice a day," Denise said. "We get to watch it in the morning *and* the afternoon."

"Lucky you."

"Yes, lucky me." Denise rolled her eyes, and Judy chuckled under her breath.

"So how are the two of you holding up?"

Denise sat up a little higher in the bed. "Well,

Kyle here is healthy as can be. From the looks of him, you'd think that nothing at all happened last night. Me, on the other hand . . . well, let's just say I could be better."

"Will you be getting out soon?"

"Tomorrow, I hope. Body willing, of course."

"If you have to stay, who's going to watch Kyle?"

"Oh, he'll stay with me. The hospital's been pretty good about that."

"Well, if you need anyone to watch him, just let me know."

"Thanks for the offer," she said, her eyes darting toward Kyle again. "But I think we'll be okay, won't we, Kyle? Mommy's had enough separation to last for a while."

On the cartoon, a mummy's tomb suddenly opened and Shaggy and Scooby were off and running again, Velma close behind. Kyle laughed, without seeming to have heard his mother.

"Besides, you've already done more than enough," Denise went on. "I'm sorry I didn't get a chance to thank you last night, but—well . . ."

Judy raised her hands to stop her. "Oh, don't worry about that. I'm just glad everything worked out the way it did. Has Carl stopped by yet?"

"Carl?"

"He's the state trooper. The one from last night."

"No, not yet. He'll be coming by?"

Judy nodded. "That's what I heard. Taylor told me this morning that Carl still had to wrap up a few things."

"Taylor? That's your son, right?"

"My one and only."

Denise struggled with the memory from the night before. "He was the one who found me, right?"

Judy nodded. "He was trying to find some downed power lines when he came across your car."

"I guess I should thank him, too."

"I'll tell him for you. But he wasn't the only one out there, you know. They had more than twenty people by the end. People from all over town went out to help."

Denise shook her head, amazed. "But they didn't even know me."

"People have a way of surprising you, don't they? But there are a lot of good people here. To tell you the truth, I wasn't surprised at all. Edenton's a small town, but it has a big heart."

"Have you lived here your whole life?"

Judy nodded.

Denise whispered conspiratorially, "I'll bet you know practically everything that goes on here."

Judy put her hand over her heart like Scarlett O'Hara and slowly drawled out the words.

"Darlin', I could tell you stories that would make your eyebrows curl."

Denise laughed. "Maybe we'll have a chance to visit sometime and you could fill me in."

Judy played the innocent southern belle to the hilt. "But that would be gossiping, and gossiping's a sin."

"I know. But I'm weak."

Judy winked. "Good. I am, too. We'll do that. And while we're at it, I'll tell you what your mom was like as a little girl."

An hour after lunch, Carl Huddle met with Denise and finished up the remaining paperwork. Lighthearted and far more alert than the evening before, Denise answered everything in detail. Even then—since the case was more or less officially closed—it didn't take more than twenty minutes. Kyle was sitting on the floor, playing with an airplane that Denise had fished from her purse. Sergeant Huddle had returned that as well.

When they were finished, Sergeant Huddle folded everything into a manila file, though he didn't rise right away. Instead he closed his eyes, stifling a yawn with the back of his hand.

"Excuse me," he said, trying to shake the drowsiness that had come over him.

"Tired?" she asked sympathetically.

"A little. I had an eventful evening."

Denise adjusted herself on the bed. "Well, I'm glad

you came by. I wanted to thank you for what you did last night. You can't imagine how much it means to me."

Sergeant Huddle nodded as if he'd been in similar situations before.

"You're welcome. That's my job, though. Besides, I have a little girl of my own, and if it had been her, I would have wanted everyone within a fifty-mile radius to drop what they were doing to help find her. You couldn't have dragged me away last night."

From his tone, Denise didn't doubt him.

"So," she asked, "you have a little girl?"

"Yeah, I do. Her birthday was last Monday. Just turned five. It's a good age."

"They're all good ages, at least that's what I've learned. What's her name?"

"Campbell. Like the soup. It's Kim's—my wife's—maiden name."

"Is she your only child?"

"So far. But in a couple of months she won't be."

"Oh, congratulations. Boy or girl?"

"Don't know yet. We'll be surprised, just like we were with Campbell."

She nodded, closing her eyes for a moment. Sergeant Huddle bounced the folder against his leg, then rose to leave.

"Well, I should be going. You probably need some rest."

Though she suspected he was speaking more for himself, Denise sat up higher in the bed. "Well . . . um . . . before you go—can I ask you a couple of questions about last night? With all the commotion then and everything this morning, I really haven't learned what went on. At least, not from the horse's mouth."

"Sure. Ask away."

"How were you able to . . . I mean, it was so dark and with the storm . . ." She paused, trying to find the right words.

"You mean, how did we find him?" Sergeant Huddle offered.

She nodded.

He glanced at Kyle, who was still playing with an airplane in the corner.

"Well, I'd like to say it was all skill and training, but it wasn't. We got lucky. Damn lucky. He could have been out there for days—it's that dense in the swamp. For a while there, we had no idea which way he'd gone, but Taylor sort of figured that Kyle would follow the wind and keep the lightning behind him. Sure enough, he was right."

He nodded toward Kyle with a look like that of a father after his son hits the game-winning home run, then went on. "You've got one tough boy there, Miss Holton. His being okay had more to do with him than any of us. Most kids—hell, every kid I know—would have been terrified, but your little boy wasn't. It's pretty amazing."

Denise's brow furrowed as she thought about what he'd just told her.

"Wait—was that Taylor McAden?"

"Yeah, the guy who found you." He reached up and scratched his jaw. "Actually, he was the one who found both of you, if you want to get right down to it. He found Kyle in a duck blind, and Kyle wouldn't let go of him until we got him to the hospital. Clamped on to him like a crab claw."

"Taylor McAden found Kyle? But I thought you did."

Sergeant Huddle picked up his trooper hat off the end of the bed. "No, it wasn't me, but you can bet it wasn't because I wasn't trying. It's just that Taylor seemed to have a bead on him all night, don't ask me how."

Sergeant Huddle seemed lost in thought. From where she was lying, Denise could see the bags under his eyes. He looked drawn, as if he wanted nothing more than to curl up in bed.

"Well . . . thank you anyway. Without you, Kyle probably wouldn't be here."

"No problem. I love a happy ending, and I'm glad we had one."

After saying good-bye, Sergeant Huddle slipped out the door. As the door closed behind him, Denise looked upward, toward the ceiling, without really seeing it.

Taylor McAden? Judy McAden?

She couldn't believe the coincidence, but then again, everything that happened last night had fluke written all over it. The storm, the deer, the seat belt over her lap but not her shoulder (she'd never done that before and wouldn't do it again, that was for sure), Kyle wandering away while Denise was unconscious and unable to stop him . . . Everything.

Including the McAdens.

One here for support, the other one finding her car. One who knew her mother long ago and one who ended up locating Kyle.

Coincidence? Fate?

Something else?

Later that afternoon, with the help of a nurse and the local telephone directory, Denise wrote out individual thank-you notes to Carl and Judy, as well as a general note (addressed in care of the fire department) to everyone involved in the search.

Last, she wrote out her note to Taylor McAden, and as she did so, she couldn't help but wonder about him.

Chapter 10

Three days after the accident and successful search for Kyle Holton, Taylor McAden walked beneath the marlstone archway that served as an entrance and made his way to the headstone in Cypress Park Cemetery, the oldest cemetery in Edenton. He knew exactly where he was going, and he cut across the lawn, weaving around memorials. Some were so ancient that two centuries of rain had smoothed away nearly all the writing on the stones, and he could remember times he'd stopped to try to decipher them. It was, he soon realized, impossible.

Today, though, Taylor paid them little attention as he moved steadily beneath a cloudy sky, stopping only when he reached the shade of a giant willow tree. Here, on the west side of the cemetery, the marker he'd come to see stood twelve inches high. It was an otherwise nondescript granite block, inscribed simply on the upper face.

Grass had grown tall around the sides but was otherwise well tended. Directly in front of it, in a small tube set into the ground, was a bouquet of dried carnations. He didn't have to count them to know how many there were, nor did he wonder who had left them.

His mother had left eleven of them, one for every year of their marriage. She left them every May, on their anniversary, as she had for the past twenty-seven years. In all that time she'd never told Taylor about leaving them, and Taylor had never mentioned that he already knew. He was content to let her have her secret, if by doing so he could keep his own.

Unlike his mother, Taylor didn't visit the grave on his parents' anniversary. That was her day, the day they'd pledged their love in front of family and friends. Instead Taylor visited in June, on the day his father died. That was the day he'd never forget.

As usual, he was dressed in jeans and a short-sleeved workshirt. He'd come directly from a project he'd been working on, slipping away during the lunch break, and parts of his shirt were neatly tacked to his chest and back. No one had asked where he was going, and he hadn't bothered to explain. It was no one's business but his own.

Taylor bent and started to pull the longer blades of grass along the sides, twisting them around his hand to get a better grip and snapping them off to make them level with the surrounding lawn. He took his time, giving his mind a chance to clear, leveling all four sides. When finished, he ran his finger over the polished granite. The words were simple:

Mason Thomas McAden
Loving father and husband
1936–1972

Year by year, visit by visit, Taylor had grown older; he was now the same age his father was when he'd passed away. He'd changed from a frightened young boy to the man he was today. His memory of his father, however, had ended abruptly on that last dreadful day. No matter how hard he tried, he couldn't picture what his father would look like if he were still alive. In Taylor's mind, his father would always be thirty-six. Never younger, never older—selective memory made that clear. And so, of course, did the photo.

Taylor closed his eyes, waiting for the image to come. He didn't need to carry the photo with him to know exactly how it looked. It still sat on the fireplace mantel in the living room. He'd seen it every day for the past twenty-seven years.

The photo had been taken a week before the accident, on a warm June morning right outside their home. In the picture his father was stepping off the back porch, fishing pole in hand, on his way to the Chowan River. Though he wasn't visible, Taylor remembered that he had been trailing behind his father, still in the house collecting his lures, scrambling to find everything he needed. His mother had been hiding behind the truck, and when she had called his father's name, Mason had turned and she'd unexpectedly snapped the picture. The film had been sent away to be developed, and because of that, it hadn't been destroyed with the other photos. Judy didn't pick it up until after the funeral and had cried while looking at it, then slipped it into her purse. To others it wasn't anything special—his father walking in midstride, hair uncombed, a stain on the buttoned shirt he was wearing—but to Taylor it had captured the very essence of his father. It was there, that irrepressible spirit that defined the man he was, and that was the reason it had affected his mother so. It was in his expression, the gleam of his eye, the jaunty yet keenly alert pose.

A month after his father had died, Taylor had sneaked it out of her purse and fallen asleep while holding it. His mother had come in, found the photo pressed into his small hands, his fingers curled tightly around it. The photo itself was smudged with tears. The following day she'd taken the negative in to have a copy made, and Taylor glued four Popsicle sticks to a discarded piece of glass and mounted the photo. In all these years he'd never considered changing the frame.

Thirty-six.

His father seemed so young in the picture. His face was lean and youthful, his eyes and forehead showing only the faintest outlines of wrinkles that would never have the chance to deepen. Why, then, did his father seem so much older than Taylor felt right now? His father had seemed so . . . wise, so sure of himself, so brave. In the eyes of his nine-year-old son, he was a man of mythic proportion, a man who understood life and could explain nearly everything. Was it because he'd lived more deeply? Had his life been defined by broader, more exceptional experiences? Or was his impression simply the product of a young boy's feelings for his father, including the last moment they'd been together?

Taylor didn't know, but then he never would. The answers had been buried with his father a long time ago.

He could barely remember the weeks immediately after his father died. That time had blurred strangely into a series of fragmented memories: the funeral, staying with his grandparents in their home on the other side of town, suffocating nightmares when he tried to sleep. It was summer—school was out—and Taylor spent most of his time outside, trying to blot out what had happened. His mother wore black for two months, mourning the loss. Then, finally, the black was put away. They found a new place to live, something smaller, and even though nine-year-olds have little comprehension of death and how to deal with it, Taylor knew exactly what his mother was trying to tell him.

It's just the two of us now. We've got to go on.

After that fateful summer Taylor had drifted through school, earning decent but unspectacular grades, progressing steadily from one grade to the next. He was remarkably resilient, others would say, and in some ways they were right. With his mother's care and fortitude, his adolescent years were like those of most others who lived in this part of the country. He went camping and boating whenever he could; he played football, basketball, and baseball throughout his high school years. Yet in many ways he was considered a loner. Mitch was, and always had been, his only real friend, and in the summers they'd go hunting and fishing, just the two of them. They would vanish for a week at a time, sometimes traveling as far away as Georgia. Though Mitch was married now, they still did it whenever they could.

Once he graduated, Taylor bypassed college in favor of work, hanging drywall and learning the carpentry business. He apprenticed with a man who was an alcoholic, a bitter man whose wife had left him, who cared more about the money he'd make than the quality of the work. After a violent confrontation that nearly came to blows, Taylor quit working for him and started taking classes to earn his contractor's license.

He supported himself by working in the gypsum mine near Little Washington, a job that left him coughing almost every night, but by twenty-four he'd saved enough to start his own business. No project was too small, and he often underbid to build up his business and reputation. By twenty-eight he'd nearly gone bankrupt twice, but he stubbornly kept on going, eventually making it work. Over the past eight years he'd nurtured the business to the point where he made a decent living. Not anything grand—his house was small and his truck was six years old—but it was enough for him to lead the simple life he desired.

A life that included volunteering for the fire department.

His mother had tried strenuously to talk him out of it. It was the only instance in which he'd deliberately gone against her wishes.

Of course, she wanted to be a grandmother as well, and she'd let that slip out every now and then. Taylor usually made light of the comment and tried to change the subject. He hadn't come close to marriage and doubted whether he ever would. It wasn't something he imagined himself doing, though in the past he'd dated two women fairly seriously. The first time was in his early twenties, when he'd started seeing Valerie. She was coming off a disastrous relationship when they'd met—her boyfriend had gotten another woman pregnant, and Taylor was the one she'd turned to in her time of need. She was two years older, smart, and they had gotten along well for a time. But Valerie wanted something more serious; Taylor had told her honestly that he might never be ready. It was a source of tension without easy answers. In time they simply drifted apart; eventually she moved away. The last he'd heard, she was married to a lawyer and living in Charlotte.

Then there was Lori. Unlike Valerie, she was younger than Taylor and had moved to Edenton to work for the bank. She was a loan officer and worked long hours; she hadn't had the chance to make any friends when Taylor walked into the bank to apply for a mortgage. Taylor offered to introduce her around; she took him up on it. Soon they were dating. She had a childlike innocence that both charmed Taylor and aroused his protective interests, but eventually, she too wanted more than Taylor was willing to commit to. They broke up soon afterward. Now she was married to the mayor's son; she had three children and drove a minivan. He hadn't exchanged more than pleasantries with her since her engagement.

By the time he was thirty, he'd dated most of the single women in Edenton; by the time he was thirty-six, there weren't that many left. Mitch's wife, Melissa, had tried to set him up on various dates, but those had fizzled as well. But then again, he hadn't really been looking, had he? Both Valerie and

Lori claimed that there was something inside of him they were unable to reach, something about the way he viewed himself that neither of them could really understand. And though he knew they meant well, their attempts to talk to him about this distance of his didn't—or couldn't—change anything.

When he was finished he stood, his knees cracking slightly and aching from the position he'd been kneeling in. Before he left he said a short prayer in memory of his father, and afterward he bent over to touch the headstone one more time.

"I'm sorry, Dad," he whispered, "I'm so, so sorry."

Mitch Johnson was leaning against Taylor's truck when he saw Taylor leaving the cemetery. In his hand he held two cans of beer secured by the plastic rings—the remains of the six-pack he'd started the night before—and he pulled one free and tossed it as Taylor drew near. Taylor caught it in midstride, surprised to see his friend, his thoughts still deep in the past.

"I thought you were out of town for the wedding," Taylor said.

"I was, but we got back last night."

"What are you doing here?"

"I sort of figured that you'd need a beer about now," Mitch answered simply.

Taller and thinner than Taylor, he was six two and

weighed about 160 pounds. Most of his hair was gone—he'd started losing it in his early twenties—and he wore wire-rimmed glasses, giving him the appearance of an accountant or engineer. He actually worked at his father's hardware store and was regarded around town as a mechanical genius. He could repair everything from lawn mowers to bulldozers, and his fingers were permanently stained with grease. Unlike Taylor, he'd gone to college at East Carolina University, majored in business, and had met a psychology major from Rocky Mount named Melissa Kindle before moving back to Edenton. They'd been married twelve years and had four children, all boys. Taylor had been best man at the wedding and was godfather to their sons. Sometimes, from the way he talked about his family, Taylor suspected that Mitch loved Melissa more now than he had when they'd walked down the aisle.

Mitch, like Taylor, was also a volunteer with the Edenton Fire Department. At Taylor's urging, the two of them had gone through the necessary training together and had joined at the same time. Though Mitch considered it more a duty than a calling, he was someone Taylor always wanted along when the call came in. Where Taylor tempted danger, Mitch exercised caution, and the two of them balanced each other out in difficult situations.

"Am I that predictable?"

"Hell, Taylor, I know you better than I know my own wife."

Taylor rolled his eyes as he leaned against the truck. "How's Melissa doing?"

"She's good. Her sister drove her crazy at the wedding, but she's back to normal now that she's home. Now it's just me and the kids who are driving her crazy." Mitch's tone softened imperceptibly. "So, how you holding up?"

Taylor shrugged without meeting Mitch's eyes. "I'm all right."

Mitch didn't press it, knowing that Taylor wouldn't say anything more. His father was one of the few things they never talked about. He cracked open his beer, and Taylor did the same before leaning against the truck next to him. Mitch pulled a bandanna from his back pocket and wiped the sweat from his forehead.

"I hear you had yourself a big night in the swamp while I was gone."

"Yeah, we did."

"Wish I could've been there."

"We could have used you, that's for sure. It was one hell of a storm."

"Yeah, but if I would have been there, there wouldn't have been all that drama. I would have headed straight to those duck blinds, right off the bat. I couldn't believe it took you guys hours to figure that out."

Taylor laughed under his breath before taking a drink of his beer and glancing over at Mitch.

"Does Melissa still want you to give it up?"

Mitch put the bandanna back in his pocket and nodded. "You know how it is with the kids and all. She just doesn't want anything to happen to me."

"How do you feel about it?"

It took a moment for him to answer. "I used to think that I'd do this forever, but I'm not so sure anymore."

"So you're considering it?" Taylor asked.

Mitch took a long pull from his beer before answering. "Yeah, I guess I am."

"We need you," Taylor said seriously.

Mitch laughed aloud. "You sound like an army recruiter when you say that."

"It's true, though."

Mitch shook his head. "No, it's not. We've got plenty of volunteers now, and there's a list of people who can replace me at a moment's notice."

"They won't know what's going on."

"Neither did we in the beginning." He paused, his fingers pressing against the can, thinking. "You know, it's not just Melissa—it's me, too. I've been at it for a long time, and I guess it just doesn't mean what it used to. I'm not like you—I don't feel the need to do it anymore. I sort of like being able to spend some time with the kids without having to go out at a moment's notice. I'd like to be able to have dinner with my wife knowing that I'm done for the day."

"You sound like your mind's already made up."

Mitch could hear the disappointment in Taylor's tone, and he took a second before nodding.

"Well, actually, it is. I mean, I'll finish out the year, but that'll be it for me. I just wanted you to be the first to know."

Taylor didn't respond. After a moment Mitch cocked his head, looking sheepishly at his friend. "But that's not why I came out here today. I came out to lend you some support, not to talk about that stuff."

Taylor seemed lost in thought. "Like I said, I'm doing all right."

"Do you wanna head somewhere and have a few beers?"

"No. I gotta get back to work. We're finishing up at Skip Hudson's place."

"You sure?"

"Yeah."

"Well, how 'bout dinner, then, next week? After we're back in the swing of things?"

"Steaks on the grill?"

"Of course," Mitch answered as if he'd never considered another option.

"That I could do." Taylor eyed Mitch suspiciously. "Melissa's not bringing a friend again, is she?"

Mitch laughed. "No. But I can tell her to rustle someone up if you want her to."

"No thanks. After Claire, I don't think I trust her judgment anymore."

"Aw, c'mon, Claire wasn't that bad."

"You didn't spend all night listening to her jabber on and on. She was like one of those Energizer bunnies—she just couldn't sit quietly, even for a minute."

"She was nervous."

"She was a pain."

"I'll tell Melissa you said that."

"No, don't—"

"I'm just kidding—you know I wouldn't do that. But how about Wednesday? You want to stop over then?"

"That'd be great."

"All right, then." Mitch nodded and pushed away from the truck as he fished the keys from his pocket. After crumpling his can, he tossed it into the back of Taylor's truck with a clank.

"Thanks," Taylor said.

"You're welcome."

"I mean about you coming by today."

"I knew what you were talking about."

Chapter 11

Sitting in the kitchen, Denise Holton decided that life was like manure.

When used in a garden, manure was fertilizer. Effective and inexpensive, it provided nourishment to the soil and helped the garden become as beautiful as it could be. But outside of the garden—in a pasture, for instance—when stepped in inadvertently, manure was nothing more than crap.

A week ago, once she and Kyle were reunited in the hospital, she definitely felt as if the manure were being used in her garden. In that moment nothing else but Kyle mattered, and when she saw that he was okay, everything was right in the world. Her life, so to speak, had been fertilized.

But give it a week and suddenly everything seemed different. Reality in the aftermath of the accident had finally settled in, and fertilizer it wasn't. Denise was seated at the Formica table in her small kitchen, poring through the papers in front of her, doing her best to make sense of them. The hospital stay was covered by the insurance, but the deductible was not. Her car may have been old, but it was nonetheless reliable. Now it was totaled, and she'd had only liability insurance. Her boss, Ray, bless his heart, told her to take her time coming back, and eight days had gone by without her earning a penny. The regular bills—phone, electricity, water, gas—were due in less than a week. And to top it off, she was staring at the bill from the towing service, the people who'd been called to remove her vehicle from the side of the road.

This week Denise's life was crap.

It wouldn't be so bad, of course, if she were a millionaire. These problems would be nothing more than an inconvenience then. She could imagine some socialite explaining what a *bother* it was to have to deal with such things. But with a few hundred bucks in the bank, this wasn't a bother. It was a bona fide problem, and a big one at that.

She could cover the regular bills with what was left in the checking account and still have enough for food if she was careful. Lots of cereal this month, that was for sure, and it was a good thing Ray let them eat for free at the diner. She could use her credit card for the hospital deductible—five hundred dollars. Luckily she'd called Rhonda—another waitress at Eights—and she'd agreed to help Denise get to and from work. That left the towing service, and fortunately they'd offered to clear the bill in exchange for the pink slip. Seventy-five dollars for the remains of her car and they'd call it even.

The net result? An additional credit card bill every month and she'd have to start riding her bicycle for errands around town. Even worse, she'd be dependent on someone to drive her to and from the diner. For a gal with a college education, this wasn't much to brag about.

Crap.

If she'd had a bottle of wine, she'd have opened it. She could have used a little escapism right now. But, hey, she couldn't even afford that.

Seventy-five bucks for her car.

Even though it was fair, somehow it just didn't seem right. She wouldn't even see the money.

After writing out the checks for her bills, she sealed the envelopes and used the last of her stamps. She'd have to swing by the post office to get some more, and she made a notation on the pad by the phone before remembering that "swinging by" had taken on a whole new meaning. If it wasn't so pathetic, she would have laughed at the ridiculousness of it all.

A bicycle. Lord have mercy.

Trying to look on the bright side, she told herself that at least she'd get in shape. Within a few months she might even be a little thankful for the extra fitness. "Look at those legs," she imagined people saying, "why, they're just like *steel.* However did you get them?"

"I ride my bike."

This time she couldn't help but giggle. She was twenty-nine years old and she'd be telling people about her bike. Lord have mercy.

Denise shook off the giggles, knowing they were simply a reaction to stress, and left the kitchen to check on Kyle. Sleeping soundly. After adjusting the covers and a quick kiss on his cheek, she headed outside and sat on the back porch, wondering yet again if she'd made the right decision to move here. Even though she knew that it was impossible, she found herself wishing she'd been able to stay in Atlanta. It would have been nice sometimes to have someone to talk to, someone she'd known for years. She supposed she could use the phone, but this month it wouldn't be possible, and there was no way she was going to call collect. Even though her friends probably wouldn't care, it wasn't something she was comfortable doing.

Still, she wanted to talk to someone. But who?

With the exception of Rhonda at the diner (who was twenty and single)—and Judy McAden—Denise didn't know anyone in town. It was one thing to lose her mother a few years back, it was a completely different situation to lose everyone she knew. Nor did it help to realize that it was her own fault. She'd chosen to move, she'd chosen to leave her job, she'd chosen to devote her life to her son. Living this way had a simplicity to it—as well as a necessity—but sometimes she couldn't help thinking that the other parts of her life were slipping by without her even knowing it.

Her loneliness, though, couldn't simply be blamed on the move. In retrospect, she knew that even while she was in Atlanta, things had begun to change. Most of her friends were married now, a few had kids of their own. Some had stayed single. None, however, had anything in common with her anymore. Her married friends enjoyed spending time with other married couples, her single friends enjoyed the same life they had in college. She didn't fit into either world. Even those who had children—well, it was hard to hear how wonderful their kids were doing. And talking about Kyle? They were supportive, but they would never really understand what it was like.

Then, of course, there was the whole man thing. Brett—good old Brett—was the last man she'd dated, and in reality it hadn't even been a date. A roll in the sack, perhaps, but not a date. What a roll, though, huh? Twenty minutes and boom—her whole life changed. What would her life be like now if it hadn't happened? True, Kyle wouldn't be here . . .

but . . . But what? Maybe she'd be married, maybe she'd have a couple of kids, maybe she'd even have a house with a white picket fence around the yard. She'd drive a Volvo or minivan and spend every vacation at Disney World. It sounded good, it definitely sounded easier, but would her life be any better?

Kyle. Sweet Kyle. Simply thinking about him made her smile.

No, she decided, it wouldn't be better. If there was one bright spot in her life, he was it. Funny how he could drive her crazy and still make her love him for it.

Sighing, Denise left the porch and walked to the bedroom. Undressing in the bathroom, she stood in front of the mirror. The bruises on her cheek were still visible, but only slightly. The gash on her forehead had been closed neatly with stitches, and though she would always have a scar, it was near the hairline and wouldn't be too obvious.

Other than that, she was pleased with how she looked. Because money was always such a concern, she never kept cookies or chips in the house. And since Kyle didn't eat meat, she seldom had that, either. She was thinner now than she was before Kyle had been born—hell, she was thinner than she was in college. Without her even trying, fifteen pounds had simply melted away. If she had the time, she'd write a book and title it *Stress and Poverty: The Guaranteed Way to Lose Inches Fast!* She'd probably sell a million copies and retire.

She giggled again. *Yeah, right.*

As Judy had mentioned in the hospital, Denise did resemble her mother. She had the same dark, wavy hair and hazel eyes, they were roughly the same height. Like her mother, she was aging well—a few crow's-feet in the corners of her eyes, but otherwise smooth skin. All in all, she didn't look too bad. In fact, she looked pretty good, if she did say so herself.

At least something was going right.

Deciding to end on that note, Denise put on a pair of pajamas, set the oscillating fan on low, and crawled under the sheets before turning out the lights. The whir and rattle was rhythmic, and she fell asleep within minutes.

With early morning sunlight slanting through the windows, Kyle padded through the bedroom and crawled into bed with Denise, ready to start the day. He whispered, "Wake up, Money, wake up," and when she rolled over with a groan, he climbed over her and used his little fingers to try to lift her eyelids. Though he wasn't successful, he thought it was hilarious, and his laugh was contagious. "Open your eyes, Money," he kept saying, and despite the ungodly hour, she couldn't help but laugh as well.

To make the morning even better, Judy called a little after nine to see if they were still on for their visit. After gabbing a little while—Judy would be coming over the following afternoon, hurray!—Denise hung up the phone, thinking about her mood from the night before and the difference a good night's sleep could make.

She chalked it up to PMS.

A little later, after breakfast, Denise got the bikes ready. Kyle's was ready to go; hers was draped with cobwebs she had to wipe off. The tires on both bikes, she noticed, were low but had enough air to get into town.

After she'd helped Kyle put on his helmet, they started toward town under a blue and cloudless sky, Kyle riding out in front. Last December she'd spent a day running through the apartment complex parking lot in Atlanta, holding on to his bicycle seat until he'd gotten the hang of it. It had taken him a few hours and half a dozen falls, but overall he had a natural instinct for it. Kyle had always had above average motor skills, a fact that always surprised the doctors when they tested him. He was, she'd come to learn, a child of many contradictions.

Of course, like any four-year-old, he wasn't able to focus on much more than keeping his balance and trying to have fun. To him, riding his bike was an adventure (especially when Mom was doing it, too), and he rode with reckless abandon. Even though traffic was light, Denise found herself shouting instructions every few seconds.

"Stay close to Mommy . . ."

"Stop!"

"Don't go in the road . . ."

"Stop!"

"Pull over, honey, a car's coming . . ."

"Stop!"

"Watch out for the hole . . ."

"Stop!"

"Don't go so fast . . ."

"Stop!"

"Stop" was the only command he really understood, and whenever she said it, he'd hit the brakes, put his feet on the ground, then turn around with a big toothy grin, as if to say, *This is so much fun. Why're you so upset?*

Denise was a nervous wreck by the time they reached the post office.

She knew then and there that riding a bicycle just wasn't going to cut it, and she decided to ask Ray for two extra shifts a week for the time being. Pay off the hospital deductible, save every penny, and maybe she'd be able to afford another car in a couple of months.

A couple of months?

She'd probably go nuts by then.

Standing in line—there was always a line at the post office—Denise wiped the perspiration from her forehead and hoped her deodorant was working. That was another thing she hadn't exactly expected when she'd started out from the house this morning. Riding a bike wasn't simply an inconvenience, it was work, especially for someone who hadn't ridden in a while. Her legs were tired, she knew her butt would be sore tomorrow, and she could feel the sweat dripping between her breasts and down her back. She tried to maintain a little distance between herself and the others in line so as not to offend them. Fortunately, no one seemed to notice.

A minute later she stood in front of the counter and received her stamps. After writing a check, she slipped her checkbook and stamps into her purse and walked back outside. She and Kyle hopped on their bikes and headed toward the market.

Edenton had a small downtown, but from a historic perspective the town was a gem. Homes dated back to the early 1800s, and nearly all had been restored to their former glory over the past thirty years. Giant oak trees lined both sides of the street and shaded the roads, providing pleasant cover from the heat of the sun.

Though Edenton had a supermarket, it was on the other side of town, and Denise decided to drop into Merchants instead, a store that had graced the town since the 1940s. It was old-fashioned in every way imaginable and a marvel of supply. The store sold everything from food to bait to automotive supplies, offered videos for rent, and had a small grill off to one side where they could cook up something on the spot. Adding to the atmosphere were four rocking chairs and a bench out front, where a regular group of locals dropped by for coffee in the mornings.

The store itself was small—maybe a few thousand square feet—and it always amazed Denise when she saw how many different items they could squeeze onto the shelves. Denise filled a small plastic basket with the few things she needed—milk, oatmeal, cheese, eggs, bread, bananas, Cheerios, macaroni and cheese, Ritz crackers, and candy (for working with Kyle)—then went to the register. Her total came to less than she expected, which was good, but unlike the supermarket, the store didn't offer plastic bags to pack them in. Instead the owner—a man with neatly combed white hair and thick bushy eyebrows—packed everything into two brown paper bags.

And that, of course, was a problem she'd overlooked.

She would have preferred plastic so she could have slipped the loops over her handlebars—but bags? How was she going to get all this home? Two arms, two bags, two handles on the bike—it just didn't add up. Especially when she had to watch out for Kyle.

She glanced at her son, still pondering the problem, and noticed he was staring through the glass entrance door, toward the street, an unfamiliar expression on his face.

"What is it, honey?"

He answered, though she didn't understand what he was trying to say. It sounded like *fowman.* Leaving her groceries on the counter, she bent down so she could watch him as he said it again. Watching his lips sometimes made understanding him easier.

"What did you say? 'Fowman'?"

Kyle nodded and said it again. "Fowman." This time he pointed through the door, and Denise looked in that direction. As she did so, Kyle started toward the door, and all at once she knew what he'd meant.

Not fowman, though it was close. *Fireman.*

Taylor McAden was standing outside the store, holding the door partially open while talking to someone off to the side, someone she couldn't see. She watched as he nodded and waved, laughed again, then opened the door a little more. While Taylor ended his conversation, Kyle ran up to him and Taylor stepped inside without really paying attention to where he was going. He almost bowled Kyle over before catching his balance.

"Whoa, sorry—didn't see you," he said instinctively.

"Excuse me." He took an involuntary step backward before blinking in confusion. Then—sudden recognition crossing his face—he broke into a wide smile, squatting so he could be at eye level. "Oh, hey, little man. How are you?"

"Hello, Taylor," Kyle said happily. *(Hewwo, Tayer)*

Without saying anything else, Kyle wrapped his arms around Taylor as he had that night in the duck blind. Taylor—unsure at first—relented and hugged him back, looking content and surprised at exactly the same time.

Denise watched in stunned silence, her hand over her mouth. After a long moment Kyle finally loosened his grip, allowing Taylor to pull back. Kyle's eyes were dancing, as if he'd recognized a long-lost friend.

"Fowman," Kyle said again excitedly. "He's found you." *(Eez foun you)*

Taylor cocked his head to one side. "What's that?"

Denise finally snapped to attention and moved toward the two of them, still having trouble believing what she'd seen. Even after spending a year with his speech therapist, Kyle had hugged her only when prodded by his mother. Unlike this, it had never been voluntary, and she wasn't exactly sure how she felt about Kyle's extraordinary new attachment. Watching her child hug a stranger—even a good one—aroused somewhat contradictory feelings.

Nice, but dangerous. Sweet, but something that shouldn't become a habit. At the same time, there was something about the comfortable way that Taylor had reacted to Kyle—and vice versa—that made it seem anything but threatening. All of this was going through her head as she drew near and answered for her son.

"He's trying to say that you found him," she said. Taylor glanced up and saw Denise for the first time since the accident, and for a moment he couldn't turn away. Despite the fact he'd seen her before, she looked . . . well, more attractive than he'd remembered. Granted, she was a mess that night, but still, the way she might look under normal circumstances hadn't crossed his mind. It wasn't that she looked glamorous or elegant; it was more that she radiated a natural beauty, a woman who knew she was attractive but didn't spend all day thinking about it.

"Yes. He's found you," Kyle said again, breaking into Taylor's thoughts. Kyle nodded for emphasis, and Taylor was thankful for a reason to face him again. He wondered if Denise could tell what he was thinking.

"That's right, I did," he said with a friendly hand still on Kyle's shoulder, "but you, little man, were the brave one."

Denise watched as he spoke to Kyle. Despite the heat, Taylor was wearing jeans and Red Wing workboots. The boots were covered with a thin layer of dried mud and well worn, as if he'd used them every day for months. The thick leather was scarred and chaffed. His white shirt was short-sleeved, revealing tight muscles in his sun-darkened arms—the arms of someone who worked with his hands all day. When he stood he seemed taller than she'd remembered.

"Sorry about almost knocking him over back there," he said, "I didn't see him when I came in." He stopped, as if not knowing what else to say, and Denise sensed a shyness she hadn't expected.

"I saw what happened. It wasn't your fault. He kind of snuck up on you." She smiled. "I'm Denise Holton, by the way. I know we met before, but a lot of that night's fairly foggy."

She held out her hand and Taylor took it. She could feel the calluses on his palm.

"Taylor McAden," he said. "I got your note. Thanks."

"Fowman," Kyle said again, this time louder than before. He wrung his hands together, twisting and turning them almost compulsively. It was something he always did when excited.

"Big fowman." He put the emphasis on *big*.

Taylor furrowed his brow and reached out, grabbing Kyle on the helmet in a friendly, almost brotherly way. Kyle's head moved in unison with his hand. "You think so, huh?"

Kyle nodded. "Big."

Denise laughed. "I think it's a case of hero worship."

"Well, the feeling's mutual, little man. It was more you than me."

Kyle's eyes were wide. "Big."

If Taylor noticed that Kyle didn't understand what he'd just said, he didn't show it. Instead Taylor winked at him. Nice.

Denise cleared her throat. "I haven't had the chance to thank you in person for what you did that night."

Taylor shrugged. With some people it would have come across as arrogant, as if they knew they'd done something wonderful. With Taylor, though, it came across differently, as if he hadn't given it a second thought since that night.

"Ah, that's all right," he said. "Your note was plenty."

For a moment neither of them spoke. Kyle, meanwhile—as if already bored by the conversation—wandered toward the candy aisle. Both of them watched as he stopped halfway down, focusing intently on the brightly covered wrappers.

"He looks good," Taylor finally said into the silence. "Kyle, I mean. After all that happened, I was sort of wondering how he was doing."

Denise's eyes followed his. "He seems to be okay.

Time will tell, I guess, but right now I'm not too worried about him. The doctor gave him a clean bill of health."

"How 'bout you?" he asked.

She answered automatically, without really thinking. "The same as always."

"No . . . I mean with your injuries. You were pretty banged up when I last saw you."

"Oh . . . well, I guess I'm doing okay, too," she said.

"Just okay?"

Her expression softened. "Better than okay. Still a little sore here and there, but otherwise I'm fine. It could have been worse."

"Good, I'm glad. I was worried about you, too."

There was something in the quiet way he spoke that made Denise take a closer look at him. Though he wasn't the most handsome man she'd ever seen, there was something about him that caught her attention—a gentleness, perhaps, despite his size; an acute but unthreatening perceptiveness in his steady gaze. Though she knew it was impossible, it was almost as if he knew how difficult her life had been during the past few years. Glancing at his left hand, she noticed he wasn't wearing a ring.

At that, she quickly turned away, wondering where the thought had come from and what had brought it on. Why would that matter? Kyle was still immersed in the candy aisle and was about to open a bag of Skittles when Denise saw what he was doing.

"Kyle—no!" She took a quick step toward him, then turned back to Taylor. "Excuse me. He's getting into something he shouldn't."

He took a small step backward. "No problem."

As she moved away, Taylor couldn't help but watch her. The lovely, almost mysterious face accented by high cheekbones and exotic eyes, long dark hair pulled into a messy ponytail that reached past her shoulder blades, a shapely figure accented by the shorts and blouse she was wearing—

"Kyle, put that down. Your candy's already in the bag."

Before she caught him staring at her, Taylor shook his head and turned away, wondering again how he could have overlooked her beauty that night. A moment later Denise was back in front of him, Kyle now standing beside her. Kyle's expression was glum, caught with his hand in the cookie jar and all that.

"Sorry about that. He knows better," she said apologetically.

"I'm sure he does, but kids always press the limits."

"You sound like you're speaking from experience."

He grinned. "No, not really. Just my own. I don't have any children."

There was an awkward pause before Taylor spoke again.

"So I take it you're in town for a few errands?" Small talk, nothing talk, Taylor knew, but for some reason he was reluctant to let her leave.

Denise ran her hand through her disheveled ponytail. "Yeah, we needed to grab a few things. The cupboard was getting pretty bare, if you know what I mean. How about you?"

"I'm just here to pick up some soda for the guys."

"At the fire department?"

"No, I only volunteer there. The guys who work for me. I'm a contractor—I remodel homes, things like that."

For a moment she was confused. "You volunteer? I thought that went out twenty years ago."

"Not here it hasn't. In fact, not in most small towns, I imagine. As a general rule, it's not busy enough for a full-time crew, so they depend on people like me when emergencies come up."

"I didn't know that." The realization made what he'd done for them seem even greater than before, though she wouldn't have thought it possible.

Kyle peered up at his mother. "He's hungry," he said. *(Eez hungwy)*

"Are you hungry, sweetheart?"

"Yes."

"Well, we'll be home soon. I'll make you a grilled cheese sandwich when we get there. Does that sound okay?"

He nodded. "Yes, it's good." *(Yes, ess good)*

Denise, however, didn't move right away—or at least not fast enough for Kyle. Instead she looked at Taylor again. Kyle reached up and tugged his mother by the hem of her shorts, and her hands automatically went down to stop him. "Let's go," Kyle added. *(Wess go)*

"We're going, honey."

Kyle's and Denise's hands engaged in a little battle as she peeled his fingers away and he tried to grab the hem again. She took him by the hand to stop him.

Taylor stifled a chuckle by clearing his throat. "Well, I'd better not keep you. A growing boy needs to eat."

"Yeah, I suppose so." She gave Taylor an expression of weariness familiar to mothers everywhere and felt a strange sense of relief when she realized he didn't seem to care that Kyle was acting up.

"It was good seeing you again," she added. Even though it sounded perfunctory to her ears—all part of the "Hi. How are you? That's good. Nice seeing you!" routine—Denise hoped he could tell that she actually meant it.

"You too," he said. He grabbed Kyle's helmet and gave it a shake as before. "And you too, little man."

Kyle waved with his free hand. "Bye-bye, Tayer," he said exuberantly.

"Bye."

Taylor grinned before heading toward the refrigerators along the wall to get the soda he'd come for.

Denise turned toward the counter, sighing to herself. The owner was immersed in *Field and Stream* magazine, his lips moving slightly as he perused the article. As she started toward him, Kyle spoke again.

"He's hungry."

"I know you are. We'll be on our way soon, okay?"

The owner saw her approaching, checked to see if she needed him or just her groceries, then set his magazine aside.

She motioned toward the bags. "Would you mind if we left this here for a few minutes? We have to get some other kinds of bags that loop over the handlebars."

Despite the fact he was already halfway across the store and pulling a six-pack of Coca-Cola from the refrigerator, Taylor strained to hear what was going on. Denise continued.

"We're on our bikes, and I don't think I can get this all home. It won't take long—we'll be right back."

In the background her voice trailed off and he heard the manager answer. "Oh sure, no problem. I'll just put them behind the counter here for now."

Soda in hand, Taylor started toward the front of the store. Denise was shepherding Kyle out of the store, her hand placed gently on his back. Taylor took a couple of steps, thinking about what he'd just overheard, then made up his mind on the spot.

"Hey, Denise, wait up . . ."

She turned and stopped as Taylor approached.

"Were those your bikes outside the store?"

She nodded. "Uh-huh. Why?"

"I couldn't help but overhear what you told the manager and . . . well . . ." He paused, that steady blue gaze holding her motionless in the store. "Can I give you a hand getting your groceries home? I'm heading right by your place, and I'd be happy to drop it all off for you."

As he spoke, he motioned to the truck parked right outside the door.

"Oh no, that's all right . . ."

"Are you sure? It's right on the way. Take me two minutes, tops."

Though she knew he was trying to be kind, a product of a small-town upbringing, she wasn't sure she should accept.

He held up his hands, as if sensing her indecision, an almost mischievous grin on his face. "I won't steal anything, I promise."

Kyle took a step toward the door, and she put her hand on his shoulder to stop him. "No, it's not that . . ."

But what was it, then? Had she been on her own

so long that she didn't even know how to accept other people's kindness anymore? Or was it that he'd already done so much for her already?

Go ahead. It's not like he's asking you to marry him or anything . . .

She swallowed, thinking of the trip across town and back again, then loading up all the groceries to transport home.

"If you're sure it's not out of your way . . ."

Taylor felt as if he'd achieved some sort of minor victory.

"No—it's not out of the way at all. Just let me pay for this and I'll help you carry your things to the truck."

He returned to the counter and set the Coca-Cola by the register.

"How do you know where I live?" she asked.

He looked over his shoulder. "It's a small town. I know where everyone lives."

Later that evening, Melissa, Mitch, and Taylor were in the backyard, steaks and hot dogs already sizzling over charcoal, the first vestiges of summer lingering almost like a dream. It was a slow-moving evening, the air bruised with humidity and heat. The yellow sun hovered low in the sky just above the stationary dogwoods, the leaves motionless in the still evening air.

While Mitch stood ready, tongs in hand, Taylor nursed a beer, his third of the evening. He had a nice buzz going and was drinking at just the right pace to keep it that way. After catching them up on what had been happening recently—including the search in the swamp—he mentioned that he'd seen Denise again at the store and that he'd dropped her groceries off.

"They seem to be doing fine," he observed, slapping at a mosquito that had landed on his leg.

Though it was said in all innocence, Melissa gave him the once-over, eyeing him carefully, then leaned forward in her chair.

"So you like her, huh?" she said, not hiding her curiosity.

Before Taylor had a chance to answer, Mitch cut into the conversation.

"What did he say? That he liked her?"

"I didn't say that," Taylor said quickly.

"You didn't have to. I could see it in your face, and besides, you wouldn't have dropped her groceries off if you didn't." Melissa turned to her husband. "Yeah, he likes her."

"You're putting words in my mouth."

Melissa smiled wryly. "So . . . is she pretty?"

"What kind of question is that?"

Melissa turned to her husband again. "He thinks she's pretty, too."

Mitch nodded, convinced. "I thought he was kind of quiet when he arrived. So what's next? You gonna ask her out?"

Taylor turned from one to the other, wondering how the conversation had spun in this direction.

"I hadn't planned on it."

"You should. You need to get out of the house once in a while."

"I'm out all day long . . ."

"You know what I mean." Mitch winked at him, enjoying his discomfort.

Melissa leaned back in her chair. "He's right, you know. You're not getting any younger. You're already past your prime."

Taylor shook his head. "Thanks a lot. Next time I need some abuse, I know exactly where to come."

Melissa giggled. "You know we're just teasing."

"Is that your version of an apology?"

"Only if it makes you change your mind about asking her out."

Her eyebrows danced up and down, and despite himself Taylor laughed. Melissa was thirty-four but looked—and acted—ten years younger. Blond and petite, she was quick with a kind word, loyal to her friends, and never seemed to hold a grudge about anything. Her kids could be fighting, the dog might have messed on the rug, the car wouldn't start—it didn't matter. Within a couple minutes she'd be back to her old self. On more than one occasion Taylor had told Mitch that he was a lucky man. Mitch's answer was always the same: "I know."

Taylor took another drink from his beer. "Why are you so interested, anyway?" he asked.

"Because we love you," Melissa answered sweetly, as if that explained it all.

And don't understand why I'm still alone, Taylor thought.

"All right," he finally said, "I'll think about it."

"Fair enough," Melissa said, not bothering to hide her enthusiasm.

Chapter 12

The day after Denise had run into Taylor at Merchants, she spent the morning working with Kyle. The accident seemed to have had neither a negative nor a positive impact on his learning, though now that summer had arrived, he seemed to work best if they were able to finish before noon. After that it was too warm in the house for either of them to concentrate.

Earlier, right after breakfast, she'd called Ray and asked him for a couple of extra shifts for the time being. Fortunately he'd consented. Starting tomorrow night she'd work every evening except Sunday, as opposed to her usual four shifts. As always, she'd head in around seven and work until midnight. Though coming in a little later meant less in tips because she'd miss a good portion of the dinner rush, she couldn't in good conscience leave Kyle in the back room for an extra hour all by himself while he was still awake. By arriving later, she could put him down in the cot and he'd fall asleep within minutes.

She'd found herself thinking about Taylor McAden ever since she'd run into him at the store the day before. Just as he'd promised, the groceries had been placed on the front porch, in the shade provided by the overhang. Because it hadn't taken more than ten or fifteen minutes for her to make it back home, the milk and eggs were still cold and she'd put them in the refrigerator before they spoiled.

While Taylor had carried the bags to his truck, he'd also offered to put their bikes in the back and give them both a ride, too, but to that Denise had said no. It had less to do with Taylor than Kyle—he was already getting on his bike, and she knew he was looking forward to another ride with his mother. She didn't want to ruin that for him, especially since this would probably be a regular routine and the last thing she wanted was for him to expect a truck ride back every time they came to town.

Still, part of her had wanted to accept Taylor's offer. She'd been around long enough to know that he'd found her attractive—the way he looked at her made that plain—yet it didn't make her uncomfortable the way the scrutiny of other men sometimes did. There wasn't the usual hungry gleam in his eye while he'd stared at her—the one that implied a roll in the sack would solve everything. Nor had his eyes wandered downward while she spoke—another common problem. It was impossible to take a man seriously when he was staring at her breasts.

No, there was something different about the way he'd looked at her. It was more appreciative somehow, less threatening, and as much as she resisted the idea, she'd found herself not only flattered by it, but pleased as well.

Of course, she knew it could have been part of Taylor's shtick, his way of coming on to women, a pattern honed over time. Some men were good at that. She'd meet them and talk to them, and every nuance of their being seemed to imply that they were different, more trustworthy, than other men. She'd been around long enough to meet plenty of those types as well, and usually she'd hear little alarm bells going off. But Taylor was either the finest actor she'd ever come across or he really was different, because this time the bells were silent.

So which was it?

Of the many things she'd learned from her mother, there was one that always stood out, one that came to mind when evaluating others. "You're going to come across people in your life who say all the right words at all the right times. But in the end, it's always their actions you should judge them by. It's actions, not words, that matter."

Maybe, she thought to herself, that was the reason she'd responded to Taylor. He'd already proven that he could do heroic things, but it wasn't simply his dramatic rescue of Kyle that inspired her . . . *interest* in him, if that's what it was. Even cads could do the right thing some of the time. No—it was the little things he'd done while they were at the store. The way he'd offered to help without expecting something in return . . . the way he seemed to care about how Kyle and she were doing . . . the way he'd treated Kyle . . .

Especially that.

Even though she didn't want to admit it, over the last few years she'd come to judge people by the way they treated her son. She remembered compiling lists in her mind of the friends who tried with Kyle and the ones that hadn't. "She sat on the floor and played blocks with him"—*she was good.* "She barely even noticed he was there"—*she was bad.* The list of "bad" people was far longer than the "good."

But here was a guy who had for whatever reason formed a bond with her son, and she couldn't stop thinking about it. Nor could she forget Kyle's reaction to him. *Hewwo, Tayer* . . .

Even though Taylor didn't understand everything Kyle had said—Kyle's pronunciations took a while to get used to—Taylor kept talking to him as if he did. He winked, he grabbed his helmet in a playful way, he hugged him, he looked Kyle in the eye when he spoke. He'd made sure to say good-bye.

Little things, but they were incredibly important to her.

Actions.

Taylor had treated Kyle like a normal little boy.

Ironically, Denise was still thinking about Taylor even as Judy pulled up the long gravel driveway and parked in the shade of a looming magnolia tree. Denise, who was just finishing up the dishes, spotted Judy and waved before making a quick scan of the kitchen. Not perfect, but clean enough, she decided as she moved to meet Judy at the front door.

After the traditional preliminaries—how each was doing and all that—Denise and Judy seated themselves on the front porch so they could keep an eye on Kyle. He was playing with his trucks near the fence, rolling them along make-believe roads. Right before Judy had arrived, Denise had liberally coated him with sunscreen and bug spray, and the lotions acted like glue when he played in the dirt. His shorts and tank top were streaked a dusty brown, and his face looked as if it hadn't been washed in a week, reminding Denise of the dust bowl children Steinbeck had described in *The Grapes of Wrath*.

On the small wooden table *(picked up at a garage sale for three dollars—another excellent buy for bargain-shopping ace Denise Holton!)* sat two glasses of sweet tea. Denise had made it that morning in a typically southern fashion—brewed Luzianne with lots of sugar added while still hot so it could dissolve completely, then chilled in the refrigerator with ice. Judy took a drink from her glass, her eyes never leaving Kyle.

"Your mother used to love getting dirty, too," Judy said.

"My mother?"

Judy glanced at her, amused. "Don't look so surprised. Your mother was quite a tomboy when she was young."

Denise reached for her glass. "Are you sure we're talking about the same lady?" she asked. "My mother wouldn't even collect the morning paper without putting makeup on."

"Oh, that happened right around the time she discovered boys. That was when your mom changed her ways. She turned into the quintessential southern lady, complete with white gloves and perfect table manners, practically overnight. But don't let that fool you. Before that, your mother was a regular Huckleberry Finn."

"You're kidding, right?"

"No—really. Your mother caught frogs, she cussed like a shrimper who'd lost his net, she even got in a few fights with boys to show how tough she was. And she was a good fighter, let me tell you. While a boy was trying to figure out whether it was okay to hit a girl, she'd sock 'em right in the nose. One time, the other kid's parents actually called the sheriff. That poor boy was so ashamed, he didn't go back to school for a week, but he never teased your mother again. She was one tough young lady."

Judy blinked, her mind clearly wandering between the present and the past. Denise stayed silent, waiting for her to go on.

"I remember we used to hike down by the river to collect blackberries. Your mother wouldn't even wear shoes in those prickly things. She had the toughest feet I'd ever seen. She'd go the whole summer without wearing shoes, except when she had to go to church. Her feet would be so dirty by September that her mother couldn't get the stains out unless she used a Brillo pad and Ajax. When school started up again, your mother would limp for the first couple of days. I never figured out whether it was because of the Brillo pad or simply the fact that she wasn't used to wearing shoes."

Denise laughed in disbelief. This was a side of her mother she'd never even heard about. Judy continued.

"I used to live right down the road from here. Do you know the Boyle place? That white house with the green shutters—big red barn out back?"

Denise nodded. She passed by it on the way into town.

"Well, that was where I lived when I was little. Your mom and I were the only two girls who lived out this way, so we ended up doing practically everything together. We were the same age, too, so we studied the same things at school. This was in the forties, and back then everyone sat in the same classroom until the eighth grade, but they still tried to group us together with people the same age. Your mother and I sat next to each other in school the whole way through. She was probably the best friend I ever had."

Staring toward the distant trees, Judy seemed lost in the throes of nostalgia.

"Why didn't she keep in touch after she moved?" Denise began. "I mean . . ."

She paused, wondering how to ask what she really meant, and Judy cast her a sidelong glance.

"You mean why, if we were such good friends, didn't she tell you about it?"

Denise nodded, and Judy collected her thoughts.

"I guess it mainly had to do with her moving away. It took me a long time to understand that distance can ruin even the best of intentions."

"That's sad . . ."

"Not really. I suppose it depends on how you look at it. For me . . . well, it just adds a richness you wouldn't otherwise get. People come, people go—they'll drift in and out of your life, almost like characters in a favorite book. When you finally close the cover, the characters have told their story and you start up again with another book, complete with new characters and adventures. Then you find yourself focusing on the new ones, not the ones from the past."

It took a moment for Denise to respond as she remembered the friends she'd left in Atlanta.

"That's pretty philosophical," she finally said.

"I'm old. What did you expect?"

Denise set her glass of tea on the table and absently wiped the moisture from the sweating glass on her shorts. "So you never talked to her again? After she left?"

"Oh no—we kept in touch for a few years, but back then your mother was in love, and when women fall in love, it's all they can think about. That was why she left Edenton in the first place. A boy—Michael Cunningham. Did she ever tell you about him?"

Denise shook her head, fascinated.

"I'm not surprised. Michael was kind of a bad boy, not exactly the kind of guy you want to remember way longer than you have to. He didn't have the greatest reputation, if you know what I mean, but a lot of girls found him attractive. I guess they thought him exciting and dangerous. Same old story, even today. Well, your mother followed him to Atlanta right after she graduated."

"But she told me she moved to Atlanta to go to college."

"Oh, that may have been somewhere in the back

of her mind, but the real reason was Michael. He had some kind of hold on her, that's for sure. He was also the reason she didn't come back here to visit."

"How so?"

"Well, her mom and dad—your grandparents—they just couldn't forgive her for running off that way. They saw Michael for what he was and said that if she didn't come home right away, she wasn't welcome here anymore. They were from the old school, as stubborn as can be, and your mom was just the same. It was like a couple of bulls staring at each other, waiting for the other one to give in. But neither of them ever did, even after Michael went by the wayside for someone else."

"My father?"

Judy shook her head. "No . . . someone else—your father came along after I lost contact with her."

"So you didn't know him at all?"

"No. But I do remember your grandparents heading off to the wedding and being a little hurt that your mother hadn't sent me an invitation. Not that I could have gone, of course. I was married by then, and like a lot of young couples, my husband and I were struggling financially, and with the new baby—well, it just would have been impossible to make it."

"I'm sorry about that."

Judy set her glass of tea on the table. "Nothing to be sorry for. It wasn't you, and in some way, it wasn't even your mom anymore—or at least the one I used to know. Your father came from a very respectable family in Atlanta, and by that point in her life, I think your mom was a little embarrassed about where she'd come from. Not that your father minded, obviously, since he married her. But I remember that your grandparents didn't say much after they returned from the wedding. I think they were a little embarrassed, too, even though they shouldn't have been. They were great people, but I think they knew they didn't fit into their daughter's world anymore, even after your father passed away."

"That's terrible."

"It's sad, but like I said, it went both ways. They were stubborn, your mom was stubborn. And little by little, they sort of drifted apart."

"I knew Mom wasn't close to her parents, but she never told me any of this."

"No, I wouldn't expect that she did. But please don't think poorly of your mother. I certainly don't. She was always so full of life, so passionate—she was exciting to be around. And she had the heart of an angel, she really did. She was as sweet a person as I ever knew."

Judy turned to face her. "I see a lot of her in you."

Denise tried to digest this new information about her mother as Judy took another sip of her tea. Then, as if knowing she'd said too much, Judy added, "But listen to me, droning on like some senile old woman. You must think I'm two steps from an old folks' home. Let's talk about you for a while."

"Me? There's not much to tell."

"Then why not start with the obvious? Why did you move to Edenton?"

Denise watched Kyle playing with his trucks, wondering what he was thinking.

"There's a couple of reasons."

Judy leaned forward and whispered conspiratorially, "Man trouble? Some psycho stalker like you see on *America's Most Wanted?*"

Denise giggled. "No, nothing that dramatic." She stopped, her brow furrowing slightly.

"If it's too personal, you don't have to tell me. It's none of my business anyway."

Denise shook her head. "I don't mind talking about it—it's just tough to know where to start." Judy stayed silent, and Denise sighed, collecting her thoughts. "I guess mainly it has to do with Kyle. I think I told you he has trouble speaking, right?"

Judy nodded.

"Did I tell you why?"

"No."

Denise looked in Kyle's direction. "Well, right now they say he has an auditory processing problem, specifically expressive and receptive language delay.

Basically, it means that for some reason—no one knows why—understanding language and learning to speak is hard for him. I guess the best analogy is that it's like dyslexia, only instead of processing visual signals, it has to do with processing sounds. For some reason, the sounds seem to get all mixed up—it's like he's hearing Chinese one second, German the next, nonsense chatter after that. Whether the problem's in the connection between the ear and the brain or within the brain itself no one knows. But in the beginning, they weren't sure how to diagnose him, and, well . . ."

Denise ran her hand through her hair and faced Judy again. "Are you sure you want to hear all of this? It's kind of a long story."

Judy reached over and patted Denise on the knee. "Only if you feel like telling me."

Judy's earnest expression suddenly reminded Denise of her mother. Strangely, it felt good to tell her about it, and she hesitated only briefly before going on.

"Well, at first the doctors thought he was deaf. I spent weeks taking Kyle to appointments with audiologists and ENTs—you know, ear, nose, and throat specialists—before they found out that he could hear. Then, they thought he was autistic. That diagnosis lasted for about a year—probably the most stressful year of my life. After that came PDD, or pervasive development disorder, which is sort of like autism, only less severe. That too lasted a few months until they'd run more tests on him. Then, they said he was retarded, with ADD—attention deficit disorder—thrown in for good measure. It wasn't until maybe nine months ago that they finally settled on this diagnosis."

"It must have been so hard on you . . ."

"You can't imagine how hard it was. They tell you something awful about your child, and you go through all these stages—disbelief, anger, grief, and finally acceptance. You learn everything you can about it—you research and read and talk to whoever you can—and just when you're ready to confront it head-on, they change their minds and the whole thing starts all over again."

"Where was the father during all of this?"

Denise shrugged, an almost guilty expression on her face. "The father wasn't around. Suffice it to say, I hadn't expected to get pregnant. Kyle was an 'oops,' if you know what I mean."

She paused again, and the two of them watched Kyle in silence. Judy seemed neither surprised nor shocked by the revelation, nor did her expression register any judgment. Denise cleared her throat.

"After Kyle was born, I took a leave of absence from the school where I was teaching. My mom had died, and I wanted to spend the first year or so with the baby. But after all this started happening, I couldn't go back to work. I was shuttling him all day long to doctors and evaluation centers and therapists until I finally came up with a therapy program that we could do at home. None of that left me with enough time for a full-time job. Working with Kyle is full-time. I'd inherited this house, but I couldn't sell it, and eventually the money just ran out."

She glanced at Judy, a rueful expression on her face. "So I guess the short answer to your question is that I had to move here out of necessity, so that I could keep working with Kyle."

When she finished, Judy stared at her before finally patting her on the knee again. "Pardon the expression, but you're a helluva mother. Not many people would make those kinds of sacrifices."

Denise watched her son play in the dirt. "I just want him to get better."

"From what you've told me, he sounds like he already has." She let that sink in before leaning back in her chair and continuing. "You know, I remember watching Kyle when you were using the computer in the library, but never once did the thought occur to me that he was having any problems at all. He seemed like every other little boy there, except that he was probably better behaved."

"But he still has trouble speaking."

"So did Einstein and Teller, but they turned out to be the greatest physicists in history."

"How would you know about their speech problems?" Though Denise knew (she'd read nearly everything on the subject), she was surprised—and impressed—that Judy knew it as well.

"Oh, you'd be amazed at the amount of trivia I've picked up over the years. I'm like a vacuum cleaner with that stuff, don't ask me why."

"You should go on *Jeopardy!*"

"I would, but that Alex Trebek is so cute, I'd probably forget everything I know as soon as he said hello. I'd just stare at him the whole time, trying to figure out a way to get him to kiss me, like that Richard Dawson did on *Family Feud.*"

"What would your husband think if he knew you'd said that?"

"I'm sure he wouldn't mind." Her voice sobered slightly. "He passed away a long time ago."

"I'm sorry," Denise began, "I didn't know."

"It's okay."

In the sudden quiet, Denise fidgeted with her hands. "So . . . you never remarried?"

Judy shook her head. "No. I just didn't seem to have time to meet someone. Taylor was a handful—it was all I could do to keep up with him."

"Boy, does that sound familiar. It seems like all I do is work with Kyle and work at the diner."

"You work at Eights? With Ray Toler?"

"Uh-huh. I got the job when I moved here."

"Has he told you about his kids?"

"Only a dozen times or so," Denise answered.

From there, the conversation drifted easily to Denise's job and the endless projects that seemed to occupy Judy's time. The rhythm of conversation was something Denise hadn't experienced in a while, and she found it unexpectedly soothing. A half hour later Kyle tired of playing with his trucks, and he put them under the porch (without being asked, Judy couldn't help but notice) before wandering up to his mother. His face was red from the heat, his bangs plastered against his forehead. "Can I have some macaroni and cheese?" *(Ca-ah haf son concor cheese?)*

"Macaroni and cheese?"

"Yes."

"Sure, sweetie. Let me go make some."

Denise and Judy stood and went into the kitchen, Kyle leaving dusty footprints on the floor. He went to the table and sat while Denise opened up the cupboard.

"Would you like to stay for lunch? I can throw together a couple of sandwiches."

Judy checked her watch. "I'd love to, but I can't. I have a meeting downtown about the festival this weekend. We still have some last-minute details we've got to iron out."

Denise was filling the saucepan with hot water and looked over her shoulder. "Festival?"

"Yeah, this weekend. It's an annual event and sort

of gets everyone in the mood for summer. I hope you're going."

Denise set the pan on the burner, and the gas range clicked to life. "I hadn't planned on it."

"Why not?"

"Well, for one thing, I hadn't even heard about it."

"You really *are* out of the loop."

"Don't remind me."

"You should go, then—Kyle would love it. They have food and crafts, contests, a carnival is in town—there's something for everyone."

Denise's mind immediately leapt to the costs involved.

"I don't know if we can," she finally said, thinking of an excuse. "I have to work Saturday night."

"Oh, you don't have to stay long—just come by during the day if you'd like. But it is a lot of fun, and if you want, I could introduce you to some people your own age."

Denise didn't respond right away, and Judy sensed her hesitation.

"Just think about it, okay?"

Judy picked up her purse from the counter, and Denise checked the water—not boiling yet—before they walked toward the front door and stepped out on the porch again.

Denise ran her hand through her hair, adjusting a few loose strands that had fallen in her face.

"Thanks for coming by. It was nice to have an adult conversation for a change."

"I enjoyed it," Judy said, leaning in to give her an impulsive hug. "Thanks for inviting me."

As Judy turned to leave, Denise realized what she'd forgotten to mention.

"Oh, by the way, I didn't tell you that I ran into Taylor yesterday at the store."

"I know. I talked to him last night."

After a beat of awkward silence, Judy adjusted her purse strap. "Let's do this again sometime, okay?"

"I'd like that."

Denise watched as Judy made her way down the steps and onto the gravel walkway. When Judy reached her car she turned to face Denise again.

"You know, Taylor's gonna be at the festival this weekend with the rest of the fire department," Judy called out conversationally. "Their softball team plays at three."

"Oh?" was all Denise could think to say.

"Well, just in case you do come by, that's where I'll be."

A moment later Judy opened her car door. Denise stood in the doorway and waved as Judy slipped behind the seat and cranked the engine to life, the faint outlines of a smile playing softly on her lips.

Chapter 13

"Hey there! I wasn't sure you two were going to make it," Judy called out happily.

It was Saturday afternoon, a little after three, when Denise and Kyle made their way up the bleachers toward Judy, stepping around the other spectators.

The softball game hadn't been hard to find—it was the only area of the park with bleachers, the field itself surrounded by a low chain-link fence. As they'd parked their bikes, Denise had easily spotted Judy sitting in the stands. Seeing them as well, Judy had waved as Denise held on to Kyle, doing her best to keep her balance as she made her way toward the upper seats.

"Hey, Judy . . . we made it all right. I didn't know that Edenton had so many people. It took us a while to make it through the crowds."

The streets downtown had been closed to traffic and were teeming with people. Banners stretched across the road, booths lining both sidewalks, as people examined the handmade crafts and drifted in and out of shops, carrying their recent purchases.

Near Cook's Drugstore, an area had been set up for children. There they could assemble their own crafts using Elmer's glue, pinecones, felt, Styrofoam, balloons, and anything else people had donated. In the center square the carnival was in full swing. The lines, Denise had noticed, were already long.

Denise and Kyle had taken their time walking their bikes through town, both of them enjoying the energy of the festival. On the far side of town, the park was alive with more food and games. A barbecue contest was under way in the shaded area near the road, and the Shriners were operating a fish fry in the near corner. Everywhere else, people had brought their own food and were preparing hot dogs and hamburgers on small grills for family and friends.

Judy scooted over to make room for the two of them, and Kyle wedged himself between them. As he did so, he leaned into Judy almost flirtatiously and laughed as if he thought the whole thing were funny. Then, settling himself, he pulled out one of the toy airplanes he'd brought with him. Denise had insisted he put them in his pockets before he left the house. She didn't even pretend that she could explain the game to him enough to keep him interested and wanted him to have something to play with.

"Oh, people come from all over for the festival," Judy said in explanation. "It pretty much draws from the whole county. It's one of the few times where people can count on seeing friends they haven't seen in a while, and it's a nice way for everyone to catch up."

"It sure looks that way."

Judy nudged Kyle in the ribs. "Hi, Kyle. How are you?"

With a serious expression, he pressed his chin to his chest before holding up his toy for her to see. "Owpwane," he said enthusiastically, making sure Judy could see it. Though Denise knew it was his way of trying to communicate on a level he understood—something he often did—she nonetheless prodded him to answer correctly. She tapped his shoulder.

"Kyle, say, 'I'm fine, thanks.'"

"I'm fine, thanks." *(I'n fie, kenks)* He bobbed his head back and forth in rhythm with the syllables, then turned his attention back to his toy. Denise slipped her arm around him and nodded toward the action on the field.

"So who exactly are we rooting for?"

"Either team, really. Taylor's in the field now at third base for the red team—that's the Chowan Volunteers. They're with the fire department. The blue team—that's the Chowan Enforcers. That's the police, the sheriffs, and local troopers. They play for charity every year. The losing team has to pony up five hundred dollars for the library."

"Whose idea was that?" Denise inquired knowingly.

"Mine, of course."

"So the library wins either way?"

"That's the whole point," Judy said. "Actually, though, the guys take it very seriously. There are a lot of egos on the line out there. You know how men are."

"What's the score?"

"Four to two, the fire department is leading."

On the field, Denise saw Taylor, crouched in his baseball stance, absently tapping his throwing hand into his glove, ready. The pitcher lobbed a painfully high pitch, and the batter connected with the ball cleanly, driving it to center field. It landed safely—a runner from third reached home plate, bringing the score to within one.

"Was that Carl Huddle who just hit that?"

"Yes. Carl's actually one of the better players. He and Taylor played together in high school."

For the next hour Denise and Judy watched the game, chatting about Edenton and cheering for both teams. The game was only seven innings and was actually more exciting than Denise thought it would be—lots of scoring and not nearly as many dropped balls as she'd expected. Taylor made a couple of plays to throw the runners out at first, but for the most part it was a hitter's game, and the lead went back and forth every inning. Nearly every player succeeded in smashing the ball into the outfield, giving the outfielders some serious exercise. Denise couldn't help but notice that the men in the outfield tended to be a good deal younger—and sweating far more profusely—than those in the infield.

Kyle, however, had grown bored with the game after only an inning and had taken to playing under and on top of the bleachers, climbing and jumping, running here and there. With so many people around, it made Denise nervous to lose sight of him, and she stood up to look for him on more than a few occasions.

Whenever she did, Taylor found his eyes darting that way. Earlier he'd seen her arrive with Kyle, holding his hand and walking slowly as she scanned the bleachers, oblivious of the fact that men were turning their heads as she strode past them. But Taylor had seen the stares, had seen them admiring the way she looked: her white shirt tucked into black shorts, long legs stretching down to matching sandals, dark windblown hair flowing past her shoulders. And for a reason he didn't quite understand, he found himself envious of the fact that his mother—not he—would be sitting with her.

Her presence was distracting, and not only because he kept thinking about the things Melissa had said. The bleachers where she was sitting were between home and first base; his position at third base made it impossible not to see her sitting in the stands. Still, he couldn't seem to stop glancing her way, as if to make sure she hadn't left. He chided himself whenever he did it—wondering why it mattered—but would catch himself at it a moment later. Once, his stare had lasted a little too long, and she waved.

He waved back with an embarrassed grin and turned away, wondering why on earth he suddenly felt like a damn teenager again.

"So that's her, huh?" Mitch asked as they were sitting in the dugout between innings.

"Who?"

"Denise, the one sitting with your mother."

"I didn't really notice," Taylor said as he absently twirled his bat, doing his best to appear uninterested.

"You were right," Mitch said.

"About what?"

"She is pretty."

"I didn't say that. Melissa said it."

"Oh," Mitch said, "right."

Taylor turned his attention to the game, and Mitch followed his eyes.

"Then why were you staring at her?" he finally asked.

"I wasn't staring at her."

"Oh," Mitch said again, nodding. He didn't even try to hide his smirk.

* * *

In the seventh inning, with the score 14–12, the Volunteers were trailing when Taylor was waiting for his turn at bat. Kyle had taken a break from his activities and was standing near the fence when he saw Taylor taking his practice swings.

"Hewwo, Tayer," he said happily, just as he'd done when he'd seen him at Merchants.

Taylor turned at the sound of his voice and approached the fence.

"Hey there, Kyle. Good to see you. How you doing?"

"He's fowman," Kyle said, pointing.

"I sure am. Are you having fun watching the game?"

Instead of answering, Kyle held up his airplane for Taylor to see.

"Whatcha got there, little man?"

"Owpwane."

"You're right. That's a nice airplane."

"You can hold it." *(You kin hode it)*

Kyle handed it through the fence, and Taylor hesitated before taking it. He examined it as Kyle watched him, a look of pride on his little face. Over his shoulder, Taylor heard his name being called to the plate.

"Thanks for showing me your airplane. Do you want it back?"

"You can hold it," Kyle said again.

Taylor debated for a moment before deciding. "Okay, this'll be my good-luck charm. I'll bring it right back." He made sure that Kyle could see him put it in his pocket, and Kyle rolled his hands together.

"Is that all right?" Taylor asked.

Kyle didn't answer, but he seemed to be fine with it.

Taylor waited to make sure, then finally jogged home. Denise nodded in Kyle's direction. Both she and Judy had seen what just transpired.

"I think Kyle likes Taylor," Denise said.

"I think," Judy answered, "the feeling's mutual."

On the second pitch, Taylor smashed the ball into right field—he batted left-handed—and took off at a full clip toward first base while two others in scoring position made their way around the bags. The ball hit the ground and bounced three times before the fielder could reach it, and he was off balance when he threw the ball. Taylor rounded second, charging hard, considering whether to try for home. But his better judgment won out in the end, and the ball reached the infield just as Taylor arrived safely at third. Two runs had scored, the game was tied, and Taylor scored when the next person batted. On his way to the dugout, he handed Kyle the airplane, a big grin on his face.

"I told you it would make me lucky, little man. That's a good airplane."

"Yes, the airplane is good." *(Yes, ee owpwane ess goo)*

It would have been the perfect way to end the game, but alas, it wasn't meant to be. In the bottom of the seventh, the Enforcers scored the winning run when Carl Huddle knocked one out of the park.

After the game was over, Denise and Judy made their way down from the bleachers with the rest of the crowd, ready to head over to the park where food and beer were waiting. Judy pointed out where they'd be sitting.

"I'm already late," Judy explained. "I was supposed to be helping set up. Can I meet you over there?"

"Go ahead—I'll be there in a couple of minutes. I have to get Kyle first."

Kyle was still standing near the fence, watching Taylor gather his gear in the dugout, when Denise approached him. He didn't turn, even after Denise had called his name, and she had to tap him on the shoulder to get his attention.

"Kyle, c'mon, let's go," Denise said.

"No," he answered with a shake of his head.

"The game's over."

Kyle looked up at her, a concerned expression on his face.

"No, he's not." *(No, eez not)*

"Kyle, would you rather go play?"

"He's not," he said again, frowning now, his tone dropping an octave. Denise knew exactly what that meant—it was one of the ways he showed frustration at his inability to communicate. It was also the first step toward what often led to a genuine, knock-down, drag-out screamfest. And boy oh boy, could Kyle scream.

Of course, all children threw tantrums now and then, and Denise didn't expect Kyle to be perfect. But for Kyle, tantrums sometimes arose because he couldn't get his point across well enough to be understood. He'd get mad at Denise for not understanding, Denise would get angry because he couldn't say what he meant, and the whole thing would spiral downward from there.

Even worse, though, were the feelings that those incidents triggered. Whenever it happened, it always reminded Denise point-blank that her son still had a serious problem, and despite the fact she knew it wasn't his fault, despite the fact she knew it was wrong, if the tantrum went on long enough, she sometimes found herself screaming at her son in the same irrational way he was screaming at her. *How hard is it to just run a few simple words together? Why can't you do that? Why can't you be like every other kid? Why can't you be normal, for God's sake?*

Afterward, once things had calmed down, she'd

feel terrible. How on earth, if she loved him so much, could she say those things to him? How could she even *think* them? Never able to sleep afterward, she would stare at the ceiling for hours, honestly believing herself to be the most mean-spirited mother on the planet.

More than anything, she didn't want to have that happen here. She steadied herself, vowing not to raise her voice.

Okay, start with what you know . . . take your time . . . he's trying his best . . .

"He's not," Denise said, repeating after Kyle.

"Yes."

She held his arm gently, in anticipation of what would come. She wanted to keep his attention focused.

"Kyle, he's not what?"

"No . . ." The word came out with a whine, and Kyle made a low growling sound in his throat. He tried to pull away.

Definitely on the verge of a screamfest.

She tried again with things she knew he understood.

"Do you want to go home?"

"No."

"Are you tired?"

"No."

"Are you hungry?"

"No."

"Kyle—"

"No!" he said, shaking his head and cutting her off. He was angry now, his cheeks turning red.

"He's not what?" she asked with as much patience as possible.

"He's not . . ."

"He's not, what?" Denise repeated.

Kyle shook his head in frustration, groping for the words.

"He's not . . . Kye," he finally said.

Denise was completely lost now.

"You're not Kyle?"

"Yes."

"You're not Kyle," she repeated, this time as a statement. Repetition, she'd learned, was important. It was something she did to find out whether or not they were both on the same wavelength.

"Yes."

Huh?

Denise thought about it, trying to figure it all out, before focusing on him again.

"What's your name? Is it Kyle?"

Kyle shook his head. "He's not Kye. He's linno man."

She ran through it again, making sure she understood what he was saying.

"Little man?" she asked.

Kyle nodded triumphantly and smiled, his anger suddenly receding as quickly as it had come.

"Eez linno man," he said again, and all Denise could do was stare at him.

Little man.

Oh Lord, how long was *this* going to last?

At that moment Taylor approached them, his gear bag thrown over his shoulder.

"Hey, Denise, how are you?" He took off his hat and wiped his forehead with the back of his hand.

Denise turned her attention to him, still flummoxed. "I'm not exactly sure," she answered honestly.

The three of them began walking across the park together, and Denise recounted her exchange with Kyle. When she was finished Taylor patted Kyle on the back.

"Little man, huh?"

"Yes. Eez linno man," Kyle said proudly in response.

"Don't encourage him," Denise said with a rueful shake of the head.

Taylor seemed to find the whole thing extremely humorous and didn't bother trying to hide it. Kyle, on the other hand, was gazing at Taylor as though he were one of the seven wonders of the world.

"But he is a little man," Taylor said in Kyle's defense. "Aren't you?"

Kyle nodded, pleased to have someone on his side. Taylor unzipped his gear bag and dug around inside before pulling out an old baseball. He handed it to Kyle.

"Do you like baseball?" he asked.

"It's a ball," Kyle answered. *(Ess a baw)*

"It's not just a ball. It's a baseball," he said seriously.

Kyle considered it.

"Yes," he whispered. "It's a baseball." *(Yes . . . Ess a bessbaw)*

He held the ball tightly in his small hand and seemed to study it, as if looking for a secret that only he could understand. Then, glancing up, he spotted a children's slide in the distance. All of a sudden that took priority over everything else.

"He wants to run," Kyle said, looking expectantly at his mother, "over there." He pointed to where he wanted to go. *(Ee wanta wun . . . O'er dare)*

"Say, '*I want to run.*'"

"I want to run," he said softly. *(I wanta wun)*

"Okay, go ahead," she said. "Just don't go too far."

Kyle dashed toward the kids' play area, a bundle of unharnessed energy. Luckily it was right next to the tables where they would be sitting—Judy had chosen the spot for just that reason, since nearly everyone involved in the game brought their children with them. Both Denise and Taylor watched Kyle as he ran.

"That's one cute kid," Taylor offered with a grin.

"Thanks. He's a good boy."

"That little man thing isn't really a problem, is it?"

"It shouldn't be . . . he went through a phase where he pretended to be Godzilla a couple of months ago. He wouldn't answer to anything else."

"Godzilla?"

"Yeah, it's pretty funny when you think back on it. But at the time, oh my. I remember we were at the store once and Kyle slipped away. I was walking through the aisles calling for Godzilla, and you wouldn't believe the looks that people were giving me. When Kyle finally came back, there was this one lady—she stared at me like I was an alien. I knew she was wondering what kind of mother names her kid Godzilla."

Taylor laughed. "That's great."

"Yeah, well . . ." She rolled her eyes, communicating a mixture of contentment and exasperation. As she glanced at him, her eyes caught his and lingered just an instant too long before each of them turned away. They walked on in silence, looking exactly like one of the other young couples in the park.

From the corner of his eye, however, Taylor still watched her.

She was radiant in the warm June sunlight. Her eyes, he noticed, were the color of jade, exotic and mysterious. She was shorter than he was—maybe five six, he guessed—and she moved with the easy grace of people who were confident of their place in the world. More than that, he sensed her intelligence in the patient way she dealt with her son and, most of all, how much she loved him. To Taylor those were the things that really mattered.

Melissa, he knew, had been right after all.

"You played a good game," Denise finally said, interrupting his thoughts.

"We didn't win, though."

"But you played well. That counts for something."

"Yeah, well, we didn't win."

"That's such a man thing to say. I hope Kyle doesn't turn out that way."

"He will, though. He won't be able to help it. It's in our genes."

Denise laughed, and they took a few steps in silence.

"So why did you get involved with the fire department?" she asked him.

The question brought his father's image to mind. Taylor swallowed, forcing the thought away.

"It's just something I've wanted to do since I was a kid," he answered.

Though she heard a slight change in his tone, his expression seemed neutral as he studied the crowds in the distance.

"How does that work? Since you volunteer, I mean. Do they just call you up when there's an emergency?"

He shrugged, suddenly relieved for some reason. "Pretty much."

"Is that how you found my car that night? Did someone call it in?"

Taylor shook his head. "No, that was just lucky. Everyone at the station had been called in earlier because of the storm—there were already downed power lines on the roads, and I was out setting flares so that people could stop in time. I just happened to come across your car and pulled over to see what was wrong."

"And there I was," she said.

At this he stopped and met her gaze, his eyes the same color as the sky. "And there you were."

The tables were piled high with enough food to feed a small army, which about equaled the number of people milling about in the area.

Off to the side, over by the grills where burgers and franks were being cooked, were four large coolers filled with ice and beer. As they neared the coolers, Taylor tossed his gear bag to one side, piling it with the others, and grabbed a beer for himself. Still bent over, he held up a can of Coors Light.

"Would you like one?"

"Sure, if you have enough."

"There's plenty. If we get through all these coolers, you'd better hope nothing happens in town tonight. No one would be able to respond."

He handed the can to her, and she opened it. She'd never been a big drinker even in the years before Kyle, but the beer was refreshing on such a hot day.

Taylor took a long pull just as Judy spotted them. She put a stack of paper plates in the center of one of the tables, then walked over to meet them.

She gave Taylor a quick squeeze. "Sorry your team lost," she said playfully. "But you owe me five hundred bucks."

"Thanks for the moral support."

Judy laughed. "Oh, you know I'm just playing with you." She squeezed him again before turning her attention to Denise.

"Well, now that you're here, can I introduce you around?"

"Sure, but let me check on Kyle first."

"He's fine. I saw him when he came up. He's playing on the slide."

Like radar, Denise was able to zero in on him almost immediately. He was indeed playing, but he looked hot. She could see how red his face was, even at a distance.

"Um . . . do you think it would be okay if I got him something to drink? A soda or something?"

"Absolutely. What kind does he like? We've got Coke, Sprite, root beer . . ."

"Sprite."

From the corners of his eyes, Taylor saw Melissa and Kim—Carl Huddle's pregnant wife—coming over to say hello. Melissa was wearing the same triumphant expression that she'd had the night he'd been over for dinner. No doubt she'd seen them walk up together.

"Here, let me bring it to him," Taylor offered hurriedly, not wanting to face her gloating. "I think a few people are coming over to say hello."

"Are you sure?" Denise asked.

"I'm positive," he answered. "Should I bring him a can, or would he like it in a cup?"

"A cup."

Taylor took another pull from his beer as he headed for the table to prepare Kyle's drink, narrowly avoiding Melissa and Kim.

Judy introduced Denise around the circle, and after visiting for a few minutes, they dragged her off to meet some other people.

Though Denise had never been comfortable meeting strangers, in this case it wasn't as difficult as she imagined. The casual setting—kids were running from here to there, everyone was dressed for summer, people were laughing and joking—made it easy for her to relax. It felt like a reunion, where anyone and everyone was welcome.

Over the next half hour or so she met a few dozen people, and as Judy had mentioned, nearly every one of them had children. Names were coming quickly—their own and their kids'—making it impossible for her to remember them all, though she did her best for those who seemed to be the closest to her own age.

Lunch for the kids came next, and after the hot dogs were pulled from the grills, kids came rushing to the tables from all over.

Kyle, of course, didn't come to the table with the rest of the children, but strangely, she didn't see Taylor, either. She hadn't seen him since he'd headed off to the play area, and she scanned the crowd, wondering if he'd slipped back unnoticed. She didn't find him.

Curious, she looked toward the play area, and it was then that she saw the two of them, facing each other a few feet apart. When she realized what they were doing, her breath caught in her throat.

She almost didn't believe it. She closed her eyes for a long moment, then opened them again.

Frozen, she watched as Taylor gently lobbed the baseball in Kyle's direction. Kyle stood with both arms straight out, his forearms close together. He didn't move a muscle as the ball sailed through the air. But as if by some magic, the ball dropped directly into his little hands.

All she could do was stare in wonder.

Taylor McAden was playing catch with her son.

* * *

Kyle's latest throw was off the mark—as many of them had been—and Taylor scrambled as the ball went past him, finally coming to a stop in the short grass. As he stepped over to retrieve it, he saw Denise approaching.

"Oh, hey," he said casually. "We were just playing catch." He picked up the ball.

"Have you been doing this the whole time?" she asked, still unable to hide her amazement. Kyle had never wanted to play catch before. She'd tried numerous times to get him interested in it, but he'd never even made the attempt. Her surprise, though, wasn't limited simply to Kyle; it had to do with Taylor. It was the first time that someone else had ever taken the time to teach Kyle something new, something that other children did.

He was playing with Kyle. Nobody played with Kyle.

Taylor nodded. "Pretty much. He seems to like it."

At the same time, Kyle saw her and waved. "Hewwo, Money," he called out.

"Are you having fun?" she asked.

"He throws it," he said excitedly. *(Ee frows it)*

Denise couldn't help but smile. "I see that. It was a good throw."

"Ee frows," Kyle said again, agreeing with her.

Taylor pushed up the bill of his hat. "He's got quite an arm sometimes," he said, as if to explain why he'd missed Kyle's throw.

Denise could only stare at him. "How did you get him to do it?"

"What? Play catch?" He shrugged, clearly unaware of his accomplishment. "Actually, it was his idea. After he finished his soda, he sort of sailed one at me. Almost hit me in the head. So I tossed it back and gave him some pointers on how to catch it. He caught on pretty fast."

"Frow it," Kyle called out impatiently. His arms were straight out again.

Taylor looked at her to see if it was all right.

"Go ahead," Denise said. "I've got to see this again."

Taylor took his position a few feet from Kyle.

"You ready?" Taylor asked.

Kyle, concentrating hard, didn't respond. Denise crossed her arms in nervous anticipation.

"Here it comes," he said, lobbing the ball. It hit Kyle on the wrist and bounced toward his chest like a pinball, before finally falling to the ground. Kyle immediately picked it up, aimed, then threw the ball back. This time the ball was on target, and Taylor was able to catch it without moving.

"Good one," Taylor said.

The ball went back and forth a few more times before Denise finally spoke.

"You ready for a break?" she asked.

"Only if he is," Taylor responded.

"Oh, he could keep doing this for a while. Once he finds something he likes, he doesn't like to stop."

"So I've noticed."

Denise called out to Kyle, "Okay, sweetie, last one."

Kyle knew what that meant, and he eyed the ball carefully before throwing it. It went off to the right, and once again Taylor wasn't able to catch it. It came to a stop near Denise, and she retrieved it just as Kyle started toward her.

"That's it? No argument?" Taylor asked, obviously impressed by Kyle's good-naturedness.

"No, he's pretty good at things like that."

When Kyle reached her, she picked him up and gave him a hug. "Good job playing catch."

"Yes," Kyle said happily.

"Would you like to play on the slide?" she asked.

Kyle nodded, and she lowered him to the ground. Kyle immediately turned and headed toward the play area.

Once they were alone, Denise faced him.

"That was really nice of you, but you know you didn't have to stay out here the whole time."

"I know I didn't. I wanted to. He's a lot of fun."

She smiled gratefully, thinking how seldom she'd heard someone say that about her son. "The food's ready if you want to go grab something," she said.

"I'm not all that hungry yet, but I would like to finish my beer, if that's okay."

His can was sitting on the bench, near the edge of the play area, and Taylor and Denise walked that way. Taylor picked it up and took a long pull. From the angle of the can, she knew he'd barely been able to touch it. She could see beads of perspiration dripping down his cheek. His dark hair peeked out from under his hat, curling slightly, and his shirt was tacked to his chest. Her son had kept him busy.

"Would you like to sit for a minute?" he asked.

"Sure."

Kyle, meanwhile, had turned his attention from the slide to the jungle gym. He climbed up, stretched his arms as high as they would go, then began to cross the monkey bars.

"Mommy, watch!" Kyle suddenly yelled out. *(Money, wash!)*

Denise turned away and watched Kyle jump down from the bars, a fall of three or four feet, landing with a crash. He stood up quickly and brushed the dirt from his knees, a big grin on his face.

"Be careful, okay?" she called out.

"He jumped," Kyle responded. *(Ee jumped)*

"Yes, you did."

"He jumped," Kyle said again.

While Denise's attention was focused on her son, Taylor could see her chest rising and falling with every breath, and he watched as she crossed one leg over the other. The movement, for some reason, seemed oddly sensual.

When she turned back to him, he made sure to keep the conversation on safe ground.

"So, did you get a chance to meet everyone?" he asked.

"I think so," she answered. "They seem like good people."

"They are. I've known most of 'em since I was a kid."

"I like your mom, too. She's been a real friend lately."

"She's a sweet lady."

For the next few minutes they continued to watch Kyle as he made the circuit through everything the playground had to offer. Sliding, climbing, jumping, and crawling, Kyle seemed to have saved an untapped energy source for something like this. Despite the heat and humidity, he never seemed to slow down at all.

"I think I'm ready for a burger now," Taylor said. "I take it you already ate."

Denise checked her watch. "Actually, I haven't, but we can't stay. I've got to work tonight."

"You're leaving already?"

"In a few minutes. It's almost five, and I've still got to feed Kyle and get ready for work."

"He can eat here—there's plenty of food."

"Kyle doesn't eat hot dogs or chips. He's kind of a picky eater."

Taylor nodded. For a long moment he seemed to be lost in thought.

"Can I give you a lift home?" he finally asked.

"We rode our bikes here."

Taylor nodded. "I know."

As soon as he said it, she knew it to be a moment of recognition for both of them. She didn't need the ride, and he knew it; he'd asked despite the fact that friends and food were waiting just a few steps away. It was obvious that he wanted her to say yes; his expression made that clear. Unlike his offer to bring her groceries home, this time, she knew, his offer had less to do with being kind than it did with what might happen between them.

It would have been easy to say no. Her life was complex enough—did she really need to add something more to the mix? Her mind was telling her that she didn't have the time, that it wouldn't be a good idea, that she barely knew him. The thoughts registered in quick succession, making perfect sense, but despite them all, she surprised herself by saying, "I'd like that."

Her answer seemed to surprise him as well. He took another drink of beer, then nodded without a word. It was then that Denise recognized the same shyness in him that she'd seen at Merchants, and she suddenly acknowledged the very thing she'd been denying to herself all along.

She hadn't come to the festival to visit with Judy, nor had she come to meet new people.

She'd come to see Taylor McAden.

Mitch and Melissa watched as Taylor and Denise departed. Mitch leaned toward his wife's ear, so that others wouldn't overhear him.

"So, what did you think of her?"

"She's nice," Melissa said honestly. "But it's not just up to her. You know how Taylor is. Where this all goes from here will really depend on him."

"Do you think they'll get together?"

"You know him better than I do. What do you think?"

Mitch shrugged. "I'm not sure."

"Yes, you are. You know how charming Taylor can be when he sets his sights on someone. I just hope that this time he doesn't hurt anyone."

"He's your friend, Melissa. You don't even know Denise."

"I know. And that's why I've always forgiven him."

Chapter 14

Monster truck!" Kyle exclaimed. *(Monstew twuck!)*

A Dodge four-by-four, it was black with oversize wheels. It had two spotlights mounted on a roll bar, a heavy-duty tow cable hooked to the front bumper, a gun rack mounted above the seats in the cab, and a silver toolbox in the bed.

Unlike others she'd seen, however, this one was no showpiece. The paint job had dulled, with deep scratches throughout, and there was a dent in the front side panel, right near the driver's-side door. One of the rearview mirrors had been torn off, leaving a hole that had rusted around the edges, and the entire lower half of the truck was crusted with a thick layer of mud.

Kyle wrung his hands together, excited. "Monster truck," he said again.

"Do you like it?" Taylor asked.

"Yes," he said, nodding enthusiastically.

Taylor loaded the bikes into the bed of the truck,

then held the door open for them. Because the truck was high, he had to help Kyle scramble inside. Denise was next, and Taylor accidentally brushed against her as he showed her where to grab to pull herself up.

He started the engine, and they headed toward the outskirts of town with Kyle propped up between them. As if knowing she wanted to be alone with her thoughts, Taylor didn't say anything, and she was grateful for that. Some people were uncomfortable with silence, considering it a void that needed to be filled, but he obviously wasn't one of them. He was content simply to drive.

The minutes passed, and her mind wandered. She watched pine trees whistle by, one right after the other, still amazed she was in the truck with him. From the corner of her eye, she could see him concentrating on the road. As she'd noted initially, Taylor wasn't typically handsome. Had she passed him on the street in Atlanta, she wouldn't have given him a second glance. He didn't have that pretty look some men had, but there was something about him she found ruggedly appealing. His face was tan and lean; the sun had carved small lines in his cheeks and around his eyes. His waist was narrow, and his shoulders were heavily muscled, as if from years of heavy load bearing. His arms looked as if he'd pounded thousands of nails, which no doubt he had.

It was almost as if his job as a contractor had molded his appearance.

She wondered if he'd ever been married. Neither he nor Judy had mentioned it, but that didn't mean anything. People were often reluctant to talk about past mistakes. Lord knew she didn't bring up Brett unless she had to. Still, there was something about him that made her suspect he'd never made the commitment. At the barbecue, she couldn't help but notice that he seemed to be the only one who was single.

Up ahead was Charity Road, and Taylor slowed the truck, making the turn and then accelerating again. They were almost home.

A minute later Taylor reached the gravel driveway and turned in, gradually applying the brakes until the truck came to a complete stop. Pushing the clutch in, he let the car idle, and Denise turned toward Taylor curiously.

"Hey, little man," he said. "You wanna drive my truck?"

It took a moment before Kyle turned.

"C'mon," he said, motioning. "You can drive it."

Kyle hesitated, and Taylor motioned again. Kyle moved slightly before Taylor finally pulled him into his lap. He placed Kyle's hands on the upper part of the steering wheel while keeping his own hands close enough to grab it if necessary.

"You ready?"

Kyle didn't answer, but Taylor slowly let the clutch out and the truck began to inch forward.

"All right, little man, let's go."

Kyle, a little unsure, held the wheel steady as the truck began to roll up the drive. His eyes widened as he realized he really had control, and all at once he turned the wheel hard to the left. The truck responded and moved onto the grass, bouncing slightly and heading toward the fence before Kyle turned the wheel the other way. The turn was erratic, but eventually he crossed the gravel driveway to the other side.

They were moving no more than five miles an hour, but Kyle broke into a wide grin and turned toward his mother, a "look what I'm doing" expression on his face. He laughed in delight before turning the wheel once more.

"He's driving!" Kyle exclaimed. *(Eez dryfeen!)*

The truck rolled toward the house like a big figure S, missing every tree (thanks to Taylor's slight but necessary adjustments in course), and when Kyle laughed aloud for the second time, Taylor winked at Denise.

"My dad used to let me do this when I was little. I just figured Kyle might like it, too."

Kyle, with Taylor's verbal—and manual—guidance, pulled the truck into the shade of the magnolia tree before finally stopping. After opening the driver's-side door, Taylor lifted Kyle down. Kyle scrambled to keep his balance before starting toward the house.

As they watched him, neither of them said anything, and at last Taylor turned away, clearing his throat.

"Let me go get your bikes," he said, and jumped out of the cab. As he moved to the back of the truck and opened the rear latch, Denise sat unmoving, feeling slightly unraveled. Once again Taylor had surprised her. Twice in a single afternoon he'd done something kind for Kyle, something considered normal in the lives of other children. The first time had caused her to stare in wonder; the second time, however, had touched her in a place she'd never expected. As his mother, she could do only so much—she could love and protect Kyle, but she couldn't make other people accept him. It was obvious, though, that Taylor already did, and she felt her throat close up just a little.

After four and a half years Kyle had finally made a friend.

She heard a thud and felt the truck tilt slightly as Taylor climbed into the bed. She composed herself before opening her door and jumping down.

Taylor lowered the bikes to the ground, then hopped out of the bed in one easy, fluid movement. Still feeling less than steady, Denise glanced toward

Kyle and saw him standing by the front door. With the sun peeking over the trees behind him, Taylor's face seemed hidden by shadows.

"Thanks for driving us home," she said.

"I was glad to do it," he replied quietly.

Standing close to him, she couldn't escape the images of Taylor playing catch with her son or letting Kyle steer the truck, and she knew then that she wanted to know more about Taylor McAden. She wanted to spend more time with him, she wanted to get to know the person who'd been so kind to her child. Most of all, she wanted him to feel the same way.

She could feel herself beginning to blush as she brought her hand to her forehead, shading the sun from her eyes.

"I've still got a little time before I've got to start getting ready for work," she said, following her instincts. "Would you like to come in for a glass of tea?"

Taylor pushed his hat up higher on his head. "That sounds good, if it's okay."

They rolled the bikes around to the back of the house, leaving them on the porch, then walked inside, pushing through a door whose paint had cracked and peeled over the years. The house wasn't much cooler, and Denise left the back door open to help circulate the air. Kyle followed them inside.

"Let me get your tea," she said, trying to hide the sudden nervousness in her voice.

From the refrigerator she pulled out the jar of tea, then added a few ice cubes to glasses she retrieved from the cupboard. She passed Taylor the glass, leaving her own on the counter, conscious of how close she was to him. She turned to Kyle, hoping that Taylor wouldn't guess what she was feeling.

"Do you want something to drink?"

Kyle nodded. "He wants some water." *(Eee wonse sum wonner)*

Thankful for the interruption of her thoughts, she got that as well and handed it to him.

"You ready for a tub? You're all sweaty."

"Yes," he said. He took a drink from his small plastic cup, spilling part of it down his shirt.

"Can you give me a minute to get his tub ready?" she asked, glancing at Taylor.

"Sure, take your time."

Denise led Kyle from the kitchen, and a few moments later, beneath the distant murmur of her voice, Taylor heard the water start up. Leaning against the counter, he took in the kitchen with a contractor's eye. The house, he knew, had been vacant for at least a couple of years before Denise had moved in, and despite her best efforts the kitchen still showed signs of neglect. The floor was warped slightly, and the linoleum had turned yellow with age. Three of the cupboard doors were hanging crooked, and the sink had a slow drip that over the years had left rust marks on the porcelain. The refrigerator, no doubt, had come with the house—it reminded him of the one he'd had as a kid. He hadn't seen one like it in years.

Still, it was obvious that Denise had done her best to make it as presentable as possible. It was clean and well kept, that much was clear. Every dish was put away, the countertops had been wiped down, a ragged washcloth was folded neatly in the sink. Over by the phone was a stack of mail that looked as if it had already been sorted through.

By the back door he saw a small wooden table with a series of textbooks arranged across the top, held in place by two small flowerpots, each housing a small geranium. Curious, he walked over and scanned the titles. Every one of them had to do with child development. On the shelf below was a thick blue binder, labeled with Kyle's name.

The water shut off and Denise returned to the kitchen, conscious of how long it had been since she'd been alone with a man. It was a strange feeling for her, one that reminded her of her life from long ago, before her world had changed.

Taylor was perusing the titles when she picked up her glass and made her way toward him.

"Interesting reading," he said.

"Sometimes." Her voice sounded different to her ears, though Taylor didn't seem to notice.

"Kyle?"

She nodded, and Taylor motioned toward the binders. "What are those?"

"Those are his journals. Whenever I work with Kyle, I record what he's able to say, how he says it, what he's having trouble with, things like that. That way I can follow his progress."

"It sounds like a lot of work."

"It is." She paused. "Would you like to sit?"

Taylor and Denise sat at the kitchen table, and though he didn't ask, she explained what—as far as she could tell—Kyle's problem was, just as she'd done with Judy. Taylor listened without interruption until she was finished.

"So you work with him every day?" he asked.

"No, not every day. We take Sundays off."

"Why is language so hard for him?"

"That's the magic question," she answered. "Nobody really knows the answer to that."

He nodded toward the shelf. "What do the books say?"

"For the most part, they don't say much. They talk a lot about language delays in children, but when they do, it's usually just one aspect of a bigger problem—like autism, for instance. They recommend therapy, but they're not specific in what kind of therapy is best. They simply recommend a program of some sort, and there are different theories as to which is most useful."

"And the doctors?"

"They're the ones who write the books."

Taylor stared into his glass, thinking back on his exchanges with Kyle, then looked up again. "You know, he doesn't talk all that bad," he said sincerely. "I understood what he was saying, and I think he understands me, too."

Denise ran her fingernail through one of the cracks in the table, thinking it was a kind—if not completely true—thing to say. "He's come a long way in the last year."

Taylor leaned forward in his seat. "I'm not just saying it," he said earnestly. "I mean it. When we were throwing the ball back and forth? He was telling me to throw the ball, and whenever he caught it, he would say, 'Good job.'"

Four words, essentially. *Throw it. Good job.* Denise could have said, *That's not much if you think about it, is it?* and she would have been right. But Taylor was being kind, and right now she didn't really want to get into a discussion about the limitations of Kyle's language abilities. Instead she was more interested in the man sitting across from her. She nodded, collecting her thoughts.

"I think that has a lot to do with you, not just

Kyle. You're very patient with him, which most people aren't. You remind me of some of the teachers I used to work with."

"You were a teacher?"

"I taught for three years, right up until Kyle was born."

"Did you like it?"

"I loved it. I worked with second-graders, and that's just such a great age. Kids like their teachers and are still eager to learn. It makes you feel like you can really make a difference in their lives."

Taylor took another sip, watching her closely over the rim of his glass. Sitting in the kitchen surrounded by her things, observing her expressions as she talked about the past—it all made her seem almost softer, somehow less guarded than she had been before. He also sensed that talking about herself wasn't something she was used to.

"Are you going to go back to it?"

"Someday," she answered. "Maybe in a few years. We'll have to see what happens in the future." She sat a little straighter in her seat. "But what about you? You said you were a contractor?"

Taylor nodded. "Twelve years now."

"And you build homes?"

"I have in the past, but generally I focus on remodeling. When I first started, those were the only types of jobs I could get because no one else wanted them. I like it, too—to me, it's a little more challenging than building something new. You have to work with what's already there, and nothing is ever as easy as you suspected it would be. Plus, most people have a budget, and it's fun to try to figure out how to get them the most for their money."

"Do you think you could do anything with this place?"

"I could make it look brand-new if you wanted. It depends on how much you wanted to spend."

"Well," she said gamely, "I just happen to have ten bucks burning a hole in my pocket."

Taylor brought his hand to his chin. "Mmm." His face assumed a serious expression. "We might have to eliminate the Corian countertops and the Sub-Zero refrigerator," he said, and they both laughed.

"So how do you like working at Eights?" he asked.

"It's all right. It's what I need right now."

"How's Ray?"

"He's wonderful, actually. He lets Kyle sleep in the back while I work, and that takes care of a lot of problems."

"Has he told you about his kids?"

Denise raised her eyebrows slightly. "Your mother asked that exact same question."

"Well, once you live here long enough, you'll find out that everyone knows everything about everyone, and in time, everyone's going to ask the same questions. It's a small town."

"Hard to stay anonymous, huh?"

"Impossible."

"What if I keep to myself?"

"Then people will talk about that, too. But it's not so bad, once you get used to it. Most people aren't mean, they're just curious. As long as you're not doing anything immoral or illegal, most people don't really care, and they certainly don't dwell on it. They're just passing the time because there's not much else to do around here."

"So what do you like to do? In your spare time, I mean?"

"My job and the fire department keep me fairly busy, but if I can get away, I go hunting."

"That wouldn't be popular with some of my friends back in Atlanta."

"What can I say? I'm just a good ol' boy from the South."

Again Denise was struck by how different he was compared with the men she used to date. Not only in the obvious things—what he did and how he looked—but because he seemed content in the world he'd created for himself. He wasn't yearning for fame or glory, he wasn't striving to earn zillions of dollars, full of hungry plans to get ahead. In a way, he almost seemed to be a throwback to an earlier time, a time when the world didn't seem as complicated as it did now, when simple things were what mattered most.

While she was thinking about him, Kyle called out from the bathroom, and Denise turned at the sound of his voice. Glancing at her watch, she saw that Rhonda would be by to pick her up in half an hour and she wasn't ready yet. Taylor knew what she was thinking, and he finished the last of his glass.

"I should probably be going."

Kyle called out again, and this time Denise answered.

"I'll be there in a second, sweetie." Then to Taylor: "Are you going back to the barbecue?"

Taylor nodded. "They're probably wondering where I am."

She gave him a mischievous smile. "Do you think they're whispering about us?"

"Probably."

"I'm going to have to get used to this, I guess."

"Don't worry. I'll make sure they know that it didn't mean anything."

Her eyes leapt to his, and under his gaze she felt something stir inside, something sudden and unexpected. Before she could stop the words, they were already out.

"It meant something to me."

Taylor seemed to study her in silence, considering what she'd said, as an embarrassed blush began to surge through her cheeks and neck. He looked around the kitchen, then toward the floor, before finally focusing on her again.

"Are you working tomorrow evening?" he finally asked.

"No," she said a little breathlessly.

Taylor took a deep breath. *God, she was pretty.*

"Can I take you and Kyle to the carnival tomorrow? I'm sure Kyle would love the rides."

Despite the fact that she'd suspected he would ask, she still felt a rush of relief when she heard the words aloud.

"I'd like that," she said quietly.

Later that night, unable to sleep, Taylor mused that what had started as simply an ordinary day had turned into something he hadn't anticipated. He didn't really understand how it had happened . . . the whole situation with Denise had just sort of snowballed, almost beyond his control.

Sure, she was attractive and intelligent—he admitted that. But he'd met attractive and intelligent women before. There was just something about Denise, something about their relationship already, that had caused his normally tight control to slip just a notch. It was almost like *comfort*, for lack of a better word.

Which didn't make any sense, not really, he told

himself, flipping his pillow over and mashing it into shape. He barely knew her. He'd had only a few conversations with her, he'd seen her only a couple of times in his life. She probably wasn't anything he imagined her to be.

Besides, he didn't want to get involved. He'd been down that road before.

Taylor shook off his blanket in sudden irritation.

Why on earth had he asked to drive her home? Why had he asked her out tomorrow?

And more important, why did the answers to those questions leave him feeling so uneasy?

Chapter 15

Sunday was mercifully cooler than the day before. Hazy clouds had blown in that morning, keeping the sun from venting its full fury, and the evening breeze had picked up just as Taylor pulled up the driveway. It was a little before six when his truck bounced over the potholes, his wheels spinning gravel. Denise stepped out onto the porch, dressed in faded jeans and a short-sleeved shirt, just as he was climbing out of the truck.

She hoped she didn't look as nervous as she felt. It was her first date in what seemed like forever. Okay, Kyle would be with them, and it wasn't technically a *real* date, but even so, it felt like one. She'd spent almost an hour trying to find something to wear before finally making her decision, and even then she questioned it. It wasn't until she saw that he was wearing jeans as well that she breathed a little easier.

"Hey, there," he said. "I hope I'm not late."

"No, not at all," she said. "You're right on time."

Absently he scratched the side of his face. "Where's Kyle?"

"He's still in the house. Let me go get him."

It took only a minute before she was ready to go. As she locked the door on the way out, Kyle took off running across the yard.

"Hewwo, Tayer," he called out.

Taylor held the door open for him and helped Kyle up, just as he'd done the day before.

"Hey, Kyle. Are you looking forward to the carnival?"

"Ess a monstew twuck," he said happily.

Immediately after scrambling onto the seat, he climbed behind the wheel again, trying unsuccessfully to turn it from side to side.

Denise heard Kyle making engine sounds as she drew near. "He's been talking about your truck all day," she explained. "This morning, he found a Matchbox that looks like the truck you drive and he wouldn't put it down."

"What about his airplane?"

"That was yesterday's attraction. Today, it's the truck."

He nodded toward the cab. "Should I let him drive again?"

"I don't think he's going to give you the chance to say no."

As Taylor made room for her to climb up, she

caught the trace of his cologne. Nothing fancy, probably something from the local drugstore, but she was touched that he'd put it on. Kyle scooted over to make room for him, then immediately crawled into his lap once Taylor was situated.

Denise shrugged, an "I told you so" expression on her face. Taylor grinned as he turned the key.

"All right, little man, let's go."

They did the big figure S again, taking their time, bumping haphazardly over the lawn and around the trees before finally reaching the road. At that point Kyle scooted off his lap, satisfied, and Taylor turned the wheel, heading into town.

The ride to the carnival took only a few minutes. Taylor was busy explaining various items in the truck to Kyle—the CB, the radio, the knobs on the dash—and though it was clear her son didn't understand what was being said, Taylor just kept on trying anyway. She noticed, however, that Taylor seemed to be speaking more slowly than he had the day before and was using simpler words. Whether it was because of their conversation in the kitchen or whether he'd picked up on her own cadence, she wasn't sure, but she was gratified by his attentiveness.

They pulled into downtown, then turned right onto one of the side streets to find a parking space. Even though it was the last night of the festival, the crowds were light, and they found a spot close to the main road. Walking toward the carnival, Denise noticed that the booths along the sidewalks were fairly well cleaned out and the people who ran them looked tired, as if they couldn't wait to finally close down. A few of them were already doing exactly that.

The carnival was still going strong, however—mainly kids and their parents, hoping to enjoy the last couple of hours of entertainment that the carnival would provide. By tomorrow everything would be loaded up and on its way to the next town.

"So, Kyle, what do you want to do?" Denise asked.

He immediately pointed to the mechanical swing—a ride in which dozens of metal swings rotated in circles, first forward and then backward. Each child had his or her own seat—supported at each corner by a chain—and kids were screaming in terror and delight. Kyle watched it going round and round, transfixed.

"It's a swing," he said. *(Ess a sweeng)*

"Do you want to ride the swing?" Denise asked him.

"Swing," he said with a nod.

"Say, 'I want to ride the swing.'"

"I want to ride the swing," he whispered. *(Wonta wide ee sweeng)*

"Okay."

Denise spotted the ticket booth—she'd saved a few dollars from her tips the evening before—and began to reach into her purse. Taylor, however, saw what she was doing and raised his hands to stop her.

"My treat. I asked, remember?"

"But Kyle . . ."

"I asked him to come, too."

After Taylor bought the tickets, they waited in line. The ride stopped and emptied, and Taylor handed over the tickets to a man who'd come straight from Central Casting. His hands were black with grease, his arms covered in tattoos, and one of his front teeth was missing. He tore the tickets before dropping them into a locked wooden box.

"Is this ride safe?" she asked.

"Passed inspection yesterday," he answered automatically. No doubt it was the same thing he said to every parent who asked, and it didn't do much to relieve her anxiety. Parts of the ride looked as if they were stapled together.

Nervously Denise led Kyle to his seat. She lifted him up, then lowered the safety bar for him as Taylor stood outside the gate, waiting for them.

"Ess a swing," Kyle said again, once he was ready to go.

"Yes, it is." She put his hands on the bar. "Now hold on and don't let go."

Kyle's only response was to laugh in delight.

"Hold on," she said again, more seriously this time, and Kyle squeezed the bar.

She walked back to Taylor's side and took her place, praying that Kyle would listen to her. A minute later it started, and the ride slowly began to pick up speed. By the second rotation the swings were beginning to fan out, carried by their momentum. Denise hadn't taken her eyes off Kyle, and as he swung by, it was impossible not to hear him laughing, a high-pitched giggle. As he came back around, she noticed that his hands were still right where they should be. She breathed a sigh of relief.

"You seem surprised," Taylor said, leaning close so his voice could be heard over the noise of the ride.

"I am," she said. "It's the first time he's ever been on a ride like this."

"Haven't you ever taken him to a carnival?"

"I didn't think he was ready for one before."

"Because he has trouble talking?"

"Partially." She glanced at him. "There's a lot about Kyle that even I don't understand."

She hesitated under Taylor's serious gaze. Suddenly she wanted more than anything for Taylor to understand Kyle, she wanted him to understand what the last four years had been like. More than that, she wanted him to understand her.

"I mean," she began softly, "imagine a world where nothing is explained, where everything has to be learned through trial and error. To me, that's what

Kyle's world is like right now. People sometimes think that language is just about conversation, but for children, it's much more than that. It's how they learn about the world. It's how they learn that burners on the stove are hot, without having to touch them. It's how they know that crossing the street is dangerous, without having to be hit by a car. Without the ability to understand language, how can I teach him those things? If Kyle can't understand the concept of danger, how can I keep him safe? When he wandered away into the swamp that night . . . well, you yourself said he didn't seem to be frightened when you found him."

She looked at Taylor earnestly. "Well, it makes perfect sense—to me, at least. I'd never walked him through the swamp, I'd never shown him snakes; I'd never shown him what might happen if he got stuck somewhere and couldn't get out. Because I hadn't shown him, he didn't know enough to be afraid. Of course, if you take that one step further and consider every possible danger and the fact that I have to literally show him what it means, instead of being able to *tell* him—sometimes it feels like I'm trying to swim across the ocean. I can't tell you how many close calls there have been. Climbing too high and wanting to jump, riding too close to the road, wandering away, walking up to growling dogs . . . it seems like every day there's something new."

She closed her eyes for a moment, as if reliving each experience, before going on.

"But believe it or not, those are only part of my worries. Most of the time, I worry about the obvious things. Whether he'll ever be able to talk normally, whether he'll go to a regular school, whether he'll ever make friends, whether people will accept him . . . whether I'll have to work with him forever. Those are the things that keep me awake at night."

She paused then, the words coming slower, every syllable edged with pain.

"I don't want you to think that I regret having Kyle, because I don't. I love him with all my heart. I'll always love him. But . . ."

She stared at the revolving swings, her eyes blind, shuttered. "It's not exactly what I imagined raising children would be like."

"I didn't realize," Taylor said gently.

She didn't respond, seemingly lost in thought. Finally, with a sigh, she faced him again.

"I'm sorry. I shouldn't have told you those things."

"No, don't be. I'm glad you did."

As if suspecting that she'd confided too much, she offered a rueful smile. "I probably made it sound pretty hopeless, didn't I?"

"Not really," he lied. In the waning sunlight she was strangely radiant. She reached over and touched his arm. Her hand was soft and warm.

"You're not very good at that, you know. You should stick to telling the truth. I know I made it sound terrible, but that's just the dark side of my life. I didn't tell you about the good things."

Taylor raised his eyebrows slightly. "There are good things, too?" he asked, prompting an embarrassed laugh from Denise.

"Next time I need to pour my heart out, remind me to stop, okay?"

Though she tried to pass off the comment, her voice betrayed her anxiety. Immediately Taylor suspected that he was the first person she'd ever really confided in this way and that it wasn't the time for jokes.

The ride ended suddenly, the swing rotating three times before coming to a stop. Kyle called out from his seat, the same ecstatic expression on his face.

"Sweeeng!" he called out, almost singing the word, his legs pumping back and forth.

"Do you want to ride the swing again?" Denise shouted.

"Yes," he answered, nodding.

There weren't many people in line, and the man nodded that it was all right for Kyle to stay where he was. Taylor handed him the tickets, then returned to Denise's side.

As the ride started up again, Taylor saw Denise staring at Kyle.

"I think he likes it," Denise said almost proudly.

"I think you're right."

He leaned over, resting his elbows on the railings, still regretting his earlier joking.

"So tell me about the good things," he said quietly.

The ride circled twice, and she waved to Kyle each time before saying anything.

"Do you really want to know?" she finally asked.

"Yes, I do."

Denise hesitated. What was she doing? Confiding about her son to a man she barely knew, giving voice to things she'd never said in the past—she felt unsteady, like a boulder inching over the edge of a cliff. Yet somehow she wanted to finish what she had started.

She cleared her throat.

"Okay, the good things . . ." She glanced briefly at Taylor and then away. "Kyle's getting better. Sometimes it may not seem like it and others may not notice it, but he is, slowly but surely. Last year, his vocabulary was only fifteen to twenty words. This year, it's in the hundreds, and at times he puts three and four words together in a single sentence. And for the most part, he makes most of his wishes known now. He tells me when he's hungry, when he's tired, what he wants to eat—all of that's new for him. He's only been doing that for the last few months."

She took a deep breath, feeling her emotions roil to the surface again.

"You have to understand . . . Kyle works *so* hard *every* day. While other kids can play outside, he has to sit in his chair, staring at picture books, trying to figure out the world itself. It takes him hours to learn things that other kids might learn in minutes." She stopped, turning toward him, an almost defiant look in her eyes.

"But you know, Kyle just keeps on going . . . he just keeps on trying, day after day, word by word, concept by concept. And he doesn't complain, he doesn't whine, he just does it. If you only knew how hard he has to work to understand things . . . how much he tries to make people happy . . . how much he wants people to like him, only to be ignored . . ."

Feeling her throat constrict, she took a ragged breath, struggling to maintain her composure.

"You have no idea how far he's come, Taylor. You've only known him for a short while. But if you knew where he started and how many obstacles he's overcome so far—you'd be so proud of him . . ."

Despite her efforts, tears began to flood her eyes.

"And you'd know what I know. That Kyle has more *heart*, more *spirit*, than any other child I've ever known. You would know that Kyle is the most wonderful little boy that any mother could wish to have. You would know that despite everything, Kyle is the greatest thing that's ever happened to me. That's the good thing I have in my life."

All those years of having those words pent up inside, all those years of wanting to say the words to someone. All those years, all those feelings—both the good and the bad—it was such a relief to finally let it all go. She was suddenly intensely thankful that she'd done so and hoped in her heart that Taylor would somehow understand.

Unable to respond, Taylor tried to swallow the lump that had formed in his throat. Watching her talk about her son—the absolute fear and absolute love—made the next move almost instinctive. Without a word, he reached for her hand and took it in his. The feeling was strange, a forgotten pleasure, though she didn't try to pull away.

With her free hand she wiped at a tear that had drifted down her cheek and sniffled. She looked spent, still defiant, and beautiful.

"That was the most beautiful thing I think I've ever heard," he said.

When Kyle wanted to ride the swing yet a third time, Taylor had to let go of Denise's hand so he could walk over and present the additional tickets. When he returned, the moment had passed; Denise was leaning on the barrier, resting on her elbows, and he decided simply to let it go. Yet standing beside her, he could still feel the lingering sensation of her touch on his skin.

They spent another hour at the carnival, riding the Ferris wheel—the three of them crammed into the wobbly seat with Taylor pointing out some of the places that could be seen from the top—and the Octopus, a spinning, dipping, gut-twisting ride that Kyle wanted to ride over and over again.

Toward the end of the hour they headed over to the area that housed the games of chance. Pop three balloons with three darts and win a prize, shoot two baskets and win something different. Vendors barked at the passersby, but Taylor walked past all of them until reaching the shooting gallery. He used the first few shots to understand the sighting of the gun, then proceeded to make fifteen straight, trading up for larger prizes as he bought more rounds. By the time he'd finished, he'd won a giant panda only slightly smaller than Kyle himself. The vendor handed it over reluctantly.

Denise relished every minute of it. It was gratifying to watch Kyle trying—and *enjoying!*—new things, and walking around the carnival provided a pleasant change from the world in which she normally lived. There were times when she almost felt like someone else, someone she didn't know. As twilight descended, the lights from the rides blinked on; as the sky darkened even further, the energy of the crowds seemed to intensify, as if everyone knew all this would be over the following day.

Everything was just right, as she had barely dared to hope it would be.

Or, if possible, even better than that.

Once they got home, Denise got a cup of milk and led Kyle into his room. She propped the giant panda in the corner so he could see it, then helped Kyle change into his pajamas. After leading him through his prayers, she gave him his milk.

His eyes were already closing.

By the time she finished reading him a story, Kyle was breathing deeply.

Slipping from the room, she left the door partially open.

Taylor was waiting for her in the kitchen, his long legs stretched out under the table.

"He's down for the count," she said.

"That was fast."

"It's been a big day for him. He's not usually up this late."

The kitchen was lit by a single overhead bulb. The other had burned out the week before, and she suddenly wished she had changed it. It seemed just a little too dim, a little too intimate, in the small kitchen. Seeking space, she fell back on tradition.

"Would you like something to drink?"

"I'll take a beer if you have one."

"My selection isn't quite that big."

"What do you have?"

"Iced tea."

"And?"

She shrugged. "Water?"

He couldn't help but smile. "Tea's fine."

She poured two glasses and handed one to him, wishing she had something stronger to serve both of them. Something to take the edge off the way she was feeling.

"It's a little warm in here," she said evenly, "would you like to sit on the porch?"

"Sure."

They made their way outside and sat in the rockers, Denise closest to the door so she could listen for Kyle if he woke up.

"Now this is nice," Taylor said after making himself comfortable.

"What do you mean?"

"This. Sitting outside. I feel like I'm on an episode of *The Waltons*."

Denise laughed, feeling some of her nervousness disperse. "Don't you like to sit on the porch?"

"Sure, but I hardly ever do it. It's one of those things that I never seem to have time for anymore."

"A good ol' boy from the South like yourself?"

she said, repeating the words he'd used the day before. "I would have thought a guy like you would sit outside on your porch with a banjo, playing song after song, a dog lying at your feet."

"With my kinfolk and a jar of moonshine and a spittoon o'er yonder?"

She grinned. "Of course."

He shook his head. "If I didn't know you were from the South, I'd think you were insulting me."

"But because I'm from Atlanta?"

"I'll let it slide this time." He felt the corners of his mouth curling into a smile. "So what do you miss the most about the big city?"

"Not a lot. I suppose if I were younger and Kyle wasn't around, this place would drive me crazy. But I don't need big malls, or fancy places to eat, or museums anymore. There was a time when I thought those things were important, but they weren't really an option during the last few years, even when I was living there."

"Do you miss your friends?"

"Sometimes. We try to keep in touch. Letters, phone calls, things like that. But how about you? Didn't you ever get the urge to just pack up and move away?"

"Not really. I'm happy here, and besides, my mom is here. I'd feel bad leaving her alone."

Denise nodded. "I don't know that I would have

moved if my mom were still alive, but I don't think so."

Taylor suddenly found himself thinking about his father.

"You've been through a lot in your life," he said.

"Too much, I sometimes think."

"But you keep going."

"I have to. I've got someone counting on me."

Their conversation was interrupted by a rustle in the bushes, followed by an almost catlike scream. Two raccoons scurried out of the woods, across the lawn. They scampered past the light reflected from the porch, and Denise stood, trying to get a better view. Taylor joined her at the porch railing, peering into the darkness. The raccoons stopped and turned, finally noticing two people on the porch, then continued across the lawn before vanishing from sight.

"They come out almost every night. I think they're scrounging for food."

"Probably. Either that or your garbage cans."

Denise nodded knowingly. "When I first moved here, I thought dogs were the ones who kept digging through them. Then I caught those two in the act one night. At first I didn't know what they were."

"You've never seen a raccoon before?"

"Of course I have. But not in the middle of the night, not crawling through my garbage, and certainly not on my porch. My apartment in Atlanta didn't have a real big wildlife problem. Spiders, yes; varmints, no."

"You're like that kid's story about the city mouse that hops on the wrong truck and gets stuck in the country."

"Believe me, I feel that way sometimes."

With her hair moving slightly in the breeze, Taylor was struck again by how pretty she was. "So what was your life like? Growing up in Atlanta, I mean?"

"Probably a little bit like yours."

"What do you mean?" he asked curiously.

She met his eyes, drawing out the words as if they were a revelation. "We were both only children, raised by widowed mothers who grew up in Edenton."

At her words, Taylor felt something unexpectedly flinch inside. Denise went on.

"You know how it is. You feel a little different because other people have two parents, even if they're divorced. It's like you grow up knowing that you're missing something important that everyone else has, but you don't know exactly what it is. I remember hearing my friends talking about how their fathers wouldn't let them stay out late or didn't like their boyfriends. It used to make me so angry because they didn't even realize what they had. Do you know what I mean?"

Taylor nodded, realizing with sudden clarity how much they had in common.

"But other than that, my life was pretty typical. I lived with my mom, I went to Catholic schools, shopped with my friends, went to the proms, and worried every time I got a pimple that people wouldn't like me anymore."

"You call that typical?"

"It is if you're a girl."

"I never worried about things like that."

She shot him a sidelong glance. "You weren't raised by my mother."

"No, but Judy's mellowed some in her old age. She was a little more stern when I was younger."

"She said that you were always getting into trouble."

"And I suppose you were perfect."

"I tried," she said playfully.

"But you weren't?"

"No, but obviously I was better at fooling my mother than you were."

Taylor chuckled. "That's good to hear. If there's one thing I can't stand, it's perfection."

"Especially when it's someone else, right?"

"Right."

There was a brief lull in the conversation before Taylor spoke again.

"Do you mind if I ask you a question?" he said almost tentatively.

"It depends on the question," she answered, trying not to tense up.

Taylor glanced away, toward the edge of the property again, pretending to look for the raccoons. "Where's Kyle's father?" he asked after a moment.

Denise had known it was coming.

"He's not around. I didn't really even know him. Kyle wasn't supposed to happen."

"Does he know about Kyle?"

"I called him when I was pregnant. He told me straight up he didn't want anything to do with him."

"Has he ever seen him?"

"No."

Taylor frowned. "How can he not care about his own child?"

Denise shrugged. "I don't know."

"Do you ever wish he was around?"

"Oh, heavens, no," she said quickly. "Not him. I mean, I would have liked Kyle to have a father. But it wouldn't have been someone like him. Besides, for Kyle to have a father—the right kind, I mean, and not just someone who calls himself that—he'd also have to be my husband."

Taylor nodded in understanding.

"But now, Mr. McAden, it's your turn," Denise said, turning to face him. "I've told you everything about me, but you haven't reciprocated. So tell me about you."

"You already know most of it."

"You haven't told me anything."

"I told you I'm a contractor."

"And I'm a waitress."

"And you already knew that I volunteer with the fire department."

"I knew that the first time I saw you. It's not enough."

"But there's really not much more than that," he protested, throwing up his hands in mock frustration. "What did you want to know?"

"Can I ask whatever I want?"

"Go ahead."

"Well, all right." She was silent for a moment, then met his eyes. "Tell me about your father," she said softly.

The words startled him. It wasn't the question he'd expected, and Taylor felt himself stiffen slightly, thinking he didn't want to respond. He could have ended it with something simple, a couple of sentences that meant nothing, but for a moment he didn't say anything.

The evening was alive with sound. Frogs and insects, the rustling of leaves. The moon had risen and now hovered above the treeline. In the milky light, an occasional bat skittered by. Denise had to lean in close to hear him.

"My father passed away when I was nine," he began.

Denise watched him carefully as he spoke. He was

speaking slowly, as if gathering his thoughts, but she could see his reluctance on every line of his face.

"But he was more than just my father. He was my best friend, too." He hesitated. "I know that sounds strange. I mean, I was just a little kid and he was grown, but he was. He and I were inseparable. As soon as five o'clock would roll around, I'd camp out on the front steps and wait for his truck to come up the driveway. He worked in the lumber mill, and I'd run for him as soon as he opened his door and jump into his arms. He was strong—even when I got bigger, he never told me to stop. I'd put my arms around him and take a deep breath. He worked hard, and even in winter I could smell the sweat and sawdust on his clothes. He called me 'little man.'"

Denise nodded in recognition.

"My mom always waited inside while he asked me what I did that day or how school went. And I'd just talk so fast, trying to say as much as I could before he went inside. But even though he was tired and probably wanting to see my mom, he never rushed me. He'd let me say everything on my mind, and only when I was all talked out would he finally put me down. Then he'd grab his lunch pail, take my hand, and we'd head inside."

Taylor swallowed hard, doing his best to think about the good things.

"Anyway, we used to go fishing every weekend. I

can't even remember how old I was when I first started going with him—probably younger than Kyle. We'd go out in the boat and sit together for hours. Sometimes he'd tell me stories—it seemed like he had thousands of them—and he'd answer whatever questions I asked as best he could. My father never graduated from high school, but even so he was pretty good at explaining things. And if I asked him something he didn't know, he'd say that, too. He wasn't the kind of person who had to be right all the time."

Denise almost reached out to touch him, but he seemed lost in the past, his chin resting on his chest.

"I never saw him get angry, I never once heard him raise his voice at anyone. When I'd act up, all he had to do was say, 'That's enough now, son.' And I'd stop because I knew I was disappointing him. I know that probably sounds strange, but I guess I just didn't want to let him down."

When he finished, Taylor took a long, slow breath.

"He sounds like a wonderful man," Denise said, knowing she'd stumbled upon something important about Taylor, but uncertain of its shape and meaning.

"He was."

The finality of his voice made it clear that the subject was closed to further discussion, although Denise suspected there was far more left to be said. They stood without speaking for a long time, listening to the music of the crickets.

"How old were you when your father died?" he asked finally, breaking the silence.

"Four."

"Do you remember him like I remember mine?"

"Not really, not the way you do. I just remember images, really—him reading me stories or the feeling of his whiskers when he kissed me good night. I was always happy when he was around. Even now, not a day goes by when I don't wish I could turn back the clock and change what happened."

As soon as she said it, Taylor turned to her with a startled expression, knowing she'd hit it right on the head. In just a few words, she'd explained the very thing he'd tried to explain to Valerie and Lori. But even though they'd listened with compassion, they'd never really understood. They couldn't. Neither of them had ever awakened with the terrible realization that they'd forgotten the sound of their father's voice. Neither had cherished a single photograph as the only means of remembrance. Neither one of them felt the urge to tend to a small granite stone in the shade of a willow tree.

All he knew was that he'd finally heard someone else echo the things that he had known, and for the second time that evening he reached for her hand.

They held hands in silence, fingers loosely intertwined, each afraid that speaking would break the spell. Lazy clouds, silver in the moon, lay scattered in the sky. Standing close, Denise watched shadows play over his features, feeling slightly unstrung. On his jaw was a small scar she'd never noticed before; there was another just below his ring finger on the hand that was holding hers, a small burn, perhaps, that had healed long ago. If he was aware of her scrutiny, he gave no notice. Instead he simply stared out over the property.

The air had cooled slightly. A sea breeze had blown through earlier, leaving a stillness in its wake. Denise sipped her tea, listening as insects buzzed noisily around the porch light. An owl called from the darkness. Cicadas sang in the trees. The evening was coming to an end, she could feel that. It was almost over.

He finished his glass, the ice cubes clinking, then set it on the railing.

"I should probably go. I have an early day tomorrow."

"I'm sure," she said.

But he stood there for another minute without saying anything more. For some reason he kept remembering how she'd looked when she'd poured out her fears about her son: her defiant expression, the intense emotion as the words had flooded out. His mother had worried about him, too, but had it ever approached what Denise went through every day?

He knew it hadn't been the same.

It moved him to see that her fears had only made her love grow stronger for her son. And to witness such unconditional love, so pure in the face of difficulties—it was natural to find beauty in that. Who wouldn't? But there was more to it, wasn't there? Something deeper, a commonality he'd never found in someone else.

Even now, not a day goes by when I don't wish I could turn back the clock and change what happened.

How had she known?

Her ebony hair, made even darker by the evening, seemed to shroud her in mystery.

Taylor finally pushed back from the railing.

"You're a good mother, Denise." He was loath to release her delicate hand. "Even though it's hard, even though it's not what you expected, I can't help but believe that everything happens for a reason. Kyle needed someone like you."

She nodded.

With great reluctance he turned away from the railing, turned from the pines and oaks, turned from the feelings inside him. The floor of the porch creaked as Taylor moved to the steps, Denise beside him.

She looked up at him.

He almost kissed her then. In the soft yellow light of the porch her eyes seemed to glow with hidden intensity. Even so, he couldn't tell if she really wanted that from him, and at the last second he held back. The evening had already been more memorable than any evening he'd spent in a long time; he didn't want to spoil that.

Instead he took a small step backward, as if to give her more space.

"I had a wonderful time tonight," he said.

"So did I," she said.

He finally let go of her hand, felt longing as it slipped away from him. He wanted to tell her that she had something inside her, something impossibly rare, something he'd looked for in the past but had never hoped to find. He wanted to say all these things but found that he couldn't.

He smiled again, faintly, then turned away, making his way down the steps in the slanting moonlight, toward the darkness of his truck.

Standing on the porch, she waved one last time as Taylor headed down the drive, his headlights shining in the distance. She heard him stop at the road and wait as a solitary car approached, then passed. Taylor's truck turned in the direction of town.

After he left, Denise walked to the bedroom and sat on the bed. On her bedstand was a small reading lamp, a photo of Kyle as a toddler, a half-empty glass of water she'd neglected to bring to the kitchen that morning. Sighing, she opened her drawer. In the past it might have held magazines and books, but now it was empty except for a small bottle of perfume she'd received from her mother a few months before she'd died. A birthday gift, it had come wrapped in gold foil and ribbon. Denise had used half of it in the first few weeks after it had been given to her; since her mother's death she'd never used it again. She'd kept it as a reminder of her mother, and now it reminded her of how long it had been since she'd worn any perfume at all. Even tonight she'd forgotten to put it on.

She was a mother. Above everything else, that was how she defined herself now. Yet as much as she wanted to deny it, she knew she was also a woman, and after years of keeping it buried, she felt its presence. Sitting in the bedroom, gazing at the perfume, she was overcome with a sense of restlessness. There was something inside her that longed to be desired, to be cared for and protected, to be listened to and accepted without judgment. To be loved.

Her arms crossed, she turned out the light in her bedroom and went across the hall. Kyle was sleeping soundly. In the warmth of his room, he'd pushed his blankets aside and he slept uncovered. On his bureau, music from a plastic, glowing teddy bear continued to play softly through the room, the same melody repeated over and over. It had been his night-light since he was an infant. She turned it off, then went to his bed, working the sheet until it wasn't tangled with the blankets. Kyle rolled over as she covered him. She kissed him on the cheek, his skin soft and unblemished, and slipped from the room.

The kitchen was quiet. Outside, she could hear the crickets chirping, riding the song of summer. She looked out the window. In the moonlight the trees were glowing silver, the leaves steady and unmoving. The sky was full of stars, stretching to eternity, and she stared at them, smiling, thinking about Taylor McAden.

Chapter 16

Taylor was sitting in his kitchen two evenings later, doing paperwork, when he got the call.

An accident on the bridge between a gasoline tanker truck and an auto.

After grabbing his keys, he was out the door less than a minute later; within five minutes he was one of the first on scene. He could hear the sirens from the fire truck wailing in the distance.

Stopping his truck, Taylor wondered if they'd make it in time. He scrambled out without shutting the door and looked around. Cars were backed up in either direction on both sides of the bridge, and people were out of their cars, gawking at the horrific sight.

The cab of the tanker had rolled up onto the back of the Honda, completely crushing the rear, before smashing through the wire barrier that lined the bridge. In the midst of the accident, the driver had locked the wheel as he'd slammed on the brakes, and the truck had whipsawed across both lanes of the road, completely blocking both directions. The car, pinned beneath the front of the cab, hung off the bridge like a diving board from its flattened rear tires, balanced precariously in a downward position. Its roof had been torn open, like a partially opened can, as it ripped through the cable along the side of the bridge. The only thing that kept the Honda from falling into the river some eighty feet below was the weight of the tanker's cab, and the cab itself looked far from stable.

Its engine was smoking badly, and fluid was leaking steadily onto the Honda beneath, spreading a shiny veneer over the hood.

When Mitch saw Taylor, he came rushing forward to fill Taylor in, getting straight to business.

"The driver of the truck's all right, but there's still someone in the car. Man or woman, we can't tell yet—whoever it is is slumped over."

"What about the tanks on that truck?"

"Three-quarters full."

Smoking engine . . . leaking over the car . . .

"If that cab explodes, will the tanks go with it?"

"The driver says that it shouldn't if the lining wasn't damaged in the accident. I didn't see a leak, but I can't be sure."

Taylor looked around, adrenaline coursing through his system. "We gotta get these people out of here."

"I know, but they're bumper to bumper right now,

and I just got here a couple of minutes ago myself. I haven't had a chance."

Two fire trucks arrived—the pumper and the hook and ladder, their red lights circling the area, and seven men jumped out before they'd come to a complete stop. Already in their fire-retardant suits, they took one look at the situation, started barking orders, and went for the hoses. Having come to the scene without going by the firehouse first, Mitch and Taylor scrambled for the suits that had been brought for them. They slipped them over their clothing with practiced ease.

Carl Huddle had arrived; so did an additional two police officers from the town of Edenton. After a quick consultation they turned their attention to the cars on the bridge. A bullhorn was retrieved from the trunk; gawkers were ordered to get back behind the wheel to vacate the area. The two other officers—in Edenton it was one officer per car—went in opposite directions, toward the end of the lines of the cars backed up on the highway. The final car in the line got the first order:

"You've got to back up or turn around now. We've got a serious situation on the bridge."

"How far?"

"Half a mile."

The first driver spoken to hesitated, as if trying to decide if it really was necessary.

"Now!" the officer barked.

Taylor speculated that half a mile was just about enough distance to create a zone of safety, but even so, it would take a while for every car to move far enough away.

Meanwhile the truck was smoking more heavily.

Ordinarily the fire department would hook up hoses to the nearest fire hydrant in order to draw all the water they need. On the bridge, however, there were no hydrants. Thus the pumper truck would provide the only water available. It was plenty for the cab of the truck, but nowhere near enough to control the fire if the tanker exploded.

Controlling the fire would be critical; helping the trapped passenger, however, was foremost in people's minds.

But how to reach the passenger? Ideas were shouted as everyone prepared for the inevitable.

Climb out over the cab to reach the person? Use a ladder and crawl out? Run a cable somehow and swing in?

No matter what course of action they chose, the problem remained the same—all were fearful of putting any extra weight on the car itself. It was a wonder that it was still there at all, and jostling the car or adding weight might be enough to cause it to tip. When a blast of water from the hose was aimed toward the cab, their fears—everyone suddenly realized—were justified.

The water gushed violently toward the engine in the cab of the truck, then cascaded inside the shattered back windshield of the Honda at the rate of five hundred gallons per minute, partially filling the car's interior. It then flowed with gravity toward the engine, out of the passenger area. Within moments water began to rush out from the front grill. The nose of the car dipped slightly, raising the cab of the truck—then rose again. The firemen manning the hose saw the ravaged car teetering in the balance and without a second to spare turned the hose away, toward the open air, before shutting it down.

To a man, their faces had gone white.

Water was still pouring from the front of the car. There had been no movement from the passenger within.

"Let's use the ladder on the truck," Taylor urged. "We'll extend it out over the car and use the cable to haul the person out."

The car continued to rock, seemingly of its own accord.

"It might not support the two of you," Joe said quickly. As the chief, he was the only full-time employee of the fire department; it was his job to drive one of the trucks, and he was always the calming influence in a crisis like this.

It was obvious he had a point. Because of the angle of the wreck and the relatively narrow width of the bridge, the hook and ladder couldn't approach to within an ideal distance. From where it could be parked, the ladder would have to extend out over the car to the side the passenger was on, an extension of at least an additional twenty feet. Not much if the ladder was at an angle—but because it would have to be positioned nearly horizontally out over the river, it would test the limits of what was safe.

Had it been a new-model fire truck, it probably wouldn't have been a problem. Edenton's hook and ladder was one of the oldest operating models in the state, however, and it had originally been purchased with the knowledge that the tallest building in town was only three stories. The ladder wasn't designed to be used in a situation like this.

"What other choice do we have? I'll be out and back before you know it," Taylor said.

Joe had almost expected him to volunteer. Twelve years ago, during Taylor's second year with the crew, Joe had asked him why he was always the first to volunteer for the riskiest assignments. Though risks were part of the job, unnecessary risks were something else, and Taylor had struck him as a man with something to prove. Joe didn't want someone like that behind him—not because he didn't trust Taylor to get him out of trouble, but because he didn't want to risk his own life saving someone who tested fate unnecessarily.

But Taylor offered a simple explanation:

"My dad died when I was nine, and I know what it's like for a kid to grow up alone. I don't want that to happen to anyone else."

Not that the others didn't risk their lives, of course. Everyone involved with the fire department accepted the risks with open eyes. They knew what might happen, and there had been dozens of occasions where Taylor's offer had been declined.

But this time . . .

"All right," Joe said with finality. "You're on the point, Taylor. Now let's get to it."

Because the hook and ladder was facing forward, it had to be backed off the bridge, then onto the grass median to reach the best possible position. Once the truck was off the bridge, the driver of the fire truck moved the truck back and forth three times before he was able to reverse toward the wreck again. By the time the truck was in position, seven minutes had elapsed.

In that seven minutes the engine in the truck continued to smoke heavily. Small flames were now visible in the area beneath it, licking out, scorching the rear of the Honda. The flames looked awfully close to the gas tanks, but spraying the hose wasn't an option anymore, and they couldn't get close enough with the fire extinguishers to make a difference.

Time was running out, and all anyone could do was watch.

While the truck was moving into position, Taylor collected the rope he needed and attached it to his own harness with a clip. When the truck was in place, Taylor climbed up and secured the other end of the rope to the ladder a few rungs from the end. A cable, much longer, was also run from the rear of the hook and ladder up to the ladder itself. Attached to the hook at the far end of the cable was a soft, well-padded safety harness. Once the safety harness was secured around the passenger, the cable would slowly be rewound, lifting the passenger out.

As the ladder began to extend, Taylor lay on his belly, his mind clicking. *Keep balanced . . . stay as far back on the ladder as possible . . . when the time comes, lower quickly but carefully . . . don't touch the car . . .*

But the passenger occupied most of his thoughts. Was the person trapped? Could he be moved without risking further injury? Would it be possible to get him out without the car tipping over?

The ladder continued to snake outward, close to the car now. There were still ten or twelve feet to go, and Taylor felt the ladder growing a little unsteady, creaking beneath him, like an old barn in a windstorm.

Eight feet. He was close enough now to reach out and touch the front of the truck.

Six feet.

Taylor could feel the heat from the small flames, could see them lapping at the mangled roof of the car. As the ladder extended, it began to rock slightly.

Four feet. He was over the car now . . . getting close to the front windshield.

Then the ladder came to a rattling halt. Still lying on his belly, Taylor looked back over his shoulder when it stopped, to see if some glitch had occurred. But by the expressions on the other firemen's faces, he knew that the ladder was extended as far as it would go and that he was going to have to make do.

The ladder wobbled precariously as he untied the rope that held his own harness. Grabbing the other harness for the passenger, he began inching forward, toward the edge of the ladder, taking advantage of the last three rungs. He needed them now to position himself over the windshield and lower himself in order to reach the passenger.

Despite the chaos surrounding him, as he crawled forward he was struck by the improbable beauty of the evening. Like a dream, the night sky had opened before him. The stars, the moon, the wispy clouds . . . over there, a firefly in the evening sky. Eighty feet below, the water was the color of coal, as black as time yet somehow trapping the light of the stars. He could hear himself breathing as he moved forward; he could feel his heart thudding in his chest. Beneath him, the ladder bounced and shuddered with every movement.

He slid forward like a soldier in the grass, clinging to the cold metal rungs. Behind him, the last of the cars were backing off the bridge. In the deathly silence Taylor could hear the flames licking beneath the truck, and without warning the car beneath him started to rock.

The nose of the car dipped slightly and straightened, then dipped again before righting itself. There was no wind at all. In the split second he noticed it, he heard a low moan, the sound muffled and almost impossible to decipher.

"Don't move!" Taylor shouted instinctively.

The moan grew louder, and the Honda started to rock in earnest.

"Don't move!" Taylor shouted again, his voice full of desperation, the only sound in the darkness. All else was still. A bat brushed by in the night air.

He heard the moan again, and the car tilted forward, its nose dipping toward the river before righting itself once more.

Taylor moved quickly. He secured his rope on the final rung, tying the knot as deftly as any sailor. Pulling his legs forward, he squeezed through the rungs, doing his best to move as fluidly and slowly as possible while staying in the harness. The ladder rocked like a teeter-totter, groaning and creaking, bouncing as if it would break in two. He settled himself as firmly as he could, almost as if he were on a swing. This was as good a position as he would get. Holding on to the rope with one hand, he reached downward toward the passenger with the other, gradually testing the ladder's strength. Pushing through the windshield to the dashboard, he saw that he was too high, but he caught sight of the person he was trying to save.

A male in his twenties or thirties, about the same size he was. Seemingly incoherent, he was struggling in the wreckage, causing the car to rock violently. The passenger's movement was a double-edged sword, Taylor realized. It meant that he could probably be removed from the car without risk of spinal injury; it also meant that his movement might tip the car.

His mind racing, Taylor reached above him to the ladder and grabbed the safety harness, then pulled it toward him. With the sudden movement, the ladder bounced up and down like marbles on the pavement. The cable grew tight.

"More cable!" he shouted, and a moment later he felt it pick up slack and he began to lower it. Once it was in position, he shouted for them to stop. He unhooked one end of the safety harness so that he could try to work it around the man's body and reattach it.

He bent down again but saw with frustration that he still couldn't reach the man. He needed another couple of feet.

"Can you hear me?" Taylor called into the car. "If you can understand what I'm saying, answer me."

He heard the moan again, and though the passenger shifted, it was obvious that he was semi-conscious at best.

The flames beneath the truck suddenly flared and intensified.

Gritting his teeth, Taylor shifted his grip on the rope to the lowest spot he could, then stretched for the passenger again. Closer this time—he could reach past the dash—but the passenger was still out of reach.

Taylor heard the others calling from the bridge.

"Can you get him out of there?" Joe shouted.

Taylor evaluated the scene. The front of the car seemed to be undamaged, and the man was unbuckled, lying half on the seat, half on the floor beneath the steering wheel, wedged in but looking as if he could be pulled out through the sheared opening of the roof. Taylor cupped his free hand around his mouth, shouting so that his voice could be heard:

"I think so. The windshield's completely blown out, and the roof is wide open. There's enough room for him to come up, and I can't see anything holding him."

"Can you reach him?"

"Not yet," he called back. "I'm close, but I can't get the harness around him. He's incoherent."

"Hurry up and do what you can," came Joe's anxious voice. "From here it looks like the engine fire's getting worse."

But Taylor already knew that. The truck was radiating extreme heat now, and he heard strange popping noises coming from within. Sweat began to drip down his face.

Bracing himself, Taylor once again grasped the rope and stretched himself, his fingertips this time grazing the unconscious man's arm through the shattered windshield. The ladder was bouncing, and he tried to extend his reach with every bounce. Still inches away.

Suddenly, as if in a nightmare, he heard a loud *whoosh*ing sound, and flames suddenly exploded from the engine of the truck, leaping toward Taylor. He pulled up, covering his face instinctively as the flames receded toward the truck again.

"You okay?" Joe shouted.

"I'm fine!"

No time for any plans, no time to debate . . .

Taylor reached for the cable and pulled it toward him. Stretching his toes, he worked the hook that held the safety harness until it was centered beneath his boot. Then, supporting his weight with his foot, he lifted himself slightly and unhooked his own harness from his support rope.

Holding on for dear life, with only one small point in the center of his boot supporting him, he slid his hands down the cable until he was almost crouching. Now low enough to reach the passenger, he let go of the cable with one hand and reached for the safety harness. He had to work it around the passenger's chest, beneath his arms.

The ladder was bouncing hard now. Flames began to sear the roof of the Honda, only inches from his head. Rivulets of sweat poured into his eyes, blurring his vision. Adrenaline surged through his limbs . . .

"Wake up!" he shouted, his voice hoarse with panic and frustration. "You've got to help me here!"

The passenger moaned again, his eyes flickering open. It wasn't enough.

With flames spitting toward him, Taylor grabbed for the man, yanking hard on his arm.

"*Help* me, damnit!" Taylor screamed.

The man, finally awakened by some flicker of self-preservation, raised his head slightly.

"Put the harness under your arm!"

He didn't seem to understand, but the new angle of his body presented an opportunity. Taylor immediately worked one end of the harness toward the man's arm—the one lying across the seat—then slipped it underneath.

One down.

All the while, he kept on screaming, his cries growing even more desperate.

"Help me! Wake up! We're almost out of time here!"

The flames were gaining strength, and the ladder was bouncing dangerously.

Again the man moved his head—not much, not nearly enough. The man's other arm, wedged between his body and the steering wheel, looked stuck. Without worrying what might happen now, Taylor shoved the body, the force making him sway. The ladder dipped precariously, as did the car. The nose began pointing toward the river.

Somehow, however, the shove was enough. This time the man opened his eyes and began to struggle out from between the steering wheel and the seat. The car was rocking heavily now. Weakly the passenger freed his other arm, then raised it slightly as he tried to crawl onto the seat. Taylor worked the safety harness around him. His hand sweaty on the cable, he attached the free end of the harness, completing the circle, then cinched it tight.

"We're gonna pull you out now. We're almost out of time."

The man simply rolled his head, suddenly drifting into unconsciousness again, but Taylor could see that the path was finally clear.

"Bring him up!" he screamed. "Passenger is secure!"

Taylor worked his hands up the cable until he was in a standing position. The firefighters slowly began to unwind the cable, careful not to jerk it for fear of the stress it would put on the ladder.

The cable tightened, and the ladder began to groan and shudder. But instead of the passenger coming up, the ladder seemed to be lowering.

Lowering . . .

Oh, crap . . .

Taylor could feel it on the verge of buckling, then they both began to rise.

Up an inch. Then another.

Then, with nightmarish deliberateness, the cable stopped recoiling. Instead the ladder began to descend again. Taylor knew instantly that the ladder couldn't support both of them.

"Stop!" he shouted. "The ladder's gonna go!"

He had to get off the cable, and he had to get off the ladder. After making sure once more that the man wouldn't get snagged, he reached for the ladder rungs above him. Then he carefully removed his foot from the hook, letting his legs dangle free, praying that the additional jostling wouldn't break the ladder in two.

He decided to go hand over hand across the ladder, like a kid crossing the monkey bars. One rung . . .

two . . . three . . . four. The car was no longer beneath him, yet he could still feel the ladder creeping lower.

It was while he was crossing the rungs that the flames ripped into a frenzy, straining with deadly intensity at the gas tanks. He'd seen engine fires numerous times—and this one was seconds away from blowing.

He looked toward the bridge. As if in slow motion, he saw the firemen, his friends, motioning frantically with their arms, screaming at him to hurry, to get off the ladder, to get to safety before the truck exploded. But he knew that there was no way he could make it back to the truck in time and still get the passenger out.

"Pull him out!" Taylor shouted hoarsely. "He's got to come up now!"

Dangling high above the water, he loosened his grip, then let go completely. In an instant he was swallowed by the evening air.

The river was eighty feet below.

"That was the dumbest, most moronic thing I've ever seen you do," Mitch said matter-of-factly. It was fifteen minutes later, and they were sitting on the banks of the Chowan River. "I mean, I've seen some stupid stunts in my life, but that one takes the cake."

"We got him out, didn't we?" Taylor said. He was

drenched and had lost one boot while kicking for safety. In the aftermath, after the adrenaline drained away, he felt his body retreating into a kind of exhausted lull. He felt as if he hadn't slept for days, his muscles seemed rubbery, his hands were shaking uncontrollably. Thankfully the accident on the bridge was being tended to by the others—he wouldn't have had the strength to help. Though the engine had blown, the seals around the main tanks had held and they were able to control the fire relatively easily.

"You didn't have to let go. You could have made it back."

Even as he said it, Mitch wasn't quite sure it was true. Right after Taylor let go, the firemen shook off their shock and began to rewind the cable in earnest. Without Taylor's weight, the ladder had enough tensile strength to allow the passenger to be lifted through the windshield. As Taylor predicted, he was pulled out without a snag. Once he was free, the ladder swung out, away from the accident, rotating back toward the bridge. Just as the ladder reached the bridge, the engine of the truck blew, churning white-and-yellow flames spewing violently in every direction. The car was tossed free and followed Taylor into the water below. Taylor had had enough sense after hitting the water to make his way beneath the bridge, foreseeing just such an occurrence. As it was, the car had come down close, too close.

After he hit the water, the pressure sucked him under and held him for several seconds, then several more. Taylor was spun and twisted like a rag in a washing machine, but he was finally able to fight his way to the surface, where he drew a gasping breath.

When Taylor had come to the surface the first time, he'd shouted that he was okay. After the car hit the water and he'd narrowly avoided being crushed by the hulking wreckage, he'd shouted it again. But by the time he'd swum to the bank, he was nauseated and dizzy, the events of the past hour finally hitting home. That was when his hands had begun to tremble.

Joe didn't know whether to be livid because of the jump or relieved that the whole thing had worked out. The passenger, it seemed, was going to be fine, and Joe had sent Mitch down to talk to Taylor.

Mitch had found him sitting in the mud, legs drawn up, hands and head resting on his knees. He hadn't moved at all since Mitch had sat beside him.

"You shouldn't have jumped," Mitch finally said after Taylor hadn't responded.

Taylor raised his head sluggishly, wiping the water from his face. "It just looked dangerous," he said flatly.

"That's because it *was* dangerous. But I was

thinking more about the car that followed you into the water. You could have been crushed."

I know . . .

"That's why I swam under the bridge," he answered.

"But what if it had fallen sooner? What if the engine had blown twenty seconds earlier? What if you'd hit something submerged in the water, for God's sake?"

What if?

Then I'd be dead.

Taylor shook his head, numb. He knew he'd have to answer these questions again, when Joe grilled him in earnest. "I didn't know what else to do," he said.

Mitch studied him with concern, hearing the flat discomfort in his voice. He'd seen this look before, the shell-shocked appearance of someone who knew he was fortunate to be alive. He noticed Taylor's shaking hands and reached over, patting him on the back. "I'm just glad you're all right."

Taylor nodded, too tired to speak.

Chapter 17

Later that evening, once the situation on the bridge was fully under control, Taylor got in his car to head home. As he'd suspected, Joe had asked every question Mitch had and more, walking him through every decision and the reasons for it, covering everything two or three times. Though he was still as angry as Taylor had ever seen him, Taylor did his best to convince him that he hadn't acted recklessly. "Look," he said, "I didn't want to jump. But if I hadn't, neither of us would have made it."

To that, Joe had no reply.

His hands had stopped shaking, and his nervous system had gradually returned to normal, though he still felt drained. He was still shivering as he made his way down the quiet rural roads.

A few minutes later Taylor walked up the cracked cement steps to the small place he called home. He'd left the lights on in his haste to leave, and the house was almost welcoming when he entered. The paper-work from his business was still spread on the table, the calculator had been left on. The ice in his water glass had melted.

In the living room he could hear the television playing in the background; a ball game he'd been listening to had given way to the local news.

He set his keys on the counter and pulled off his shirt as he walked through the kitchen to the small room where he kept the washer and dryer. Holding open the lid, he dropped the shirt in the washer. He slipped off his shoes, then kicked them against the wall. Pants, socks, and underwear went in with the shirt, followed by detergent. After starting the washer, he grabbed a folded towel from the top of the dryer, made his way to the bathroom, and took a quick hot shower, rinsing the brackish water from his body.

Afterward he ran a quick brush through his hair, then walked through the house, turning everything off before slipping into bed.

He turned out the lights almost reluctantly. He wanted to sleep, he needed to sleep, but despite his exhaustion he suddenly knew that sleep wouldn't come. Instead, immediately upon closing his eyes, the images of the past several hours began to replay in his mind. Almost like a movie, some moved in fast-forward, others in reverse, but in each case they were different from what had actually happened. His were not the images of success—his were more like nightmares.

In one sequence after another, he watched helplessly as everything went wrong.

He saw himself reaching for the victim, he heard the crack and felt a sickening shudder as the ladder snapped in two, sending both of them to their death—

Or . . .

He watched in horror as the victim reached for his out-stretched hand, his face contorting in terror, just as the car tipped over the bridge, Taylor unable to do anything to stop it—

Or . . .

He felt his sweaty hand suddenly slipping from the cable as he plunged downward, toward the bridge supports, toward his death—

Or . . .

While hooking the harness, he heard a strange ticking immediately before the truck engine exploded, his skin tearing and burning, the sound of his own screams as his life was taken from him—

Or . . .

The nightmare he'd been living with since childhood—

His eyes snapped open. His hands were trembling again, his throat dry. Breathing rapidly, he could feel another adrenaline surge, though this time the surges made his body ache.

Turning his head, he checked the clock. The red glowing digital lights showed that it was nearly eleven-thirty.

Knowing he wouldn't sleep, he turned on the lamp by his bedside and began to dress.

He didn't understand his decision, not really. All he knew was that he needed to talk.

Not to Mitch, not to Melissa. Not even to his mother.

He needed to talk to Denise.

The parking lot at Eights was mostly empty when he arrived. One car was parked off to the side. Taylor pulled his truck into the space nearest the door and checked his watch. The diner would be closing in ten minutes.

He pushed open the wooden door and heard a small bell jingle, signaling his entrance. The place was the same as always. A counter ran along the far wall; it was here that most truckers sat during the early morning hours. There were a dozen square tables in the center of the room beneath a circulating ceiling fan. On either side of the door beneath the windows were three booths, the seats covered in red vinyl, small tears in every one of them. The air smelled of bacon despite the lateness of the hour.

Beyond the far counter, he saw Ray cleaning up in the back. Ray turned at the sound of the door and recognized Taylor as he stepped in. He waved, a greasy dishtowel in his hand.

"Hey, Taylor," he said. "Long time no see. You comin' in to eat?"

"Oh, hey, Ray." He looked from side to side. "Not really."

Ray shook his head, chuckling to himself. "Somehow, I didn't think so," he said almost mischievously. "Denise'll be out in a minute. She's putting some stuff in the walk-in. You here to ask if you can drive her home?"

When Taylor didn't answer right away, Ray's eyes gleamed. "Did you think you were the first one to come in here, that lost puppy-dog look on your face? There's one or two a week comin' in here, looking just like you do now, hoping for the same thing. Truckers, bikers, even married guys." He grinned. "She's somethin', that's for sure, ain't she? Pretty as a flower. But don't worry, she ain't said yes to one of 'em yet."

"I wasn't . . ." Taylor stammered, suddenly at a loss for words.

"Of course you were." He winked, letting it sink in, then lowered his tone. "But like I said, don't worry. I've got a funny feeling she just might say yes to you. I'll tell her you're here."

All Taylor could do was stare as Ray vanished from sight. Almost immediately Denise came out from the kitchen area, pushing through a swinging door.

"Taylor?" she said, clearly surprised.

"Hi," he said sheepishly.

"What are you doing here?" She started toward him, smiling curiously.

"I wanted to see you," he said quietly, not knowing what else to say.

As she walked toward him he took in her image. She wore a white, work-stained apron over her marigold yellow dress. The dress, short-sleeved and V-necked, was buttoned as high as it would go; the skirt reached just past her knees. She wore white sneakers, something her feet would be comfortable in, even after standing for hours. Her hair was pulled back into a ponytail, and her face was shiny from her own perspiration and the grease in the air.

She was beautiful.

She was aware of his appraisal, but as she neared, she saw something else in his eyes, something she'd never seen before.

"Are you okay?" she asked. "You look like you've seen a ghost."

"I don't know," he muttered, almost to himself.

She stared up at him, concerned, then looked over her shoulder.

"Hey, Ray? Can I take a quick break here for a second?"

Ray acted as if he hadn't even noticed that Taylor had come in. He continued to clean the grill as he spoke.

"Take your time, sweetheart. I'm just about done here, anyway."

She faced Taylor again. "Do you want to sit down?"

It was exactly the reason he'd come, but Ray's comments had thrown him off. All he could think about were the men who came to the diner looking for her.

"Maybe I shouldn't have come," he said.

But Denise, as if knowing exactly what to do, smiled sympathetically.

"I'm glad you did," she said softly. "What happened?"

He stood silently before her, everything rushing at him at once. The faint smell of her shampoo, his desire to put his arms around her and tell her everything about the evening, the waking nightmares, how he longed for her to listen . . .

The men who came to the diner looking for her . . .

Despite everything, that thought erased those of the night's drama. Not that he had any reason to be jealous. Ray had said she'd always turned the others down, and he hadn't established a serious relationship with her. Yet the feeling gripped him anyway. What men? Who wanted to take her home? He wanted to ask her but knew it wasn't his place.

"I should go," he said, shaking his head. "I shouldn't be here. You're still working."

"No," she said, seriously this time, sensing that something was troubling him. "Something happened tonight. What was it?"

"I wanted to talk to you," he said simply.

"About what?"

Her eyes searched his, never turning away. Those wonderful eyes. God, she was lovely. Taylor swallowed, his mind whirling. "There was an accident on the bridge tonight," he said abruptly.

Denise nodded, still uncertain of where this was going. "I know. It was quiet here all night. Hardly anyone came in because the bridge was closed. Were you there?"

Taylor nodded.

"I heard it was terrible. Was it?"

Taylor nodded again.

She reached out, her fingers gently taking hold of his arm. "Hold on, okay? Let me see what still needs to be done before we close up."

She turned from him, her touch slipping from his skin, and went back to the kitchen. Taylor stood in the diner, alone with his thoughts for a minute, until Denise came back out.

Surprisingly, she walked past him toward the front door, where she reversed the "Open" sign. Eights was closed.

"Everything in the kitchen's shut down," she explained. "I've got a few things to do and then I'll be ready to go. Why don't you wait for me, okay? We can talk at my house."

Taylor carried Kyle to the truck, his head on Taylor's shoulder. Once inside, he immediately curled around Denise, never awaking in the process.

Once they were home, the procedure was reversed, and after sliding Kyle from Denise's lap, Taylor carried him into the house to his bedroom. He put Kyle in his bed, and Denise immediately pulled the sheet over him. On the way out the door, she pushed the button on his plastic glowing teddy bear, hearing the music come on. She left the door halfway open as they both crept out of his room.

In the living room, Denise turned on one of the lamps as Taylor sat on the couch. After a slight hesitation, Denise sat in a separate chair, catercorner to the couch.

Neither one of them had said anything on the way home for fear of waking Kyle, but once they were seated Denise went straight to the point.

"What happened?" she asked. "On the bridge tonight."

Taylor told her everything: about the rescue, what Mitch and Joe had said, the images he'd been tormented by afterward. Denise sat quietly as he talked, her eyes never leaving his face. When he was finished, she leaned forward in her seat.

"You saved him?"

"I didn't. We all did," Taylor said, automatically making the distinction.

"But how many of you went out on the ladder? How many of you had to let go because the ladder wouldn't hold?"

Taylor didn't answer, and Denise rose from her seat to sit next to him on the couch.

"You're a hero," she said, a small grin on her face. "Just like you were when Kyle was lost."

"No, I'm not," he said, images of the past surfacing against his will.

"Yes, you are." She reached for his hand. For the next twenty minutes they talked about inconsequential things, their conversation wandering here and there. At last Taylor asked about the men who wanted to drive her home; she laughed and rolled her eyes, explaining it away as part of the job. "The nicer I am, the more tips I get. But some men, I suppose, take it the wrong way."

The simple drift of the conversation was soothing; Denise did her best to keep Taylor's thoughts away from the accident. As a child, when she'd had nightmares, her mother used to do the same thing. By talking about something else, anything else, she would finally be able to relax.

It seemed to be working for Taylor as well. He gradually began to speak less, his answers coming more slowly. His eyes closed and opened, closed again. His breaths settled into a deeper rhythm as the demands of the day began to take their toll.

Denise held his hand, watching until he nodded off. Then she rose from the couch and retrieved an extra blanket from her bedroom. When she gave him a nudge, Taylor lay down and she was able to drape the blanket over him.

Half-asleep, he mumbled something about having to go; Denise whispered that he was fine where he was. "Go to sleep," she murmured as she turned off the lamp.

She went to her own room and slipped out of her workclothes, then into her pajamas. She untied her ponytail, brushed her teeth, and scrubbed the grease from her face. Then, after crawling into bed, she closed her eyes.

The fact that Taylor McAden was sleeping in the other room was the last thing she remembered before she, too, nodded off.

"Hewwo, Tayer," Kyle said happily.

Taylor opened his eyes, squinting against the early morning sunlight streaming in the living room window. Wiping the sleep from his eyes with the back of his hand, he saw Kyle standing over him, his face very close. Kyle's hair, clumped and matted, pointed off in various directions.

It took a second for Taylor to register where he was. When Kyle pulled back, smiling, Taylor sat up. He ran both hands through his hair. Checking his watch, he saw that it was a little after six in the morning. The rest of the house was quiet.

"Good morning, Kyle. How are you?"

"He's sleeping." *(Eez sweepeen)*

"Where's your mom?"

"He's on the couch." *(Eez on-ah coush)*

Taylor straightened up, feeling the stiffness in his joints. His shoulder ached as it always did when he woke.

"I sure was."

Taylor stretched his arms out to the side and yawned.

"Good morning," he heard behind him. Over his shoulder he saw Denise coming out of her room, wearing long pink pajamas and socks. He stood up from the couch.

"Good morning," he said, turning around. "I reckon I must have dozed off last night."

"You were tired."

"Sorry about that."

"It's okay," she said. Kyle had wandered to the corner of the living room and sat down to play with his toys. Denise walked over to him and bent, kissing him on the top of the head. "Good morning, sweetie."

"Morning," he said. *(Mawneen)*

"Are you hungry?"

"No."

"Do you want some yogurt?"

"No."

"Do you want to play with your toys?"

Kyle nodded, and Denise returned her attention to Taylor. "How about you? Are you hungry?"

"I don't want you to have to cook up something special."

"I was going to offer you some Cheerios," she said, eliciting a smile from Taylor. She adjusted her pajama top. "Did you sleep okay?"

"Like a rock," he said. "Thanks for last night. You were more than patient with me."

She shrugged, her eyes catching the morning light. Her hair, long and tangled, grazed her shoulders. "What are friends for?"

Embarrassed for some reason, he reached for the blanket and began folding it, glad for something to do. He felt out of place here, at her house, so early in the morning.

Denise came and stood next to him. "You sure you don't want to stay for breakfast? I've got half a box."

Taylor debated. "And milk?" he finally asked.

"No, we use water in our cereal here," she said seriously.

He looked at her as if wondering whether or not

to believe her, when Denise suddenly laughed, the sound melodic.

"Of course we have milk, you goob."

"Goob?"

"It's a term of endearment. It means that I like you," she said with a wink.

The words were strangely uplifting. "In that case, I'd be glad to stay."

"So what's on your agenda today?" Taylor asked.

They'd finished breakfast, and Denise was walking him to the door. He still had to make it home to change before heading off to meet his crew.

"Same as always. I'll work with Kyle for a few hours, and then I'm not sure. It sort of depends on what he wants to do—play in the yard, ride bikes, whatever. Then it's off to work tonight."

"Back to serving those lecherous men?"

"A gal's gotta pay the bills," she said archly, "and besides, they're not all so bad. The one who came in last night was pretty nice. I let him stay over at my place."

"A real charmer, huh?"

"Not really. But he was so pathetic, I didn't have the heart to turn him down."

"Ouch."

As they reached the door, she leaned against him, nudging him playfully.

"You know I'm kidding."

"I hope so." The sky was cloudless, and the sun was beginning to peek over the trees in the east as they stepped out onto the porch. "Hey, listen, about last night . . . thanks for everything."

"You already thanked me earlier, remember?"

"I know," Taylor said earnestly, "but I wanted to do it again."

They stood together without speaking until Denise finally took a small step forward. Glancing down, then up at Taylor again, she tilted her head slightly, her face drawing nearer to his. She could see the surprise in his eyes when she kissed him softly on the lips.

It wasn't more than a peck, really, but all he could do was stare at her afterward, thinking how wonderful it was.

"I'm glad I was the one you came to," she said.

Still dressed in pajamas, her hair a tangled mess, she looked absolutely perfect.

Chapter 18

Later that day, at Taylor's request, Denise showed him Kyle's journal.

Sitting in the kitchen beside him, she flipped through the pages, commenting every now and then. Each page was filled with Denise's goals, as well as specific words and phrases, pronunciations, and her final observations.

"See, it's just a record of what we do. That's all."

Taylor flipped to the very first page. Across the top was written a single word: Apple. Beneath that, toward the middle of the page and continuing onto the back side, was Denise's description of the very first day she'd worked with him.

"May I?" he asked, motioning to the page. Denise nodded and Taylor read slowly, taking in every word. When he finished he looked up.

"Four hours?"

"Yes."

"Just to say the word *apple?*"

"Actually, he didn't say it exactly right, even in

the end. But it was close enough to understand what he was trying to say."

"How did you finally get him to do it?"

"I just kept working with him until he did."

"But how did you know what would work?"

"I didn't, really. Not in the beginning. I'd studied a lot of different things about how to work with kids like Kyle; I'd read up on different programs that universities were trying, I learned about speech therapy and the things they do. But none of them really seemed to be describing Kyle—I mean, they'd get parts of it right, but mostly they were describing other kids. But there were two books, *Late-Talking Children* by Thomas Sowell and *Let Me Hear Your Voice* by Catherine Maurice, that seemed to come the closest. Sowell's book was the first one that let me know that I wasn't alone in all this; that a lot of children have trouble speaking, even though nothing else seems to be wrong with them. Maurice's book gave me an idea of how to actually teach Kyle, even though her book primarily dealt with autism."

"So what do you do?"

"I use a type of behavioral modification program, one that was originally designed out at UCLA. They've had a lot of success with autistic children over the years by rewarding good behavior and punishing negative behavior. I modified the program for speech, since that was really Kyle's only problem.

Basically, when Kyle says what he's supposed to, he gets a tiny piece of candy. When he doesn't say it, no candy. If he doesn't even try or he's being stubborn, I scold him. When I taught him how to say 'apple,' I pointed to a picture of an apple and kept repeating the word. I'd give him candy whenever he made a sound; after that, I gave him candy only when he made the right sound—even if it was just part of the word. Eventually, he was rewarded only when he said the whole word."

"And that took four hours?"

Denise nodded. "Four incredibly long hours. He cried and fussed, he kept trying to get out of the chair, he screamed like I was stabbing him with pins. If someone had heard us that day, he probably would have thought I was torturing him. I must have said the word, I don't know, five or six hundred times. I kept repeating it over and over, until we were both absolutely sick of it. It was terrible, truly awful for both of us, and I never thought it would end, but you know . . ."

She leaned a little closer.

"When he finally said it, all the terrible parts suddenly went away—all the frustration and anger and fear that both of us were experiencing. I remember how excited I was—you can't even begin to imagine it. I started crying, and I had him repeat the word at least a dozen times before I really believed he'd done it. That was the first time that I ever knew for certain that Kyle had the ability to learn. I'd done it, on my own, and I can't even describe how much that meant, after all the things the doctors had said about him."

She shook her head wistfully, remembering that day.

"Well, after that, we just kept trying new words, one at a time, until he got those, too. He got to the point where he could name every tree and flower there was, every type of car, every kind of airplane . . . his vocabulary was huge, but he still didn't have the ability to understand that language was actually *used* for something. So then we started with two-word combinations, like 'blue truck' or 'big tree,' and I think that helped him grasp what I was trying to teach him—that words are the way people communicate. After a few months, he could mimic almost everything I said, so I started trying to teach him what questions were."

"Was that hard?"

"It's still hard. Harder than teaching him words, because now he has to try to interpret inflections in tone, then understand what the question is, then answer it appropriately. All three parts of that are difficult for him, and that's what we've been working on for the last few months. At first, questions presented a whole new set of challenges, because Kyle wanted to simply mimic what I was saying. I'd point to a picture of an apple and say, 'What is this?' Kyle would respond, 'What is this?' I'd say, 'No, say, "It's an apple,"' and Kyle would answer, 'No, say, "It's an apple."' Eventually, I started whispering the question, then saying the answer loudly, hoping he could understand what I wanted. But for a long time, he'd whisper the question like I did, then answer loudly, repeating my words and tones exactly. It took weeks before he would say only the answer. I'd reward him, of course, whenever he did."

Taylor nodded, beginning to grasp just how difficult all this must have been. "You must have the patience of a saint," he said.

"Not always."

"But to do it every day . . ."

"I have to. Besides, look at how far he's come."

Taylor flipped through the notebook, toward the end. From a nearly blank page with only a single word on it, Denise's notes about the hours spent with Kyle now covered three and four pages at a time.

"He's come a long way."

"Yes, he has. He's got a long way to go, though. He's good with some questions, like 'what' and 'who,' but he still doesn't understand 'why' and 'how' questions. He doesn't really converse yet, either—he usually just makes a single statement. He's also got trouble with the phrasing of questions. He knows what I mean when I say, 'Where's your toy?' But if I ask him, 'Where did you put your toy?' all I get is a blank stare. Things like that are the reason I'm glad I've kept that journal. Whenever Kyle has a bad day—and he does, quite often—I'll open this up and remind myself of all the challenges he's made it through so far. One day, once he's better, I'm going to give this to him. I want him to read it, so that he knows how much I love him."

"He already knows that."

"I know. But someday, I also want to hear him say that he loves me, too."

"Doesn't he do that now? When you tuck him in at night?"

"No," she answered. "Kyle's never said that to me."

"Haven't you tried to teach him that?"

"No."

"Why?"

"Because I want to be surprised on the day that he finally does it on his own."

During the next week and a half Taylor spent more and more time at Denise's house, always dropping by in the afternoons once he knew she'd finished working with Kyle. Sometimes he stayed for an hour, other times a little longer. On two afternoons he played catch with Kyle while Denise watched from the porch; on the third afternoon he taught Kyle to hit the ball with a small bat and tee that Taylor had used when he was young. Swing after swing, Taylor retrieved the ball and set it back on the tee, only to encourage Kyle to try again. By the time Kyle was ready to stop, Taylor's shirt was soaked through. Denise kissed him for the second time after handing him a glass of water.

On Sunday, the week after the carnival, Taylor drove them to Kitty Hawk, where they spent the day at the beach. Taylor pointed out the spot where Orville and Wilbur Wright made their historic flight in 1903, and they read the details on a monument that had been erected to honor them. They shared a picnic lunch, then waded in and out of the surf on a long walk down the beach as terns fluttered overhead. Toward the end of the afternoon Denise and Taylor built sand castles that Kyle delighted in ruining. Roaring like Godzilla, he stomped through the mounds almost as quickly as they were molded.

On the way home, they stopped at a farmer's road stand, where they picked up some fresh corn. While Kyle ate macaroni and cheese, Taylor had his first dinner at Denise's house. The sun and wind at the beach had worn Kyle out, and he fell asleep immediately afterward. Taylor and Denise talked in the kitchen until almost midnight. On the doorstep they kissed again, Taylor's arms wrapped around her.

A few days later Taylor let Denise borrow his truck to head into town to run some errands. By the time she got back, he'd rehung the sagging cabinet doors in her kitchen. "I hope you don't mind," he said, wondering if he'd overstepped some invisible line.

"Not at all," she cried, clapping her hands together, "but can you do anything about the leaky sink?" Thirty minutes later that was fixed as well.

In their moments alone, Taylor found himself mesmerized by her simple beauty and grace. But there were also times when he could see written in her features the sacrifices she'd made for her son. It was an almost weary expression, like that of a warrior after a long battle on the plains, and it inspired an admiration in him that he found difficult to put into words. She seemed to be one of a slowly vanishing breed; a stark contrast to those who were always chasing, running, on the go, searching for personal fulfillment and self-esteem. So many people these days, it seemed, believed that these things could come only from work, not from parenting, and many people believed that having children had nothing to do with raising them. When he said as much, Denise had simply looked away, out the window. "I used to believe that, too."

On Wednesday of the following week, Taylor invited both Denise and Kyle to his home. Similar to Denise's in many ways, it was an older house that sat on a large parcel of land. His, however, had been remodeled over the years, both before and after he'd bought the place. Kyle loved the toolshed out back, and after pointing out the "tractor" (actually a lawn mower), Taylor took him for a ride around the yard without engaging the blade. As he'd done when he'd driven Taylor's truck, Kyle beamed as he zigzagged across the yard.

Watching them together, Denise realized that her initial impression of Taylor being shy wasn't completely accurate. But he did hold things back about himself, she reflected. Though they'd talked about his job and his time with the fire department, he remained strangely silent about his father, never volunteering more than he had that first night. Nor had he said anything about the women he'd known in the past, not even in a casual way. It didn't really matter, of course, but the omission perplexed her.

Still, she had to admit she was drawn to him. He'd stumbled into her life when she'd least expected it, in the most unlikely of ways. He was already more than a friend. But at night, lying under the sheet with the oscillating fan rattling in the background, she found herself hoping and praying that the whole thing was real.

"How much longer?" Denise asked.

Taylor had surprised her by bringing over an old-fashioned ice-cream maker, complete with all the ingredients needed. He was cranking the handle, sweat running off his face, as the cream churned, thickening slowly.

"Five minutes, maybe ten. Why, are you hungry?"

"I've never had homemade ice cream before."

"Would you like to claim some ownership? You can take over for a while . . ."

She held up her hands. "No, that's okay. It's more fun watching you do it."

Taylor nodded as if disappointed, then played the martyr as he pretended to struggle with the handle. She giggled. When she stopped, Taylor wiped his forehead with the back of his hand.

"Are you doing anything Sunday night?"

She knew he was going to ask. "Not really."

"Do you want to go out for dinner?"

Denise shrugged. "Sure. But you know how Kyle is. He won't eat anything at most places."

Taylor swallowed, his arm never stopping. His eyes met hers.

"I meant, could I take just you? Without Kyle this time? My mom said she'd be happy to come over and watch him."

Denise hesitated. "I don't know how he'd do with her. He doesn't know her too well."

"How about if I pick you up after he's already asleep? You can put him in bed, tuck him in, and we won't leave until you're sure it's okay."

She relented then, unable to disguise her pleasure. "You've really thought this through, haven't you?"

"I didn't want you to have the opportunity to say no."

She grinned, leaning in to within inches of his face. "In that case, I'd love to go."

Judy arrived at seven-thirty, a few minutes after Denise had put Kyle in bed. She'd kept him busy outside all day in the hope that he'd sleep while she was out. They'd ridden their bikes into town and stopped at the playground; they'd played in the dirt out back. It was hot and steamy, the kind of day that saps the energy, and Kyle started yawning right before dinner. After giving him a bath and putting on his pajamas, Denise read three books in his room while Kyle drank his milk, his eyes half-open. After pulling the shades closed—it was still light outside—she closed the door; Kyle was already sound asleep.

She took a shower and shaved her legs, then stood with a towel wrapped around her, trying to decide what to wear. Taylor had said they were going to Fontana, a wonderfully quiet restaurant in the heart of downtown. When she'd asked him what she should wear, he'd said not to worry about it, which didn't help at all.

She finally decided on a simple black cocktail dress that seemed appropriate for almost any occasion. It had been in the back of her closet for years, still draped in a plastic sheath from a dry cleaner in Atlanta. She couldn't remember the last time she'd worn it, but after slipping it on, she was pleased to see that it still fit well. A pair of black pumps came next; she considered wearing black stockings, too, but that idea was dropped as quickly as she'd thought of it. It was too warm a night, and besides, who ever wore black stockings in Edenton, except for a funeral?

After drying and styling her hair, she put on a little makeup, then pulled out the perfume that sat in her bedstand drawer. A little on her neck and hair, then a dab on her wrists, which she rubbed together. In her top drawer she kept a small jewelry box from which she withdrew a pair of hoop earrings.

Standing in front of the bathroom mirror, she evaluated herself, pleased with how she looked. Not too much, not too little. Just right, in fact. It was then that she heard Judy knocking. Taylor arrived two minutes later.

Fontana's Restaurant had been in business for a dozen years. It was owned by a middle-aged couple originally from Berne, Switzerland, who had moved to Edenton from New Orleans, hoping for a simpler life. In the process, however, they'd also brought a touch of elegance to the town. Dimly lit, with first-rate service, it was popular with couples celebrating anniversaries and engagements; its reputation had been established when an article on the place had appeared in *Southern Living*.

Taylor and Denise were seated at a small table in the corner, Taylor nursing a Scotch and soda, Denise sipping Chardonnay.

"Have you eaten here before?" Denise asked, scanning the menu.

"A few times, but I haven't been here in a while."

She flipped through the pages, unused to so many choices after years of one-pot dinners. "What do you recommend?"

"Everything, really. The rack of lamb is the house specialty, but they're also known for their steaks and seafood."

"That doesn't really narrow it down."

"It's true, though. You won't be disappointed with anything."

Studying the appetizer listings, she twirled a strand of her hair between her fingers. Taylor watched with a mixture of fascination and amusement.

"Have I told you how nice you look tonight?" he asked.

"Only twice," she said, playing it cool, "but don't feel you have to stop. I don't mind."

"Really?"

"Not when it comes from a man dressed as spiffy as you."

"Spiffy?"

She winked. "It means the same thing as goob."

The dinner that followed was wonderful in every

detail, the food delicious and the setting undeniably intimate. Over dessert, Taylor reached for her hand across the table. He didn't let go for the next hour.

As the evening wore on, they immersed themselves in each other's lives. Taylor told Denise about his past with the fire department and some of the more dangerous blazes he'd helped to battle; he also talked about Mitch and Melissa, the two friends who'd been with him through it all. Denise shared stories of her college years and went on to describe the first two years she'd spent teaching and how utterly unprepared she'd felt the first time she'd stepped into a classroom. To both of them, this night seemed to mark the beginning of their life as a couple. It was also the first time they'd ever had a conversation in which Kyle's name never came up.

After dinner, as they stepped out onto the deserted street, Denise noted how different the old town seemed at night, like a place lost in time. Aside from the restaurant they'd been in and a bar on the corner, everything was closed. Meandering along brick sidewalks that had cracked over time, they passed an antique shop and an art gallery.

It was perfectly silent on the street, neither of them feeling the urge to speak. Within a couple of minutes they'd reached the harbor, and Denise could make out the boats settled into their slips. Large and small, new and old, they ran the gamut from wooden sailboats to weekend trawlers. A few were illuminated from within, but the only sound came from the water lapping against the seawall.

Leaning against a railing that had been set up near the docks, Taylor cleared his throat and took Denise's hand.

"Edenton was one of the earliest settled ports in the South, and even though the town was nothing more than an outpost, trading ships used to stop here, either to sell their wares or to replenish their supplies. Can you see those railings on top of the houses over there?"

He motioned to some of the historic homes along the harbor, and Denise nodded.

"In colonial days, shipping was dangerous, and wives would stand on those balconies, waiting for their husbands' ships to enter the harbor. So many husbands died, however, that they became known as widows' walks. But here in Edenton, the ships would never come directly into port. Instead, they used to stop out there in the middle of the harbor, no matter how long the voyage had been, and women standing on the widows' walks would strain their eyes, searching for their husbands as the ship came to a stop."

"Why did they stop out there?"

"There used to be a tree, a giant cypress tree,

standing all by itself. That's one of the ways that ships knew they'd reached Edenton, especially if they'd never been here before. It was the only tree like it anywhere along the East Coast. Usually cypress trees grow close to the banks—within a few feet or so—but this one was at least two hundred yards from shore. It was like a monument because it seemed so out of place. Well, somehow it became a custom for ships to stop at the tree whenever they entered the harbor. They'd get in a small boat, row over to the tree, and put a bottle of rum in the trunk of the tree, thankful that they'd made it back to port safely. And whenever a ship left the harbor, the crew would stop at the tree and members of the crew would drink a dram of the rum in the hopes of a safe and prosperous voyage. That's why they call it the dram tree."

"Really?"

"Sure. The town is ripe with legends of ships that neglected to stop for their 'dram' of rum that were subsequently lost at sea. It was considered bad luck, and only the foolish ignored the custom. Sailors disregarded it at their own peril."

"What if there wasn't any rum there when a ship was on its way out? Would they turn the ship around?"

"As legend has it, it never happened." He looked over the water, his tone changing slightly. "I remember my dad telling me that story when I was a kid. He took me out there, too, to the very spot where the tree had been and told me all about it."

Denise smiled. "Do you have any other stories about Edenton?"

"A few."

"Any ghost stories?"

"Of course. Every old town in North Carolina has ghost stories. On Halloween, my father would sit me and my friends down after we'd gone trick-or-treating and tell us the story of Brownrigg Mill. It's about a witch, and it's got everything needed to terrify children. Superstitious townsfolk, evil spells, mysterious deaths, even a three-legged cat. By the time my dad was done, we'd be too scared to sleep. He could spin a yarn with the best of them."

She thought about life in a small town, the ancient stories, and how different it all was from her own experiences in Atlanta.

"That must have been neat."

"It was. If you'd like, I could do the same for Kyle."

"I doubt if he'd understand what you're saying."

"Maybe I'll tell him the one about the haunted monster truck of Chowan County."

"There's no such thing."

"I know. But I could always make one up."

Denise squeezed his hand again. "How come you never had kids?" she asked.

"I'm not the right sex."

"You know what I mean," she said, nudging him. "You'd be a good father."

"I don't know. I just haven't."

"Did you ever want to?"

"Sometimes."

"Well, you should."

"You sound like my mother now."

"You know what they say. Brilliant minds think alike."

"If you do say so yourself."

"Exactly."

As they left the harbor and started toward downtown again, Denise was struck by how much her world had changed recently; and all of it, she realized, could be traced to the man beside her. Yet never once, despite all he'd done for her, had he pressured her for anything in return, something she might not be ready for. She was the one who'd kissed him first, and it was she who'd kissed him the second time. Even when he'd stayed late at her house after their day at the beach, he'd left when he sensed that it was time to go.

Most men wouldn't have done that, she knew. Most men seized the initiative as soon as the opportunity presented itself. Lord knew that was what had happened with Kyle's father. But Taylor was different. He was content to get to know her first, she mused, to listen to her problems, to hang crooked cabinet doors and make homemade ice cream on the porch. In every way he had presented himself as a gentleman.

But because he'd never pushed her, she found herself wanting him with an intensity that surprised her. She wondered what it would feel like when he finally took her in his arms or what it would be like to have him touch her body, his fingers tracing over her skin. Thinking about it made something tighten inside, and she squeezed his hand reflexively.

As they neared the truck, they passed a storefront whose glass door had been propped open. Stenciled on it was "Trina's Bar." Aside from Fontana, it was the only place open downtown; when she peeked in, Denise saw three couples talking quietly over small circular tables. In the corner was a jukebox playing a country song, the nasal baritone of the singer quieting as the final lyrics wound down. There was a short silence until the next song rotated through: "Unchained Melody." Denise stopped in her tracks when she recognized it, pulling on Taylor's hand.

"I love this song," she said.

"Would you like to go inside?"

She debated as the melody swirled around her.

"We could dance if you'd like," he added.

"No. I'd feel funny with all those people watching," she said after a beat. "And there's not really enough room, anyway."

The street was devoid of traffic, the sidewalks deserted. A single light, set high on a pole, flickered slightly, illuminating the corner. Beneath the strains of the music from the bar drifted the sound of intimate conversations. Denise took a tentative step, away from the open door. The music was still evident behind them, playing softly, when Taylor suddenly stopped. She looked up at him curiously.

Without a word, he slipped one arm around her back, pulling her closer to him. With an endearing smile, he raised her hand to his mouth and kissed it, then lowered it into position. Suddenly realizing what was happening, but still not believing it, Denise took an awkward step before beginning to follow his lead.

For a moment, both were slightly embarrassed. But the music played steadily in the background, dispelling the awkwardness, and after a couple of turns Denise closed her eyes and leaned into him. Taylor's arm drifted up her back, and she could hear his breathing as they rotated in slow circles, swaying gently with the music. Suddenly it didn't matter whether anyone was watching. Except for his touch and the feel of his warm body against hers, nothing mattered at all, and they danced and danced, holding each other close beneath a flickering streetlight in the tiny town of Edenton.

Chapter 19

Judy was reading a novel in the living room when the two of them returned. Kyle, she said, hadn't even stirred while they'd been away.

"Did you two have a good time?" she asked, eyeing Denise's flushed cheeks.

"Yes, we did," Denise answered. "Thanks for watching Kyle."

"My pleasure," she said sincerely, slinging her purse over her shoulder and getting ready to leave.

Denise went back to check on Kyle as Taylor walked Judy to the car. He didn't say much as they walked, and Judy hoped that it meant Taylor was as taken with Denise as she seemed to be with him.

Taylor was in the living room, squatting by a small cooler he'd removed from the back of the truck, when Denise emerged from Kyle's room. He didn't hear her close her son's door, lost in what he was doing. Silently Denise watched as he slid open the top of the cooler and removed two crystal flutes. They clinked together as he shook the water off them, then he set them on the small table in front of the couch. He reached in again, this time pulling out a bottle of Champagne.

After peeling the foil off the top, he untwisted the wire that held the cork and popped the cork free in one easy movement. The bottle went onto the table, next to the flutes he'd brought. Once again he reached into the cooler, then fished out a plate of strawberries neatly wrapped in cellophane. Once the strawberries were unwrapped, he straightened everything on the table and pushed the cooler off to the side. After leaning back to get a better perspective, he seemed satisfied. He rubbed his hands on his pants, wiping the moisture from them, and glanced toward the hallway. At the sight of Denise standing there, he froze, an embarrassed expression on his face. Then, smiling bashfully, he stood.

"I thought this would be a nice surprise," he said.

She looked toward the table and back at Taylor again, realizing she'd been holding her breath.

"It is," she said.

"I didn't know whether you liked wine or Champagne, so I just took a chance."

Taylor's eyes were fixed on her.

"I'm sure it's wonderful," she murmured. "I haven't had Champagne in years."

He reached for the bottle. "Can I pour you a glass?"

"Please."

Taylor poured two glasses as Denise approached the table, suddenly a little unsteady. He handed one to her wordlessly, and all she could do was stare at him, wondering how long it had taken him to plan this.

"Wait, okay?" Denise said quickly, knowing exactly what was missing. Taylor watched as she set down her glass and ran to the kitchen. He listened as she rifled through a drawer, then saw her emerge again with two small candles and a book of matches. She set them on the table beside the Champagne and strawberries, then lit them. As soon as she turned out the lamp, the room was transformed, shadows dancing against the wall as she picked up her glass. In the glowing light she was more beautiful than ever.

"To you," he said as they tapped their glasses together. She took a sip. The bubbles made her nose twitch, but it tasted wonderful.

He motioned to the couch, and they sat close to each other, her knee pulled up and resting against his thigh. Outside the window, the moon had risen and its light spilled through the clouds, turning them silver white. Taylor took another sip of Champagne, watching Denise.

"What are you thinking?" she asked. Taylor glanced away briefly before facing her again.

"I was thinking about what would have happened had you never been in the accident that night."

"I would have had my car," she declared, and Taylor laughed before growing serious again.

"But do you think I'd be here now, if it hadn't happened?"

Denise considered it. "I don't know," she said at last. "I'd like to think so, though. My mom used to believe that people were destined for one another. That's a romantic idea that young girls have, and I guess part of me still believes it."

Taylor nodded. "My mom used to say that, too. I think that's one of the reasons why she never remarried. She knew there could never be anyone to replace my father. I don't think my mom's even considered dating anyone since the day he died."

"Really?"

"That's how it always seemed to me, anyway."

"I'm sure you're wrong about that, Taylor. Your mom's only human, and we all need companionship."

As soon as she'd said it, she realized she was talking about herself as much as she was about Judy. Taylor, however, didn't seem to notice.

Instead he smiled. "You don't know her as well as I do."

"Maybe, but remember, my mother went through the same things your mom did. She mourned my father always, but I know she still felt the desire to be loved by someone."

"Did she date?"

Denise nodded, taking a sip of her Champagne. Shadows flickered across his features.

"After a couple of years, she did. She saw a few men seriously, and there were times I thought I'd have a new stepfather soon, but none of them ever worked out."

"Did that make you angry? Her dating, I mean?"

"No, not at all. I wanted my mom to be happy."

Taylor raised an eyebrow before draining the last of his Champagne. "I don't know if I would have been as mature about it as you were."

"Maybe not. But your mom's still young. There may still come a time when it happens."

Taylor brought the glass to his lap, realizing he'd never even imagined the possibility.

"What about you? Did you think you'd be married by now?" he asked.

"Of course," she said wryly. "I had it all worked out. Graduate at twenty-two, married by twenty-five, my first child at thirty. It was a great plan, except that absolutely none of it worked out the way I thought it would."

"You sound disappointed."

"I was," she admitted, "for a long time. I mean, my mom always had this idea of what my life would be like and never missed the opportunity to remind me. And she meant well, I know she did. She wanted me to learn from her mistakes, and I was willing to do that. But when she died . . . I don't know. I guess for a while there I forgot everything she'd taught me."

She stopped, a pensive look on her face.

"Because you got pregnant?" he asked gently.

Denise shook her head. "No, not because I got pregnant, though that was part of it. It was more that after she died, I felt like she wouldn't be looking over my shoulder all the time, evaluating everything in my life. And of course, she wasn't, and I took advantage of that. It wasn't until later that I realized the things my mom said weren't meant to hold me back, they were for my own benefit so that all my own dreams could come true."

"We all make mistakes, Denise—"

She held up a hand, cutting him off. "I'm not saying it because I feel sorry for myself now. Like I said, I'm not disappointed anymore. These days, when I think about my mom, I know she'd be proud of the decisions I've made over the last five years."

She hesitated before taking a deep breath. "I think she'd also like you."

"Because I'm nice to Kyle?"

"No," she answered. "My mom would like you because you've made me happier in the last two weeks than I have been in the last five years."

Taylor could only stare at her, humbled by the emotion behind her words. She was so honest, so vulnerable, so incredibly beautiful . . .

In the glowing candlelight, sitting close, she looked at him squarely, her eyes lit with mystery and compassion, and it was at that moment that Taylor McAden fell in love with Denise Holton.

All the years of wondering exactly what that meant, all the years of loneliness, had led to this place, this here and now. He reached out and took her hand, feeling the softness of her skin as a well of tenderness rose within him.

As he touched her cheek, Denise closed her eyes, willing this memory to last forever. She knew intuitively the meaning of Taylor's touch, the words he'd left unspoken. Not because she'd come to know him so well. She knew because she'd fallen in love with him at exactly the same time.

In the late evening, moonlight spilled through the bedroom. The air was silver as Taylor lay on the bed, Denise resting her head on his chest. She had turned on the radio, and the faint strains of jazz muted the sounds of their whispers.

Denise lifted her head from his chest, marveling at the naked beauty of his form, seeing at once the man she loved and the blueprint of the young boy she never knew. With guilty pleasure, she recalled the sight of their bodies intertwined in passion, her own soft whimpers as they'd become one, and how she'd buried her face in his neck to stifle her screams.

And she'd done so knowing that it was what she both needed and wanted; she'd closed her eyes, giving herself to him without reserve.

When Taylor saw her staring, he reached over and traced her cheek with his fingers, a melancholy smile playing on his lips, his eyes unreadable in the soft gray light. She moved her cheek closer to his fingers as he opened his hand.

In silence they lay together as the digital numbers on the clock radio blinked forward steadily. Later Taylor rose. He threw on his pants and walked to the kitchen to get two glasses of water. When he came back, he saw Denise's figure intertwined with the sheet, covering part of her. As she lay on her back, Taylor took a drink of water, then set both glasses on the bedstand. When he kissed her between her breasts, she could feel the cool temperature of his tongue against her. "You're perfect," he whispered.

She put one arm around his neck, then ran her hand down his back, feeling all of it: the fullness of the evening, the silent weight of their passion.

"I'm not, but thank you. For everything." He sat on the bed then, his back against the headrest. Denise moved up and he draped one arm around her, pulling her close to him.

It was in that position that the two of them finally fell asleep.

Chapter 20

When she woke the following morning, Denise was alone. The bedcovers on Taylor's side had been pulled up, his clothes nowhere to be seen. Checking the clock, she saw that it was a little before seven. Puzzled, she got out of bed, put on a short silk bathrobe, and checked the house quickly before glancing out the window.

Taylor's truck was gone.

Frowning, Denise returned to the bedroom to check the bed-stand: no note. Not in the kitchen, either.

Kyle, who'd heard her puttering around the house, staggered sleepily out of his bedroom as she was pondering the situation, plopping down on the living room couch.

"Hewwo, Money," he mumbled, his eyes half-closed. Just as she answered, she heard Taylor's truck coming up the drive. A minute later Taylor was slowly opening the front door, a grocery bag in his arms, as if wary of waking a sleeping household.

"Oh, hey," he said, whispering as soon as he saw them, "I didn't think you two would be up yet."

"Hewwo, Tayer," Kyle cried, suddenly alert.

Denise pulled her robe a little tighter. "Where did you go?"

"I ran to the store."

"At this hour?"

Taylor closed the door behind him and walked across the living room. "It opens at six."

"Why're you whispering?"

"I don't know." He laughed, and his tone returned to normal. "Sorry about leaving this morning, but my stomach was growling."

She looked at him questioningly.

"So anyway, since I was already up, I decided that I would make you two a real breakfast. Eggs, bacon, pancakes, the works."

Denise smiled. "You don't like my Cheerios?"

"I love your Cheerios. But today is special."

"Why is today so special?"

He glanced toward Kyle, who was now focused on the toys piled in the corner. Judy had organized them neatly the night before, and he was doing his best to rectify that. Certain his attention was occupied, Taylor simply raised his eyebrows.

"Do you have anything on under that robe, Miss Holton?" he murmured, obvious desire in his tone.

"Wouldn't you like to know," she teased.

Taylor set the bag of groceries on the end table and put his arms around her, his hands running down her back, then inching lower. She looked momentarily embarrassed, her eyes flashing toward Kyle.

"I think I just found out," he said conspiratorially.

"Stop," she said, meaning it, but not really wanting him to. "Kyle's in the room."

Taylor nodded and pulled away with a wink. Kyle hadn't turned his attention from his toys.

"Well, today is special for the obvious reason," he said conversationally as he picked up the bag again. "But even more, after I make your gourmet breakfast, I'd like to take you and Kyle to the beach today."

"But I have to work with Kyle and then head into the diner tonight."

As he walked past her toward the kitchen, he stopped, leaning toward her ear as if sharing a secret.

"I know. I'm supposed to go over to Mitch's this morning to help fix his roof. But I'm willing to play hooky once if you are."

"But I took the morning off at the store," Mitch protested gamely. "You can't back out on me now. I've already pulled everything out of the garage."

Dressed in jeans and an old shirt, he had been waiting for Taylor to pull up when he heard the phone ring.

"Well, put it all back in," Taylor said good-naturedly. "Like I said, I'm not going to be able to make it."

As Taylor talked, he moved the bacon around with a fork in the sizzling pan. The aroma filled the house. Denise was standing close by, still in her short robe, scooping coffee grounds into the filter. The sight of her made Taylor wish that Kyle would disappear for the next hour or so. His mind was barely on the conversation.

"But what if it rains?"

"You already told me it's not leaking yet. That's why you let me put it off this long."

"Four cups or six?" Denise asked.

Lifting his chin away from the receiver, Taylor answered. "Make it eight. I love coffee."

"Who's that?" Mitch asked, everything suddenly coming clear now. "Hey . . . are you with Denise?"

Taylor looked toward her admiringly. "Not that it's any of your business, but yes."

"So you were with her all night?"

"What kind of question is that?"

Denise smiled, knowing exactly what Mitch was saying on the other end.

"You sly dog . . ."

"So about your roof," Taylor said loudly, trying to get the subject back on track.

"Oh, don't worry about it," Mitch said, suddenly

affable. "You just have yourself a nice time with her. It's about time you finally found someone—"

"Good-bye, Mitch," Taylor said, cutting him off. Shaking his head, he hung up the phone while Mitch was still talking.

Denise pulled the eggs from the grocery bag. "Scrambled?" she asked.

He grinned. "With you looking so good, how could I not feel scrambled?"

She rolled her eyes. "You really are a goob."

Two hours later they were sitting on a blanket at the beach near Nags Head, Taylor applying sunscreen to Denise's back. Kyle was using a plastic shovel nearby, scooping sand from one spot on the beach and moving it to another. Neither Taylor nor Denise had any idea what he was thinking as he did it, but he seemed to be enjoying it.

For Denise, the memories of the previous evening were revived as she felt the lotion being caressed into her skin.

"Can I ask you a question?" she said.

"Sure."

"Last night . . . after we'd . . . well . . ." She paused.

"After we'd done the horizontal tango?" Taylor offered.

She elbowed him in the ribs. "Don't make it sound

so romantic," she protested, and Taylor laughed. She shook her head but was unable to repress a grin.

"Anyway," she went on, regaining her composure. "Afterward, you got sort of quiet, like you were . . . sad or something."

Taylor nodded, looking out to the horizon. Denise waited for him to say something, but he didn't.

Watching the waves as they rolled up the shore, Denise gathered her courage.

"Was it because you regretted what happened?"

"No," he said quietly, his hands on her skin again. "It wasn't that at all."

"Then what was it?"

Without answering directly, Taylor followed her eyes, tracking the waves. "Do you remember back when you were a kid? Around Christmas? And how the anticipation was sometimes even more exciting than opening the presents?"

"Yes."

"That's what it reminds me of. I'd been dreaming about what it would finally be like . . ."

He stopped, considering how best to communicate what he meant.

"So the anticipation was actually more exciting than last night?" she asked.

"No," he said quickly. "You've got it all wrong. It was just the opposite. Last night was wonderful—you were wonderful. The whole thing was so perfect . . .

I guess it makes me sad to think that there's never going to be a first time with you again."

At that, he grew quiet once more. Denise, musing on his words and the sudden stillness in his gaze, decided to let the subject go. Instead she leaned back against him, comforted by the reassuring warmth of his encircling arms. They sat that way for a long time, each lost in thought.

Later, as the sun began its midafternoon march across the sky, they packed up their things, ready to head home. Taylor carried the blanket, towels, and picnic basket they'd brought with them. Kyle was walking ahead of them, his body covered in sand, carrying his pail and shovel as he weaved through the last of the sand dunes. All along the footpath, a sea of orange and yellow blossoms bloomed, their colors spectacular. Denise bent and plucked a blossom, bringing it to her nose.

"Around here, we call it the Jobellflower," Taylor said, watching her. She handed it to him, and Taylor wagged a finger at her in mock reproach.

"You know it's against the law to pick flowers on the dunes. They help protect us from the hurricanes."

"Are you going to turn me in?"

Taylor shook his head. "No, but I'm going to make you listen to the legend of how they got their name."

She pushed away the hair that had blown into her eyes. "Is this another story like the dram tree?"

"Sort of. It's a little more romantic, though."

Denise took a step closer to him. "So tell me about the flower."

He twirled it between his fingers, and the petals seemed to blend together.

"The Jobellflower was named for Joe Bell, who lived on this island a long time ago. Supposedly, Joe had been in love with a woman, but she ended up marrying someone else. Heartbroken, he moved to the Outer Banks, where he intended to live the life of a recluse. On his first morning in his new home, however, he saw a woman walking along the beach in front of his house, looking terribly sad and alone. Every day, at the same time, he would see her, and eventually he went out to meet her, but when she saw him, she turned and ran away. He thought he'd frightened her off for good, but the next morning she was walking along the beach again. This time, when he went to see her, she didn't run, and Joe was immediately struck by how beautiful she was. They talked all day, then the next, and soon they were in love. Surprisingly, at the same time he was falling in love, a small batch of flowers began to grow right behind his house, flowers never seen before in this area. As his love grew, the flowers continued to spread, and by the end of the summer, they'd become a beautiful ocean of color. It was there that Joe knelt and asked her to marry him. When she agreed, Joe picked a dozen blossoms and handed them to her, but strangely, she recoiled, refusing to take them. Later, on their wedding day, she explained her reason. 'This flower is the living symbol of our love,' she said. 'If the flowers die, then our love will die as well.' This terrified Joe—for some reason, he knew in his heart that truer words had never been spoken. So he began to plant or seed Jobellflowers all along the stretch of beach where they'd first met, then eventually throughout the Outer Banks, as a testimony to how much he loved his wife. And every year, as the flowers were spread, they fell deeper and deeper in love."

When he was finished, Taylor bent and picked a few more of the blossoms, then handed the bunch to Denise.

"I like that story," she said.

"I do, too."

"But didn't you just break the law, too?"

"Of course. But I figure that this way, we'll each have something to keep the other in line."

"Like trust?"

"That too," he said as he leaned in and kissed her on the cheek.

Taylor drove her into work that night, though Kyle didn't stay with her. Instead Taylor offered to watch him at Denise's house.

"We'll have fun. We'll play a little ball, watch a movie, eat some popcorn."

After hemming and hawing, Denise finally agreed, and Taylor dropped her off right before seven. As their truck pulled away, Taylor winked at Kyle.

"Okay, little man. First stop is my house. If we're going to watch a movie, we're going to need a VCR."

"He's driving," Kyle responded vigorously, and Taylor laughed, well used to Kyle's form of communication by now.

"We've also got one more stop to make, okay?"

Kyle simply nodded again, seemingly relieved that he didn't have to go into the diner. Taylor picked up his cellular phone and made a call, hoping the guy on the other end wouldn't mind doing him a favor.

At midnight Taylor loaded Kyle into the car, then went to pick up Denise. Kyle woke only briefly when Denise got in, then curled up onto her lap as he usually did. Fifteen minutes later everyone was in bed; Kyle in his room, Denise and Taylor in hers.

"I've been thinking about what you said earlier," Denise said, slipping off the marigold work dress.

Taylor found it difficult to concentrate as it fell to the floor. "What did I say?"

"About you being sad that there will never be a first time again."

"And?"

In her bra and panties, she moved closer, nuzzling up to him. "Well, I was just thinking that if we make this time even better than last night, your anticipation might come back."

Taylor felt her body sidle up against his. "How so?"

"If every time is better than the last, you'll always be looking forward to the next time."

Taylor put his arms around her back, becoming aroused. "Do you think that'll work?"

"I have no idea," she said, beginning to unbutton his shirt, "but I'd sure like to find out."

Taylor slipped out of her room just before dawn, as he'd done the day before, though this time he stopped at the couch. Not wanting Kyle to see them sleeping together, he dozed on and off for another couple of hours until Denise and Kyle came wandering out of their bedrooms. It was nearly eight o'clock—Kyle hadn't slept that late in a long time.

Denise scanned the room and immediately understood the reason. From the looks of things, it was obvious that he'd been up late. The TV was at an odd angle, the VCR was on the floor beside it, cables snaking out everywhere. Two half-empty cups sat on the end table with three cans of Sprite alongside them. Pieces of popcorn were scattered on the floor and on the couch; a Skittles wrapper had wedged itself between the pillows on the chair. On top of the television were two movies, *The Rescuers* and *The Lion King*, the cases open, videos on top.

Denise put her hands on her hips, taking in the mess.

"I didn't notice the mess you two made last night when I came in. It looks like you two had yourselves a good old time."

Taylor sat up from the couch and wiped his eyes. "We had fun."

"I'll bet," she groaned.

"But did you see what else we did?"

"You mean aside from spraying popcorn all over my furniture?"

He laughed. "C'mon. Let me show you. I'll get this stuff cleaned up in a minute."

He got up from the couch and stretched his arms over his head. "You too, Kyle. Let's show your mom what we did last night."

To Denise's surprise, Kyle seemed to understand what Taylor had said and obediently followed Taylor to the back door. Taylor led them across the porch to the rear steps, motioning to the garden on either side of the door.

When Denise saw what awaited her, she was speechless.

All along the back of the house were freshly planted Jobellflowers.

"You did this?" she asked.

"Kyle did, too," he said, a touch of pride in his voice, seeing that she was pleased.

"That feels wonderful," Denise said softly.

It was past midnight, long after Denise had once again finished with her shift at Eights. During the past week, Denise and Taylor had seen each other virtually every day. On the Fourth of July Taylor had taken them out on his rebuilt ancient motorboat; later they had set off their own fireworks, to Kyle's delight. They picnicked on the banks of the Chowan River and dug clams at the beach. For Denise, it was the kind of interlude she could never have allowed herself to imagine, sweeter than any dreams.

Tonight, like so many recent nights, she lay on the bed, naked, Taylor beside her. His hands were slick with oil, and the sensation of his hands sliding over her slippery body was unbearably tantalizing.

"You feel like heaven," Taylor whispered.

"We can't keep doing this," she groaned.

He kneaded the muscles in her lower back, applying gentle pressure, then relaxing his hands. "Doing what?"

"Staying up this late every night. It's killing me."

"For a dying woman, you still look good."

"I haven't had more than four hours of sleep since last weekend."

"That's because you can't keep your hands off me."

With her eyes almost closed, she felt a smile tugging at the corners of her mouth. Taylor bent over and kissed her on the spine between her shoulder blades.

"Would you like me to leave so you can get your rest?" he asked, his hands moving up to her shoulders again.

"Not just yet," she purred. "I'll let you finish first."

"Just using me now?"

"If that's okay."

"It is."

"So what's happening with Denise?" Mitch asked. "Melissa ordered me not to let you leave until you filled me in on all the details."

They were at Mitch's house on Monday, finally repairing the roof that Taylor had so successfully put off last week. The sun was blisteringly hot, and both had their shirts off as they worked their crowbars, prying off the torn shingles one by one. Taylor reached for his bandanna and wiped the sweat from his face.

"Not much."

Mitch waited for more, but Taylor said nothing else.

"That's it?" he snorted. "'Not much'?"

"What do you want me to say?"

"The works. Just start rambling and I'll stop you if I need something explained."

Taylor glanced from side to side as if making sure no one else was around. "Can you keep a secret?"

"Of course."

Taylor leaned a little closer. "So can I," he said with a wink, and Mitch burst out laughing.

"So you're going to keep all of this to yourself?"

"I didn't know I had to fill you in on everything," he retorted with mock indignation. "I guess I just assumed it was my own business."

Mitch shook his head. "You know, you can use that line on other people. The way I figure it—you're going to tell me sooner or later, so it may as well be sooner."

Taylor looked over at his friend, a smirk on his face. "You think so, huh?"

Mitch began prying a nail from the roof. "I don't think so. I *know* so. And besides, like I said, Melissa won't let you out of here until you do. Trust me, that gal can throw a frying pan with deadly accuracy."

Taylor laughed. "Well, you can tell Melissa that we're doing fine."

Mitch grabbed a damaged shingle with his gloved hands and began to tug at it, feeling as it ripped in half. He tossed it to the ground and started working the other half.

"And?"

"And what?"

"Does she make you happy?"

It took a moment for Taylor to answer. "Yeah," he said finally, "she really does." He searched for the right words as he continued to work the crowbar. "I've never met anyone like her before."

Mitch reached for his jug of ice water and took a sip, waiting for Taylor to continue.

"I mean, she's got everything. She's pretty, she's intelligent, she's charming, she makes me laugh . . . And you should see the way she is with her son. He's a great kid, but he's got some problems with talking, and the way she works with him—she's so patient, so dedicated, so loving . . . It's really something, that's for sure."

Taylor pried another nail loose, then tossed it over the side.

"She sounds great," Mitch said, impressed.

"She is."

Suddenly Mitch reached over, grabbing Taylor on the shoulder and giving him a good shake.

"Then what's she doing with a slacker like you?" he joked. Instead of laughing, however, Taylor simply shrugged.

"I have no idea."

Mitch set the jug of water aside. "Can I give you some advice?"

"Could I stop you?"

"No, not really. I'm like Ann Landers when it comes to things like this."

Taylor adjusted his position on the roof, making his way toward another shingle. "Then go ahead."

Mitch tensed slightly, anticipating Taylor's reaction. "Well, if she's everything you say she is and she makes you happy, don't screw it up this time."

Taylor stopped in midmotion. "What's that supposed to mean?"

"You know how you are in things like this. Remember Valerie? Remember Lori? If you don't, I do. You go out with 'em, you pour on the charm, you spend all your time with them, you get them to fall in love with you . . . and then wham—you end it."

"You don't know what you're talking about."

Mitch watched as Taylor's mouth tightened into a grim line. "No? Then go ahead and tell me where I'm mistaken."

Reluctantly Taylor considered what Mitch had said.

"They were different from Denise," he said slowly. "I was different. I've changed since then."

Mitch held up his hands to stop him from continuing. "It's not me you have to convince, Taylor. Like they say, don't shoot the messenger—I'm only telling you because I don't want to see you kicking yourself later."

Taylor shook his head. For a few minutes they

worked in silence. Finally: "You're a pain in the ass, do you know that?"

Mitch brushed at a couple of nails. "Yeah, I know. Melissa tells me that, too, so don't take it personally. It's just the way I am."

"So did you two finish the roof?"

Taylor nodded. He was holding a beer in his lap, nursing it slowly, a couple of hours before Denise began her shift. They were sitting on the front steps as Kyle played with his trucks in the yard. Despite his best efforts to the contrary, his thoughts kept returning to the things Mitch had said. There was some truth in his friend's words, he knew, but he couldn't help wishing he hadn't brought the matter up. It nagged at him like a bad memory.

"Yeah," he said, "it's done."

"Was it harder than you thought it would be?" Denise asked.

"No, not really. Why?"

"You just seem distracted."

"I'm sorry. Just a little tired, I guess."

Denise scrutinized him. "Are you sure that's all?"

Taylor brought the beer to his lips and took a drink. "I guess so."

"You guess?"

He set the can on the steps. "Well, Mitch said some things to me today . . ."

"Like what?"

"Just stuff," Taylor said, not wanting to elaborate. Denise read the concern in his eyes.

"Like what?"

Taylor drew a deep breath, wondering whether or not to answer but deciding to anyway. "He told me that if I'm serious about you, I shouldn't mess things up this time."

Denise felt her breath catch in her throat at the bluntness of his comment. Why would Mitch need to warn him this way?

"What did you say?"

Taylor shook his head. "I told him he didn't know what he was talking about."

"Well . . ." She hesitated. "Does he?"

"No, of course not."

"Then why is it bothering you?"

"Because," he said, "it just pisses me off that he'd think I might. He doesn't know anything about you, or us. And he doesn't know how I feel, that's for damn sure."

She squinted up at him, caught in the dying rays of the sun. "How do you feel?"

He reached for her hand.

"Don't you know?" he said. "Haven't I made it obvious yet?"

Chapter 21

Summer rose in full fury in mid-July, the temperature creeping past the century mark, then finally it began to cool. Toward the end of the month Hurricane Belle threatened the coast of North Carolina near Cape Hatteras before turning out to sea; in early August Hurricane Delilah did the same. Mid-August brought drought conditions; by late August crops were withering in the heat.

September opened with an unseasonal cold front, something that hadn't happened in twenty years. Jeans were pulled from the bottoms of drawers, light jackets were donned in the early evening hours. A week later another heat wave arrived and the jeans were put away, hopefully for the next couple of months.

Throughout the summer, however, the relationship between Taylor and Denise remained constant. Settled into a routine, they spent most afternoons together—to escape the heat, Taylor's crew started early in the morning and would finish by two o'clock—and Taylor continued to shuttle Denise to and from her job at the diner, whenever he could. Occasionally they ate dinner at Judy's house; sometimes Judy came by to baby-sit Kyle again, so they could have some time alone.

During those three months, Denise came to enjoy Edenton more and more. Taylor, of course, kept her busy as her guide, exploring the sights around town, going out in the boat, and heading to the beach. In time Denise came to see Edenton for what it was, a place that operated on its own slow schedule, a culture tied to raising kids and spending Sundays in church, to working the waters and tilling the fertile soil; a place where home still meant something. Denise caught herself gazing as he stood in her kitchen, holding his coffee cup, wondering idly whether he would look the same way to her in the distant future, when his hair had turned to gray.

She looked forward to everything they did; on a warm night toward the end of July, he took her up to Elizabeth City and they went dancing, another first in too many years. He moved her around the floor with surprising grace, waltzing and two-stepping to the drumming bass of a local country band. Women, she couldn't help but notice, were naturally drawn to him, and occasionally one would smile at him from across the floor and Denise would feel a quick hot pang of jealousy, even though Taylor never seemed to notice. Instead his arm never left her lower back, and he looked at her that night as if she were the only person in the world. Later, while eating cheese sandwiches in bed, Taylor pulled her close as a thunderstorm raged outside the bedroom window. "This," he confided, "is as good as it gets."

Kyle, too, blossomed under his attention. Gaining confidence in his speech, he began to talk more frequently, though much of it didn't make sense. He'd also stopped whispering when running more than a few words together. By late summer he'd learned to hit the ball off the tee consistently, and his ability to throw the ball had improved dramatically. Taylor set up makeshift bases in the front yard, and though he did his best to teach Kyle the rules of the game, it wasn't something Kyle was interested in at all. He just wanted to have fun.

But as idyllic as everything seemed, there were moments in which Denise sensed an undercurrent of restlessness in Taylor she couldn't exactly pin down. As he had during their first night together, Taylor would sometimes get that unreadable, almost distant look after they made love. He would hold her and caress her as usual, but she could sense something in him that made her vaguely uncomfortable, something dark and unknowable that made him seem older and more tired than Denise had ever felt. It scared her sometimes, although when daylight came she often berated herself for letting her imagination run away with her.

Toward the end of August Taylor left town to help fight a major fire in the Croatan forest for three days, a dangerous situation made more deadly by the searing August heat. Denise found it difficult to sleep while he was gone. Worrying about him, she called Judy and they spent an hour talking on the phone. Denise followed the coverage of the fire in the newspaper and on television, searching in vain for any glimpse of Taylor. When Taylor finally returned to Edenton, he drove straight to her house. With Ray's permission, she took the evening off, but Taylor was exhausted and fell asleep on the couch soon after the sun had gone down. She covered him with a blanket, thinking he'd sleep until the morning, but in the middle of the night he crept into her room. Again, he had the shakes, but this time they didn't stop for hours. Taylor refused to talk about what had happened, and Denise held him in her arms, concerned, until he was finally able to nod off again. Even in his sleep his demons gave him no relief. Twisting and turning, he called out in his sleep, his words incomprehensible, except for the fear she heard in them.

The next morning, sheepish, he apologized. But he offered nothing by way of explanation. He didn't have to. Somehow she knew it wasn't simply memories of the fire that were eating him up; it was something else, naked and dark, bubbling to the surface.

Her mother had once told her that there were men who kept secrets bottled up inside and that it spelled trouble for the women who loved them. Denise instinctively knew the truth of her mother's statement, yet it was hard to reconcile her words with the love she felt for Taylor McAden. She loved the way he smelled; she loved the rough texture of his hands upon her and the wrinkles around his eyes whenever he laughed. She loved the way he stared at her as she got off work, leaning against the truck in the parking lot, one leg crossed over the other. She loved everything about him.

Sometimes she also found herself dreaming of someday walking down the aisle with him. She could deny it, she could ignore it, she could tell herself that neither of them was ready yet. And maybe the last part of that was true. They hadn't been together very long, and if he asked her tomorrow, she liked to think that she would have the wisdom to say exactly that. Yet . . . she wouldn't say those words, she admitted to herself in her most brutally candid moments. She would say *Yes . . . yes . . . yes.*

In her daydreams, she could only hope that Taylor felt the same.

* * *

"You seem nervous," Taylor commented, studying Denise's reflection in the mirror. He was standing behind her in the bathroom as she put the finishing touches on her makeup.

"I am nervous."

"But it's only Mitch and Melissa. There's nothing to be nervous about."

Holding up two different earrings, one to each ear, she debated between the gold hoop and the simple stud.

"For you, maybe. You already know them. I only met them one time, three months ago, and we didn't talk all that long. What if I make a bad impression?"

"Don't worry." Taylor gave her arm a squeeze. "You won't."

"But what if I do?"

"They won't care. You'll see."

She put the hoops aside, choosing the studs. She slipped one into each ear.

"Well, it wouldn't be so nerve-racking if you'd taken me to meet them sooner, you know. You've waited an awful long time to start bringing me to meet your friends."

Taylor held up his hands. "Hey, don't blame me. You're the one who works six nights a week, and I'm sorry if I want you all to myself on the one night you have off."

"Yeah, but . . ."

"But what?"

"Well, I was beginning to wonder whether you were embarrassed to be seen with me."

"Don't be ridiculous. I assure you that my intentions were purely selfish. I'm greedy when it comes to spending time with you."

Looking over her shoulder, she asked, "Is this something I'm going to have to worry about in the future?"

Taylor shrugged, a sly grin on his face. "It depends if you keep working six nights a week."

She sighed, finishing with the earrings. "Well, it should be coming to an end fairly soon. I've almost saved enough for a car, and then, believe me, I'll be begging Ray to scale back my shifts."

Taylor slipped both arms around her, still staring at her in the mirror. "Hey, have I told you how wonderful you look?"

"You're changing the subject."

"I know. But damn, look at you. You're beautiful."

After eyeing their reflection in the mirror, she turned to face him.

"Good enough for a barbecue with your friends?"

"You look fantastic," he said sincerely, "but even if you didn't, they'd still love you."

Thirty minutes later Taylor, Denise, and Kyle were walking toward the door when Mitch appeared from around the back of the house, beer in hand.

"Hey, y'all," he said. "Glad you could make it. The gang's out back."

Taylor and Denise followed him through the gate, past the swing set and azalea bushes, before reaching the deck.

Melissa was sitting at the outdoor table, watching her four boys jump in and out of the swimming pool, their noisy cries blending into one jumbled roar punctuated by sharp outbursts. The pool had been installed the summer before, after one too many water moccasins had been spotted near the dock on the river. Nothing like a venomous snake to sour a person on nature's beauty, Mitch liked to say.

"Hey there," Melissa called out, getting to her feet. "Thanks for coming."

Taylor drew Melissa into a bear hug and gave her a quick kiss on the cheek.

"You two have met, right?" he said.

"At the festival," Melissa said easily. "But that was a long time ago, and besides, you met a lot of people that day. How are you doing, Denise?"

"Good, thanks," she said, still feeling a little nervous.

Mitch motioned to the cooler. "You two want a beer?"

"That sounds great," Taylor answered. "Would you like one, Denise?"

"Please."

As Taylor went to fetch the beers, Mitch settled himself at the outdoor table, adjusting the umbrella to keep the sun off them. Melissa made herself comfortable again, followed by Denise. Kyle, wearing a bathing suit and T-shirt, stood shyly by his mother's side, a towel draped over his shoulders. Melissa leaned toward him.

"Hi, Kyle, how are you?"

Kyle didn't answer.

"Kyle, say, 'I'm fine, thanks,'" Denise said.

"I'm fine, thanks." *(I'n fine, kenks)*

Melissa smiled. "Well, good. Would you like to go get in the pool with the other boys? They've been waiting all day for you to show up."

Kyle looked from Melissa to his mother.

"Do you want to swim?" Denise asked, rephrasing the question.

Kyle nodded excitedly. "Yes."

"Okay, go ahead. Be careful."

Denise took his towel as Kyle ambled toward the water.

"Does he need a float?" Melissa asked.

"No, he can swim. I have to keep my eye on him, of course."

Kyle reached the pool and stepped down, the water up to his knees. He bent over and splashed, as if testing the temperature, before breaking into a wide grin. Denise and Melissa watched him as he waded in.

"How old is he now?"

"He'll be five in a few months."

"Oh, so will Jud." Melissa pointed toward the far end of the pool. "That's him over there, holding on to the side, by the diving board."

Denise saw him. Same size as Kyle, buzz haircut. Melissa's four boys were jumping, splashing, screaming—in short, having themselves a great time.

"All four kids are yours?" Denise asked, amazed.

"Today they are. You let me know if you want to take one home, though. I'll give you the pick of the litter."

Denise felt herself relaxing a little. "Are they a handful?"

"They're boys. They've got energy coming out their ears."

"How old are they?"

"Ten, eight, six, and four."

"My wife had a plan," Mitch said, cutting into the conversation while peeling the label from his bottle. "Every other year, on our anniversary, she'd let me sleep with her, whether she wanted me to or not."

Melissa rolled her eyes. "Don't listen to him. His conversation skills aren't meant for civilized people."

Taylor returned with the beers, opening Denise's bottle before setting it in front of her. His was already open. "What are y'all talking about?"

"Our sex life," Mitch said seriously, and this time Melissa punched him in the arm.

"Watch it, buster. We've got a guest here. You don't want to make a bad impression, do you?"

Mitch leaned toward Denise. "I'm not making a bad impression. Am I?"

Denise smiled, deciding that she liked these two immediately. "No."

"See, I told you, honey," Mitch said victoriously.

"She's just saying that because you put her on the spot. Now leave the poor lady alone. We were talking here, having a perfectly nice conversation, until you butted in."

"Well—"

It was all Mitch could say before Melissa cut him off. "Don't push it."

"But—"

"Do you want to sleep on the couch tonight?"

Mitch's eyebrows went up and down. "Is that a promise?"

She gave him the once-over. "It is now."

Everyone at the table laughed, and Mitch leaned toward his wife, resting his head on her shoulder.

"I'm sorry, honey," he said, looking at her like a puppy who'd messed on the rug.

"Not good enough," she said, feigning haughtiness.

"What if I do the dishes later?"

"We're eating off paper plates tonight."

"I know. That's why I offered."

"Why don't you two leave us alone so we can talk? Go clean the grill or something."

"I just got here," Taylor complained. "Why do I have to go?"

"Because the grill is really dirty."

"It is?" Mitch asked.

"Go on," Melissa said as if shooing a fly from her plate. "Leave us alone so we can do some girl-talk."

Mitch turned toward his friend. "I don't think we're wanted, Taylor."

"I think you're right, Mitch."

Melissa whispered conspiratorially, "These two should have been rocket scientists. Nothing gets by them."

Mitch's mouth was playfully agape. "I think she just insulted us, Taylor," he said.

"I think you're right."

"See what I mean?" Melissa said, nodding as if her point had been proven. "Rocket scientists."

"C'mon, Taylor," Mitch said, pretending to be offended. "We don't need to put up with this. We're better than that."

"Good. Go be better while you clean the grill."

Mitch and Taylor rose from the table, leaving Denise and Melissa alone. Denise was still laughing as they headed toward the grill.

"Now how long have you two been married?"

"Twelve years. It only seems like twenty."

Melissa winked, and all Denise could do was wonder why it suddenly seemed as if she'd known her forever.

"So how did you two meet?" Denise asked.

"At a party in college. The first time I ever saw him, Mitch was balancing a bottle of beer on his forehead while trying to cross the room. If he could do it without spilling it, he'd win fifty bucks."

"Did he make it?"

"No, he ended up soaked from head to toe. But it was obvious he didn't take himself too seriously. And after some of the other guys I dated, I guess that's what I was looking for. We started dating, and a couple of years later, we got married."

She looked toward her husband, obvious affection in her eyes.

"He's a good guy. I think I'll keep him."

"So how was it down in the Croatan?"

When Joe had asked for volunteers to fight the forest fire a few weeks earlier, only Taylor had raised his hand. Mitch had simply shaken his head when Taylor had asked him to come along.

What Taylor didn't know was that Mitch had learned exactly what had happened. Joe had called Mitch in confidence, telling him that Taylor had nearly been killed when the fire suddenly closed in around him. Had it not been for a slight shift in the wind, which cleared enough smoke for Taylor to find his way out, he would have been dead. His latest brush with death hadn't surprised Mitch at all.

Taylor took a drink of his beer, his eyes clouding with the memory.

"Pretty hairy at times—you know how those fires are. But luckily no one got hurt."

Yes, lucky. Again.

"Nothing else?"

"Not really," he said, downplaying any hint of danger. "But you should have come along. We could have used more men out there."

Mitch shook his head as he reached for the grate on the grill. He began to work the scraper back and forth.

"No, that's for you young guys. I'm getting too old for things like that."

"I'm older than you are, Mitch."

"Sure, if you think of it just in terms of numbers. But I'm like an old man compared to you. I have progeny."

"Progeny?"

"Crossword puzzle word. It means I have children."

"I know what it means."

"Well, then you also know that I can't just up and leave anymore. Now that the boys are getting bigger, it's not fair to Melissa if I head out of town for things like that. I mean, if there's a problem here, that's one thing. But I'm not going to search them out. Life's too short for that."

Taylor reached for a rag and handed it to Mitch to wipe the scraper.

"You're still going to give it up?"

"Yep. A few more months and then that's it."

"No regrets?"

"None." Mitch paused before going on. "You know, you might want to consider giving it up, too," he added conversationally.

"I'm not gonna quit, Mitch," Taylor said, dismissing the idea immediately. "I'm not like you. I'm not afraid of what might happen."

"You should be."

"That's how you see it."

"Maybe so," Mitch said, speaking calmly. "But it's true. If you really care about Denise and Kyle, you gotta start putting them first, like I put my family first. What we do is dangerous, no matter how careful we are, and it's a risk that we don't have to take. We've been lucky more than a few times." He was silent as he set the scraper aside. Then his eyes met Taylor's.

"You know what it's like to grow up without a father. Would you want to do that to Kyle?"

Taylor stiffened. "Christ, Mitch . . ."

Mitch raised his hands to stop Taylor from

continuing. "Before you start calling me names, it's something I had to say. Ever since that night on the bridge . . . and then again in the Croatan. Yeah, I know about that, too, and it doesn't give me warm fuzzies. A dead hero is still dead, Taylor." He cleared his throat. "I don't know. It's like over the years you've been testing fate more and more often, like you're chasing something. It scares me sometimes."

"You don't have to worry about me."

Mitch stood and put his hand on Taylor's shoulder.

"I always worry about you, Taylor. You're like my brother."

"What do you think they're talking about?" Denise asked, watching Taylor from the table. She saw the change in his demeanor, the sudden stiffness, as if someone had turned on a switch.

Melissa had seen it as well.

"Mitch and Taylor? Probably the fire department. Mitch is giving it up at the end of the year. He probably told Taylor to do the same thing."

"But doesn't Taylor enjoy being a fireman?"

"I don't know if he enjoys it. He does it because he has to."

"Why?"

Melissa looked at Denise, a perplexed expression on her face. "Well . . . because of his father," she said.

"His father?" Denise repeated.

"Didn't he tell you?" Melissa asked carefully.

"No." Denise shook her head, suddenly afraid of what Melissa was getting at. "He just told me that his father had died when he was a child."

Melissa nodded, her lips together.

"What is it?" Denise asked, her anxiety plain.

Melissa sighed, debating whether to continue.

"Please," Denise said, and Melissa glanced away. Finally she spoke.

"Taylor's father died in a fire."

At her words, a cold hand seemed to settle on Denise's spine.

Taylor had taken the grate to rinse it under the hose and returned to see Mitch opening the cooler for another two beers. As Mitch opened his, Taylor walked by without a word.

"She sure is pretty, Taylor."

Taylor put the grate back on the grill, over the charcoal. "I know."

"Her kid's cute, too. Nice little guy."

"I know."

"He looks like you."

"Huh?"

"Just seeing if you're paying attention," Mitch said, grinning. "You looked a little lost when you came back." He stepped closer. "Hey, listen, I'm sorry I said those things earlier. I didn't mean to upset you."

"It didn't upset me," Taylor lied.

Mitch handed Taylor the beer. "Sure it did. But someone's got to keep you on the straight and narrow."

"And you're the one to do it?"

"Of course. I'm the only one who can."

"No, Mitch, really, don't be so modest," Taylor said sarcastically.

Mitch raised his eyebrows. "You think I'm kidding? How long have I known you now? Thirty years? I think that entitles me to speak my mind once in a while without worrying what you think about it. And I was serious about what I said. Not so much about you quitting—I know you're not going to do that. You should try to be a little more cautious in the future, though. See this?"

Mitch pointed to his balding head. "I used to have a full head of hair. And I'd still have it if you weren't such a damn daredevil. Every time you do something crazy, I can feel my little hairs committing suicide by jumping right out of my head and plunging all the way to my shoulders. If you listen carefully, you can sometimes hear them screaming all the way down. You know what it's like going bald? Having to put sunscreen on top of your head when you go outside? Getting liver spots where you used to part your hair? It doesn't do much for the old ego, if you know what I mean. So you owe me."

Taylor laughed despite himself. "Gee, and here I thought it was hereditary."

"Oh no. It's you, buddy."

"I'm touched."

"You should be. It's not like I'd be willing to go bald for just anybody."

"All right." He sighed. "I'll try to be more cautious in the future."

"Good. Because in a while, I won't be there to bail you out."

"How's the charcoal coming?" Melissa called out.

Mitch and Taylor were standing by the grill, the kids already eating. Mitch had cooked the hot dogs first, and the five of them were at the table. Denise, who'd brought Kyle's dinner with him (macaroni and cheese, Ritz crackers, grapes), set his plate in front of him. After swimming for a couple of hours, he was famished.

"Another ten minutes," Mitch shouted over his shoulder.

"I want macaroni and cheese, too," Melissa's youngest whined when he saw that Kyle was eating something different from what the rest of them had.

"Eat your hot dog," Melissa answered.

"But Mom—"

"Eat your hot dog," she said again. "If you're still hungry after that, I'll make some, okay?"

She knew he wouldn't still be hungry, but it seemed to placate the child.

Once everything was under control, Denise and Melissa moved away from the table and sat down closer to the pool. Ever since Denise had learned about Taylor's father, she had been trying to piece the rest of it together in her mind. Melissa seemed to divine the direction of her thoughts.

"Taylor?" she said, and Denise smiled sheepishly, embarrassed that it was so obvious.

"Yeah."

"How are you two getting along?"

"I thought it was going pretty well. But now, I'm not so sure."

"Because he didn't tell you about his father? Well, I'll let you in on a secret: Taylor doesn't talk about it to anyone, ever. Not to me, not to anyone he works with, not to his friends. He's never even talked about it with Mitch."

Denise considered this, unsure how to respond.

"That makes me feel better." She paused, furrowing her brow. "I think."

Melissa put her iced tea aside. Like Denise, she'd stopped drinking beer after finishing her second.

"He's a charmer when he wants to be, isn't he? Cute, too."

Denise leaned back in her seat. "Yes, he is."

"How is he with Kyle?"

"Kyle adores him—lately, he likes Taylor more than me. Taylor's like a little boy when they're together."

"Taylor's always been good with kids. My kids feel the same way about him. They'll call him to see if he can come over to play."

"Does he come?"

"Sometimes. Not lately, though. You've been taking up all of his time."

"Sorry about that."

Melissa waved off the apology. "Don't be. I'm happy for him. You too. I was beginning to wonder if he'd ever meet somebody. You're the first person in years he's actually brought over."

"So there've been others?"

Melissa smiled wryly. "He hasn't talked to you about them, either?"

"Nope."

"Well, girl, it's a good thing you came over," she said conspiratorially, and Denise laughed.

"So what did you want to know?"

"What were they like?"

"Not like you, that's for sure."

"No?"

"No. You're a lot prettier than they were. And you've got a son."

"Whatever happened to them?"

"Now, unfortunately, that I can't tell you. Taylor

doesn't talk about that, either. All I know is that one day they seemed to be doing fine and the next thing you knew, it was over. I never did understand why."

"That's a comforting thought."

"Oh, I'm not saying it's going to happen with you. He likes you more than he liked them, a lot more. I can see it in the way he looks at you."

Denise hoped that Melissa was telling the truth.

"Sometimes . . . ," Denise began, then trailed off, not knowing exactly how to say it.

"Sometimes you're scared about what he's thinking?"

She looked at Melissa, startled by the acuity of her observation. Melissa went on.

"Even though Mitch and I have been together for a long time, I still don't understand everything that makes him tick. He's sort of like Taylor sometimes, in that regard. But in the end, it's worked out because we both want it to. As long as you two have that, you'll be able to make it through anything."

A beach ball came flying from the table where the kids were sitting, bonking Melissa on the head. A series of loud giggles broke out.

Melissa rolled her eyes but otherwise paid no attention as the beach ball rolled away. "You might even be able to put up with having four boys, like we do."

“I don’t know if I could do that.”

“Sure you could. It’s easy. All you have to do is wake up early, get the paper, and read it leisurely while drinking tequila shooters.”

Denise giggled.

“Seriously, do you ever think about having more kids?” Melissa asked.

“Not too often.”

“Because of Kyle?” They’d talked a little about his problem earlier.

“No, not just that. But it’s not something I can do alone, is it?”

“But if you were married?”

After a moment Denise smiled. “Probably.”

Melissa nodded. “Do you think Taylor would be a good dad?”

“I know he would.”

“So do I,” Melissa agreed. “Have you two ever talked about it?”

“Marriage? No. He hasn’t brought it up at all.”

“Mmm,” Melissa said. “I’ll try to find out what he’s thinking, all right?”

“You don’t have to do that,” Denise protested, flushing.

“Oh, I want to. I’m as curious as you are. But don’t worry, I’ll be subtle. He won’t even know what I’m getting at.”

* * *

"So, Taylor, are you gonna marry this wonderful girl or what?"

Denise almost dropped her fork onto her plate. Taylor was in the middle of taking a drink and he inhaled a bit of it, causing him to cough three times as he expelled it from the wrong pipe. He brought his napkin to his face, his eyes watering.

"Excuse me?"

The four of them were eating their meal—steaks, green salad, Cheddar cheese potatoes, and garlic bread. They'd been laughing and joking, having a good time, and were halfway done when Melissa dropped her bombshell. Denise felt the blood rush to her cheeks as Melissa went on matter-of-factly.

"I mean, she's a babe, Taylor. Smart, too. Girls like her don't come along every day."

Though obviously said in jest, Taylor stiffened slightly.

"I haven't really thought about it," he said almost defensively, and Melissa leaned forward, patting his arm as she laughed out loud.

"I don't expect an answer, Taylor—I was kidding. I just wanted to see your expression. Your eyes got big as saucers."

"That's because I was choking," Taylor answered.

She leaned toward him. "I'm sorry. But I just couldn't resist. You're easy to pick on. Just like Bozo over here."

"Are you talking about me, darling?" Mitch broke in, trying to offset Taylor's obvious discomfort.

"Who else calls you Bozo?"

"With the exception of you—and my three other wives, of course—no one really."

"Mmm," she said, "that's good. Otherwise I might get jealous."

Melissa leaned over and gave her husband a quick kiss on the cheek.

"Are they always like this?" Denise whispered to Taylor, praying he wouldn't think she'd put Melissa up to the question.

"Ever since I've known them," Taylor said, but it was obvious his mind was elsewhere.

"Hey, no talking behind our backs," Melissa said. Turning toward Denise, she moved the conversation back to safer ground. "So tell me about Atlanta. I've never been there . . ."

Denise took a deep breath as Melissa looked right at her, an almost imperceptible smirk on her face. Her wink was so inconspicuous that neither Mitch nor Taylor caught it.

And though Melissa and Denise chatted for the next hour, Mitch joining in whenever appropriate, Taylor, Denise noticed, didn't say much at all.

"I'm gonna get you!" Mitch shouted as he ran through the yard, chasing Jud, who was screaming as well, the high-pitched shrieks alternating between delight and fear.

"You're almost on base! Run!" Taylor yelled. Jud lowered his head, charging, as Mitch slowed down behind him, the cause lost. Jud reached base, joining the others.

It was an hour after dinner—the sun had finally set, and Mitch and Taylor were playing tag with the boys in the yard out front. Mitch, his hands on his hips, looked around the yard at the five kids, his chest heaving. They were all within a few feet of each other.

"You can't get me, Daddy!" Cameron taunted, his thumbs by his ears, fingers wagging.

"Try to get me, Daddy!" Will added, his voice joining his brother's.

"Then you've got to get off base," Mitch said, bending over and putting his hands on his knees. Cameron and Will, sensing weakness, suddenly darted in opposite directions.

"C'mon, Daddy!" Will shouted gleefully.

"Okay, now you asked for it!" Mitch said, doing his best to rise to the challenge. Mitch began trudging toward Will, heading past Taylor and Kyle, who remained safely on base.

"Run, Daddy, run!" Will teased, knowing he was agile enough to stay well away from his father.

Mitch chased one son after the other, veering

course as he needed to for the next few minutes. Kyle, who had taken a little while to pick up on the game, finally understood it well enough to run with the other kids, and soon his screams were joining with the others as Mitch made his way around the yard. After one too many near misses, Mitch surged toward Taylor.

"I need a little break here," Mitch said, the words almost lost in the wheeze of his gasps.

Taylor darted off to the side, safely out of reach. "Then you gotta catch me, pal."

Taylor let him suffer for another minute or so, until Mitch looked almost green. He finally ran toward the middle of the yard, slowed down, and allowed Mitch to tag off. Mitch bent over again, trying to catch his breath.

"They're faster than they look," Mitch said honestly, "and they change directions like jackrabbits."

"It just seems that way when you're old like you," Taylor replied. "But if you're right, I'll just tag you."

"If you think I'm leaving base, you're out of your mind. I'm just going to take a seat here for a while."

"C'mon!" Cameron shouted to Taylor, wanting the game to resume. "You can't catch me!"

Taylor rubbed his hands together. "All right, here I come!"

Taylor took a giant step toward the kids, and with a jubilant scream they scattered in different directions.

But Kyle's voice, cutting loudly through the darkness, was unmistakable and suddenly made Taylor stop his charge.

"C'mon, Daddy!" *(C'maw, Da-ee!)* Kyle shouted. "C'mon, Daddy!"

Daddy.

Taylor, frozen for a moment, simply stared in Kyle's direction. Mitch, who'd seen Taylor's reaction, teased: "Is there something you haven't told me, Taylor?"

Taylor didn't respond.

"He just called you 'Daddy,'" Mitch added, as if Taylor had missed it.

But Taylor barely heard what Mitch had said. Lost in thought, the word repeated in Taylor's mind.

Daddy.

Though he knew it was simply Kyle mimicking the other children—as if calling out Daddy were part of the game—it nonetheless brought Melissa's statement to mind again.

So are you going to marry this girl or what?

"Earth to Taylor . . . come in, big *daddy*," Mitch said, unable to suppress a grin.

Taylor finally glanced toward him. "Shut up, Mitch."

"Sure enough . . . Daddy."

Taylor finally took a step toward the kids. "I'm not his daddy," he said, almost to himself.

Though Mitch whispered the next words to

himself, Taylor heard them as clearly as he'd heard Kyle's a moment before.

"Not yet, anyway."

"Did you guys have fun?" Melissa asked as the children came pounding through the front door, finally tired enough to call it quits for the night.

"We had a blast. Dad's getting awful slow, though," Cameron offered.

"I am not," Mitch said defensively as he followed them inside. "I let you get to base."

"Right, Dad."

"I put some juice in the living room. Don't spill, okay?" Melissa said as the kids trudged past her. Mitch leaned in to kiss Melissa, but she pulled back. "Not until after you shower. You're filthy."

"This is what I get for entertaining the kids?"

"No, that's the response you get when you smell bad."

Mitch laughed and started toward the patio slider, heading toward the backyard in search of a beer.

Taylor brought up the rear, Kyle right in front of him. Kyle followed the other kids to the living room as Denise watched him go.

"How did he do?" Denise asked.

"Fine," Taylor said simply. "He had fun."

Denise looked at Taylor carefully. Something was obviously bothering him.

"Are you okay?"

Taylor glanced away. "Yeah," he said. "I'm okay."

Without saying anything else, he followed Mitch outside.

With the evening finally winding down, Denise volunteered to help Melissa in the kitchen after dinner, putting the leftovers away. The kids were watching a movie in the living room, sprawled all over the floor, while Mitch and Taylor straightened things up on the deck out back.

Denise was rinsing the silverware before putting it into the dishwasher. From where she was standing she could see the two men outside, and she watched them, her hands unmoving under the water.

"Penny for your thoughts," Melissa said, startling her.

Denise shook her head, returning to the task at hand. "I'm not sure a penny will cover it."

Melissa picked up some empty cups and brought them to the sink. "Listen, I'm sorry if I put you on the spot during dinner."

"No, I'm not mad about that. You were just having fun. We all were."

"But you're worried anyway?"

"I don't know . . . I guess . . ." She glanced at Melissa. "Maybe a little. He's been quiet all night."

"I wouldn't read too much into that. I know he

really cares about you. He lights up whenever he looks your way—even after I teased him."

She watched as Taylor pushed in the chairs around the table.

Denise nodded. "I know."

Despite her answer, she couldn't help but wonder why that suddenly didn't seem to be enough. She sealed the Tupperware bowl with a lid.

"Did Mitch say anything to you about anything that happened while they were out front with the kids?"

Melissa looked at her curiously. "No. Why?"

Denise put the salad in the refrigerator. "Just curious."

Daddy.

So are you gonna marry this girl or what?

As he nursed his beer, the words continued to echo through Taylor's mind.

"Hey, why so glum?" Mitch asked, filling a plastic garbage bag with the remains from the table.

Taylor shrugged. "Just preoccupied. That's all."

"About what?"

"Just work stuff. I'm just trying to figure out everything I've got to do tomorrow," Taylor answered, telling only the partial truth. "Since I've been spending so much time with Denise, I've let my business slide a little. I've got to get back into it."

"Haven't you been heading in every day?"

"Yeah, but I don't always stay all day. You know how it is. You do that long enough and little problems start cropping up."

"Anything I can do? Check how your orders are coming, things like that?"

Taylor placed most of his orders through the hardware store.

"No, not really, but I've got to get it squared away. One thing I've learned is that when things go wrong, they go wrong in a hurry."

Mitch hesitated as he put a paper cup in the bag, feeling a strange sense of déjà vu.

The last time Taylor had used that expression, he'd been dating Lori.

Thirty minutes later Taylor and Denise were driving home, Kyle between them, a scene that had been repeated dozens of times. Yet now, for the first time, there was an air of tension in the truck without a reason that could be easily explained by either of them. But it was there, and it had kept them quiet enough that Kyle had already fallen asleep, lulled by the silence.

For Denise, the sensation was a strange one. She kept thinking about everything that Melissa had told her, her statements rattling through her brain like senseless, ricocheting pinballs. She didn't feel like talking, but then Taylor didn't, either. He'd been strangely distant, and that only intensified her feelings. What was supposed to have been a casual, friendly night out with friends, Denise knew with certainty had become something far more important than that.

Okay, so Taylor had almost choked when Melissa had asked if marriage was in the plans. That would have surprised anyone, especially the way Melissa had blurted it out, wouldn't it? In the truck she tried to convince herself of that, but the more she thought about it, the more unsure she felt. Three months isn't a long time when a person is young. But they weren't kids. She was pushing thirty, Taylor was six years older than that. They'd already had a chance to grow up, to figure out exactly who they were, to know what they wanted in their lives. If he wasn't as serious about their future together as he seemed to be, then why the full-court press these last couple of months?

All I know is that one day they seemed to be doing fine and the next thing you knew, it was over. I never did understand why.

That was also bothering her, wasn't it? If Melissa didn't understand what had happened with Taylor's other relationships, Mitch probably didn't, either. Did that mean that Taylor didn't understand it?

And if so, was the same thing going to happen to her?

Denise felt a knot form in her stomach, and she glanced at Taylor uncertainly. From the corner of his eye, Taylor caught her glance and turned to face her, seemingly oblivious of her thoughts. Outside the car window, the trees whistling past were black and clumped together, solidified into a single image.

"Did you have a good time tonight?"

"Yeah, I did," Denise answered quietly. "I like your friends."

"So how did you and Melissa get along?"

"We got along fine."

"One thing you've probably already learned is that she'll say the first thing that pops into her head, no matter how ridiculous it is. You just have to ignore her sometimes."

His comment did nothing for her nerves. Kyle mumbled incoherently as he adjusted himself a little lower in the seat. Denise wondered why the things Taylor hadn't said suddenly seemed more important than the things he had.

Who are you, Taylor McAden?

How well do I really know you?

And where, most important, are we going from here?

She knew he would answer none of those things. Instead she drew a deep breath, willing herself to keep her voice steady.

"Taylor . . . why didn't you tell me about your father?" she asked.

Taylor's eyes widened just a little. "My father?"

"Melissa told me that he died in a fire."

She saw his hands tighten on the wheel.

"How did that come up?" he asked, his tone changing slightly.

"I don't know. It just did."

"Was it her idea to bring it up or yours?"

"Why does that matter? I don't remember how it came up."

Taylor didn't respond; his eyes were locked on the road ahead. Denise waited before realizing he wasn't going to answer her original question.

"Did you become a fireman because of your father?"

Shaking his head, Taylor expelled a sharp breath. "I'd rather not talk about it."

"Maybe I can help—"

"You can't," he said, cutting her off, "and besides, it doesn't concern you."

"It doesn't concern me?" she asked in disbelief. "What are you talking about? I care about you, Taylor, and it hurts me to think that you don't trust me enough to tell me what's wrong."

"Nothing's wrong," he said. "I just don't like to talk about my father."

She could have pressed it further but knew it wouldn't get her anywhere.

Once again silence descended in the truck. This

time, however, the silence was tainted with fear. It lasted the rest of the way home.

After Taylor carried Kyle into his bedroom, he waited in the living room until Denise had changed him into his pajamas. When she came back out, she noticed that Taylor hadn't made himself comfortable. Instead he was standing near the door, as if waiting to say good-bye.

"You're not going to stay?" she asked, surprised.

He shook his head. "No, I really can't. I've got to get to work early tomorrow."

Though he said it without a trace of bitterness or anger, his words didn't dispel her unease. He began to jingle his keys, and Denise walked across the living room to be closer to him.

"You sure?"

"Yeah, I'm sure."

She reached for his hand. "Is something bothering you?"

Taylor shook his head. "No, not at all."

She waited to see if he would add anything else, but he didn't go any further.

"All right. See you tomorrow?"

Taylor cleared his throat before answering. "I'll try, but I've got a pretty full schedule tomorrow. I don't know if I'll be able to swing by."

Denise studied him carefully, wondering.

"Even for lunch?"

"I'll do my best," he said, "but I can't make any promises."

Their eyes met only briefly before Taylor glanced away.

"Will you be able to take me into work tomorrow night?"

For a brief, flickering instant, it almost seemed to Denise as if he hadn't wanted her to ask.

Her imagination?

"Yeah, sure," he finally said. "I'll take you in."

He left after kissing her only briefly, then walked to his truck without turning around.

Chapter 22

Early the next morning, while Denise was drinking a cup of coffee, the phone rang. Kyle was sprawled on the living room floor, coloring as best he could but finding it impossible to stay in the lines. When she answered it, she recognized Taylor's voice instantly.

"Oh, hey, I'm glad you're up," he said.

"I'm always up this early," she said, feeling a strange sense of relief wash over her at the sound of his voice. "I missed you last night."

"I missed you, too," Taylor said. "I probably should have stayed. I didn't sleep too well."

"Neither did I," she admitted. "I kept waking up because I had all the covers for once."

"I don't hog the sheets. You must be thinking of someone else."

"Like who?"

"Maybe one of those men at the diner."

"I don't think so." She chuckled. "Hey, are you calling because you've changed your mind about lunch?"

"No, I can't. Not today. I'll be by after I finish up to bring you into work, though."

"How about an early supper?"

"No, I don't think I'll be able to make that, either, but thanks for the offer. I've got a load of drywall coming in late, and I don't think I'd be able to make it over in time."

She turned in place, the phone cord going taut against her.

They make deliveries after five?

She didn't say that, however. Instead she said brightly:

"Oh, all right. I'll see you this evening."

There was a longer pause than she thought there would be.

"Will do," he finally answered.

"Kyle kept asking about you this afternoon," Denise said casually.

Good to his word, Taylor was waiting in the kitchen as she collected the last of her things, though he hadn't come by with much time to spare before she had to head off. They'd kissed only briefly, and he seemed a little more distant than usual, though he'd apologized for it, attributing it to the hassles at the work site.

"Oh, yeah? Where is the little guy?"

"Out back. I don't think he heard you come up. Let me go get him."

After Denise opened the back door and called for him, Kyle came running for the house. A moment later he burst inside.

"Hewwo, Tayer," he said, a big grin on his face. Ignoring Denise, he surged toward Taylor and jumped. Taylor caught him easily.

"Hey, little man. How was your day?"

Denise couldn't help but notice the difference in Taylor's demeanor as he lifted Kyle up to eye level.

"He's here!" Kyle shouted gleefully.

"Sorry I was so busy today," Taylor said, clearly meaning it. "Did you miss me, little man?"

"Yes," he answered. "I missed you."

It was the first time he'd answered a new question properly, without being told how to do it, shocking both of them into silence.

And for just a second, Denise's worries from the night before were forgotten.

If Denise expected that Kyle's simple statement would alleviate her concerns about Taylor, however, she was mistaken.

Not that it went bad right away. In fact, in many ways things didn't seem much different at all, at least for the next week or so. Though Taylor—still citing work as the reason—had stopped coming by in the afternoons, he nonetheless continued to drive Denise to and from the diner. They'd also made love the night Kyle had spoken.

Yet things were changing, that much seemed obvious. Nothing dramatic; it was more like the unwinding of twine, a gradual unfurling of everything that had been established during the summer. Less time together meant less time to simply hold each other or talk, and because of that, it was difficult for her to ignore the warning bells that had sounded the night they'd had dinner with Mitch and Melissa.

Even now, a week and a half later, the things that had been said that night still troubled her, but at the same time, she honestly wondered if she was making too much of the whole thing. Taylor hadn't really done anything wrong, so to speak, and that's what made his recent behavior difficult to figure out. He denied that anything was bothering him, he hadn't raised his voice; they still hadn't even had an argument. On Sunday they spent the afternoon on the river, as they'd done numerous times before. He was still great with Kyle, and more than once he'd reached for her hand as he drove her into work. On the surface, everything seemed the same. All that had really changed was a suddenly intense devotion to work, which he'd already explained. Yet . . .

Yet, what?

Sitting on the porch while Kyle played with his

trucks in the yard, Denise tried to put her finger on it. She'd been around long enough to know something about the pattern of relationships. She knew that the initial feelings associated with love were almost like an ocean wave in their intensity, acting as the magnetic force that drew two people together. It was possible to be washed away in the emotion, but the wave wouldn't last forever. It couldn't—nor was it meant to—but if two people were right for each other, a truer kind of love could last forever in its wake. At least, that's what she believed.

With Taylor, however, it almost seemed as if he'd been caught in the wave, unaware of what might be left behind, and now that he realized it, he was trying to fight his way back against the current. Not all the time . . . but *some* of the time, and that's what she seemed to be noticing lately. It was almost as if he were using work as an excuse to avoid the new realities of their situation.

Of course, if people start looking for something in particular, they're more likely to find it, and she hoped that was the case now. It might simply be that Taylor was preoccupied by work, and his reasons seemed genuine enough. At night, after picking her up, he looked tired enough for Denise to know that he wasn't lying to her about working all day.

So she kept as busy as she could, doing her best not to dwell on what might be happening between them. While Taylor seemed to be losing himself in his work, Denise threw herself into her work with Kyle with renewed energy. Now that he was speaking more, she began working on more complex phrases and ideas, while also teaching him other skills associated with school. One by one she began to teach him simple directions, and she worked with him to improve his coloring. She also introduced the concept of numbers, which seemed to make no sense to him whatever. She cleaned the house, she worked her shifts, she paid her bills—in short, she lived her life much the same as she had before she'd met Taylor McAden. But even though it was a life she was used to, she nonetheless spent most of the afternoons looking out the kitchen window, hoping to see him coming up the drive.

Usually, however, he didn't.

Despite herself, she heard Melissa's words once more.

All I know is that one day they seemed to be doing fine and the next thing you knew, it was over.

Denise shook her head, forcing the thought away. Though she didn't want to believe that about him—or them—it was getting more and more difficult not to do so. Incidents like yesterday's only reinforced her doubts.

She'd taken a bike ride with Kyle to the house Taylor was working on and had seen his truck parked out front. The owners were remodeling everything inside—the kitchen, the bathrooms, the living room—and the huge pile of scrap wood that had been torn from the interior of the house served as evidence that the project was a large one. Yet when she'd popped her head in to say hello, she'd been told by his employees that Taylor was out back, under the tree, eating his lunch. When she finally found him, he looked almost guilty, as if she'd caught him doing something wrong. Kyle, oblivious of his expression, ran over to him and Taylor stood to greet them.

"Denise?"

"Hey, Taylor. How are you?"

"Fine." He wiped his hands on his jeans. "I was just having a quick bite to eat," he said.

His lunch had come from Hardee's, which meant he'd had to drive *past* her house to the far side of town in order to buy it.

"I can see that," she said, trying not to let her concern show.

"So what are you doing here?"

Not exactly what I wanted to hear.

Putting on a brave face, she smiled. "I just wanted to stop by and say hello."

After a couple of minutes Taylor led them inside, describing the remodeling project almost as if he were talking to a stranger. Deep down, she suspected it was simply his way of avoiding the obvious question as to why he'd chosen to eat here instead of with her, as he'd done all summer long, or why he hadn't stopped in on his way past her house.

But later that night, when he'd picked her up to take her to work, he didn't say much at all.

The fact that it wasn't unusual anymore kept Denise on edge throughout her entire shift.

"It's just for a few days," Taylor said, shrugging.

They were sitting on the couch in the living room while Kyle watched a cartoon on television.

Another week had gone by and nothing had changed. Or rather, everything had changed. It all depended on her perspective, and right now Denise was leaning heavily toward the latter. It was Tuesday and he'd just come by to take her into work. Her pleasure at his earlier arrival had evaporated almost immediately when he'd informed her that he was leaving for a few days.

"When did you decide this?" Denise asked.

"Just this morning. A couple of the guys are going down and asked if I wanted to go along. South Carolina opens the hunting season two weeks earlier than we do around here, so I figured I'd head down with them. I feel like I need a break."

Are you talking about me or work?

"So you're leaving tomorrow?"

Taylor shifted slightly. "Actually, it's more like the middle of the night. We'll be leaving around three."

"You'll be exhausted."

"Nothing that a thermos of coffee can't fix."

"You probably shouldn't pick me up tonight," Denise offered. "You need a little sleep."

"Don't worry about that. I'll be there."

Denise shook her head. "No, I'll talk to Rhonda. She'll bring me home."

"Are you sure she won't mind?"

"She doesn't live that far from here. And it's not like she's been doing it very much lately."

Taylor slipped his arm around Denise, surprising her. He pulled her close. "I'll miss you."

"You will?" she said, hating the plaintive note in her voice.

"Of course. Especially around midnight. I'll probably wander out to my truck through force of habit."

Denise smiled, thinking he'd kiss her. Instead he turned away, motioning with his chin toward Kyle. "And I'll miss you, too, little man."

"Yes," Kyle said, eyes glued to the television.

"Hey, Kyle," Denise said, "Taylor's leaving for a few days."

"Yes," Kyle said again, obviously not listening.

Taylor crawled down from the couch, creeping on all fours toward Kyle.

"Are you ignoring me, Kyle?" he growled.

Once Taylor was close, Kyle realized his intent and squealed as he tried to get away. Taylor grabbed him easily, and they began to wrestle on the floor.

"Are you listening to me?" Taylor asked.

"He's wrestling!" Kyle shrieked, his arms and legs flailing. *(Ees wesswing!)*

"I'm gonna get you!" Taylor bellowed, and for the next few minutes there was pandemonium on the living room floor. When Kyle finally tired, Taylor let him pull away.

"Hey, when I get back, I'm going to take you to a baseball game. If that's okay with your mom, of course."

"Bessbaw game," Kyle repeated wonderingly.

"It's fine with me."

Taylor winked, first at Denise, then at Kyle.

"Did you hear that? Your mom said we can go."

"Bessbaw game!" Kyle cried, louder this time.

At least with Kyle he hasn't changed.

Denise glanced at the clock.

"It's about that time," she said, sighing.

"Already?"

Denise nodded, then rose from the couch to collect her things. A couple of minutes later they were on their way to the diner. When they arrived Taylor walked with Denise to the front door.

"Call me?" she said.

"I'll try," Taylor promised.

They stood gazing at each other for a moment before Taylor kissed her good-bye. Denise went in, hoping that the trip would help clear his mind of whatever had been bothering him.

Perhaps it did, but Denise had no way of knowing.

For the next four days she didn't hear from him at all.

She hated waiting for the phone to ring.

It wasn't like her to be this way; the experience a new one. In college her roommate sometimes refused to go out in the evenings because she thought her boyfriend might call. Denise always did her best to convince her roommate to come with her, usually to no avail, and then would head out to meet with different friends. When she explained why her roommate wasn't with them, each of them swore up and down that they'd never do something like that.

But here she was, and suddenly it didn't seem so easy to follow her own advice.

Not that she stopped living her life, as her roommate had done. She had too many responsibilities for that. But it didn't stop her from racing to the phone every time it rang and feeling disappointed when it wasn't Taylor.

The whole thing made her feel helpless, a sensation she detested. She wasn't, nor had she ever been, the helpless type, and she refused to become that now. So he hadn't called . . . so what? Because she was working, he couldn't reach her at home in the evenings, and he was probably spending all day in the woods. When was he supposed to call her? The middle of the night? At the crack of dawn? Sure, he could call and leave a message when she wasn't there, but why did she expect that?

And why did it seem so important?

I'm not going to be like this, she told herself. After running through the explanations again and convincing herself that they made sense, Denise forged on. On Friday she took Kyle to the park; on Saturday they went for a long walk in the woods. On Sunday she took Kyle to church, then spent the early part of the afternoon running other errands.

With enough money now to begin looking for a car (old and used, cheap, but hopefully reliable), she picked up two newspapers for their classified ads. Next stop was the grocery store, and she scanned the aisles, choosing carefully, not wanting to over-load herself for the trip back home. Kyle was staring at the cartoon figure of a crocodile printed on a box of cereal when Denise heard her name being called. Turning, she saw Judy pushing her cart toward her.

"I thought that was you," Judy said cheerfully. "How are you?"

"Hi, Judy. I'm fine."

"Hey, Kyle," Judy said.

"Hewwo, Miss Jewey," he whispered, still enamored with the box.

Judy moved her cart a little off to the side. "So what have you been doing lately? You and Taylor haven't come by for dinner in a while."

Denise shrugged, feeling a pang of unease. "Just the usual. Kyle's been keeping me pretty busy these days."

"They always do. How's he coming along?"

"He's had a good summer, that's for sure. Haven't you, Kyle?"

"Yes," he said quietly.

Judy turned her attention to him, beaming. "You sure are getting handsome. And I hear you're getting pretty good at baseball, too."

"Bessbaw," Kyle said, perking up, finally looking away from the box.

"Taylor's been helping him," Denise added. "Kyle really likes it."

"I'm glad. It's a lot easier for a mother to watch her children play baseball than football. I used to cover my eyes whenever Taylor played. He used to get crunched all the time—I could hear it in the stands, and it gave me nightmares."

Denise offered a strained laugh as Kyle stared, uncomprehending. Judy went on.

"I didn't expect to see you here. I figured you

would be with Taylor right now. He told me he was going to spend the day with you."

Denise ran her hand through her hair. "He did?"

Judy nodded. "Yesterday. He came by after he got home."

"So . . . he's back?"

Judy eyed her curiously. The next words came out carefully. "Didn't he call you?"

"No."

As she answered, Denise crossed her arms and turned away, trying not to show her discomfiture.

"Well, maybe you were already at work," Judy offered softly.

But even as she spoke the words, both of them knew it wasn't true.

Two hours after she got home, she spotted Taylor coming up the drive. Kyle was playing out front and immediately started for the truck, racing across the lawn. As soon as Taylor opened the door, Kyle jumped up into his arms.

Denise stepped out onto the porch with conflicting emotions, wondering if he'd come because Judy had called him after running into her at the store. Wondering if he would have come otherwise. Wondering why he hadn't called while he was gone, and wondering why, despite all that, her heart still leapt at the sight of him.

After Taylor put Kyle down, Kyle grabbed his hand and the two of them began making their way to the porch.

"Hey, Denise," Taylor said warily, almost as if he knew what she was thinking.

"Hi, Taylor."

When she made no move off the porch toward him, Taylor hesitated before closing the gap. He hopped up the steps as Denise took a small step backward, not meeting his eyes. When he tried to kiss her, she pulled back slightly.

"Are you mad at me?" he asked.

She looked around the yard before focusing on him. "I don't know, Taylor. Should I be?"

"Tayer!" Kyle said again. "Tayer's here!"

Denise reached for his hand. "Could you go inside for a minute, sweetie?"

"Tayer's here."

"I know. But do me a favor and leave us alone, okay?"

Reaching behind her, she opened the screen door and then led Kyle inside. After making sure he was occupied with his toys, she returned to the porch.

"So what's up?" Taylor asked.

"Why didn't you call while you were gone?"

Taylor shrugged. "I don't know . . . I guess I just didn't have the time. We were out all day and I was pretty worn by the time I got back to the motel. Is that why you're mad?"

Without answering, Denise went on.

"Why did you tell your mother you were going to spend the day here if you didn't plan on doing so?"

"What's with the questions? I did come by—what do you think I'm doing now?"

Denise exhaled sharply. "Taylor, what's going on with you?"

"What do you mean?"

"You know what I mean."

"No, I don't. Look, I got back into town yesterday, I was beat, and I had a bunch of things to take care of this morning. Why are you making such a big deal out of this?"

"I'm not making a big deal out of this—"

"Yes, you are. If you don't want me around, just tell me and I'll get in my truck and leave."

"It's not that I don't want you around, Taylor. I just don't know why you're acting the way you are."

"And how am I acting?"

Denise sighed, trying to put it into words.

"I don't know, Taylor . . . it's hard to explain. It's like you're not sure what you want anymore. With us, I mean."

Taylor's expression didn't change. "Where is all this coming from? What—did you talk to Melissa again?"

"No. Melissa has nothing to do with this," she said, becoming frustrated and a little angry. "It's just that you've changed, and sometimes I don't know what to think anymore."

"Just because I didn't call? I've already explained that." He took a step closer to her, his expression softening. "There just wasn't any time, that's all."

Not knowing whether to believe him, she hesitated. Meanwhile, as if sensing something wrong, Kyle pushed open the screen door.

"C'mon, guys," he said. "Let's go inside." *(C'mon, guys. Wess go issite)*

For a moment, however, they simply stood without moving.

"C'mon," Kyle prodded, reaching for Denise's shirt.

Denise looked down, forcing a smile, before glancing up again. Taylor was grinning, doing his best to break the ice.

"If you let me in, I'll give you a surprise."

As she thought about it, Denise crossed her arms. Behind Taylor, in the yard, a bluejay called from the fencepost. Kyle looked up expectantly.

"What is it?" she finally asked, giving in.

"It's in the truck. Let me go get it." Taylor stepped backward, watching her carefully, realizing that her comment meant she was going to let him stay. Before she changed her mind, he motioned toward Kyle. "C'mon, you can help."

As they walked back to the truck, Denise watched him, her emotions warring within her. Again, his explanations seemed reasonable, as they had for the past two weeks. Again, he was great with Kyle.

So why didn't she believe him?

After Kyle was asleep that night, Denise and Taylor sat together on the couch in the living room.

"So how did you like your surprise?"

"It was delicious. But you didn't have to fill my freezer."

"Well, mine was already full."

"Your mom might want some."

Taylor shrugged. "Hers is full, too."

"How often *do* you hunt?"

"As much as I can."

Before dinner, Taylor and Kyle had played catch in the yard; for dinner, Taylor had done the cooking, or rather part of it. Along with the venison, he'd brought some potato salad and baked beans from the supermarket. Now, relaxing for the first time, Denise felt better than she had for the past couple of weeks. The only light came from a small lamp in the corner, and a radio was playing softly in the background.

"So when are you taking Kyle to his baseball game?"

"I was thinking about Saturday, if that's okay. There's a game in Norfolk."

"Oh, that's his birthday," she said, disappointed. "I was planning to throw a little party for him."

"What time's the party?"

"Probably around noon or so. I still have to work that night."

"The game starts at seven. How about if I take Kyle with me while you're at work?"

"But I kind of wanted to go, too."

"Ah, let us have another boys night out. He'd enjoy it."

"I know he would. You've already got him hooked on that game."

"So is it all right if I bring him? I'd have him home in time to pick you up."

She brought her hands to her lap. "All right, you win. But don't keep him too long if he gets tired."

Taylor raised his hand. "Scouts' honor. I'll pick him up at five, and by the end of the night, he'll be eating hot dogs and peanuts and singing 'Take Me Out to the Ball Game.'"

She nudged him in the ribs. "Yeah, sure."

"Well, maybe you're right. But it won't be for lack of trying."

Denise rested her head against his shoulder. He smelled like salt and wind.

"You're a good guy, Taylor."

"I try."

"No, I'm serious. You've really made me feel special these last couple of months."

"So have you."

For a long moment, silence filled the living room like a living presence. She could feel Taylor's chest rising and falling with every breath. As wonderful as he'd been tonight, she couldn't escape the concerns that had been troubling her for the past two weeks.

"Do you ever think about the future, Taylor?"

He cleared his throat before answering.

"Sure, sometimes. Usually it doesn't go much beyond the next meal, though."

She took his hand in hers, weaving their fingers together.

"Do you ever think about us? About where we're going with all this, I mean?"

Taylor didn't respond, and Denise went on.

"I've just been thinking that we've been seeing each other for a few months now, but sometimes I don't know where you stand on all this. I mean, these last couple of weeks . . . I don't know . . . sometimes it feels like you're pulling away. You've been working such long hours that we haven't had much time to spend together, and then when you didn't call . . ."

She trailed off, leaving the rest unspoken, knowing she'd already said these things before. She felt his body stiffen just a little as she heard his answer coming out in a hoarse whisper.

"I care about you, Denise, if that's what you're asking."

She blinked, keeping her eyes closed for a long moment before opening them again.

"No, that's not it . . . or not all of it. I guess I just want to know if you're serious about us."

He pulled her closer, running his hand through her hair.

"Of course I'm serious. But like I said, my vision of the future doesn't extend all that far. I'm not the brightest guy you've ever met."

He smiled at his own joke. Hinting wasn't going to suffice. Denise took a deep breath.

"Well, when you think about the future, are Kyle and I in it?" she asked point-blank.

It was quiet in the living room as she waited for his answer. Licking her lips, she realized her mouth had gone dry. Eventually she heard him sigh.

"I can't predict the future, Denise. No one can. But like I said, I care about you and I care about Kyle. Isn't that enough for now?"

Needless to say, it wasn't the answer she had hoped for, but she lifted her head from his shoulder and met his eyes.

"Yeah," she lied. "That's enough for now."

* * *

Later that night, after making love and falling asleep together, Denise woke and saw Taylor standing by the window, looking toward the trees but obviously thinking of something else. She watched him for a long time, before he finally crawled back into bed. As he tugged at the sheet, Denise turned toward him.

"Are you okay?" she whispered.

Taylor seemed surprised at the sound of her voice. "I'm sorry. Did I wake you?"

"No. I've been awake for a while now. What's wrong?"

"Nothing. I just couldn't sleep."

"Are you worried about something?"

"No."

"Then why can't you sleep?"

"I don't know."

"Is it something I did?"

He drew a long breath. "No. There's nothing wrong with you at all."

With that, he cuddled against her, pulling her close.

The following morning, Denise woke alone.

This time Taylor wasn't sleeping on the couch. This time he didn't surprise her with breakfast. He'd slipped out unnoticed, and calls to his house went unanswered. For a while Denise debated stopping by his work site later in the day, but the memory of her last visit kept her from doing so.

Instead she reviewed their evening, trying to get a better read on it. For every positive thing, there seemed to be something negative as well. Yes, he'd come by . . . but that may have been because his mother had said something to him. Yes, he'd been great with Kyle . . . but then he might be focusing on Kyle to avoid what was really bothering him. Yes, he'd told her he cared about her . . . but not enough to even think about the future? They'd made love . . . but he was gone first thing in the morning, without so much as a good-bye.

Analysis, debate, dissection . . . she hated reducing their relationship to that. It seemed so eighties, so grounded in psychobabble, a bunch of words and actions that might or might not mean anything. No, scratch that. They did mean something, and that's exactly what the problem was.

Yet, deep down, she realized that Taylor wasn't lying when he said he cared about her. If there was one thing that kept her going, that was it. But . . .

So many buts these days.

She shook her head, doing her best to put it all out of her mind, at least until she saw him again. He'd be by later to take her into work, and though she didn't think there'd be time to talk to him about her feelings again, she felt sure that she would know more as soon as she saw him. Hopefully he'd come by a little early.

The rest of the morning and the afternoon passed slowly. Kyle was in one of his moods—not talking, grumpy, stubborn—and that didn't help her own mood, but it did keep her from focusing all day on Taylor.

A little after five she thought she heard his truck on the road out front, but as soon as she stepped outside, she realized it wasn't Taylor. Disappointed, she changed into her workclothes, made Kyle a grilled cheese sandwich, watched the news.

Time continued to pass. Six o'clock now. Where was he?

She turned off the television and tried unsuccessfully to get Kyle interested in a book. Then she got down on the floor and started playing with his Legos, but Kyle ignored her, focusing on his coloring book. When she tried to join him in that, he told her to go away. She sighed and decided it wasn't worth the effort.

Instead she straightened up the kitchen, killing time. Not much to do there, so she folded a basket of laundry and put it away.

Six-thirty and still no sign of him. Concern was giving way to a sinking sensation in her gut.

He's coming, she told herself. *Isn't he?*

Against her better judgment she dialed his

number, but there was no answer. She went back into the kitchen, got a glass of water, then returned to the living room window. Looking out, she waited.

And waited.

Fifteen minutes to get there or she'd be late.

Then ten.

At five until seven she was holding her glass so hard that her knuckles had turned white. Loosening her grip, she felt the blood rush back into her fingers. Her lips were pressed together when seven o'clock rolled around and she called Ray, apologizing and telling him she'd be a little late.

"We've got to go, Kyle," she said after hanging up the phone. "We're going to ride our bikes."

"No," he said.

"I'm not asking, Kyle, I'm telling you. Now move!"

Hearing the tone of her voice, Kyle put down his colors and started toward her.

Cursing, she went to the back porch to get her bike. Rolling it off the porch, she noticed it wasn't gliding smoothly, and she jerked it before finally learning what the problem was.

A flat tire.

"Oh, c'mon . . . not tonight," she said almost in disbelief. As if not trusting her eyes, she checked the tire with her finger, feeling it give as she applied only a little pressure.

"Damnit," she said, kicking at the wheel. She let

the bike fall onto a couple of cardboard boxes, then went into the kitchen again just as Kyle was coming out the door.

"We're not taking our bikes," she said through gritted teeth. "Come inside."

Kyle knew enough not to press her now and did as he was told. Denise went to the phone and tried Taylor again. Not in. She slammed the phone down, then thought of who else to call. Not Rhonda—she was already at the diner. But . . . Judy? She dialed her number and let it ring a dozen times before hanging up. Who else to call? Who else did she know? Really, only one other person. She opened the cupboard and found the phone book, then thumbed to the appropriate page. After punching in the right numbers, she breathed a sigh of relief as it was answered.

"Melissa? Hi, it's Denise."

"Oh, hey, how are you?"

"Actually, I'm not too good right now. I hate to do this, but I'm really calling for a favor."

"What can I do?"

"I know it's really inconvenient, but is it possible for you to drive me into work tonight?"

"Sure, when?"

"Now? I know it's last minute and I'm sorry, but the tires on my bike are flat—"

"Don't worry about it," Melissa interrupted. "I'll be there in ten minutes."

"I'll owe you one."

"No, you won't. It's not that big a deal. I just have to grab my purse and the keys."

Denise hung up, then called Ray again, explaining with more apologies that she'd be there by seven-thirty. This time Ray laughed.

"Don't worry about it, honey. You'll get here when you do. No rush—it's kind of quiet right now anyway."

Again she breathed a sigh of relief. Suddenly she noticed Kyle, watching her without saying a word.

"Mommy's not mad at you, sweetheart. I'm sorry for yelling."

She was, however, still angry at Taylor. Any relief she was feeling was counteracted by that. How could he?

Gathering her things, she waited for Melissa to show up, then led Kyle out the door when Melissa's car rolled up the drive. Melissa rolled down the window as the car slowed to a stop.

"Hey there. C'mon in, but excuse the mess. Kids are knee-deep in soccer these days."

Denise buckled Kyle into the backseat and was shaking her head as she got in the front seat. Soon the car had made its way down the drive and had turned onto the main road.

"So what happened?" Melissa asked. "You said your tire was flat?"

"Yeah, but I didn't expect that I'd have to ride my bike in the first place. Taylor didn't show up."

"And he said he would?"

Her question made Denise hesitate before answering. *Did* she ask him? Did she still have to?

"We didn't talk about it specifically," Denise admitted, "but he's been driving me all summer, so I just assumed he'd keep doing it."

"Did he call?"

"No."

Melissa's eyes darted in Denise's direction. "I take it things have changed between you two," she said.

Denise simply nodded. Melissa faced the road again and was quiet, leaving Denise alone with her thoughts.

"You knew this was going to happen, didn't you?"

"I've known Taylor a long time," Melissa answered carefully.

"So what's going on with him?"

Melissa sighed. "To tell you the truth, I don't know. I never have. But Taylor always seems to turn gun-shy whenever he starts getting serious with someone."

"But . . . why? I mean, we get along so well, he's great with Kyle . . ."

"I can't speak for Taylor, I really can't. Like I said, I don't really understand it."

"If you had to guess, though?"

Melissa hesitated. "It's not you, trust me. When we were at dinner, I wasn't kidding when I said that Taylor really cares about you. He does—more than I've seen him care about anyone. And Mitch says the same thing. But sometimes I think that Taylor doesn't feel that he deserves to be happy, so he sabotages every opportunity. I don't think he does it on purpose—I think it's more that he can't help himself."

"That doesn't make sense."

"Maybe not. But it's the way he is."

Denise pondered that. Up ahead she saw the diner. As Ray had said, from the looks of the parking lot there weren't too many people inside. Closing her eyes, she balled her fists in frustration.

"Again, the question is why?"

Melissa didn't respond right away. She turned on the blinker and began to slow the van.

"If you ask me . . . it's because of something that happened a long time ago."

Melissa's tone made her meaning obvious.

"His father?"

Melissa nodded, then let the words out slowly. "He blames himself for his father's death."

Denise felt her stomach dip, then roll. "What happened back then?"

The van came to a stop. "You should probably talk to him about that."

"I've tried . . ."

Melissa shook her head. "I know, Denise. We all have."

Denise worked her shift, barely concentrating, but because it was slow, it didn't really matter. Rhonda, who would normally have driven her home, left early, leaving Ray as the only option to bring her and Kyle home. Though she was thankful Ray was willing to drive her, he usually spent an hour after closing cleaning up, so it meant a later night than usual. Resigning herself to that, Denise was doing her own closing work when the front door opened just before it was time to lock up.

Taylor.

He stepped inside, waved to Ray, but didn't make a move toward Denise.

"Melissa called," he said, "and told me you might need a ride home."

She was at a loss for words. Angry, hurt, confused . . . yet undeniably still in love. Though the last part seemed to be fading with each passing day.

"Where were you earlier?"

Taylor shifted from one foot to the other. "I was working," he finally answered. "I didn't know you needed a ride today."

"You've been driving me for the last three months," she said, trying to keep her composure.

"But I was gone last week. You didn't ask me to

drive you in last night, so I just figured Rhonda would bring you in. I didn't realize that I was supposed to be your personal chauffeur."

Her eyes narrowed. "That's not fair, Taylor, and you know it."

Taylor crossed his arms. "Hey, I didn't come here to get yelled at. I'm here in case you need a ride home. Do you want one or not?"

Denise pursed her lips together. "No," she said simply.

If Taylor was surprised, he didn't show it.

"All right, then," he said. He turned to look at the walls, then the floor, then back to her. "I'm sorry about earlier, if that means anything."

It does and it doesn't, Denise thought. But she didn't say anything. When Taylor realized she wasn't going to speak, he turned away, pulling the door open again.

"Do you need a ride tomorrow?" he asked over his shoulder.

Again she thought about it. "Will you be there?"

He winced. "Yes," he answered softly. "I will."

"Then, okay," she said.

He nodded, then made his way out the door. Turning around, Denise saw Ray scrubbing the counter as if his life depended on it.

"Ray?"

"Yes, honey?" he answered, pretending that he

hadn't been paying attention to what was going on.

"Can I take tomorrow evening off?"

He glanced up from the counter, looking at her as he probably would have looked at his own child.

"I think you'd better," he answered honestly.

Taylor came by thirty minutes before her shift was supposed to start and was surprised when she opened the door dressed in jeans and a short-sleeved blouse. It had been raining most of the day, and the temperature was in the sixties, too cool for shorts. Taylor, meanwhile, was clean and dry—it was obvious he'd changed before coming over.

"C'mon in," she said.

"Aren't you supposed to be dressed for work?"

"I'm not working tonight," she said evenly.

"You're not?"

"No," she replied. Taylor followed her inside, curious.

"Where's Kyle?"

Denise sat. "Melissa said she'd watch him for a while."

Taylor stopped, looking around uncertainly, and Denise patted the couch.

"Sit down."

Taylor did as she suggested. "So what's up?"

"We've got to talk," she began.

"About what?"

She couldn't help but shake her head at that. "What's going on with you?"

"Why? Is there something I don't know about?" he said, grinning nervously.

"This isn't the time for jokes, Taylor. I took tonight off in the hopes that you'd help me understand what the problem is."

"Are you talking about what happened yesterday? I said I was sorry, and I mean it."

"It's not that. I'm talking about you and me."

"Didn't we just talk about this the other night?"

Denise sighed in exasperation. "Yeah, we talked. Or rather, I talked. But you didn't say much at all."

"Sure I did."

"No, you didn't. But then, you never have. You just talk about surface things, never the things that are really bothering you."

"That's not true—"

"Then why are you treating me—us—differently than you used to?"

"I'm not . . ."

Denise stopped him by raising her hands.

"You don't come over much anymore, you didn't call while you were away, you snuck out of here yesterday morning, then didn't show up later . . ."

"I've already explained that."

"Yes, you did—you explained each and every situation. But don't you see the pattern?"

He turned toward the clock on the wall, staring at it, stubbornly avoiding her question.

Denise ran her hand through her hair. "But more than that, you don't talk to me anymore. And I'm beginning to wonder whether you ever really did."

Taylor glanced back at her, and Denise caught his gaze. She'd been down this road before with him—the denial of any problem—and didn't want to go there again. Hearing Melissa's voice, she decided to go to the heart of the matter. She took a deep breath and let it out slowly.

"What happened to your father?"

Immediately she saw him tense.

"Why does that matter?" he asked, suddenly wary.

"Because I think that it might have something to do with the way you've been acting lately."

Instead of responding, Taylor shook his head, his mood changing to something just short of anger.

"What gives you that idea?"

She tried again. "It doesn't really matter. I just want to know what happened."

"We've already talked about this," he said curtly.

"No, we haven't. I've asked you about him, and you've told me some things. But you haven't told me the whole story."

Taylor gritted his teeth. He was opening and

closing one of his hands, without seeming to realize it. "He died, okay? I've already told you that."

"And?"

"And what?" he burst out. "What do you want me to say?"

She reached toward his hand and took it in hers. "Melissa said that you blame yourself."

Taylor pulled his hand away. "She doesn't know what she's talking about."

Denise kept her voice calm. "There was a fire, right?"

Taylor closed his eyes, and when he opened them again, she saw a kind of fury there that she had never seen before.

"He died, that's all. That's all there is."

"Why won't you answer me?" she asked. "Why can't you talk to me?"

"Christ!" he spat out, his voice booming off the walls. "Can't you just drop it?"

His outburst surprised her, and her eyes widened a little.

"No, I can't," she persisted, her heart suddenly racing. "Not if it's something that concerns us."

He stood from the couch.

"It doesn't concern *us!* What the hell is all this about, anyway? I'm getting sick and tired of you grilling me all the time!"

She leaned forward, hands extended. "I'm not

grilling you, Taylor, I—I'm just trying to talk," she stammered.

"What do you want from me?" he said, not listening, his face flushed.

"I just want to know what's going on so we can work on it."

"Work on what? We're not married, Denise," he said. "Where the hell do you get off trying to pry?"

The words stung. "I'm not prying," she said defensively.

"Sure you are. You're trying to get into my head so you can try to fix what's wrong. But nothing's wrong, Denise, at least not with me. I am who I am, and if you can't handle it, maybe you shouldn't try."

He glared at her from where he was standing, and Denise took a deep breath. Before she could say anything else, Taylor shook his head and took a step backward.

"Look, you don't need a ride and I don't want to be here right now. So think about what I said, okay? I'm getting out of here."

With that, Taylor spun and made his way to the door, leaving the house as Denise sat on the couch, stunned.

Think about what I said?

"I would," she whispered, "if you'd made any sense at all."

* * *

The next few days passed uneventfully, except, of course, for the flowers that arrived the day after their argument.

The note was simple:

I'm sorry for the way I acted. I just need a couple days to think things through. Can you give me that?

Part of her wanted to throw the flowers away, another part wanted to keep them. Part of her wanted to end the relationship right now, another part wanted to plead for another chance. *So what else is new?* she thought to herself.

Outside her window, the storm had returned. The sky was gray and cold, rain sheeting itself against the windows, strong winds bending the trees almost double.

She lifted the receiver and called Rhonda, then turned her attention to the classified ads. This weekend she'd buy herself a car.

Maybe then she wouldn't feel so trapped.

On Saturday Kyle celebrated his birthday. Melissa, Mitch and their four boys, and Judy were the only ones in attendance. When asked about Taylor, Denise explained that Taylor was coming by later to take Kyle to a baseball game, which was why he wasn't here now.

"Kyle's been looking forward to it all week," she said, down-playing any problem.

It was only because of Kyle that she didn't worry. Despite everything, Taylor hadn't changed at all when it concerned her son. He would come, she knew. There was no way on earth that he wouldn't.

He'd be here around five, he'd take Kyle to the game.

The hours ticked by, more slowly than usual.

At twenty past five, Denise was playing catch with Kyle in the yard, a pit in her stomach and on the verge of crying.

Kyle looked adorable dressed in jeans and a baseball hat. With his mitt—a new one, courtesy of Melissa—he caught Denise's latest toss. Gripping the ball, he held it out in front of him, looking at Denise.

"Taylor's coming," he said. *(Tayer's cummeen)*

Denise glanced at her watch for the hundredth time, then swallowed hard, feeling nauseated. She'd called three times; he wasn't home. Nor, it seemed, was he on his way.

"I don't think so, honey."

"Taylor's coming," he repeated.

That one brought tears to her eyes. Denise approached him and squatted to be at eye level.

"Taylor is busy. I don't think he's going to take

you to the game. You can come with Mommy to work, okay?"

Saying the words hurt more than it seemed possible.

Kyle looked up at her, the words slowly sinking in.

"Taylor's gone," he finally said.

Denise reached out for him. "Yes, he is," she said sadly.

Kyle dropped the ball and walked past her, toward the house, looking as dejected as she'd ever seen him.

Denise lowered her face into her hands.

Taylor came by the following morning, a wrapped gift under his arm. Before Denise could get to the door, Kyle was outside, reaching for the package, the fact that he hadn't shown up yesterday already forgotten. If children had one advantage over their elders, Denise reflected, it was their ability to forgive quickly.

But she wasn't a child. She stepped outside, her arms crossed, obviously upset. Kyle had taken the gift and was already unwrapping it, ripping off the paper in an excited frenzy. Deciding not to say anything until he was done, Denise watched as Kyle's eyes grew wider.

"Legos!" he cried joyfully, holding up the box for Denise to see. *(Weggoes)*

"It sure is," she said, agreeing with him. Without

looking at Taylor, she brushed a loose strand of hair from her eyes. "Kyle, say, 'Thank you.'"

"Kenk you," he said, staring at the box.

"Here," Taylor said, removing a small pocketknife from his pants and squatting, "let me open that for you."

He cut the tape on the box and removed the cover. Kyle reached in and pulled out a set of wheels for one of the model cars.

Denise cleared her throat. "Kyle? Why don't you take that inside. Mommy's got to talk to Taylor."

She held open the screen door, and Kyle dutifully did as she'd asked. Setting the box on the coffee table, he was immediately engrossed in the pieces.

Taylor stood, not making a move toward her.

"I'm sorry," he said sincerely. "There's really no excuse. I just forgot about the game. Was he upset?"

"You could say that."

Taylor's expression was pained. "Maybe I could make it up to him. There's another game next weekend."

"I don't think so," she said quietly. She motioned to the chairs on the porch. Taylor hesitated before moving to take a seat. Denise sat as well but didn't face him. Instead she watched a pair of squirrels hopping across the yard, collecting acorns.

"I screwed up, didn't I?" Taylor said honestly.

Denise smiled wryly. "Yeah."

"You have every right to be angry with me."

Denise finally turned to face him. "I was. Last night, if you had come into the diner, I would have thrown a frying pan at you."

The corners of Taylor's mouth upturned slightly, then straightened again. He knew she wasn't finished.

"But I'm over that. Now I'm less angry than I am resigned."

Taylor looked at her curiously as Denise exhaled slowly. When she spoke again, her voice was low and soft.

"For the last four years, I had my life with Kyle," she began. "It's not always easy, but it's predictable, and there's something to be said for that. I know how I'm going to spend today and tomorrow and the day after that, and it helps me keep some semblance of control. Kyle needs me to do that, and I need to do it for him because he's all I've got in the world. But then, you showed up."

She smiled, but it couldn't mask the sadness in her eyes. Still, Taylor was silent.

"You were so good to him, right from the beginning. You treated Kyle differently than anyone else ever has, and that meant the world to me. But even more than that, you were good to me."

Denise paused, picking at a knot in the armrest of her old wooden rocker, her eyes focused inward.

"When we first met, I didn't want to get involved with anyone. I didn't have the time or the energy, and even after the carnival, I wasn't sure that I was ready for it. But you were so good with Kyle. You did things with him that no one else had taken the time to do, and I got swept up in that. And little by little, I found myself falling in love with you."

Taylor put both hands in his lap as he stared at the floor. Denise shook her head wistfully.

"I don't know . . . I grew up reading fairy tales, and maybe that had something to do with it."

Denise leaned back in her rocker, gazing at him from below lowered lashes.

"Do you remember that night we met? When you rescued my son? After that, you delivered my groceries and then taught Kyle how to play catch. It was like you were the handsome prince of my girlhood fantasies, and the more I got to know you, the more I came to believe it. And part of me still does. You're everything I've ever wanted in a man. But as much as I care for you, I don't think you're ready for me or my son."

Taylor rubbed his face wearily before staring up at her with pain-darkened eyes.

"I'm not blind to what's been happening with us these last few weeks. You're pulling away from me—from both of us—no matter how much you try to deny it. It's obvious, Taylor. What I don't understand is why you're doing it."

"I've been busy at work," Taylor began halfheartedly.

"That may be true, but it's not the whole truth."

Denise took a deep breath, willing her voice not to break. "I know you're holding something back, and if you can't, or don't, want to talk about it, there's not much I can do. But whatever it is, it's driving you away."

She stopped, her eyes welling with tears. "Yesterday, you hurt me. But worse than that, you hurt Kyle. He waited for you, Taylor. For two hours. He jumped up every time a car went by, thinking it was you. But it wasn't, and finally even he knew that everything had changed. He didn't say a single thing the rest of the night. Not one word."

Taylor, pale and shaken, seemed incapable of speech. Denise looked toward the horizon, a single tear drifting down her cheek.

"I can put up with a lot of things. Lord knows, I already have. The way you've been drawing me in, pushing me away, drawing me in again. But I'm a grown-up, and I'm old enough to choose whether I want to keep letting that happen. But if the same thing should start happening with Kyle . . ." She trailed off, swiping at her cheek.

"You're a wonderful person, Taylor. You've got so much to offer someone, and I hope that one day you'll finally meet the person who can make sense of all that pain you're carrying around. You deserve that. In my heart, I know you didn't mean to hurt Kyle. But I can't take the chance of that happening again, especially when you're not serious about our future together."

"I'm sorry," he said thickly.

"I am, too."

He reached for her hand. "I don't want to lose you." His voice was almost a whisper.

Seeing his haggard expression, she took his hand and squeezed it, then reluctantly let it go. She could feel the tears again, and she fought them back.

"But you don't want to keep me, either, do you?"

To that, he had no response.

Once he was gone, Denise drifted like a zombie through the house, holding on to her self-control by a thread. She'd cried most of the night already, knowing what was to come. She'd been strong, she reminded herself as she sat on the living room couch; she'd done the right thing. She couldn't allow him to hurt Kyle again. She wasn't going to cry.

Damnit, not anymore.

But watching Kyle play with his Legos and knowing that Taylor would no longer be coming by the house made a sickening knot rise in her throat.

"I'm not going to cry," she said aloud, the words coming out like a mantra. "I'm not going to cry."

With that, she broke down and wept for the next two hours.

"So you went ahead and ended it, huh?" Mitch said, clearly disgusted.

They were in a bar, a dingy place that opened its doors for breakfast, usually to a waiting crowd of three or four regulars. Now, however, it was late in the evening. Taylor hadn't called until after eight; Mitch had shown up an hour later. Taylor had started drinking without him.

"It wasn't me, Mitch," he said defensively. "She's the one who called it off. You can't pin this one on me."

"And I suppose it just came out of the blue, right? You had nothing to do with it."

"It's over, Mitch. What do you want me to say?"

Mitch shook his head. "You know, Taylor, you're a piece of work. You sit here thinking you've got it all figured out, but you don't understand anything."

"Thanks for your support, Mitch."

Mitch glared at him. "Don't give me that crap. You don't need my support. What you need is someone to tell you to get your ass back over there and fix whatever it was you did wrong."

"You don't understand—"

"Like hell I don't!" Mitch said, slamming his beer glass onto the table. "Who do you think you are? You think I don't know? Hell, Taylor, I probably know you better than you know yourself. You think you're the only one with a shitty past? You think you're the only one who's always trying to change it? I have news for you. Everyone has crap in their background, everyone has things they wish they could undo. But most people don't go around doing their best to screw up their present lives because of it."

"I didn't screw up," Taylor said angrily. "Didn't you hear what I said? *She*'s the one who ended it. Not me. Not this time."

"I tell you what, Taylor. You can go to the goddamn grave thinking that, but both you and I know, it ain't the whole truth. So get back over there and try to salvage it. She's the best thing that ever happened to you."

"I didn't ask you to come here so you can give me some of your advice—"

"Well, you're getting the best advice I've ever given you. Do me a favor and listen to it, okay? Don't ignore it this time. Your father would have wanted you to."

Taylor squinted at Mitch, everything suddenly tensing. "Don't bring him into this. You don't want to go there."

"Why, Taylor? Are you afraid of something? Afraid that his ghost is gonna start hovering around us or knocking our beers off the table?"

"That's enough," Taylor growled.

"Don't forget, I knew your father, too. I knew what a great guy he was. He was a guy who loved his family, loved his wife, loved his son. He would have been disappointed by what you're doing now, I can guarantee it."

The blood drained from Taylor's face and he gripped his glass hard.

"Screw you, Mitch."

"No, Taylor. You've already done that to yourself. If I did it, too, it would just be piling on."

"I don't need this crap," Taylor snapped, rising from the table. He started for the door. "You don't even know who I am."

Mitch pushed the table away from his body, knocking over the beers and causing a few heads to turn. The bartender looked up from his conversation as Mitch stood and came up behind Taylor, grabbing him roughly by his shirt and spinning him around.

"I don't know you? Hell, I know you! You're a goddamn coward, is what you are! You're afraid of living because you think it means giving up this cross you've been carrying around your whole life. But this time, you've gone too far. You think you're the only one in the world with feelings? You think you'll just walk away from Denise and everything's going to go back to normal now? You think you'll be happier? You won't, Taylor. You won't let yourself do that. And this time, you aren't just hurting one person, did you ever think of that? It isn't just Denise—you're hurting a little boy! God almighty, doesn't that mean anything to you? What the hell would your father say to that, huh? 'Good job, son'? 'I'm proud of you, son'? Not a chance. Your father would be sickened, just like I am now."

Taylor, his face white, grabbed Mitch and lifted him, driving him backward into the jukebox. Two men scattered off their stools, away from the melee, as the bartender rushed to the far end of the bar. After pulling out a baseball bat, he started back toward them. Taylor raised his fist.

"What are you gonna do? Hit me?" Mitch taunted.

"Knock it off!" the bartender shouted. "Take that shit outside, now!"

"Go ahead," Mitch said. "I don't really give a damn."

Biting his lip so hard that it began to bleed, Taylor pulled his arm back, ready to strike, his hand shaking.

"I'll always forgive you, Taylor," Mitch said almost calmly. "But you gotta forgive yourself, too."

Taylor, hesitating, struggling, finally released Mitch and turned away, toward the faces staring at him. The bartender was at his side, bat in hand, waiting to see what Taylor was going to do.

Stifling the curses in his throat, he strode out the door.

Chapter 23

Just before midnight Taylor returned home to a flickering message on his answering machine. Since leaving Mitch he'd been alone, doing his best to clear his mind, and had sat on the bridge where he'd plunged into the river only a few months earlier. That night, he realized, was the first night he'd needed Denise. It seemed like a lifetime ago.

Guessing that Mitch had left him a message, Taylor walked to the answering machine, regretting his outburst at his friend, and pressed the play button. To his surprise, it wasn't Mitch.

It was Joe from the fire department, his voice straining to stay calm.

"There's a warehouse fire, on the outskirts of town. Arvil Henderson's place. A big one—everyone in Edenton has been called, and additional trucks and crews are being requested from the surrounding counties. Lives are in danger. If you get the message in time, we'll need your help . . ."

The message had been left twenty-four minutes ago.

Without listening to the rest of the message, Taylor hung up the phone and raced to the truck, cursing himself for having turned off his cell phone when he left the bar. Henderson's was a regional wholesaler of housepaint and one of the larger businesses in Chowan County. Trucks were loaded day and night; every hour of the day saw at least a dozen people working inside the warehouse.

It would take him about ten minutes to get there.

Everyone else was probably already on the scene, and he'd be rolling in some thirty minutes late. Those thirty minutes could mean the difference between life and death to any number of trapped people inside.

Others were fighting for their lives while he'd been out feeling sorry for himself.

Gravel shot from his tires as he turned around in the driveway, barely slowing as he turned on the road. His tires squealed and the engine roared as Taylor punched the gas, still cursing. The truck slid through numerous turns on the way to Henderson's as he took every shortcut he knew. When he hit a straight stretch of road, he accelerated until he was traveling at nearly ninety miles an hour. Tools rattled in the back; he heard a thump of something heavy as it slid across the bed of the truck while it made another turn.

Minutes ticked by, long minutes, eternal minutes.

In time he could see the sky glowing orange in the distance, an ungodly color in the darkness. He slammed his hand on the steering wheel when he realized how large the fire was. Over the sound of the engine, he could hear the distant wailing of sirens.

He slammed on the brakes, the truck tires almost refusing to catch, then fishtailed onto the road that ran toward Henderson's. The air was already thick with greasy black smoke, fueled by the petroleum in the paint. Without a breeze, the smoke hung languidly all around him; he could see the flames rising from the warehouse. It was blazing violently when Taylor made a final turn, coming to a halt, his tires screeching.

Pandemonium everywhere.

Three pumper trucks were already on the scene . . . hoses hooked to hydrants, blowing water toward one side of the building . . . the other side still undamaged but looking as if it wouldn't stay that way for long . . . two ambulances, their lights flashing on and off . . . five people on the ground being attended by others . . . two others being helped out of the warehouse, supported on either side by men who seemed as weak as they were . . .

As he scanned the hellish scene, he noticed Mitch's car off to one side, although it was impossible to make him out in the chaos of bodies and vehicles.

Taylor leapt from the truck and scrambled toward Joe, who was barking orders, trying and failing to gain control of the situation. Another fire truck arrived, this one from Elizabeth City; six more men jumped out and started unwinding the hose while another ran toward another hydrant.

Joe turned and saw Taylor rushing toward him. His face was covered with black soot, and he pointed toward the hook and ladder.

"Get your gear!" he shouted.

Taylor followed his orders, climbing up and pulling out a suit, then tearing off his boots. Two minutes later, fully outfitted, Taylor ran toward Joe again.

As he moved, the evening was suddenly shattered by a series of explosions, dozens, one right after the other. A black cloud mushroomed from the center of the building, the smoke curling as if a bomb had gone off. People nearest the building hit the ground as burning portions of the roof and building shot toward them, deadly in their aim.

Taylor dove and covered his head.

Flames were everywhere now, the building being consumed from within. More explosions erupted, rocketing debris as firemen scattered backward, away from the heat. From the inferno emerged two men, limbs on fire; hoses were trained on them, and they fell to the ground, writhing.

Taylor pushed up from the ground and ran toward

the heat, toward the blaze, toward the men on the ground . . . Seventy yards, running wildly, the world suddenly resembling a war zone . . . more explosions as paint can after paint can exploded inside, the fire raging out of control . . . breathing difficult because of the fumes . . . an external wall suddenly collapsed outward, barely missing the men.

Taylor squinted, his eyes tearing and burning as he finally reached the two men. Both were unconscious, flames lapping within inches of them now. He grabbed both of them by the wrists and began to pull them back, away from the flames. The heat from the fire had melted part of their gear, and Taylor could see them almost smoldering as he dragged them to safety. Another fireman arrived, someone Taylor didn't know, and took charge of one of the wounded men. They doubled their pace, pulling them toward the ambulances as a paramedic rushed over.

Only one part of the building was left untouched now, though judging by the smoke pouring through the small rectangular windows that had been blown out, that section was getting ready to blow as well.

Joe was motioning frantically for everyone to get back, to move away to a safe distance. No one could hear him above the roar.

The paramedic arrived and immediately knelt before the wounded men. Their faces were singed and their clothes were still smoldering, the oil-fired flames having defeated the fire-retardant suits. The paramedic pulled a pair of sharp scissors from his box and began to cut open the suit of one of the firemen, peeling it off. Another paramedic appeared from nowhere and began the same procedure on the other man.

Both were moaning in agony now, conscious again. As their suits were cut, Taylor helped to tear them away from the men's skin. Up one leg, then the next, followed by their arms and torso. They were helped into a sitting position, and their suits were stripped from their bodies. One man had worn jeans and two shirts beneath; he'd escaped largely unburned except for his arms. The second, however, had only worn a T-shirt beneath his suit—that too had to be cut away from his skin. His back was blistered with second-degree burns.

Looking up from the injured men, Taylor saw Joe waving wildly again; three men were crowded around him, and three others were closing in. It was then that Taylor turned toward the building and knew that something was terribly wrong.

He rose and began to rush toward Joe, a wave of nausea breaking over him. Drawing near, he heard the soul-numbing words.

"They're still inside! Two men! Over there!"

Taylor blinked, a memory rising from the ashes.

A boy, nine years old, in the attic, calling from the window . . .

It stopped him cold. Taylor looked toward the flaming ruins of the warehouse, now only partially standing; then, as if in a dream, he started toward the only portion of the building left intact, the part that housed the offices. Gaining speed, he rushed past the men holding the hoses, ignoring their calls to stop.

The warehouse flames engulfed nearly everything; their flames had spread to the surrounding trees, and those were now ablaze. Straight ahead was a doorway that had been torn open by the firemen, and black smoke poured out the opening.

He was at the door before Joe saw him and began screaming for him to stop.

Unable to hear above the roar, Taylor rushed through the door, propelled like a cannonball, his gloved hand over his face, flames lapping at him. Nearly blind, he turned toward the left, hoping nothing would block his way. His eyes burned as he inhaled a breath of acrid air and held it.

Fire was everywhere, beams crashing down, the air itself becoming poisonous.

He knew he could hold his breath a minute, no longer.

To the left he charged, the smoke almost impenetrable, fires providing the only light.

Everything blazed with unearthly fury. The walls, the ceiling . . . above him, the splintering sound of a beam crashing. Taylor leapt aside instinctively as part of the ceiling collapsed beside him.

His lungs straining, he moved quickly toward the south end of the building, the only area left standing. He could feel his body was growing weaker; his lungs seemed to be folding in as he staggered forward. To his left he spied a window, the glass unshattered, and he lurched toward it. From his belt he removed his ax and broke the window in one swift motion, then immediately leaned his head out, drawing a new breath.

Like a living being, the fire seemed to sense the new influx of oxygen, and seconds later the room exploded behind him with new fury.

The scorching heat of the new flames propelled him away from the window, toward the south again.

After the sudden surge, the fire receded momentarily, a few seconds at most. But it was enough for Taylor to get his bearings—and to see the figure of a man lying on the ground. From the shape of his gear, Taylor could see it was a fireman.

Taylor staggered toward him, narrowly avoiding another falling beam. Trapped in the last standing corner of the warehouse now, he could see the wall of flames closing in around them.

Almost out of breath again, Taylor reached the man. Bending over, he grabbed the man's wrist and then hauled him up over his shoulder, struggling back to the only window he could see.

Moving on instinct alone, he rushed toward the window, his head growing light, closing his eyes to keep the smoke and heat from damaging them any further. He made it to the window and in one quick motion threw the man through the shattered window, where he landed in a heap. His damaged vision, however, prevented him from seeing the other firemen rushing toward the body.

All Taylor could do was hope.

He took two harsh breaths and coughed violently. Then, taking another breath, he turned and made his way inside one more time.

Everything was a roaring hell of acid-tongued flames and suffocating smoke.

Taylor pushed through the wall of heat and smoke, moving as if guided by a hidden hand.

One more man inside.

A boy, nine years old, in the attic, calling from the window that he was afraid to jump . . .

Taylor closed one of his eyes when it began to spasm in pain. As he pushed forward, the wall of the office collapsed, topping in on itself like a stack of cards. The roof above him sagged as flames sought out new weakness and began to surge upward, toward the gap in the ceiling.

One more man inside.

Taylor felt as if he were dying inside. His lungs

screamed for him to take a breath of the burning, poisonous air around him. But he ignored the need, growing dizzier.

Smoke snaked around him and Taylor dropped to his knees, his other eye beginning to spasm now. Flames surrounded him in three directions, but Taylor pressed onward, heading for the only area where someone might still be alive.

Crawling now, the heat like a sizzling anvil . . .

It was then that Taylor knew he was going to die.

Hardly conscious, he continued to crawl.

He started to black out, could feel the world beginning to slip away.

Take a breath! his body screamed.

Crawling, inching forward, praying automatically. Ahead of him, still more flames, an unending wall of rippling heat.

It was then that he came across the body.

With smoke completely surrounding him, he couldn't tell who it was. But the man's legs were trapped beneath a collapsed wall.

Feeling his insides weakening, his vision going black, Taylor groped the body like a blind man, seeing it in his mind's eye.

The man lay on his stomach and chest, the arms out to either side. His helmet was still fastened firmly on his head. Two feet of rubble covered his legs from the thighs down.

Taylor went to the head of the body, gripped both arms, and pulled. The body didn't budge.

With the last vestiges of his strength, Taylor stood and painstakingly began to move the rubble off the man. Two-by-fours, drywall, pieces of plywood, one item of charred debris after another.

His lungs were about to explode.

Flames closing in now, licking at the body.

Piece by piece, he lifted off the wreckage; luckily none of the pieces were too heavy to move. But the exertion had taken nearly everything out of him. He moved to the head of the body and tugged.

This time the body moved. Taylor put his weight into it and pulled again, but out of air completely, his body reacted instinctively.

Taylor expelled his breath and inhaled sharply, strangled for air.

His body was wrong.

Taylor suddenly went dizzy, coughing violently. He let go of the man and rose, staggering in pure panic now, still without air in the oxygen-depleted room; all his training, every conscious thought, had seemingly evaporated in a rush of unadulterated survival instinct.

He stumbled back the way he had come, his legs moving of their own volition. After a few yards, however, he stopped, as if waking forcibly from a daze. Turning back, he took a step in the direction of the body. At that second the world suddenly exploded into fire. Taylor nearly fell.

Flames engulfed him, setting his suit on fire, as he lunged for the window. He threw himself blindly through the opening. The last thing he felt was his body hitting the earth with a thud, a scream of despair dying on his lips.

Chapter 24

Only one person died that early Monday morning.

Six men were injured, Taylor among them, and all were taken to the hospital, where they were treated. Three of the men were able to leave that night. Two of the men who stayed were the ones Taylor had helped drag to safety—they were to be transferred to the burn unit at Duke University in Durham as soon as the helicopter arrived.

Taylor lay alone in the darkness of his hospital room, his thoughts filled with the man he had left behind who had died. One eye was heavily bandaged, and he was lying on his back, staring up at the ceiling with the other, when his mother arrived.

She sat with him in his hospital room for an hour, then left him alone with his thoughts.

Taylor McAden never said a word.

Denise showed up Tuesday morning, when visiting hours began. As soon as she arrived, Judy looked up from her chair, her eyes red and exhausted. When Judy called, Denise had come immediately, Kyle in tow. Judy took Kyle's hand and silently led him downstairs.

Denise entered Taylor's room, seating herself where Judy had been. Taylor turned his head the other way.

"I'm sorry about Mitch," she said gently.

Chapter 25

The funeral was to be held three days later, on Friday.

Taylor had been released from the hospital on Thursday and went straight to Melissa's.

Melissa's family had come in from Rocky Mount, and the house was filled with people Taylor had met only a few times in the past: at the wedding, at baptisms, and at various holidays. Mitch's parents and siblings, who lived in Edenton, also spent time at the house, though they all left in the evening.

The door was open as Taylor stepped inside, looking for Melissa.

As soon as he saw her across the living room, his eyes began to burn and he started toward her. She was talking to her sister and brother-in-law, standing by the framed family photo on the wall, when she saw him. She immediately broke off her conversation and made her way toward him. When they were close he wrapped his arms around her, putting his head on her shoulder as he cried into her hair.

"I'm so sorry," he said, "I'm so, so, sorry."

All he could do was to repeat himself. Melissa began to cry as well. The other family members left them alone in their grief.

"I tried, Melissa . . . I tried. I didn't know it was him . . ."

Melissa couldn't speak, having already learned what had happened from Joe.

"I couldn't . . . ," he finally choked out, before breaking down completely.

They stood holding each other for a long, long time.

He left an hour later, without talking to anyone else.

The funeral service, held at Cypress Park Cemetery, was overflowing with people. Every fireman from the surrounding three counties, as well as every law enforcement official, made an appearance, as did friends and family. The crowd was among the largest ever for a service in Edenton; since Mitch had grown up here and ran the hardware store, nearly everyone in town came to pay their respects.

Melissa and her four children sat weeping in the front row.

The minister spoke a little while before reciting the Twenty-third Psalm. When it came time for eulogies, the minister stepped aside, allowing close friends and family to come forward.

Joe, the fire chief, went first and spoke of Mitch's dedication, his bravery, and the respect he would always hold in his heart. Mitch's older sister also said a few words, sharing a few remembrances from their childhood. When she finished, Taylor stepped forward.

"Mitch was like a brother to me," he began, his voice cracking, his eyes cast downward. "We grew up together, and every good memory I have growing up included him. I remember once, when we were twelve, Mitch and I were fishing when I stood up too quickly in the dinghy. I slipped and hit my head, then fell into the water. Mitch dove in and pulled me to the surface. He saved my life that day, but when I finally came to, he only laughed. 'You made me lose the fish, you clumsy oaf,' was the only thing he said."

Despite the solemnity of the afternoon, a low murmur of chuckles rose, then faded away.

"Mitch—what can I say? He was the kind of man who added something to everything he touched and everyone he came in contact with. I was envious of his view on life. He saw it all as a big game, where the only way to win was to be good to other people, to be able to look at yourself in the mirror and like what you see. Mitch . . ."

He closed his eyes hard, pushing back the tears.

"Mitch was everything I've ever wanted to be . . ."

Taylor stepped back from the microphone, his head bowed, then made his way back into the crowd. The minister finished with the service, and people filed by the coffin, where a picture of Mitch had been placed. In the photo he was smiling broadly, standing over the grill in his backyard. Like the picture of Taylor's father, it captured the very essence of who he was.

Afterward Taylor drove alone back to Melissa's house.

It was crowded at the house as people came by after the funeral to offer Melissa their condolences. Unlike the day before—a gathering of close friends and family—this time everyone who'd been at the service was there, including some Melissa barely knew.

Judy and Melissa's mother tended to the busywork of feeding the masses; because it was so packed inside, Denise wandered into the backyard to watch Kyle and the other children who'd also attended the funeral. Mainly nephews and nieces, they were young and, like Kyle, unable to fully understand everything that was going on. Dressed in formal clothes, they were running around, playing with each other as if the situation were nothing more than a family reunion.

Denise had needed to get out of the house. The grief could be stifling at times, even to her. After hugging Melissa and sharing a few words of sympathy, she had left Melissa to the care of her family and Mitch's. She knew that Melissa would have the support she needed today; Melissa's parents intended to stay for a week. While her mother would be there to listen and hold her, Melissa's father could begin with the numbing paperwork that always followed an event like this.

Denise stood from her chair and walked to the edge of the pool, her arms crossed, when Judy saw her through the kitchen window. She opened the sliding glass door and started toward her.

Denise heard her approaching and glanced over her shoulder, smiling warily.

Judy laid a gentle hand on her back. "How're you holding up?" she asked.

Denise shook her head. "I should be asking you that. You knew Mitch a lot longer than I did."

"I know. But you look like you need a friend right now."

Denise uncrossed her arms and glanced toward the house. People could be seen in every room.

"I'm okay. Just thinking about Mitch. And Melissa."

"And Taylor?"

Despite the fact that it was over between them, she couldn't lie.

"Him too."

* * *

Two hours later the crowd was finally thinning. Most of the distant friends had come and gone; a few members of the family had flights to catch and had left as well.

Melissa was sitting with her immediate family in the living room; her boys had changed their clothes and had gone outside, to the front yard. Taylor was standing in Mitch's den alone when Denise approached him.

Taylor saw her, then returned his attention to the walls of the den. The shelves were filled with books, trophies the boys had won in soccer and Little League baseball, pictures of Mitch's family. In one corner was a rolltop desk, the cover pulled shut.

"Your words at the service were beautiful," Denise said. "I know Melissa was really touched by what you said."

Taylor simply nodded without responding. Denise ran her hand through her hair.

"I'm really sorry, Taylor. I just wanted you to know that if you need to talk, you know where I am."

"I don't need anyone," he whispered, his voice ragged. With that he turned from her and walked away.

What neither of them knew was that Judy had witnessed the whole thing.

Chapter 26

Taylor bolted upright in bed, his heart pounding, his mouth dry. For a moment he was inside the burning warehouse again, adrenaline surging through his system. He couldn't breathe, and his eyes stung with pain. Flames were everywhere, and though he tried to scream, no sounds escaped from his throat. He was suffocating on imaginary smoke.

Then, just as suddenly, he realized he was imagining it. He looked around the room and blinked hard as reality pressed in around him, making him ache in a different way, weighing heavily on his chest and limbs.

Mitch Johnson was dead.

It was Tuesday. Since the funeral he hadn't left his house, hadn't answered the phone. He vowed to change today. He had things to do: an ongoing job, small problems at the site that needed his attention. Checking the clock, he saw that it was already past nine. He should have been there an hour ago.

Instead of getting up, however, he simply lay back down, unable to summon the energy to rise.

On Wednesday, midmorning, Taylor sat in the kitchen, dressed only in a pair of jeans. He'd made scrambled eggs and bacon and had stared at the plate before finally rinsing the untouched food down the disposal. He hadn't eaten anything in two days. He couldn't sleep, nor did he want to. He refused to talk to anyone; instead he let his answering machine pick up his calls. He didn't deserve those things. Those things could provide pleasure, they could provide escape—they were for people who deserved them, not for him. He was exhausted. His mind and body were being drained of the things they needed to survive; if he wanted, he knew he could continue along this path forever. It would be easy, an escape of a different sort. Taylor shook his head. No, he couldn't go that far. He wasn't worthy of that, either.

Instead he forced down a piece of toast. His stomach still growled, but he refused to eat any more than necessary. It was his way of acknowledging the truth as he saw it. Each hunger pang would remind him of his guilt, his own self-loathing. Because of him, his friend had died.

Just like his father.

Last night, while sitting on the porch, he had tried to bring Mitch to life again, but strangely, Mitch's face was already frozen in time. He could remember the picture, he could see Mitch's face, but for the life of him he couldn't remember what Mitch looked like when he laughed or joked or slapped him on the back. Already his friend was leaving him. Soon his image would be gone forever.

Just like his father.

Inside, Taylor hadn't turned on any lights. It was dark on the porch, and Taylor sat in the blackness, feeling his insides turn to stone.

He made it into work on Thursday; he spoke with the owners and made a dozen decisions. Fortunately his workers were present when he spoke with the owners and knew enough to proceed on their own. An hour later Taylor remembered nothing about the conversation.

Early Saturday morning, awakened by nightmares once more, Taylor forced himself out of bed. He hooked up the trailer to his truck, then loaded his riding mower onto it, along with a weed whacker, edger, and trimmer. Ten minutes later he was parked in front of Melissa's house. She came out just as he finished unloading.

"I drove by and saw the lawn was getting a little high," he said without meeting her eyes. After a moment of awkward silence, he ventured, "How're you holding up?"

"Okay," she said without much emotion. Her eyes were rimmed with red. "How about you?"

Taylor shrugged, swallowing the lump in his throat.

He spent the next eight hours outside, working steadily, making her yard look as if a professional landscaper had come by. In the early afternoon a load of pine straw was delivered, and he placed it carefully around the trees, in the flower beds, along the house. As he worked he made mental lists of other things to do, and after loading the equipment back on the trailer, he donned his tool belt. He reattached a few broken planks in the fence, caulked around three of the windows, mended a screen that had been broken, changed the burned-out light bulbs in the outdoor lights. Focusing next on the pool, he added chlorine, emptied the baskets, cleared the water of debris, and back-washed the filter.

He didn't go inside to visit with Melissa until he was finally ready to leave, and even then he stayed only briefly.

"There are a few more things to do," he said on his way out the door. "I'll be by tomorrow to take care of them."

The next day he worked until nightfall, possessed.

Melissa's parents left the following week, and Taylor filled the void in their absence. As he'd done with Denise during the summer months, he began swinging by Melissa's home nearly every day. He brought dinner with him twice—pizza first, then fried chicken—and though he still felt vaguely uncomfortable around Melissa, he felt a sense of responsibility regarding the boys.

They needed a father figure.

He'd made the decision earlier in the week, after yet another sleepless night. The idea, however, had initially come to him while he was still in the hospital. He knew he couldn't take Mitch's place and didn't intend to. Nor would he hinder Melissa's life in any way. In time, if she met someone new, he would slip quietly from the picture. In the meantime he would be there for them, doing the things that Mitch had done. The lawn. Ball games and fishing trips with the boys. Odds and ends around the house. Whatever.

He knew what it was like to grow up without a father. He remembered longing for someone besides his mother to talk to. He remembered lying in his bed, listening to the quiet sounds of his mother's sobbing in the adjoining room, and how difficult it had been to talk to her in the year following his father's death. Thinking back, he saw clearly how his childhood had been stripped away.

For Mitch's sake, he wouldn't let that happen to the boys.

He was sure it was what Mitch would have wanted

him to do. They were like brothers, and brothers watched out for each other. Besides, he was the godfather. It was his duty.

Melissa didn't seem to mind that he'd begun to come over. Nor had she asked the reason why, which meant that she too understood why it was important. The boys had always been at the forefront of her concerns, and now with Mitch gone, Taylor felt sure that those feelings had only increased.

The boys. They needed him now, no doubt about it.

In his mind, he didn't have a choice. The decision made, he began to eat again, and all at once the nightmares stopped. He knew what he had to do.

The following weekend, when Taylor arrived to take care of the lawn, he inhaled sharply when he pulled up to Mitch and Melissa's driveway. He blinked hard, to make sure his eyes weren't deceiving him, but when he looked again it hadn't moved at all.

A realty sign.

"For Sale."

The house was for sale.

He sat in his idling truck as Melissa emerged from the house. When she waved to him, Taylor finally turned the key and the engine sputtered to a halt. As he started toward her he could hear the boys in the yard out back, though he couldn't see them.

Melissa gave him a hug.

"How are you, Taylor?" she asked, searching his face. Taylor took a small step back, avoiding her gaze.

"All right, I guess," he answered, distracted. He nodded in the direction of the road.

"What's with the sign?"

"Isn't it obvious?"

"You're selling the house?"

"Hopefully."

"Why?"

Melissa's whole body seemed to sag as she turned to face the house.

"I just can't live here anymore . . ." she finally answered, trailing off. "Too many memories."

She blinked back tears and stared wordlessly at the house. She suddenly looked so tired, so defeated, as if the burden of carrying on without Mitch were crushing the life force out of her. A ribbon of fear twisted inside him.

"You're not moving away, are you?" he asked in disbelief. "You're still going to live in Edenton, right?"

After a long moment, Melissa shook her head.

"Where're you going?"

"Rocky Mount," she answered.

"But why?" he asked, his voice straining. "You've lived here for a dozen years . . . you've got friends here . . . I'm here . . . Is it the house?" he asked quickly, searching. He didn't wait for a reply. "If the house is too much, there might be something I could do. I could build you a new one for cost, anywhere you want."

Melissa finally turned to face him.

"It's not the house—that has nothing to do with it. My family's in Rocky Mount, and I need them right now. So do the boys. All their cousins are there, and the school year just started. It won't be so hard for them to adjust."

"You're moving right away?" he asked, still struggling to make sense of this news.

Melissa nodded. "Next week," she said. "My parents have an older rental house they said I could use until I sell this place. It's right up the street from where they live. And if I do have to take a job, they can watch my boys for me."

"I could do that," Taylor said quickly. "I could give you a job doing all the billing and ordering if you need to earn some money, and you could do it right here from the house. You could do it on your own time."

She smiled sadly at him. "Why? Do you want to rescue me, too, Taylor?"

The words made him flinch. Melissa looked at him carefully before going on.

"That's what you're trying to do, isn't it? Coming over last weekend to take care of the yard, spending time with the boys, the offer for a house and a job . . . I appreciate what you're trying to do, but it's not what I need right now. I need to handle this my own way."

"I wasn't trying to rescue you," he protested, trying to hide how pained he felt. "I just know how hard it can be to lose someone, and I didn't want you to have to handle everything alone."

She slowly shook her head. "Oh, Taylor," she said in almost a motherly tone, "it's the same thing." She hesitated, her expression at once knowing and sad. "It's what you've been doing your whole life. You sense that someone needs help, and if you can, you give her exactly what she needs. And now, you're turning your sights on us."

"I'm not turning my sights on you," he denied.

Melissa wasn't dissuaded. Instead she reached for his hand.

"Yes, you are," she said calmly. "It's what you did with Valerie after her boyfriend left her, it's what you did with Lori when she felt so alone. It's what you did with Denise when you found out how hard her life was. Think of all the things you did for her, right from the very beginning." She paused, letting that sink in. "You feel the need to make things better, Taylor. You always have. You may not believe it, but everything in your life proves that over and over. Even your jobs. As a contractor, you fix things that are broken. As a fireman, you save people. Mitch never understood that about you, but to me, it was obvious. It's who you are."

To that, Taylor had no response. Instead he turned away, his mind reeling from her words. Melissa squeezed his hand.

"That's not a bad thing, Taylor. But it's not what I need. And in the long run, it's not what you need, either. In time, once you think I'm saved, you'd move on, looking for the next person to rescue. And I'd probably be thankful for everything you did, except for the fact that I would know the truth about why you did it."

She stopped there, waiting for Taylor to say something.

"What truth is that?" he rasped out finally.

"That even though you rescued me, you were trying to rescue yourself, because of what happened to your father. And no matter how hard I try, I'll never be able to do that for you. That's a conflict you're going to have to resolve on your own."

The words hit him with almost physical force. He felt breathless as he tried to focus on his feet, unable to feel his body, his mind a riot of warring thoughts. Random memories flashed through his mind in dizzying succession: Mitch's angry face at the bar; Denise's eyes filled with tears; the flames at the warehouse, licking at his arms and legs; his father turning in the sunlight as his mother snapped his picture . . .

Melissa watched a host of emotions play across Taylor's face before pulling him close. She wrapped her arms around him, hugging him tightly.

"You've been like a brother to me, and I love the fact that you would be here for my boys. And if you love me, too, you'll understand that I didn't say any of these things to hurt you. I know you want to save me, but I don't need it. What I need is for you to find a way to save yourself, just like you tried to save Mitch."

He felt too numb to respond. In the early morning sunlight, they stood together, simply holding each other in the soft morning sunlight.

"How?" he finally croaked out.

"You know," she whispered, her hands on his back. "You already know."

He left Melissa's home in a daze. It was all he could do to stay focused on the road, not knowing where he wanted to go, his thoughts unconnected. He felt as if the remaining strength he'd had to go on had been stripped away, leaving him naked and drained.

His life, as he knew it, was over, and he had no idea what to do. As much as he wanted to deny the things that Melissa had said, he couldn't. At the same time, he didn't believe them, either. At least, not completely. Or did he?

Thinking along these lines exhausted him. In his life he'd tried to see things as concrete and clear, not ambiguous and steeped in hidden meanings. He didn't search for hidden motivations, either in himself or in others, because he had never really believed that they mattered.

His father's death had been something concrete, something horrible, but real nonetheless. He couldn't understand why his father had died, and for a time he'd talked to God about the things he was going through, wanting to make sense of it. In time, though, he gave up. Talking about it, understanding it . . . even if the answers eventually came, would make no difference. Those things wouldn't bring his father back.

But now, in this difficult time, Melissa's words were making him question the meaning of everything he had once thought so clear and simple.

Had his father's death really influenced everything in his life? Were Melissa and Denise right in their assessment of him?

No, he decided. They weren't right. Neither one of them knew what happened the night his father had died. No one, besides his mother, knew the truth.

Taylor, driving automatically, paid little attention to where he was going. Turning now and then, slowing at intersections, stopping when he had to, he obeyed the laws but didn't remember doing so.

His mind clicked forward and backward with the shifting transmission of his truck. Melissa's final words haunted him.

You already know . . .

Know what? he wanted to ask. *I don't know anything right now. I don't know what you're talking about. I just want to help the kids, like when I was a child. I know what they need. I can help them. I can help you, too, Melissa. I've got it all worked out . . .*

Are you trying to rescue me, too?

No, I'm not. I just want to help.

It's the same thing.

Is it?

Taylor refused to chase the thought down to its final conclusion. Instead, really seeing the road for the first time, he realized where he was. He stopped the truck and began the short trek to his final destination.

Judy was waiting for him at his father's grave.

"What are you doing here, Mom?" he asked.

Judy didn't turn at the sound of his voice. Instead, kneeling down, she tended the weeds around the stone as Taylor did whenever he came.

"Melissa called me and told me you'd come," she said quietly, hearing his footsteps close behind her. From her voice he could tell she'd been crying. "She said I should be here."

Taylor squatted beside her. "What's wrong, Mom?"

Her face was flushed. She swiped at her cheek, leaving a torn blade of grass on her face.

"I'm sorry," she began. "I wasn't a good mother . . ."

Her voice seemed to die in her throat then, leaving Taylor too surprised to respond. With a gentle finger he removed the blade of grass from her cheek, and she finally turned to face him.

"You were a great mother," he said firmly.

"No," she whispered, "I wasn't. If I were, you wouldn't come here as much as you do."

"Mom, what are you talking about?"

"You know," she answered, drawing a deep breath before going on. "When you hit bad patches in your life, you don't turn to me, you don't turn to friends. You come here. No matter what the question or the problem, you always come to the decision that you're better off alone, just like you are now."

She stared at him almost as if seeing a stranger.

"Can't you see why that hurts me? I can't help but think how sad it must be for you to live your life without people—people who could offer you support or simply lend an ear when you need it. And it's all because of me."

"No—"

She didn't let him finish, refusing to listen to his protests. Looking toward the horizon, she seemed lost in the past.

"When your father died, I was so caught up in my own sadness that I ignored how hard it was for you. I tried to be everything for you, but because of that, I didn't have time for myself. I didn't teach you how wonderful it is to love someone and have them love you back."

"Sure you did," he said.

She fixed him with a look of inexpressible sorrow. "Then why are you alone?"

"You don't have to worry about me, okay?" he muttered, almost to himself.

"Of course I do," she said weakly. "I'm your mother."

Judy moved from her knees to a sitting position on the ground. Taylor did the same and reached out his hand. She took it willingly and they sat in silence, a light wind moving the trees around them.

"Your father and I had a wonderful relationship," she finally whispered.

"I know—"

"No, let me finish, okay? I may not have been the mother that you needed back then, but I'm going to try now." She squeezed his hand. "Your father made me happy, Taylor. He was the best person that I ever knew. I remember the first time he ever spoke to me. I was on my way home from school and I'd stopped to get an ice-cream cone. He came in the store right behind me. I knew who he was, of course—Edenton was even smaller than it is now. I was in the third grade, and after getting my ice-cream cone, I bumped into someone and dropped it. That was my last nickel, and I got so upset that your father bought me a new one. I think I fell in love with him right there. Well . . . as time went on, I never did get him out of my system. We dated in high school, and after that we got married, and never once did I ever regret it."

She stopped there, and Taylor let go of her hand before slipping his arm around her.

"I know you loved Dad," he said with difficulty.

"That wasn't my point. My point is that even now, I don't regret it."

He looked at her, uncomprehending. Judy met his gaze, her eyes suddenly fierce.

"Even if I knew what would eventually happen to your father, I would have married him. Even if I'd known that we'd only be together for eleven years, I wouldn't have traded those eleven years for anything. Can you understand that? Yes, it would have been wonderful to have grown old together, but that doesn't mean I regret the time we spent together. Loving someone and having them love you back is the most precious thing in the world. It's what made it possible for me to go on, but you don't seem to realize that. Even when love is right there in front of you, you choose to turn away from it. You're alone because you want to be."

Taylor rubbed his fingers together, his mind growing numb again.

"I know," Judy went on with fatigue in her voice, "that you feel responsible for your father's death. All my life I've tried to help you understand that you shouldn't, that it was a horrible accident. You were just a child. You didn't know what was going to happen any more than I did, but no matter how many ways I tried to say it, you still believed you were at fault. And because of that, you've shut yourself off from the world. I don't know why . . . maybe you don't think you deserve to be happy, maybe you're afraid that if you finally allow yourself to love someone, you'd be admitting that you weren't responsible . . . maybe you're afraid of leaving your own family behind. I don't know what it is, but all those things are wrong. I can't think of another way to tell you."

Taylor didn't respond, and Judy sighed when she realized he wasn't going to.

"This summer, when I saw you with Kyle, do you know what I thought? I thought about how much you looked like your father. He was always good with kids, just like you. I remember how you used to tag along behind him, everywhere he went. Just the way you used to look at him always made me smile. It was an expression of awe and hero worship. I'd forgotten about that until I saw Kyle when you were with him. He looked at you in exactly the same way.

I'll bet you miss him."

Taylor nodded reluctantly.

"Is that because you were trying to give him what you thought you missed growing up, or is it because you like him?"

Taylor considered the question before answering.

"I like him. He's a great kid."

Judy met his eyes. "Do you miss Denise, too?"

Yeah, I do . . .

Taylor shifted uncomfortably. "That's over now, Mom," he said.

She hesitated. "Are you sure?"

Taylor nodded, and Judy leaned into him, resting her head on his shoulder.

"That's a shame, Taylor," she whispered. "She was perfect for you."

They sat without speaking for the next few minutes, until a light autumn shower began to fall, forcing them back to the parking lot. Taylor opened her door, and Judy got in the front seat. After closing the door, he pressed his hands against the glass, feeling the cool drops on his fingertips. Judy smiled sadly at her son, then pulled away, leaving Taylor standing in the rain.

He'd lost everything.

He knew that as he left the cemetery and began the short trip home. He drove past a row of old Victorian houses that looked gloomy in the soft hazy sunlight, through ankle-deep puddles in the middle of the road, his wipers flashing back and forth with rhythmic regularity. He continued through downtown, and as he passed the commercial landmarks he'd known since childhood, his thoughts were drawn irresistibly to Denise.

She was perfect for you.

He finally admitted to himself that despite Mitch's death, despite everything, he hadn't been able to stop thinking about her. Like an apparition, her image had flashed through his mind over and over, but he'd forced it away with stubborn resolve. Now, though, it was impossible. With startling clarity he saw her expression as he'd fixed her cupboard doors, he heard her laughter echo across the porch, he could smell the faint scent of her shampoo in her hair. She was here with him . . . and yet she wasn't. Nor would she ever be again. The realization made him feel emptier than he'd ever felt before.

Denise . . .

As he drove along, the explanations he'd made to himself—and to her—suddenly rang hollow. What had come over him? Yes, he'd been pulling away. Despite the denials, Denise had been right about that. Why, he wondered, had he let himself? Was it for the reasons his mother had said?

I didn't teach you how wonderful it is to love someone and have them love you back . . .

Taylor shook his head, suddenly unsure of every decision he'd ever made. Was his mother right? If his father hadn't died, would he have acted the same way over the years? Thinking back to Valerie or Lori—would he have married them? Maybe, he thought, uncertainly, but probably not. There were other things wrong with the relationships, and he couldn't honestly say that he'd ever really loved either of them.

But Denise?

His throat tightened as he remembered the first night they'd made love. As much as he wanted to deny it, he knew now that he'd been in love with her, with everything about her. So why, then, hadn't he told her so? And more important, why had he forcibly ignored his own feelings in order to pull away?

You're alone because you want to be . . .

Was that it? Did he really want to face the future alone? Without Mitch—and soon Melissa—who else did he have? His mother and . . . and . . . The list trailed off. After her, there was no one. Is that what he really wanted? An empty house, a world without friends, a world without someone who cared about him? A world where he avoided love at all costs?

In the truck, rain splashed against the windshield as if driving that thought home, and for the first time in his life, he knew he was—and had been—lying to himself.

In his daze, snatches of other conversations began to replay themselves in his mind.

Mitch warning him: *Don't screw it up this time . . .*

Melissa teasing: *So are you gonna marry this wonderful girl or what? . . .*

Denise, in all her luminous beauty: *We all need companionship . . .*

His response?

I don't need anyone . . .

It was a lie. His entire life had been a lie, and his lies had led to a reality that was suddenly impossible to fathom. Mitch was gone, Melissa was gone, Denise was gone, Kyle was gone . . . he'd lost it all. His lies had become reality.

Everyone is gone.

The realization made Taylor grip the steering wheel hard, fighting to keep control. He pulled the truck to the side of the road and slipped the stick shift into neutral, his vision blurring.

I'm alone . . .

He clung to the steering wheel as the rain poured down around him, wondering how on earth he'd let it happen.

Chapter 27

Denise pulled into the drive, tired from her shift. The steady rain had kept business slow all night. There'd been just enough to keep her constantly moving, but not enough to make decent tips. More or less a wasted evening, but on the bright side, she'd been able to leave a little early, and Kyle hadn't stirred as she'd loaded him into the car. He'd become used to curling up around her on the ride home over the past few months, but now that she had her own car again (hurray!), she had to buckle him into the backseat. Last night he'd fussed so much that he hadn't been able to fall asleep again for a couple of hours.

Denise stifled a yawn as she turned up the drive, relieved that she'd be in bed soon. The gravel was wet from the earlier rains, and she could hear small pinging sounds as the wheels kicked up pebbles that ricocheted off her car. A few more minutes, a nice cup of cocoa, and she'd be under the covers. The thought was almost intoxicating.

The night was black and moonless, dark clouds blocking the light from the stars. A light fog had settled in, and Denise moved up the drive slowly, using the porch light as a beacon. As she neared the house and things came into better focus, she nearly slammed on the brakes at the sight of Taylor's truck parked out front.

Glancing toward the front door, she saw Taylor sitting on the steps, waiting for her.

Despite her exhaustion, her mind snapped to attention. A dozen possibilities raced through her head as she parked and shut off the engine.

Taylor approached the car as she got out, careful not to slam the door behind her. She was about to ask him what he wanted when the words died on her lips.

He looked terrible.

His eyes were red rimmed and raw looking, his face pale and drawn. As he pushed his hands deep into his pockets, he seemed unable to meet her gaze. Frozen, she searched for something to say.

"I see you got yourself a car," Taylor offered.

The sound of his voice triggered a flood of emotions in her: love and joy, pain and anger, the loneliness and quiet desperation of the past few weeks.

She couldn't go through all this again.

"What are you doing here, Taylor?"

Her voice was edged with more bitterness than

Taylor had expected. Taylor took a deep breath.

"I came to tell you how sorry I was," he began haltingly. "I never meant to hurt you."

She'd wanted to hear those words at one time, but strangely they meant nothing now. She glanced over her shoulder at the car, spying Kyle's sleeping figure in the back.

"It's too late for that," she said.

He lifted his head slightly. In the light of the porch he looked far older than she remembered, almost as if years had passed since she'd last seen him. He forced a thin-lipped smile, then lowered his gaze again before pulling his hands from his pockets. He took a hesitant step toward his truck.

Had it been any other day, had it been any other person, he would have kept moving, telling himself that he'd tried. Instead he forced himself to stop.

"Melissa's moving to Rocky Mount," he said into the darkness, his back to her.

Denise absently ran her hand through her hair. "I know. She told me a couple of days ago. Is that why you're here?"

Taylor shook his head. "No. I'm here because I wanted to talk about Mitch." He murmured the words over his shoulder; Denise could barely hear him. "I was hoping that you'd listen because I don't know who else to turn to."

His vulnerability touched and surprised her, and

for a fleeting moment she almost went to his side. But she couldn't forget what he had done to Kyle—or to her, she reminded herself.

I can't go through this again.

But I also said I'd be there if you needed to talk.

"Taylor . . . it's really late . . . maybe tomorrow?" she suggested softly. Taylor nodded, as if he had expected her to say as much. She thought he would leave then, yet strangely he didn't move from his spot.

In the distance Denise heard the faint rumble of thunder. The temperature was dropping, and the moisture in the air made it seem colder than it really was. A misty halo encircled the porch light, glittering like tiny diamonds, as Taylor turned to face her again.

"I also wanted to tell you about my father," he said slowly. "It's time you finally knew the truth."

From his strained expression, she knew how hard it had been for him to say the words. He seemed on the verge of tears as he stood before her; this time it was her turn to look away.

Her mind flashed back to the day of the festival when he'd asked to drive her home. She'd gone against her instincts, and as a result she'd eventually received a painful lesson. Here again was another crossroads, and once more she hesitated. She sighed.

It's not the right time, Taylor. It's late, and Kyle's

already asleep. I'm tired and don't think I'm ready for this just yet.

That's what she imagined herself saying.

The words that came out, however, were different.

"All right," she said.

He didn't look at her from his position on the couch. With the room lit by only a single lamp, dark shadows hid his face.

"I was nine years old," he began, "and for two weeks, we were practically buried in heat. The temperature had hovered near a hundred, even though it was still early in the summer. It had been one of the driest springs on record—not a single drop of rain in two months, and everything was splinter dry. I remember my mother and father talking about the drought and how farmers were already beginning to worry about their crops because summer had supposedly just begun. It was so hot that time just seemed to slow down. I'd wait all day for the sun to go down for some relief, but even then it didn't help. Our house was old—it didn't have air-conditioning or much insulation—and just lying in bed would make me sweat. I remember that my sheets would get soaked; it was impossible to sleep. I kept moving around to get comfortable, but I couldn't. I'd just toss and turn and sweat like crazy."

He was staring at the coffee table as he spoke, his

eyes unfocused, his voice subdued. Denise watched as one hand formed into a fist, then relaxed, then formed again. Opening and closing like the door to his memory, random images slipping through the cracks.

"Back then, there was this set of plastic army soldiers that I saw in the Sears catalog. It came with tanks, jeeps, tents, and barricades—everything a kid needs to have a little war, and I don't remember ever wanting anything more in my whole life. I used to leave the catalog open to that page so that my mom wouldn't miss it, and when I finally got the set for my birthday, I don't think I'd ever been more excited about a gift. But my bedroom was real small—it used to be a sewing room before I came along—and there wasn't enough space to set it up the way I wanted, so I put the whole collection up in the attic. When I couldn't sleep that night, that's where I went."

He finally looked up, a rueful sigh escaping from him, something bitter and long repressed. He shook his head as if he still didn't believe it. Denise knew enough not to interrupt.

"It was late. It was past midnight when I snuck past my parents' door to the steps at the end of the hall. I was so quiet—I knew where every squeak in the floor was, and I purposely avoided them so my parents wouldn't know I was up there. And they didn't."

He brought his hands to his face and bent forward, hiding his face before letting his hands fall away again. His voice gained momentum.

"I don't know how long I was up there that night. I could play with those soldiers for hours and not even realize it. I just kept setting them up and fighting these imaginary battles. I was always Sergeant Mason—the soldiers had their names stamped in the bottom—and when I saw that one of them had my father's name, I knew he had to be the hero. He always won, no matter what the odds were. I'd pit him against ten men and a tank, and he'd always do exactly the right thing. In my mind, he was indestructible; I'd get lost in Sergeant Mason's world, no matter what else was going on. I'd miss dinner or forget my chores . . . I couldn't help it. Even on that night, hot as it was, I couldn't think of anything else but those damn soldiers. I guess that's why I didn't smell the smoke."

He paused, his fist finally closing for good. Denise felt the muscles in her neck tighten as he continued.

"I just didn't smell it. To this day, I don't know why—it seems impossible to me that I could have missed it—but I did. I didn't realize anything was happening at all until I heard my parents come scrambling out of their bedroom, making a huge ruckus. They were yelling and screaming for me, and I remember thinking that they'd found out that I wasn't where I was supposed to be. I kept hearing them call my name over and over, but I was too afraid to answer."

His eyes pleaded for understanding.

"I didn't want them to find me up there—they'd already told me a hundred times that once I was in bed, I was supposed to stay there all night. If they found me, I figured I'd get in big trouble. I had a baseball game that weekend, and I knew they'd ground me for sure, so instead of coming out when they called, I came up with a plan to wait until they were downstairs. Then I was going to sneak into the bathroom and pretend that I'd been in there the whole time. It sounds dumb, I know, but at the time, it made sense to me. I turned out the light and hid behind some boxes to wait it out. I heard my father open the attic door, shouting for me, but I kept quiet until he finally left. Eventually, the sounds of them tearing through the house died down, and that was when I went for the door. I still had no idea of what was going on, and when I opened it, I was stunned by a blast of heat and smoke. The walls and ceiling were on fire, but it seemed so completely unreal; at first I didn't really understand how serious it was. Had I rushed through it then, I probably could have made it out, but I didn't. I just stared at the fire, thinking how strange it was. I wasn't even afraid."

Taylor tensed, hunching over the table in an almost protective position, his voice rasping on.

"But that changed almost immediately. Before I knew it, everything seemed to catch on fire at once and the way out was blocked. That was when I first realized that something awful was happening. It had been so dry that the house was burning like kindling. I remember thinking that the fire seemed so . . . alive. The flames seemed to know exactly where I was, and a burst of fire shot toward me, knocking me down. I began to scream for my father. But he was already gone, and I knew it. In a panic, I scrambled to the window. When I opened it, I saw my parents on the front lawn. My mom was wearing a long shirt and my dad was in his boxers, and they were running around in a panic, looking and calling for me. For a moment I couldn't say a thing, but my mom seemed to sense where I was, and she looked up at me. I can still see her eyes when she realized I was still in the house. They got real wide, and she brought her hand to her mouth and then she just started screaming. My dad stopped what he was doing—he was over by the fence—and he saw me, too. That was when I started to cry."

On the couch, a tear spilled out of the corner of his unblinking eye, though he didn't seem to realize it. Denise felt sick to her stomach.

"My dad . . . my big strong dad came rushing across

the lawn in a flash. By then, most of the house was on fire, and I could hear things crashing and exploding downstairs. It was coming up through the attic, and the smoke started getting really thick. My mom was screaming for my dad to do something, and he ran to the spot right beneath the window. I remember him screaming, '*Jump, Taylor! I'll catch you! I'll catch you, I promise!*' But instead of jumping, I just started to cry all the harder. The window was at least twenty feet up, and it just seemed so high that I was sure I'd die if I tried. '*Jump, Taylor! I'll catch you!*' He just kept shouting it over and over: '*Jump! Come on!*' My mom was screaming even louder, and I was crying until I finally shouted out that I was afraid."

Taylor swallowed hard.

"The more my dad called for me to jump, the more paralyzed I became. I could hear the terror in his voice and my mom was losing it and I just kept screaming back that I couldn't, that I was afraid. And I was, even though I'm sure now he would have caught me."

A muscle in his jaw twitched rhythmically, his eyes were hooded, opaque. He slammed his fist into his leg.

"I can still see my father's face when he realized I wasn't going to jump—we both came to the realization at exactly the same time. There was fear there, but not for himself. He just stopped shouting and he lowered his arms, and I remember that his eyes never left mine. It was like time stopped right then—it was just the two of us. I couldn't hear my mom anymore, I couldn't feel the heat, I couldn't smell the smoke. All I could think about was my father. Then, he nodded ever so slightly and we both knew what he was going to do. He finally turned away and started running for the front door.

"He moved so fast that my mom didn't have time to stop him. By then, the house was completely in flames. The fire was closing in around me, and I just stood in the window, too shocked to scream anymore."

Taylor pressed the heels of his palms against his closed eyes, applying pressure. When he dropped his hands into his lap, he leaned back into the far corner of the couch, as if unwilling to finish the story. With great effort he went on.

"It must have been less than a minute before he got to me, but it seemed like forever. Even with my head out the window, I could barely breathe. Smoke was everywhere. The fire was deafening. People think they're quiet, but they're not. It sounds like devils screaming in agony when things are consumed by flames. Despite that, I could hear my father's voice in the house, calling that he was coming."

Here Taylor's voice broke, and he turned away to hide the tears that began to spill down his face.

"I remember turning around and seeing him rushing toward me. He was on fire. His skin, his arms, his face, his hair—everything. Just this human fireball rushing at me, being eaten away, bursting through the flames. But he wasn't screaming. He just barreled into me, pushing me toward the window, saying, 'Go, son.' He forced me out the window, holding on to my wrist. When the entire weight of my body was dangling, he finally let go. I landed hard enough to crack a bone in my ankle—I heard the snap as I fell onto my back, looking upward. It was like God wanted me to see what I'd done. I watched my father pull his flaming arm back inside . . ."

Taylor stopped there, unable to go on. Denise sat frozen in her chair, tears in her own eyes, a lump in her throat. When he spoke again, his voice was barely audible and he was shivering as if the effort of choking back sobs were tearing his body apart.

"He never came back out. I remember my mom pulling me away from the house, still screaming, and by then I was screaming, too."

His eyes closed tightly, he lifted his chin to the ceiling.

"Daddy . . . no—" he called out hoarsely.

The sound of his voice echoed like a shot in the room.

"Get out, Daddy!"

As Taylor seemed to crumple into himself, Denise moved instinctively to his side, wrapping her arms around him as he rocked back and forth, his broken cries almost incoherent.

"Please, God . . . let me do it over . . . please . . . I'll jump . . . please, God . . . I'll do it this time . . . please let him come out . . ."

Denise hugged him with all her strength, her own tears falling unheeded onto his neck and back as she pressed her face into him. After a while she heard nothing but the beating of his heart, the creak of the sofa as he rocked himself into a rhythmic trance, and the words he kept whispering over and over—

"I didn't mean to kill him . . ."

Chapter 28

Denise held Taylor until he finally fell silent, spent and exhausted. Then she released him and went to the kitchen, returning a moment later with a can of beer, something she'd splurged on when she'd bought her car.

She didn't know what else to do, nor did she have any idea what to say. She'd heard terrible things in her life, but nothing like this. Taylor looked up from the couch as she handed him the beer; with an almost deadened expression, he opened the beer and took a drink, then lowered it to his lap, both hands wrapped around the can.

She reached over, resting her hand on his leg, and he took hold of it.

"Are you okay?" she asked.

"No," he answered earnestly, "but then maybe I never was."

She squeezed his hand.

"Probably not," she agreed. He smiled wanly. They sat in silence for a few moments before she spoke again.

"Why tonight, Taylor?" Though she could have tried to talk him out of the guilt he still felt, she knew intuitively that now wasn't the time. Neither of them was ready to face those demons.

He absently rotated the can in his hands. "I've been thinking about Mitch ever since he died, and with Melissa moving away . . . I don't know . . . I felt like it was starting to eat me alive."

It always was, Taylor.

"Why me, then? Why not someone else?"

He didn't answer right away, but when he glanced up at her, his blue eyes registered nothing but regret.

"Because," he said with unmistakable sincerity, "I care about you more than I ever cared about anyone."

At his words, her breath caught in her throat. When she didn't speak, Taylor reluctantly withdrew his hand the same way he once had at the carnival.

"You have every right not to believe me," he admitted. "I probably wouldn't, given the way I acted. I'm sorry for that—for everything. I was wrong." He paused. With his thumbnail, he flicked the tab on the can in his hands. "I wish I could explain why I did the things I did, but I honestly don't know. I've been lying to myself for so long that I'm not even sure I'd know the truth if I saw it. All I know for sure is that I screwed up the best thing I've ever had in my life."

"Yeah, you did," she agreed, prompting a nervous laugh from Taylor.

"I guess a second chance is out of the question, huh?"

Denise was silent, suddenly aware that at some point this evening, her anger toward Taylor had dissipated. The pain was still there, though, and so was the fear of what might come. In some ways she felt the same anxiety she'd felt when she was getting to know him for the first time. And in a way, she knew she was.

"You used that one a month ago," she said calmly. "You're probably somewhere in the twenties by now."

He heard an unexpected glimmer of encouragement in her tone and looked up at her, his hope barely disguised.

"That bad?"

"Worse," she said, smiling. "If I were the queen, I probably would have had you beheaded."

"No hope, huh?"

Was there? That was what it all came down to, wasn't it?

Denise hesitated. She could feel her stubborn resolve crumbling as his eyes held her gaze, speaking more eloquently than any words he might say. All at once she was flooded with memories of all the kind things he'd done for her and Kyle, reviving the feelings she had worked so hard to repress these past few weeks.

"I didn't exactly say that," she finally answered. "But we can't just pick up where we left off. There's a lot we have to figure out first, and it isn't going to be easy."

It took a moment for the words to sink in, and when he realized that the possibility was still there—faint though it was—Taylor felt a wave of sudden relief wash over him. He smiled briefly before setting the can on the table.

"I'm sorry, Denise," he repeated earnestly. "I'm sorry for what I did to Kyle, too."

She simply nodded and took his hand.

For the next few hours they talked with a new openness. Taylor filled her in on the last few weeks: his conversations with Melissa and what his mother had said; the argument he'd had with Mitch the night he'd died. He spoke about how Mitch's death had resurrected the memories of his father's death and—despite everything—his lingering guilt about both deaths.

He talked steadily as Denise listened, offering support as he needed it, occasionally asking questions. It was nearly four in the morning when he rose to leave; Denise walked him to the door and watched him drive away.

While putting on her pajamas, she reflected that she still didn't know where their relationship would go from here—talking about things didn't always translate into actions, she cautioned herself. It might mean nothing, it might mean everything. But she knew it wasn't simply up to her to give him another chance. As it had been from the beginning, it was—she thought as her eyelids drooped shut—still up to Taylor.

The following afternoon he called to ask if it would be all right for him to stop by.

"I'd like to apologize to Kyle, too," he said. "And besides, I have something to show him."

Still exhausted from the night before, she wanted time to mull things over. She needed that. So did he. But in the end she reluctantly consented, more for Kyle's sake than her own. She knew that Kyle would be overjoyed to see him.

As she hung up the phone, however, she wondered if she'd done the right thing. Outside, the day was blustery; cool autumn weather had arrived in full force. The leaves were dazzling in their color: reds, oranges, and yellows exploding on the branches, preparing for their final descent to the dew-covered grass. Soon the yard would be covered with faded remnants of the summer.

An hour later Taylor arrived. Though Kyle was in the yard out front, she could hear his excited screams over the sound of the faucet.

"Money! Tayer's here!"

Setting her dishrag aside—she'd just finished washing the morning dishes—she went to the front door, still feeling a little uneasy. Opening it, she saw

Kyle charging Taylor's truck; as soon as Taylor stepped out, Kyle jumped into his arms as if Taylor had never stayed away, his face beaming. Taylor hugged him for a long time, putting him down just as Denise walked up.

"Hey there," he said quietly.

She crossed her arms. "Hi, Taylor."

"Tayer's here!" Kyle said jubilantly, latching on to Taylor's leg. "Tayer's here!"

Denise smiled thinly. "He sure is, sweetie."

Taylor cleared his throat, sensing her unease, and motioned over his shoulder.

"I grabbed a few things from the store on my way over here. If it's okay to stay awhile."

Kyle laughed aloud, completely enamored by Taylor's presence. "Tayer's here," he said again.

"I don't think I have much of a choice," she answered honestly.

Taylor grabbed a grocery bag from the cab of the truck and carried it inside. The bag contained the makings for stew: beef, potatoes, carrots, celery, and onions. They spoke for a couple of minutes, but he seemed to sense her ambivalence about his presence and finally went outside with Kyle, who refused to leave his side. Denise started preparing the meal, thankful to be left alone. She browned the meat and peeled the potatoes, cut the carrots, celery, and onions, throwing everything into a big pot with water and spices. The monotony of the work was soothing, calming her roiling emotions.

As she stood over the sink, however, she glanced outside occasionally, watching Taylor and Kyle play in the dirt pile, where they each pushed Tonka trucks back and forth, building imaginary roads. Yet despite how well they seemed to be getting along, she was struck once more with a paralyzing sense of uncertainty about Taylor; the memories of the pain he had caused her and Kyle surfaced with new clarity. Could she trust him? Would he change? Could he change?

As she watched, Kyle climbed on to Taylor's squatting figure, covering him with dirt. She could hear Kyle laughing; she could hear Taylor laughing as well.

It's good to hear that sound again . . .

But . . .

Denise shook her head. *Even if Kyle has forgiven him, I won't forget. He hurt us once, he could hurt us again.* She wouldn't allow herself to fall for him so deeply this time. She wouldn't let herself go.

But they look so cute together . . .

Don't let yourself go, she warned herself.

She sighed, refusing to allow the internal conversation to dominate her thoughts. With the stew cooking over low heat, she set the table, then straightened up the living room before running out of things to do.

Deciding to sit outside, she walked out into the

crisp, fresh air and sat on the porch steps. She could see Taylor and Kyle, still immersed in their playing.

Despite her thick turtleneck sweater, the nip in the air made her cross her arms. Overhead, a flock of geese in triangular formation flew overhead, heading south for the winter. They were followed by a second group that seemed to be struggling to catch up. As she watched them, she realized her breaths were coming out in little puffs. The temperature had dropped since the morning; a cold front blowing in from the midwest had descended through the low country of North Carolina.

After a while, Taylor glanced toward the house and saw her, letting her know with a smile. With a quick flick of her hand, she waved before burying her hand back in the warmth of her sleeves. Taylor leaned close to Kyle and motioned with his chin, prompting Kyle to turn in her direction. Kyle waved happily, and both of them stood. Taylor brushed off his jeans as they started toward the house.

"You two look like you were having fun," she said.

Taylor grinned, stopping a few feet from her. "I think I'll give up contracting and just build dirt cities. It's a lot more fun, and the people are easier to deal with."

She leaned toward Kyle. "Did you have fun, sweetie?"

"Yes," he said, nodding enthusiastically. "It was fun." *(Ess fun)*

Denise looked up at Taylor again. "The stew won't be ready for a while. I just got it all going, so you've got plenty of time if you want to stay outside."

"I figured as much, but I need a glass of water to wash down some of the dirt."

Denise smiled. "Do you want something to drink, too, Kyle?"

Instead of answering, however, Kyle moved closer, his arms outstretched. Almost molding into her, he wrapped his arms around Denise's neck.

"What's wrong, honey?" Denise asked, suddenly concerned. With his eyes closed, Kyle squeezed more tightly, and she instinctively put her arms around him.

"Thank you, Mommy. Thank you . . ." *(Kenk you, Money. Kenk you)*

For what?

"Honey, what's wrong?" she asked again.

"Kenk you," Kyle said again, not listening. "Kenk you, Money."

He repeated it a third and fourth time, his eyes closed. Taylor's grin left his face.

"Honey . . . ," Denise tried again, a little more desperately this time, suddenly feeling a flash of fear at what was happening.

Kyle, lost in his own world, continued to hold her tight. Denise shot a "See what you've done now" look at Taylor when all of a sudden Kyle spoke again, the same grateful tone in his voice.

"I wuff you, Money."

It took a moment to understand what he was trying to say, and she felt the hairs on her neck stand up.

I love you, Mommy.

Denise closed her eyes in shock. As if knowing she still didn't believe it, Kyle tightened his grip around her, squeezing with ferocious intensity, and said it a second time.

"I wuff you, Money."

Oh, my God . . .

Unexpected tears suddenly began to spill from her eyes.

For five years she'd waited to hear the words. For five long years she'd been deprived of something other parents take for granted, a simple declaration of love.

"I love you, too, sweetie . . . I love you so much."

Lost in the moment, she hugged Kyle as tightly as he was holding her.

I'll never forget this, she thought, memorizing the feel of Kyle's body, his little-boy smell, his halting miraculous words. *Never*.

Watching them together, Taylor stood off to the side, as mesmerized by the moment as she was. Kyle, too, seemed to know he'd done something right, and as she finally released him, he turned to Taylor, a grin on his face. Denise laughed at his expression, her cheeks flushed. She turned to gaze at Taylor, her expression full of wonder.

"Did you teach him to say that?"

Taylor shook his head. "Not me. We were just playing."

Kyle turned from Taylor back to his mother again, the same joyous expression on his face.

"Kenk you, Money," he said simply. "Tayer's home."

Taylor's home . . .

As soon as he said it, Denise wiped the tears from her cheeks, her hand shaking slightly, and it was quiet for a moment. Neither Denise nor Taylor knew what to say. Though Denise's shock was evident, to Taylor she looked absolutely wondrous, as beautiful as anyone he'd ever seen. Taylor dropped his eyes and reached for a twig on the ground, then twirled it absently in his fingers. He looked up at her, back to the twig, then over to Kyle before meeting and holding her gaze with steady determination.

"I hope he's right," Taylor said, his voice cracking slightly. "Because I love you, too."

It was the first time he'd ever said the words to her, or to anyone. Though he'd imagined they would be hard to say, they weren't. He'd never been so sure about anything.

Denise could almost feel Taylor's emotion as he reached for her hand. In a daze, she took it, allowing him to pull her to her feet, drawing her close. He tilted his head, slowly moving it closer, and before she knew it, she felt his lips against hers, mingling with the warmth of his body. The tenderness of the kiss seemed to last forever until he finally buried his face in her neck.

"I love you, Denise," he whispered again. "I love you so much. I'll do anything for another chance, and if you give it to me, I promise I'll never leave you again."

Denise closed her eyes, letting him hold her, before finally, reluctantly, pulling back. With a little space between them, she turned away, and for a moment Taylor didn't know what to think. He squeezed her hand, listening as she took a breath. Still, she didn't speak.

Above them, the autumn sun was bearing down. Cumulus clouds, rolling white and gray, were drifting steadily, moving with the wind. On the horizon, dark clouds loomed black and thick. In an hour the rain would come, full and heavy. But by then they would be in the kitchen, listening as raindrops pelted the tin roof, watching as the steam from their plates curled toward the ceiling.

Denise sighed and faced Taylor again. He loved her. It was as simple as that. And she loved him. She moved into his arms, knowing that the coming storm had nothing to do with them.

Epilogue

Earlier that morning Taylor had taken Kyle fishing. Denise opted to stay behind; she had a few things to do around the house before Judy came over for lunch, and besides, she needed a bit of a break. Kyle was in kindergarten now, and though he'd come a long way in the past year, he was still having a little trouble adjusting to school for the first time. She continued to work with him on his speech every day, but she was also doing her best to help him with other skills so that he'd be able to keep up with his peers. Fortunately the recent move to their new house hadn't seemed to bother him at all. He loved his new room, which was much bigger than it had been in their first house in Edenton, and delighted in the fact that it overlooked the water. She had to admit, she loved it, too. From where she was sitting on the porch, she could see Taylor and Kyle perched on the seawall, fishing poles in hand. She smiled wistfully, thinking how natural they looked together. Like father and son, which of course they were.

After the wedding Taylor had legally adopted Kyle. Kyle had served as the ring bearer in a small, private service held at the Episcopal church. A few friends had come in from Atlanta, and Taylor had invited a dozen others from around town. Melissa served as maid of honor, and Judy dabbed at her tears from her seat in the front row as the rings were exchanged. After the ceremony Taylor and Denise drove to Ocracoke and honeymooned in a small bed-and-breakfast that overlooked the ocean. On her first wedded morning, they rose before the sun came up and took a walk on the beach. As porpoises rode the waves just offshore, they watched the sunrise. With Taylor standing behind her, his arms around her waist, Denise simply leaned her head back, feeling warm and safe, as a new day unfolded.

When they returned from the honeymoon, Taylor surprised Denise with a set of blueprints he'd had drawn up. The plans were for a graceful, low-country home on the water with wide porches, complete with window seats, a modern kitchen, and hardwood floors. They purchased a lot on the outskirts of town and began building within a month; they'd moved in just before the school year started.

Denise had stopped working at Eights as well; she and Taylor went in for dinner now and then, simply to visit with Ray. He was the same as always; he never seemed to age, and as they left he always joked that she could have her job back anytime she wanted. She didn't miss it, despite Ray's good humor.

Though Taylor still suffered from the occasional nightmare, he'd surprised her with his devotion over the past year. Despite the responsibilities of building the house, he came home for lunch every day and refused to work any later than six. He coached Kyle's T-ball team last spring—Kyle wasn't the best player, but he wasn't the worst, either—and they spent every weekend as a family. During the summer they'd taken a trip to Disney World; for Christmas they'd purchased a used Jeep Cherokee.

The only thing left was the white picket fence, and that was going up next week.

She heard the timer go off in the kitchen and rose from her chair. An apple pie was in the oven, and she took it out, setting it on the counter to cool. On the stove, stewed chicken was boiling, and the salty smell of broth wafted through the house.

Their house. The McAdens. Even though she'd been married a little over a year, she still relished the sound of that. *Denise and Taylor McAden*. It had a nice ring to it, if she did say so herself.

She stirred the stew—it had been cooking for an hour now, and meat was beginning to fall off the bones. Though Kyle still avoided eating meat for the most part, a few months earlier she'd made him try chicken. He'd fussed for an hour but had finally taken a bite;

over the next few weeks he'd gradually started eating a little more. Now, on days like these, they ate as a family, everyone sharing the same food. Just as a family should.

A *family*. She liked the sound of that, too.

Glancing out the window, she saw Taylor and Kyle walking up the lawn, toward the shed where they kept their fishing poles. She watched as Taylor hung his pole, then took Kyle's as well. Kyle put the tackle box on the floor inside, and Taylor scooted it out of the way with a tip of his boot. A moment later they were mounting the steps to the porch.

"Hey, Mom," Kyle chirped.

"Did you catch anything?" she asked.

"No. No fish."

Like everything else in her life, Kyle's speech had improved dramatically. It wasn't perfect by any means, but he was gradually closing the gap between himself and his peers at school. More important, she'd stopped worrying about it so much.

Taylor kissed Denise as Kyle made his way inside.

"So, where is the little fella?" Taylor asked.

She nodded toward the corner of the porch. "Still asleep."

"Shouldn't he be awake by now?"

"In a few minutes. He'll be getting hungry soon."

Together they approached the basket in the corner, and Taylor bent over, peering closely, something he still did often, as if he couldn't believe he'd been responsible for helping to create a new life. He reached out and gently ran his hand over his son's hair. At seven weeks there was barely anything at all.

"He seems so peaceful," he whispered, almost in awe. Denise put her hand on Taylor's shoulder, hoping that one day he'd look just like his father.

"He's beautiful," she said.

Taylor looked over his shoulder at the woman he loved, then turned back to his son. He leaned in close, kissing his son on his forehead.

"Did you hear that, Mitch? Your mom thinks you're beautiful."